FOXBAT

James Barrington is a trained military pilot who has worked in covert operations and espionage. He now lives in Andorra and this is his third novel. His previous novels, *Overkill* and *Pandemic*, also featured Paul Richter.

Also by James Barrington

OVERKILL
PANDEMIC

JAMES
BARRINGTON

FOXBAT

PAN BOOKS

First published 2007 by Macmillan

First published in paperback 2008 by Pan Books
an imprint of Pan Macmillan, a division of Macmillan Publishers Limited
Pan Macmillan, 20 New Wharf Road, London N1 9RR
Basingstoke and Oxford
Associated companies throughout the world
www.panmacmillan.com

ISBN 978-0-330-51940-3

1 3 5 7 9 8 6 4 2

A CIP catalogue record for this book is available from
the British Library.

Typeset by IntypeLibra, London
Printed and bound in the UK by
CPI Mackays, Chatham ME5 8TD

Visit **www.panmacmillan.com** to read more about all our books
and to buy them. You will also find features, author interviews and
news of any author events, and you can sign up for e-newsletters
so that you're always first to hear about our new releases.

Acknowledgements

A substantial part of this novel is set on board Her Majesty's Ship *Illustrious*, a Royal Navy aircraft carrier on which I served for some two years. Times change, memories fade, and subtle alterations are made to such vessels, and I'm indebted to Lieutenant Craig Howe, Royal Navy, a front-line pilot on 814 Squadron, both for reminding me of some things I should have remembered, and pointing out the more significant of those changes that have taken place on board this ship. Craig makes a couple of cameo appearances in this novel, and even gets to survive the experience!

I'd also like to thank Lieutenant Commander Paul Tremelling, Royal Navy, for his invaluable and expert guidance on modern Harrier operations and weapons – the GR9 is a far cry from the old FA2 version.

Finally, I must thank my good friend and wonderful agent, Luigi Bonomi, for his continued enthusiasm and encouragement, Peter Lavery for his exhaustive and talented editing, and all the rest of the team at Macmillan.

And, as ever, Sally.

James Barrington
Principality of Andorra, 2007

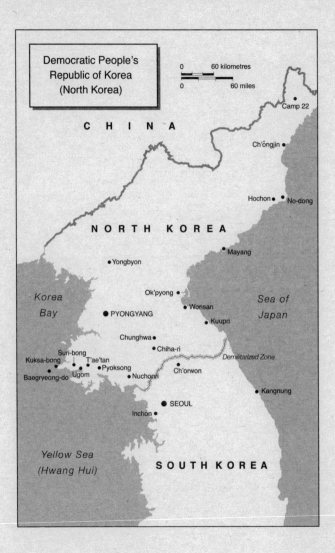

Democratic People's
Republic of Korea
(North Korea)

0   60 kilometres
0   60 miles

C H I N A

Camp 22

Ch'öngjin

Hochon   No-dong

N O R T H   K O R E A

Mayang

Yongbyon

Ok'pyong

*Korea
Bay*

Wonsan

PYONGYANG

Kuupri

*Sea of
Japan*

Chunghwa

Chiha-ri

Suri-bong

Demilitarized Zone

Kuksa-bong   T'ae'tan

Pyoksong

Ch'orwon

Ugom

Baegryeong-do   Nuchonri

Kangnung

SEOUL

Inchon

*Yellow Sea
(Hwang Hui)*

S O U T H   K O R E A

Prologue

'Can we accomplish this?'

The question was uttered softly, barely above a sibilant whisper, by the short man sitting in a large padded chair at the head, but it fell across the long conference table like a sudden dark shadow on a sunny day. There was no response from any of the six men sitting near him along the sides of the table, all wearing almost identical light-coloured Mao-style jackets. Instead they swivelled slightly in their seats to stare at an eighth man in a chair set apart at the other end.

He was slightly younger than the others but, despite the similarity in dress, his physical separation from them marked him out as a supplicant. For a few moments he didn't reply, but stared down at the papers laid out on the table in front of him.

'We have a very narrow window of opportunity,' he said eventually, 'but the crucial factor is that we will only get this one chance. If the Americans do succeed in perfecting the new technology they have announced, we will never be able to risk such a venture again.'

'That was not the question I asked you, Pak Je-San. Kindly confine yourself to matters of fact. I myself will decide on strategy.'

1

Pak flushed slightly. 'I'm sorry, sir. Yes, I believe we can achieve this.'

'Pak is, I suggest, being over-optimistic, and he seems strangely ill-informed about certain aspects of our technological development.' The speaker – Kim Yong-Su – was sitting right next to the man at the head of the table. 'In particular, he appears to be unaware that our nuclear devices are at present much too large to comprise the payload of the Taep'o-dong 2 missile. So how, then, does he intend to make our demands sound credible to the Americans?'

Seven impassive faces stared down the length of the table.

'We do not need to mount a weapon on a missile,' Pak Je-San explained quickly. 'We only need to convince the Americans that we have the *ability* to do so. Securing their belief in that will be sufficient for our purposes.'

'And how do you propose to achieve this?' Kim demanded. 'Simply telling them so will not be enough. And, as you appear to be planning some kind of deception operation, don't forget their satellites are overflying us constantly. Their technical intelligence specialists will be scrutinizing all the images they obtain.'

'I'm counting on that, Comrade Kim,' Pak replied.

'Explain,' hissed the man at the head of the table.

That didn't take long. Pak had rehearsed his presentation more than a dozen times, and had pared it down to the bare minimum necessary to explain precisely what his scheme entailed.

When he'd finished, Kim Yong-Su was the first to speak. 'If I understand you correctly, Pak, you propose to spend several million dollars *and* use almost all of our plutonium supplies to achieve this . . . this conjuring trick you've devised.'

'But if it works,' Pak replied, 'I believe it would be well worth it.'

'I agree.' Again the words were barely more than a whisper.

'But there's another aspect you seem to have forgotten.' Kim Yong-Su wasn't prepared to let Pak Je-San off the hook so easily. The younger man was the head of Central Committee Bureau 39, the North Korean government department responsible for coordinating the production of hard drugs within the country, and also the associated smuggling network. But his background was military, and he'd reached the rank of *tab-ryong* – full colonel in the army – before being transferred to Bureau 39.

'Suppose this scheme of yours actually works,' Kim said. 'Suppose you do manage to make the Americans believe what you want them to. How do you think they'll react?'

'They'll probably try to apply diplomatic pressure, and if that doesn't work they might consider a military option.'

'I don't think the words "might consider" are accurate in this situation, Pak. They have ICBMs in silos all over America that can easily reach this country. They have cruise missiles on their warships and submarines that can carry out what they call surgical strikes. They have aircraft based on Guam that could carpet-bomb the entire peninsula. They could destroy all of our missile pads before we could launch a single weapon.'

Pak had expected opposition to his plan, but he hadn't

anticipated the direction from which it was coming. He'd thought his biggest job would be convincing the leader himself: yet that individual had seemed to favour the plan from the first, whereas now Kim Yong-Su appeared most opposed to it.

Kim was the Deputy General Secretary of the Workers' Party of Korea and Deputy Chairman of the DPRK National Defence Commission – effectively second-in-command of the whole country – and a man who quite literally held the power of life and death over almost every citizen of North Korea. Pak had once witnessed him use that power, and the experience had frightened him all the more for the quiet, casual, almost indifferent manner Kim had adopted for its implementation.

'I think the Americans would tread carefully, Comrade Kim, for several reasons,' Pak suggested. 'If convinced by our demonstration, they will hesitate to attack us directly for fear of retaliation. They are cowards underneath, and the possibility that we could visit upon America a level of devastation far worse than they inflicted on Iraq might be enough to deter them. If we can thus eliminate American support, our armed forces could easily crush and obliterate the armies of South Korea on the battlefield, but it probably wouldn't ever come to that.

'We know – more importantly, they know – that we can flatten Seoul using conventional munitions fired from weapons we already have in place. Almost half the population of the South live in and around the capital city. I believe the threat of a massive bombardment causing huge loss of life, plus our ability to deploy chemical and biological weapons, would soon convince Seoul that opposition is futile – especially with no American cavalry riding to the rescue.'

Pak was pleased with this analogy, and was sure it would appeal to the leader, who was known to have a fondness for old-style American movies.

'And what about their bombers and missiles if the Americans decide not to react as you expect?'

'The bombers would be more of a problem,' Pak conceded, 'since our Air Force does not currently possess modern air-superiority fighters. But we do have adequate surface-to-air missile systems to defend our principal sites, and I don't think they would attempt a first strike using nuclear weapons, for fear of offending our Chinese friends. But I have another suggestion that might address your concerns on both counts. And I also have a proposal that would permanently remove any possibility of Seoul interfering with our plan.'

All seven men listened attentively as Pak outlined the second part of the strategy he'd spent the last month devising. When he finished speaking, even Kim Yong-Su seemed stunned, so Pak wondered if he'd overreached himself. But the man heading the table appeared unfazed by the sheer enormity of Pak's suggested course of action. Instead, he seemed concerned only with the details of the scheme.

'You've proposed a tight schedule, Pak. Can you guarantee your agents would manage to obtain the assets you require by the time we'd need to make our final decision? And what about the funding?'

'I can't totally predict how successful our efforts might be, sir, simply because the sources are presently beyond our control. But we would still be in a win–win situation, for if we don't manage to obtain enough assets in time, we are not committed to proceeding, yet our military will be significantly strengthened.'

'At a cost,' Kim interjected.

'Agreed, comrade, but perhaps not as much as you might expect. We would have to pay in American dollars, because that's the only currency likely to be acceptable. But because of the nature of the financial transactions, the money would not be deposited in a bank, so we can seed all the payments with counterfeit notes, reducing our total outlay by as much as twenty or thirty per cent. Already the Bureau holds significant amounts of forged currency – mainly "superdollars" – that could be utilized.'

'Has anyone any further questions?' the leader asked softly, after a few moments' silence. Nobody responded. 'Very well. Wait outside while we discuss your proposal further.'

Fifteen minutes later, Pak Je-San was called back into the room, to see only two men now sitting at the table – the leader himself and Kim Yong-Su.

'You have our approval, Pak, therefore proceed at once. You are authorized to use the funds currently held by the Bureau – both genuine and counterfeit – to achieve your objectives, but you are to keep an accurate accounting. This operation is to be considered highly classified and you will not discuss it with anyone else. All the agents you recruit are to be told only enough to allow them to achieve their immediate objectives. You will report direct to Kim Yong-Su at least once every month for the remainder of this year, and subsequently once a week until the operation is concluded.'

And that, Pak Je-San thought to himself as he left the building, was the only real problem. He had no doubts that he could achieve exactly what he had promised, but reporting to Kim Yong-Su was something he had not anticipated, and did not look forward to.

Because of all the members of the North Korean government he had ever met, Kim Yong-Su was the only one who frankly terrified him.

Chapter One

One of the standing jokes about the venerable C-130 Hercules transport aircraft – colloquially known as a 'Fat
Albert' – is that Lockheed solved the noise problem by
putting it all inside the fuselage. After the long flog south
to Meknes from Lyneham via Gibraltar, Paul Richter fully
appreciated the point. It was incredibly noisy in the back
of the Herc: a constant, nerve-jangling, whining roar that
penetrated all too easily through the headset he was
wearing. It was better in the enormous cockpit, and he
could now see why the two loadmasters stayed up there
with the pilots instead of occupying the pull-down seats
that lined the cavernous hold.

In front of him, and clearly visible even with only
the red 'night-vision' lights illuminated, were two open
long-wheelbase Land Rover Defender 110s, lashed down
along the centreline of the hold and facing aft towards the
loading ramp. Known as 'Pink Panthers' or just 'Pinkies'
from the strange shade of camouflage paint SAS vehicles
had sported during the Second World War, these two had
been specially prepared for this one particular mission,
their engine and chassis numbers removed, and all their
identifying marks stripped off. They were fitted with

8

diesel engines, long-range fuel tanks, water containers, emergency rations – though nobody expected to have time to eat anything – ruggedized satellite navigation systems, and plenty of ammunition for the half-inch Browning M2 machine-guns. They were also carrying Mark 19 40-millimetre grenade launchers and Milan anti-tank missiles.

The 47 Squadron Special Forces Flight aircraft had lifted off from Meknes, with full tanks, just under an hour earlier and headed east at about ten thousand feet. Now, Richter realized from the angle of the floor and the popping in his ears, it was in a steep descent.

'Border in ten,' the pilot declared laconically over the intercom, and the Hercules began turning to port, as it levelled at just over two hundred feet. Eleven minutes later, the pilot spoke again: 'Welcome to Algeria, gentlemen. We're now in breach of international law, and things are about to get bumpy.'

Richter grinned at the man sitting next to him. 'Here we go again,' he said, almost at a shout.

Colin Dekker smiled, but didn't respond. Short, wiry and compact, like a lot of SAS personnel, he was a captain in the Royal Artillery and the commander of Troop 3, D Squadron, 22 Special Air Service Regiment. He was also in overall charge of this mission, and was using a pencil torch to examine a high-definition satellite photograph of their objective. It was force of habit rather than any particular need – the eight SAS men had studied all the available maps and photographs when they'd been given their briefing back at Hereford, and they'd had plenty of time to remind themselves of the route and terrain during the flight south to Morocco. But

Dekker was a professional, and professionals check everything repeatedly.

The last time Richter had worked with the Special Air Service had been in France, with appalling penalties for failure. This operation, in contrast, was low-risk and relatively straightforward. As the briefing officer – a lanky bespectacled desk jockey from Vauxhall Cross – had put it: 'Fly in, take a look and fly out. A piece of piss.'

It had sounded so easy in the Hereford briefing room, but both Richter and Dekker knew – from intimate personal experience – that the simplest operation could, and frequently did, turn to rat-shit in the blink of an eye. So Dekker was checking the photograph again, looking for anything they might previously have missed.

The pilot hadn't been kidding about the flight. Richter didn't know if it was heat rising from the desert or wind shear or something else, but the Hercules was bouncing violently as it tracked east. And the hard turns the pilot kept making didn't help either. For obvious reasons, the route into Algeria had been carefully plotted to bypass all military establishments, and even every settlement the satellites had identified, while simultaneously having to stay at low level to keep below radar cover. The result was a flight path like the meanderings of a drunken snake, the pilot barely ever able to fly straight and level, but twisting constantly to avoid one potential hazard or another.

'I'm going up-front,' said Richter, leaning across to Dekker, who nodded that he'd understood.

Richter unbuckled his seatbelt, stood up and inched his way forward. There was no need, operationally or otherwise, for him to visit the cockpit, but the truth was that, like many qualified pilots, he was a lousy passenger. He knew the two men in the driving seats had been picked from the cream of the Royal Air Force for the Special Forces Flight, but he'd still rather be flying the aircraft himself.

He pulled open the cockpit door, surprised as before at how spacious the Hercules' flight deck was, and how quiet it was compared to the noise at the rear. The co-pilot, a senior flight lieutenant, glanced back to acknowledge him, but the pilot didn't take his gaze away from the view through the cockpit windows, as he pulled the Hercules into yet another turn to starboard.

'Problem?' Adam Johnson asked.

'No,' Richter shook his head. 'I just felt like a change of scene. It's not a lot of fun back there. Where are we just now?'

The co-pilot pointed to the screen of the navigation computer on the console located between the two seats. 'Right here. We're about forty-five minutes from Aïn Oussera flying in a straight line, or around ninety minutes on our selected route.'

Richter gazed through the windscreen at the terrain a bare two hundred feet below them. The moon was low in the eastern sky but illuminated the landscape reasonably well, and what he could see of it didn't look inviting. The word 'desert' tends to conjure up images of golden sand dunes extending in gentle waves to a cloudless blue horizon, but the Algerian desert was very different. It was fairly flat, which was the good news, but the ground was studded with rocks that cast long shadows in the moonlight. It looked like the kind of surface where Richter would have thought twice about landing a helicopter, far less a seventy-ton fixed-wing aircraft, even one optimized for rough-ground operations.

'Are you going to be able to land safely on that crap?' he asked.

'On that, no,' Johnson replied, 'but the area the eyes in the sky have located for us is fairly clear of rocks. We'll do a pass over it first, just to check, and if it looks OK we'll put the Herc down.'

'And if it isn't?'

'We'll opt for Plan B, head on to the second landing area, and try there. It'll mean a longer drive for you and the Regiment guys, that's all. And if we can't land there either, we'll turn round and fly you back to Morocco in time for breakfast.'

'That isn't really an option,' Richter argued. 'We *have* to do this. Somehow you have to get us down there.'

'I know, but trust us, we've done this before. This Herky-bird can land pretty much anywhere.' Johnson paused for a few seconds. 'Look, we weren't privy to your briefing, but what the hell's going on in Algeria that's caused half the Mobility Troop of an SAS Sabre Squadron to be scrambled? We aren't at war with these guys, are we?'

'Not yet, as far as I know, but the Algerians are on edge. There's an extremist terrorist group called GIA operating within the country. They consider anybody who isn't a Muslim as fair game, so they've assassinated tens of thousands of fellow Algerians and a bunch of foreigners since ninety-two. According to some authorities, Algeria is the single most dangerous country in the world to visit, including Iraq and Afghanistan.'

'That must be a real comfort to you.'

Richter grinned at him. 'You said it. To answer your question, this is a classified mission, but it's really pretty simple: we're doing the Americans a favour. Their Keyhole birds have picked up unusual activity at several Algerian military bases – increased patrols by fighter planes, extra guards posted, that kind of thing – and at Aïn Oussera they've cordoned off one particular hangar and posted armed guards around it. The Americans are worried that Algeria might be working up its forces to launch an attack on Libya, or maybe Morocco.'

'You're kidding.'

Richter smiled grimly in the gloom of the cockpit. 'Unfortunately not, though I don't think the Yanks have any real clue about this region.'

'Or anywhere else east of New York.'

'There's that too. But *something*'s going on out here, which is why we're bouncing around in this bag of bolts instead of tucked up in bed back at home.'

'So what's with the hangar?'

'That's what we're here to find out. The Americans reckon the Algerians might have a bunch of new aircraft, or maybe even a nuke or two, tucked away at Aïn Oussera. The only way to find out is to get someone to take a peep inside the building. And that someone is me.'

'But you're not SAS, right?' Johnson asked. 'You're a spook.'

'I've been called worse,' Richter admitted. 'If I was still in the Navy, I'd be the SLJO.'

'Right – "Shitty Little Jobs Officer"? We've got one of those.'

'Everyone has. And in my section it's usually me.'

Yellow Sea, south of Suri-bong, North Korea

Yi Min-Ho opened the wheelhouse door of the fishing boat and stepped inside. He nodded to the skipper and walked over to the radar display, dimly illuminated by red lighting, and peered at the screen.

'We're clear,' the captain confirmed. A middle-aged South Korean who'd spent his entire life as a professional fisherman, he was quietly pleased that his vessel had been selected for this task. However, he wouldn't ever admit that either to his crew or to the slightly arrogant junior NIS officer now in front of him, who would be carrying out the mission itself.

'No contacts within five miles of us, and nothing moving on the coast. We're tracking south-east, speed just over two knots.'

Yi Min-Ho was tall for a Korean, with pleasant, regular features, but his ingrained air of authority – or perhaps superiority – had already caused some friction on board. 'And the radar detector?' he demanded.

Although in most respects the craft was just a fishing boat, and would pass any routine inspection by a North Korean patrol, it had been fitted with several extra items of equipment, all either cleverly concealed or designed to be easily ditched if the vessel looked likely to be boarded. The radar-warning receiver was one of these items.

'We're currently being illuminated by normal coastal surveillance radars, but no signs of anything unusual.'

The fishing boat had made exactly the same journey three times a week for the last month, leaving Inchon in South Korea in mid-afternoon and sailing west into the Yellow Sea. Its route took it to a point about twenty miles north-west of the island of Baegryeong-do, before the craft turned south-east, passing between that island and the mainland, and then paralleling the North Korean coast for a while before returning to its home port.

On every one of those trips, except this one, all the crew had done was catch fish. Twice patrol boats had approached them closely, but on neither occasion was the vessel boarded. Two days earlier, the National Intelligence Service – South Korea's espionage agency – had decided that the mission was a 'go', and Yi Min-Ho had finally embarked on the fishing boat. With him came two bulky containers, each of which had needed two men to lift, and a single haversack holding his personal equipment.

The boat had already made the turn north-west of Baegryeong-do, so the vessel was now about midway between the island and the largely uninhabited peninsula of Kuksa-bong, virtually the most westerly point of North Korea, jutting out sharply into the Yellow Sea.

'It's time,' Yi said.

The skipper nodded agreement, set the autopilot, and followed the NIS officer out onto the deck, where three crewmen stood waiting.

'Open them,' Yi ordered.

One of the seamen produced a knife and sliced through the cord securing the lid of the container. He swiftly unlaced the cord from the eyelets, then flipped off the fabric lid to reveal the contents. In the glow cast by the deck lights – for obvious reasons the fishing boat was displaying the normal lights any patrol craft's captain would expect to see – it appeared to contain just a single lump of black rubber.

Protruding from one corner of it was a short but rigid hose, which another crewman now attached to a petrol-powered compressor standing ready on deck. Having secured it, he bent over the compressor, flicked a switch and pulled the starter cord. The engine roared into life, then settled down to a steady thrum. Almost immediately the black object began expanding, as the air rushed into it. An inflatable boat was already beginning to take shape.

Yi Min-Ho watched its progress for a few seconds, then turned his attention to the second container. After the lid was flipped back, two of the crewmen bent over to extract an outboard motor, and placed it carefully on the deck. A small toolkit followed it, then a twenty-five-litre can of ready-mixed fuel. The outboard had a bulky and unfamiliar look to it, caused partly by its silenced exhaust but mainly by a thick, soft cover enveloping the entire motor apart from the control arm. This was made of anechoic fabric, designed to absorb radar waves. The NIS had calculated that, despite the mass of metal in the outboard motor, the boat would have an insignificant radar signature, about the same as a large bird.

Yi nodded to the skipper, and headed back to the wheelhouse to make a last check of both the radar screen and the radar-warning receiver, and finally to pick up his haversack. He was wearing an all-black jumpsuit, under which were a camouflage-pattern jacket and trousers. In the haversack was all the equipment he hoped he might need to survive for a week in North Korea: a Kyocera SS66K Iridium satellite phone and spare battery, providing his lifeline to the boat due to pick him up once his mission was over; a Czechoslovakian CZ75 nine-

millimetre semi-automatic pistol with two spare magazines, both fully charged; a GPS receiver; a pair of compact binoculars; a map; a notebook and pencil; seven
days' worth of American-issue MRE rations and five
bottles of water.

By the time he walked back onto the deck, the compressor had fallen silent. The four-metre-long boat was
now fully inflated, and had already been lowered over
the side of the fishing vessel facing away from the mainland, just in case anyone there was watching them
through night-vision glasses. The inflatable was carefully secured by a line, while two of the crewmen, one
wearing an all-black jumpsuit identical to Yi's, were fix-
ing the outboard motor to the wooden transom of the
little rubber boat.

With the motor safely in place, the crewmen filled up
its tank from the fuel can, and then both climbed back
into the fishing boat.

'Are you ready?' the skipper asked. As Yi nodded, he
continued, 'We'll see you in about a week.'

The two black-clad figures then scrambled over the
side into the inflatable, and one of the other crewmen
passed down Yi's haversack. The outboard motor started
at first pull, the engine barely audible. The inflatable
eased away from the side of the fishing boat and turned
east towards the coast of North Korea. The sea was calm,
which was just as well, because the inflatable had a long
way to go. About twenty miles to the drop-off point, and
another fifteen back to where the fishing boat would then
be waiting.

Within seconds the small craft and its occupants were
invisible against the darkness of the water.

Algeria

The loadmaster reappeared in the hold, checked that everyone there was wearing a headset, and then gave Richter a thumbs-up as he sat down.

'We're about sixty seconds from the first landing strip,' the captain announced, his voice clear enough through the intercom. 'We'll do a low-level fly-by to check the surface, and if it looks OK we'll land. Check your belts are tight and hold on.'

The Hercules sank even lower, then lurched up slightly, levelling at about one hundred feet.

In the cockpit, the captain had switched on the set of landing lights filtered for NVG use, and was peering through his night-vision glasses at the ground below the aircraft. If he was going to land here, he wanted to be absolutely sure he could do so safely and, even more important, take off again afterwards.

From the cockpit, the desert surface looked firm, and though there were plenty of rocks and a few stunted shrubs evident, none of them looked big enough to do the aircraft any damage.

'Good enough,' the captain said. 'Let's put her down.'

He discarded his NVGs, pulled the aircraft round in a tight turn to starboard, climbed back up to three hundred feet and started what at an airfield would have been called the downwind leg.

'Landing checks.'

The co-pilot ran through the list, as the rumble of the main landing gear being lowered echoed through the hold, audible even over the howl of the engines. The Hercules banked steeply to starboard, the pilot holding the turn and easing it onto a final approach heading. He levelled the wings, switched on the normal landing lights and pulled the throttles back, and the C-130 sank gently towards the ground.

The SAS troops rapidly checked their equipment and weapons. Then they held on tight.

'Alpha and Bravo, check in,' Dekker ordered, and was rewarded by seven voices responding on their secure radios in proper sequence. Richter was the odd man out, in more ways than one, and he found himself using the radio callsign 'Spook', simply because Dekker liked the sound of it.

Touchdown was much bumpier than Richter had expected, the Hercules bouncing violently several times as its speed dropped away. Even before the aircraft came to rest, and the piercing whine of the engines had fallen to a more bearable level, the SAS troopers had unclipped their seatbelts and stood up. Two of them were already releasing the securing straps on the Land Rovers before the loadmaster stepped across to the ramp controls. The remaining five men, plus Richter and Dekker, headed to the rear of the hold and waited. The loadmaster studied the group, noting that all the men had their Heckler & Koch MP5 submachine-guns cocked and held ready, then began lowering the ramp.

Immediately, the lights in the hold extinguished, and they saw a slowly extending oblong open up in front of them, a dark blue sky studded with stars. Then the surface of the desert itself appeared. The moment the ramp grounded, the SAS troopers thundered down it and fanned out, alert for any sign of danger.

In the hold, the engines of the two Pinkies started

simultaneously, then they rolled down the ramp and stopped side by side. Once everyone had climbed on board, Dekker checked that all the GPS units were indicating the same location, and that both the satellite navigation systems were working properly. They had to be able to find their objective swiftly and, equally important, find their way back to the Hercules once this operation was over.

Dekker carried out a final radio check to ensure that everyone was on the net, then gave the order to advance. Behind them, the ramp closed and the noise of the C-130's engines rose to a roar as the pilot began manoeuvring the aircraft into a take-off position. Once he was satisfied, he would shut down the engines and simply wait for the team to return.

They knew it was going to be an uncomfortable ten miles – the satellite photographs had made that abundantly clear – but they weren't prepared for just how rough the desert terrain actually was. Picking a suitable path through the rocks and boulders tested both drivers to the limit, and they weren't helped by the covers over their headlamps that reduced the normal beam by about eighty per cent. Richter was hoping to get in and out of Algeria undetected, and bright lights can show up a long way off in the desert. Sound travels far as well, so the vehicles' engines were fitted with additional silencers, and the engine bays packed with sound-insulating material to reduce the risk of being heard.

Under normal conditions, driving this distance should have taken about twenty to thirty minutes, but it was nearly three quarters of an hour before Dekker looked up from his navigation system and ordered the vehicles to stop. They were now just under a mile from the airfield boundary, nine miles from the waiting Hercules, and that was as close as they could risk taking the Pinkies.

Dekker ordered the two drivers to stay with their vehicles, then led the rest of his men, Richter tagging along behind, towards the east and to Aïn Oussera.

Twenty minutes later they were lying prone on the summit of a slight rise, as Dekker and Richter studied the layout of the airfield directly in front of them.

South of Suri-bong, North Korea

The north coast of the Kuksa-bong peninsula is partially cultivated, but west of Kama-san the south coast is essentially uninhabited. The reason almost nobody lived there was the same reason that Yi Min-Ho couldn't land there: an extremely inhospitable terrain cut through with deep, heavily wooded valleys ending in steep cliffs overlooking the sea. Instead, the plan called for him to be landed south of Suri-bong, on the north side of the bay known as Daito-wan. Yi himself would have preferred a location even further east, but that was impossible because of the logistics of getting the inflatable back to the fishing boat, and it would also have greatly increased the possibility of detection.

About five hundred metres off the coast the crewman eased the inflatable to a virtual standstill and cut the engine. The boat rocked gently on the waves while the two men scanned the shore through image-intensifying binoculars, looking and listening for any sign of life or movement, but the coastline appeared almost deserted.

They could see a few lights – probably from oil lamps, since the mains electricity supply in North Korea is, to put it mildly, erratic – signifying isolated dwellings, but there were no large settlements in this region.

At a gesture from Yi Min-Ho, the crewman restarted the engine and steered towards the beach. This was perhaps the most dangerous phase of the entire operation, and they proceeded very cautiously, checking all around them – not just on the beach ahead – as they neared landfall. Both knew the fate that would await them if they were caught by the North Korean security forces.

The moment the inflatable touched the beach, the crewman jumped out and held the bow steady while Yi Min-Ho shrugged his haversack onto his back and climbed out, his boots crunching on the pebbles. Without a backward glance, the crewman immediately pushed the inflatable away from the beach, and climbed back into it.

Yi looked back once, checking that the boat was well clear of the strand and already heading south-west to rendezvous with the fishing boat, then he tramped across to the cover of the trees that bordered the shore. There he stopped, put down his haversack and took out the Kyocera satellite phone and the GPS receiver to check precisely his current position. He'd landed almost exactly where they'd calculated, and this he hoped was a good omen. He next switched on the Kyocera, made a call that lasted less than fifteen seconds, then turned the unit off.

Yi hefted the haversack onto his back again, tucked the GPS receiver into one of his pockets, and started walking. His destination lay some fifteen kilometres directly to the east, but he would probably have to walk about double that distance. He couldn't cover the entire route in darkness, but the final section of his journey would be in the hill country south of Kungnak-san, where he could probably travel safely in daylight. If nothing unexpected occurred, he should be in position sometime the following morning.

Aïn Oussera Air Base, Algeria

The base looked almost deserted in the ghostly green light of the image intensifier, but Richter could see at least a dozen sentries posted around the hangars ranged inside the boundary fence. Most seemed to be smoking, the sudden flares of brightness unmistakable through the NVGs. That was good news from the point of view of the SAS team, because sentries with lighted cigarettes give away their positions every time they draw in a lungful of tobacco smoke, but also have degraded night vision and are less likely to be fully alert.

'That's it,' Richter murmured into his boom microphone, 'the second one from the left.'

The satellite pictures they'd studied at Hereford had clearly identified the hangar that Six and the Americans wanted investigating. They'd also shown, on three separate passes, that it normally had sentries posted on all of its four sides, which presented a problem, but Richter thought he'd worked out a way around that.

'Still happy with the plan?' Dekker asked.

'I'm not happy with any of this, but I don't see any other way of getting a look inside. Do you?'

'No, not unless we take out about half those sentries first. And since the Head-shed's very keen to ensure nobody knows we were here, that's not an option.'

'Right,' Richter said, 'we'd better get on with it.'

To the front of their position, a wadi ran diagonally towards the airfield's boundary fence. It looked around four or five feet deep, enough to conceal a crouching man, and was the obvious way to reach the fence undetected, which now made Dekker nervous.

'If I was in charge of security at this place,' he said, 'I'd stick a handful of Claymores in that ditch. I think our best approach is straight to the fence, keeping low. The guards are positioned around the hangars, not on the boundary, and there aren't any watchtowers or dogs to cause a problem.'

Dekker turned aside for a short conversation with his number two – a small wiry sergeant-major named Wallace – then he briefed his men. Just he and Richter, accompanied by a trooper carrying a collapsible aluminium ladder, would cross the open ground to the airfield boundary, while the rest of the men stayed well back. If they reached the fence undetected, Richter would use the ladder to get inside. Then it had to be all up to him, since he was the deniable asset, carrying no possible means of identification. The SAS troopers would protect his progress, of course, but under no circumstances would they themselves enter the base. That had been made very clear at Hereford. Richter must get inside, carry out his surveillance, and get out again, alone.

Richter checked his gear. Like the SAS troopers, he was wearing all-black combat clothing, but he wasn't carrying the usual assortment of weapons, ammunition and equipment. He had a Sig 226 in a holster strapped to his thigh, which he really hoped he wouldn't have to use, because that would blow the mission; a set of compact binoculars; a collapsible jemmy; a coil of thin but very strong climbing rope, two webbing straps and a harness; and a high-specification digital camera inside his jacket. And that, apart from a slim leather wallet containing a selection of specialized lock-picking tools, was pretty much all he had. Stealth, not firepower, was his most important weapon here.

'Ready?' Dekker asked, and Richter nodded. 'Right, let's go. All callsigns, heads-up. Spook's going in, immediate.'

Dekker led the way, sliding backwards from the top of the rise until he could stand up safely out of sight of the air base. A trooper appeared beside him and placed his 203 against a rock. The ladder, folded and fitted to the frame of his Bergen, was a cumbersome and bulky load, and he didn't want to carry the rifle as well.

There were dips and rises on the desert floor, and clumps of rocks between their position and the perimeter of the air base. Dekker quickly sketched out a route that would make the best possible use of what cover there was available, then set off. Richter followed, the trooper with the ladder behind him. The three men proceeded slowly, only one at a time, so as to minimize the possibility that their movements would be seen. The nearest sentry was only about one hundred yards away, which was far too close for comfort.

They were forty yards from the fence when Dekker suddenly dropped flat, followed by the others. He'd seen headlights approaching from inside the airfield. The vehicle came closer, apparently following the perimeter track. It passed directly in front of them without slowing down, and they could see it was an open jeep or similar with a machine-gun mounted on the back.

'Probably just a roving patrol,' Dekker suggested, his voice sounding alarmingly loud in Richter's earpiece. 'No doubt checking that all the sentries are still awake.'

'Which they are, unfortunately,' Richter replied.

They resumed their slow and steady progress, and five minutes later the three of them were crouching in a slight dip in the ground only fifteen feet from the fence. It was a typical low-security barrier: steel posts about ten feet high set into concrete bases, with heavy-duty wire netting strung between them, supported by horizontal steel cables.

'No sign of sensors,' Dekker observed, 'and it's definitely not electrified, so you won't fry when you touch it.'

'That's encouraging, at least.'

Dekker slid the folding ladder from the trooper's Bergen frame and laid it out flat on the ground. Most collapsible ladders have joints that click loudly when they snap into place, but this one had been specially manufactured for the Regiment. It was absolutely rigid when assembled, but the joints closed in complete silence.

In less than a minute the ladder was ready. They checked in all directions, making sure that they were still unobserved, then Dekker stepped forward and leant the ladder against one of the steel posts supporting the fence. The ladder itself was twelve feet long, since the analysts at JARIC had calculated the height of the fence at ten feet, based upon the length of the shadows they'd observed on the satellite imagery.

Richter climbed up swiftly, swung his leg over so that he straddled the fence, his feet resting safely on one of the horizontal steel cables, pulled the ladder up and over, then lowered its base to the ground inside the airfield. Then he slid down it, lifted the ladder away from the fence and placed it flat on the ground.

Outside the wire, Dekker gave him a thumbs-up, then the two men melted away into the night.

Richter was inside. Now all he had to do was complete the mission and get out again. It sounded easy enough if you said it quickly.

Chapter Two

Monday
Pyoksong, North Korea

North Korea maintains a huge standing army of just over a million men – almost as many as the United States – with a further five million troops in reserve. It has some eight hundred combat aircraft, three thousand five hundred tanks and over ten thousand artillery pieces. Almost without exception, these men, aircraft and weapons are located within forty miles of the border with South Korea, not least because technically the two nations are still at war, despite the armistice signed in 1953. Virtually every battle plan that the North Korean forces have prepared is aimed at either repelling an invasion from the south, or actually launching an attack on its more prosperous neighbour.

The gulf between the two countries is vast. South Korea is about twenty per cent smaller than its brother nation, but has twice the population, a gross domestic product *four hundred* times greater, and the average worker there earns about twenty times more than a North Korean. The North spends around thirty per cent of its national income on the military budget: the South less than three per cent. South Korea is a major manufacturing nation, selling its products – everything from cars to computer components – around the world. North

Korea has only one major export: hard drugs, produced with the active support and compliance of the government and frequently shipped out using diplomatic privilege to avoid confiscation.

What North Korea hates – and fears – more than anything is the nation immediately south of the Demilitarized Zone. Or, more precisely, that nation's huge silent partner, America.

For any country with an extensive coastline, and especially one suffering from what amounts to government-orchestrated paranoia, radar surveillance of all its borders and seaward approaches is essential. In the southeast of its territory, North Korea has radar heads located on the Kuksa-bong peninsula, the island of Sunwi-do, and on the promontory extending due west of the South Korean island of Gyodong-do. All are left unmanned, their signals fed through a combination of cables and microwave links to a central radar station just outside Pyoksong.

The South Korean National Intelligence Service had been absolutely right: the silenced outboard motor *did* have about the same radar signature as a large bird. But what Yi Min-Ho hadn't considered, as he made his clandestine approach to the landfall south of Suri-bong, was that birds very rarely fly in a straight line.

The signal generated by the intruders' motor was detected by the Kuksa-bong radar head immediately the inflatable moved away from the fishing boat, but at first the operator at Pyoksong had ignored it, just as he ignored all other small and intermittent returns. It was only when this 'bird' began following an arrow-straight track directly towards the North Korean coastline that he called over his watch supervisor to investigate.

The *so-ryong* – the rank equivalent to major – stared at the radar screen for a couple of minutes, then issued a curt instruction. 'Keep tracking it,' he snapped, 'and tell me the moment it makes landfall.'

Then he strode back to his own desk and picked up the telephone.

Aïn Oussera Air Base, Algeria

The task was simple enough. There were three hangars in front of him, and Richter needed to get himself into the middle one, or at least take a look inside it. The problem was that while the two hangars on either side each had a single guard stationed in front of its huge sliding doors, the middle building had six men watching it – one posted at each of its four sides and a two-man roving patrol. Getting in undetected was not a viable option from the ground, so he was going to have to try the roof. Or, to be precise, the lighting gantry.

The satellite photographs supplied by the Americans had revealed one single dark line cutting across the fronts of all three buildings, and their analysts' best guess had been an overhead duct carrying power cables. Looking from where Richter now lay, concealed behind a stack of empty oil drums near the perimeter fence, their assumption was clearly correct, but the structure also carried banks of spotlights to illuminate the hardstanding immediately in front of the three hangars. Since it carried massive lights whose bulbs would periodically need replacing, this meant the gantry had to be strong enough to support a man's weight, and therefore Richter could crawl along it to reach the target hangar. The trick now was getting up onto the roof of the first one in line.

All three hangars had been built to the same design: windowless brick walls supporting a metal roof, with aircraft-width doors at the front, pedestrian doors at the back and on both sides – each with a single light burning above it. These doors would obviously be locked, but that wasn't an insurmountable problem. The difficult bit would be managing to open one of them without collecting a bullet from a sentry.

For a while Richter just waited and watched what the guards were up to. From his confined position he could see only the rear and one side of the left-hand hangar, and the backs of the two others further along. The sentry guarding the nearest hangar occasionally appeared at the far end, glancing directly along the side of the building before returning to his post at the front. But while Richter watched he never bothered to walk the full distance to check round the back. The rear door at first seemed to offer the best chance of getting inside without this particular guard spotting him, but that wasn't going to work because of the roving patrol and the single sentry stationed at the back of the middle hangar. The moment Richter approached he'd be seen by one or other of them.

The side door therefore was his best, in fact his only, option. He'd just have to somehow crack the lock on the door as quickly as possible. For almost half an hour Richter patiently watched the sentry's routine, trying to work out a pattern to his timing, but there didn't seem to be any. Sometimes the man would check the side of the hangar twice inside five minutes, then he might not reappear for another ten. There was no point, Richter decided, in waiting any longer. The guard's unpredictable movements were working against him, and he was just going to have to take his chances.

He carefully studied the side door through his binoculars. It appeared to have both a mortise and a Yale-type lock, which was irritating, since two locks would obviously take longer to crack than just one. Richter opened his leather wallet and selected two picks – a snake and a half-diamond – and also a tension wrench. From another pocket he took a device that looked something like an electric toothbrush, actually a SouthOrd Model E100C Electric Pick, then inserted a thin steel probe called a needle into the pivot arm at the end, and tightened the hexagonal screw.

Then he checked in with Dekker, so the SAS man would know what he was planning. 'Alpha One, Spook. I'm going in through the side door, after I next see the guard check this side of the building.'

The voice in his earphones was quiet and reassuring. 'Roger, Spook. We're watching your back.'

Three minutes later the sentry stuck his head around the far corner of the hangar and glanced along the side of the building, then again retreated.

'Spook. I'm going in now.'

The moment the guard vanished, Richter moved, sprinting across the fifty-odd yards of short-cropped grass that separated him from his objective. The side door was slightly recessed into the brickwork, but not enough to hide him from sight. He had to make sure he got the door open before the guard decided to take another look this way.

The first thing he did was check for wires or sensors, or any kind of an alarm system. He wasn't really expecting to find one, since the hangar lay inside an airfield constantly patrolled by armed guards, but it was his practice to check everything, and usually twice over. Then he tried the door handle, just in case somebody had forgotten to lock it, but that got him nowhere. He slid the tension wrench – a slim steel tool shaped like an elongated 'L' – into the keyway of the mortise lock and exerted gentle turning pressure, then inserted the snake pick and started probing.

Lock-picking was a skill Richter had only recently acquired, while attending a short course in Camberwell conducted by a professional locksmith employed as a consultant by the Security Service, MI5. That instruction had been arranged solely in preparation for this operation.

The lock was an exterior-quality five-lever unit, but it felt old and worn and, more importantly, loose. Holding the snake pick lightly between forefinger and thumb, he began twisting it gently, locating the various wards and trying to visualize the shape of the key that would fit, then moving the levers gently, guided by the pressure of the tension wrench. It was a delicate, highly tactile process, and here Richter was trying to rush it. Suddenly he felt the wrench move slightly in his hand, and he continued turning. With a faint click, the pick and wrench rotated through a complete circle. The first lock was now open.

He tried the door handle again, but it still didn't

budge. Richter transferred the tension wrench to the other lock, and took the electric pick out of his pocket. This type of lock was known as a pin-tumbler, and he saw with some surprise that it wasn't just Yale-pattern: it was actually a genuine Yale. According to the MI5 man, unless there was something very unusual about the design, opening a pin-tumbler would normally take only a few seconds. This realization had persuaded Richter to replace the entire security system for the entrance door of his attic apartment in Stepney.

Through his night-vision goggles, Colin Dekker lay watching the figure crouching at one side of the hangar. Beside him, outside the Aïn Oussera boundary fence, Sergeant-Major Wallace was doing much the same, but he was peering through a Davin Optical Starlight scope fitted to a 7.62mm Accuracy International PM sniper rifle, with a bulky suppressor attached to the end of the barrel.

Wallace wasn't concentrating on Richter, though. His weapon was aimed towards the front of the hangar, at the corner where the sentry would appear if he suddenly decided to take another look along that side of the build-ing. If the Algerian guard spotted Richter, then Dekker's instructions were perfectly clear: Wallace was to take him out at once, before he could raise the alarm. Then it would be up to Richter to conceal the body, probably by hauling it inside the hangar, assuming he could get the door open. It wasn't much of a plan, admittedly, but it was the only one they had, under the circumstances.

*

Richter inserted the needle all the way into the keyway then eased it back a fraction in order to allow it to move freely, exerting gentle pressure on the wrench and then pressing the button to activate the pick. The unit hummed and shifted slightly in his hand as the vibrating needle impacted the pins, and only seconds later he was able to rotate the wrench. He released the button on the pick and turned the lock against the pressure of the spring holding the latch. With his left hand he reached for the door handle, turned it and pushed with his shoulder. Immediately the door swung open and he stepped inside the hangar. Quickly he pushed the door closed behind him, the latch clicking back into place.

'You can relax, Dave,' Dekker murmured into his headset microphone, after he watched Richter disappear. 'He's inside now.'

Beside him, Wallace eased the sniper rifle off his shoulder and rested the butt on the ground, while the front of the weapon was still supported on its bipod. 'Just remind me, boss. How's he going to get himself into the right hangar?'

Dekker still didn't take his eyes off the scene in front of him. 'He's got a plan – but it all depends on what he finds in there.'

Inside the hangar, three hundred yards away, Richter was beginning to hope that he hadn't wasted his time. In the light from his torch he could see three aircraft: two MiG-25PDS, the up-rated export model of the Foxbat

interceptor; and a two-seat trainer, the MiG-25U, probably belonging to the 110th Escadron de Chasse, if the Six
briefing officer had got it right. But Richter had no interest in the fighters: he was looking for something much
smaller.

The thing about hangars is that they're very large and
tall, designed to accommodate one or more aircraft while
they're undergoing maintenance, and to facilitate this
work they need banks of powerful lights mounted high
up. Since lights periodically need their bulbs replacing,
what Richter was looking for was the cherry-picker hoist,
or whatever the Algerians used to do this. What he was
hoping now was that they kept one in each hangar, rather
than rely on a single hoist shared between them.

Then he saw it, tucked back against one wall: a standard electric-powered cherry-picker with controls in the
cradle itself. The only problem was that it probably
didn't have the height for him to reach the very top of
the building, but that wouldn't matter. Up there, Richter
could see a latticework of girders supporting the gently
curved roof of the hangar and knew that if he could at
least reach the top of one of the steel side-pillars, he could
climb up the rest of the way. So as long as he was quiet,
the guard outside shouldn't hear anything, but if the
cherry-picker was fitted with a petrol engine, he'd just
have to do it the hard way.

Moving the contraption was an unnecessary risk, so
Richter left it in position, climbed into its cradle, and ran
the beam of his torch over the controls. Fortunately, they
looked simple enough. He flicked on the master switch,
shifted the joystick lever forward, and the cradle began
to move upwards and, to his relief, almost silently. As he

neared the top of the side-pillar, he adjusted the elevation angle slightly so that the cradle stopped, virtually at its upper limit, right beside one end of a steel rafter.

Shining his torch across the underside of the roof, he observed that its structure was strong and simple. The main support was a single central steel beam running all the way from the front to the back of the hangar, with about a dozen girders positioned like ribs on either side of it, and additional longitudinal supports to carry the roof panels.

He calculated it would necessitate a fifty-foot climb – at about a fifteen-degree upward angle all the way, and hanging upside down underneath the rafter, in order to reach the central supporting span.

Richter secured a webbing strap to the harness he had already strapped around his torso, looped it over the rafter and clipped it to the D-ring. That would now be his safety line. Then he pulled on a pair of custom-made leather gloves with yellow mesh webbing on the palms and fingers, designed to provide the maximum possible grip, checked that all his equipment was secure, grasped the rafter with both hands and swung his feet up, digging his heels into the recessed sides of the steel beam.

Immediately he could feel the strain on his arms and legs, and knew he had to get this climb over with as quickly as possible. He reached out with his left hand, grasped the central beam, about six inches beyond his head, and repeated the manoeuvre with his right hand. Then he slid his feet along the beam in the same direction. It was slow, hard work, but every time he completed these three movements, he was another foot closer to his objective.

And, he consoled himself, coming back it would be downhill all the way.

Pyongyang, North Korea

Almost in the centre of the city of Pyongyang stood a plain six-storey concrete building. Like most of the other structures in the vicinity, it carried no sign or logo to enlighten the curious about what activity might be carried on inside it. Here, as elsewhere in North Korea, curiosity was not encouraged, and anyone considering just walking in would get little further than the double doors of the entrance. The armed guards posted there would guarantee that.

This was the headquarters of Central Committee Bureau 39, a deliberately innocuous title obscuring the fact that the organization was the hub of North Korea's government-sponsored drug production and smuggling network. The building now appeared almost deserted, lights burning only in the entrance hall, and in the one office currently occupied.

After Pak Je-San's proposal had been accepted, he'd worked with Kim Yong-Su – not an enjoyable experience – in putting a number of procedures in place to ensure that all details of their operation remained totally secret. Approving his suggestions, Kim had then issued instructions to the Supreme Commander of the Armed Forces. Those orders, in turn, had filtered down through the various levels of command, their content becoming progressively less informative as they descended, until at the very bottom level every troop commander and radar

officer had received little more than the briefest possible
instructions and a telephone number.

But that was enough. The call from the radar-watch
supervisor at Pyoksong reached the switchboard at
Bureau 39 headquarters, and was automatically diverted
to Pak's phone because tonight, not unusually, he was
sleeping in his office.

The call had awoken him from a deep slumber, and on
answering it he was somewhat confused. He hadn't
expected to be disturbed, but if anyone was going to call
him, it was likely to be someone from Russia. So it took
him a few seconds to grasp what the *so-ryong* was telling
him.

'We think it might be an attempt to land an agent, sir.'

'Where, exactly, *so-ryong*?' Pak was now fully awake.

The major carefully explained where they'd lost contact with the radar return, some three kilometres off the
coast.

'Projecting the track, sir, we think the vessel must have
made landfall somewhere to the south of Suri-bong.'
He started to say something else, then broke off with
a muttered apology as something distracted his attention. In a few seconds he resumed his report. 'I've just
been advised by one of my staff that the contact has reappeared on radar, and is now heading south-west. We
believe it's a small powerboat, and that it's currently
returning to its parent vessel.'

'Which is what?' Pak asked. 'A submarine?'

'Not likely so close inshore, sir, and we've already pro-
visionally identified the larger vessel as a fishing boat
with South Korean registry. It's sailed out of Inchon on
the same route about a dozen times over the last month,

and our patrol boats have already checked it twice. We could intercept it before it gets back to Inchon.'

'No, that vessel is unimportant. Even if we did stop it, we would find nothing of interest on board, and our action would just warn Seoul that we know what they're up to. We must forget the fishing boat and concentrate on finding the man they've dropped off.'

'I don't understand. Why would they infiltrate a spy *there*?'

'There's a lot you don't understand about this situation, *so-ryong*. I know exactly why they landed their man where they did, and I know where he's currently heading.'

Aïn Oussera Air Base, Algeria

Richter reached the steel centre span of the hangar and swung himself up onto it. There was just enough space between the beam and the roof panels to allow him to crouch down. His arms and legs were trembling from the strain of the climb, and he needed a few seconds' respite before tackling the next phase.

He looped his safety strap around the beam, out of the way, then tested the roof with his gloved hand: it was made from corrugated iron panels. Taking the collapsible jemmy from his pocket, he extended it and eased the point between two of these panels and pulled gently. With a faint creak, the lower one gave slightly. He repositioned the tool and applied pressure again, and this time it lifted far enough for him to see the sky. It would, he reckoned, be a big enough gap for him to climb through.

He checked his equipment to make sure everything was properly attached, then seized the sides of the opening he'd created, and pulled himself up. He wriggled through the gap and lay flat on the roof, checking all around him before moving on.

At that moment Colin Dekker was still looking in the wrong place, at the nearer edge of the roof, but he now spotted Richter within seconds of him emerging. He nudged Wallace and gestured towards the hangar.

'Alpha and Bravo, look sharp,' he said into his microphone. 'Spook's just climbed onto the roof. Let me know if any of the guards spot him.'

Beside him, Wallace trained his sniper rifle on the roof of the hangar, pinpointed Richter through the scope, then dropped the muzzle of the weapon so that it would cover the sentries on the ground.

'Spook. I'm moving forward towards the gantry,' Richter said softly. He was confident that the roof would take his weight – having seen the immensely strong steel skeleton supporting it – and now his biggest concern was to avoid making any noise.

He stayed in a crouch, just in case any of the guards looked up: the sight of a man standing upright on top of the hangar in the moonlight would bring an instant burst of fire from the ground. Not only would he be less noticeable on all fours, but it would also enable him to spread his weight more evenly on the rooftop.

The panel he'd forced open was close to the front of the hangar, so it took only a couple of minutes, even moving slowly and with the greatest care, for him to reach the lighting gantry. From the satellite pictures, the structure had looked fairly substantial, but Richter guessed that at least some of its apparent width was actually shadow, because when he stopped directly above the main doors and looked down, the gantry seemed incredibly narrow.

He glanced over the edge of the high building, looking straight down. The guard was visible below, leaning back against the main entrance doors, a cigarette burning in his mouth, and his rifle slung over one shoulder. The advantage for Richter was that human beings are very limited in their normal field of view: most regard the world at eye level and below, and rarely bother looking up. The bad news is that people in some occupations, pilots and professional soldiers in particular, *are* trained to look up, and if the guard below did so while Richter was crossing the gantry over to the adjacent hangar, he'd be a sitting duck.

Stepping back from the edge, Richter murmured into his microphone. 'Spook. I'm starting across now.'

'Alpha One. Roger that.'

The gantry wasn't going to get any wider however long he hesitated, so Richter took a deep breath and lowered himself onto it. He deliberately ignored the guard below, and also the two sentries standing in front of the target hangar, because clearly there was nothing he could do about them. If any of them spotted him, the first he'd know about it would be a bullet. He concentrated on moving steadily and silently, taking care not to kick against anything – a floodlight or the gantry itself – or trip over the cables, and focused, instead, on getting to the far end.

Halfway across, a sudden gust of wind rattled the entire structure, and for a minute or so Richter paused, just in case a sentry heard the noise and looked up, but then the breeze died away and he continued his careful progress.

Less than four minutes after he'd stepped onto the gantry, he climbed off it thankfully at the other end, and began crawling up the gently sloping roof towards the central ridge. He wouldn't need to get into this hangar: merely force a panel and look carefully inside, and record whatever he saw there with the camera.

More or less reaching the centre of the roof, he took out his jemmy, and began to lever up a panel. The sound of tearing metal was not loud enough to be heard by the guards below, and soon Richter was able to lift the entire panel free and peer down, along the narrow but powerful beam of his torch as it illuminated the interior of the hangar.

Directly below him was a small electric-powered towing truck, normally used to manoeuvre aircraft in and out of the hangar or around the hardstandings. To one side of that, closer to the wall of the building, was another cherry-picker, but what astonished Richter was what else occupied the hangar.

'Shit a brick,' he muttered as he fished the Nikon out of his pocket. 'Six will never believe this.'

Chapter Three

Well before he left Seoul, Yi Min-Ho had spent several hours with his colleagues at Naegok-dong working out the optimum route to his objective, though there had actually been little choice. The coastal area was mainly flat, but cultivated and inhabited, and therefore potentially dangerous. The hills extending north of the coast provided very difficult terrain and, although taking that route would guarantee the least chance of being detected, it would take him an unacceptable length of time to reach his objective.

So Yi stayed near the coast, and followed the main – almost the only – road. He walked along the grass verge because the sound of footsteps – even those made by his rubber-soled boots – risked alerting someone to his presence. Every fifty paces or so he stopped and listened for a short while, in case his ears might detect something his eyes had missed.

Twice he froze into immobility on hearing the sound of movement nearby, his hand reaching for his pistol, but each time the noises faded away. Animals, he assumed, resuming his solitary march. Once a vehicle – an old truck lacking one of its headlamps – rattled past the ditch where he'd already taken cover. He stayed motionless for a few minutes after it had passed him, just in case anyone was following it on foot.

His GPS unit told him that he'd covered almost three kilometres in the first hour, and he calculated that he should reach the vicinity of Ugom in another two. Yi stopped between two stunted bushes for a brief rest, ate a small chocolate bar and washed it down with a mouthful of water, then resumed his steady progress eastward.

Aïn Oussera Air Base, Algeria

Richter held the Nikon firmly by the strap and aimed it at the far end of the hangar, pressed the button, then moved the digital camera slightly to cover the next section of the floor of the large building. Because of the filter, the electronic flash was invisible to his eyes – and more importantly, invisible to the sentries standing outside the building – but was ideally matched to the infrared-sensitive media inside the camera.

He took a dozen pictures, then another couple just in case, switched off the Nikon and replaced it in his pocket. There was no way he could refit the metal roof panel, so he just pushed it down until it was more or less level with those either side of it.

'Spook. I'm on the way back,' he murmured into his microphone, then started crawling across the roof back towards the lighting gantry.

*

'Roger,' Dekker replied. 'Heads up, all callsigns. Watch the guards, but don't fire unless you've no other option.'

Wallace settled the stock of the rifle comfortably into his shoulder and aimed it along the left-hand side of the nearest hangar, looking out for the sentry.

Before stepping out on to the lighting gantry, Richter checked below for the current positions of the guards, who still appeared totally unaware of his presence. The return trip seemed to take less time than before, and within five minutes he was crouching on the roof of the first hangar to make a final check all round him, before re-entering the building itself.

He slid his legs into the gap where he'd lifted the panel, his feet locating the steel beam. He crouched down on it and did his best to pull the panel back into place behind him. It wasn't a good fit, and would be obvious to anyone doing an inspection of the roof, but from the ground it would probably pass muster.

Rather than crawl precariously back down the sloping roof girder, Richter decided it would be quicker to use his climbing rope, and go straight down to the floor of the hangar. He draped it over the main roof spar, both ends of it easily reaching the ground. He looped the safety strap around the beam, clipped it to his harness, and altered his position until he was lying flat across the steel spar.

Trapping the two lengths of the dangling rope between his boots, he also gripped it firmly with his right hand before totally letting go of the beam itself. The safety strap immediately tugged at his harness, and he reached down and released the clip, allowing the strap to slide around and off the steel beam and dangle loose below him. The descent was fast and easy, Richter letting the doubled-over climbing rope slide through his gloved hands, till in seconds he was standing on the hangar floor.

He tugged one end of the rope, pulling it clear of the beam, then coiled it and looped it back over his shoulder. He next walked over to the cherry-picker and lowered its cradle to ground level, then checked around with his torch that he wasn't leaving anything behind him. Seeing nothing out of place, he crossed over to the side door he'd used to enter. At least he wouldn't have to pick the lock this time, nor was he going to bother relocking the five-lever mortise. He'd merely close the door behind him and walk away.

Richter pressed his ear to the door and just listened for a few seconds. 'Spook. I'm coming out,' he said into the microphone, and waited for Dekker's acknowledgement. Then he turned the handle of the Yale lock and eased the door open.

Wallace moved the rifle across to cover the side door of the hangar, watching for Richter to re-emerge. He saw the doorway turn black as the door opened inwards, then a dark shape appeared and looked cautiously in both directions. The sentry wasn't in sight, and within seconds the door was closed again behind him.

But as Richter started to sprint across the open ground towards the cover of the oil drums, the guard suddenly stepped around the corner, then froze as he saw a running man.

'Boss,' Wallace hissed urgently.

'I see him. Alpha Two – take him out.'

Wallace shifted his aim fractionally, centring the crosshairs on the sentry's chest. Above the sight picture, he saw the Algerian open his mouth to shout as he began unslinging his AK47 assault rifle. Then Wallace squeezed the trigger. The sniper rifle bucked against his shoulder, but the suppressor reduced the noise to a muffled thud, and the guard tumbled backwards, the Kalashnikov falling from his lifeless hands.

Hearing the faint noise of the shot coming from outside the boundary fence, Richter glanced round even as he ran. He absorbed the scene in an instant. Time was now crucial, as sooner or later one of the other guards would be bound to notice that the sentry was missing, and head around the side of the hangar to check on him. The team had minutes at best to get away from here.

Richter raced straight for the section of fence where he'd stashed the ladder, lifted it up and leant it against a post. In front, he could see Dekker moving quickly towards him in a crouch, another SAS soldier right behind him. Richter climbed up and perched for a moment on top of the fence, while he swung the ladder over, then slid down to the open ground outside.

'Time we got out of here,' Dekker observed.

'Roger that.'

As they turned away from the fence, Richter felt a slight tug on his left boot. He glanced down and spotted what they'd all missed, but it was now too late. The thin silver trip-wire gleamed in the darkness.

'Oh, shit.'

Behind him security lights suddenly flared into life, illuminating the boundary fence and the open ground outside it. Simultaneously, sirens started their atonic wailing. Their supposedly covert insertion and surveillance operation had just turned very *overt* indeed.

North Korea

The truck seemed to come out of nowhere. One minute the road was empty as far as Yi Min-Ho could see. Then headlights came stabbing through the darkness directly towards him. The unmistakable sound of a big diesel engine shattered the silence of the night.

He'd just crossed the bridge over the river that drains into the Teiton Wan bay at Ugom, and was about to leave the road and strike out across country, heading for a narrow gap through the double line of hills that lay north of the town.

For an instant Yi didn't move, a combination of fatigue and surprise momentarily dulling his reactions, then he stepped unhurriedly off the verge – if the truck contained police or soldiers, a sudden movement would immediately attract their attention – and headed into the adjacent field. But the moment he was clear of the headlight beams, he ran like hell.

The truck growled to a halt and Yi could clearly hear

men shouting, followed by the sound of their boots clumping loudly on the metalled surface of the road. He concentrated totally on keeping his footing on the uneven soil, and covering the ground as swiftly as possible.

The sudden flare of the truck's headlights had impaired his night vision, and Yi stumbled and almost fell three times in his desperate escape. But the men behind him experienced exactly the same problem, and the dancing beams of their torches were of little help because he already had a substantial lead of about one hundred metres.

The ground beneath his feet began to change as scrubby farmland gave way to the uncultivated terrain leading up to the foothills. Running across rough ground is very tiring, and Yi's breath now came in short, painful gasps. He would be forced to stop soon, despite his desperate situation.

Around him were clumps of bushes and stunted trees, and he realized that these offered the best cover he was likely to find. He slowed down and skidded behind two trees growing close together, looking back down the slope towards the lights of his pursuers. They were now even further away, probably two hundred metres, but Yi could clearly sense the determination in their pursuit.

What had started out seemingly as a simple chase was now transformed into a methodical search, with about fifteen men spread out in a line and walking up the hill towards him. Making a conscious effort to slow his breathing, Yi pulled out his binoculars and focused them.

The moonlight was bright enough for him to detect that they were soldiers, assault rifles slung over their shoulders. He'd obviously been unlucky enough to run into a North Korean Army patrol, but the surprise was that they hadn't already started firing in his direction. Because these were military, rather than the police, he didn't imagine they would give up the chase easily, but whatever happened, he mustn't get caught. Realizing he would now have to put as much distance as possible between himself and such a determined pursuit, Yi replaced the binoculars in his pocket, turned northwards and jogged on up the hill.

In fact, luck had nothing to do with this encounter. The moment Pak Je-San ended the call from the radar-watch supervisor at Pyoksong, he had proceeded to mobilize troops from the closest military establishment, which was the fighter airfield at T'ae'tan. There were very few roads in that part of the country, so anyone landing south of Suri-bong had little option but to head east. And therefore Pak had guessed exactly where his quarry was going.

Aïn Oussera Air Base, Algeria

Suddenly the base came alive with the sound of vehicle engines revving up and with loudly shouted orders. The sentries around the various hangars left their posts and began running towards the perimeter fence. It was only a matter of seconds, Richter realized, before they started shooting.

'All callsigns, Alpha One,' Dekker shouted. 'Let's get the fuck out of here. Break, break. Delta One and Two, get the Pinkies moving, immediate.'

The response from the two SAS troopers guarding

the Land Rovers was instant. 'Deltas mobile, heading straight for you.'

The six SAS men were already up and running, weaving and dodging unpredictably from side to side to make themselves as difficult targets as possible, but all the time heading away from the fence and the glare of the security lights.

'Regroup in two hundred yards,' Dekker instructed, as the metallic clatter of a couple of Kalashnikovs on full auto echoed behind them, bullets spraying randomly in their direction. 'But don't return fire.'

They were already well away from the fence, so he knew the Algerians had to be firing blind. Shooting back would just confirm their position, giving the enemy something definite to aim at.

Richter could see two pairs of headlights approaching, half a mile away to their right, the vehicles bouncing wildly over the desert floor.

'Regroup on me,' Dekker called out, as he slid to a halt behind an outcrop of rock. 'Anyone hurt? Any problems?' It took less than ten seconds to confirm that none of them had suffered any injuries, then they started running again, this time in two loose groups heading directly towards the approaching Land Rovers.

Behind them, the main gates of Aïn Oussera were open, and the first of the Algerian Air Force trucks, loaded with heavily armed soldiers, were heading out in pursuit. Unfortunately the headlights of the SAS Pinkies would soon give them a clear target.

'Delta One and Two, kill the lights,' Dekker ordered. 'Home in on our torches.'

Immediately the headlights were extinguished, which

would obviously slow their escape, but not having the lights blazing might buy them a few precious seconds, or even minutes, while the Algerians tried to locate them. Meanwhile two of the troopers took out their torches and shone them steadily, like beacons, in the direction of the approaching Land Rovers.

Dekker called a halt for a few seconds, while he looked back towards the airfield, checking the disposition of the enemy troops. A couple of large trucks had emerged and were now heading in their general direction, but obviously the drivers had no firm idea where their quarry was located. Richter wasn't bothered about such vehicles – the Pinkies could outrun them, no problem – but the three smaller ones were a definite concern. In the lights from the perimeter fence, they looked like either open jeeps or Land Rovers, and in each one he could discern the unmistakable shape of a heavy machine-gun, set on a pillar right behind the driver. Whatever those vehicles were, they had pretty much the same armament as the Pinkies, and could also probably match them for speed. But before Richter could suggest any action against them or their occupants, Dekker was already issuing orders.

'Alpha Two, Bravo One, take out their jeeps.'

'Roger.'

As Richter watched, Wallace unslung his sniper rifle, dropped into a prone position and rested the bipod on an almost flat rock in front of him. He paused for a few seconds, slowing his breathing as he took aim at the moving target still nearly a quarter of a mile away. Then the rifle kicked in his hands, the sound of it a flat slap in the desert night. Outside the gate, the front tyre on one of the jeeps suddenly exploded, the vehicle lurching to one side and stopping immediately. It was a hell of a shot in the circumstances.

'Brilliant shot,' Richter muttered.

'I was aiming at the driver,' Wallace confessed.

At that moment the other sniper fired but missed: the bullet's impact with a rock somewhere near the gates was clearly audible. The Algerian soldiers reacted immediately. Half a dozen of them moved forward to whatever cover they could find, and began loosing off shots from their Kalashnikov assault rifles towards the SAS troops. They weren't aimed rounds, just supporting fire designed to make their unknown attackers keep their heads down. Behind them, the two remaining jeeps manoeuvred to the rear of the three-ton trucks and out of sight.

'One down, two to go,' Dekker muttered. Behind him, the two Land Rovers lurched to a halt side by side amid swirling dust. 'Mount up and let's get the hell out of here.'

Inside thirty seconds, the two Pinkies were on the move again, the drivers pushing them as hard as they could which, without lights, wasn't very fast. The terrain was rocky and uneven, strewn with boulders the size of small cars, which loomed up faster than Richter, for one, was comfortable about. But just as dangerous were the smaller rocks, any one of which could smash a sump or transmission housing, or burst a tyre. The drivers kept swerving violently from side to side, picking the best path they could through the tortured landscape.

'We're trading speed for invisibility,' Dekker said, 'but once we're clear of this area we can use the headlights.

And,' he added, pointing east, where the first fingers of red and yellow grew visible against the dark blue of the sky, 'it looks like the sun will be up in about thirty minutes.'

At that moment two sets of headlights suddenly stabbed through the darkness towards them from behind. The Algerians had sent their two jeeps ahead in pursuit, and they were approaching fast. Like the SAS vehicles, they'd been driving without lights until confident they were getting near to their quarry, but now they were only about a hundred yards behind, and closing quickly. So the moment one of the escaping Land Rovers was briefly illuminated by the pursuers' dancing headlamp beams, the shooting started.

Dekker glanced back, and made the obvious decision. 'Hit the lights,' he ordered. 'Now we need the speed, and let's try to frighten them off.'

Wallace stood up awkwardly in the bucking vehicle, and seized the grip of the Browning machine-gun. He took the best aim he could and loosed a short burst at their pursuers. Unsurprisingly, none of the bullets appeared to hit its target, but within seconds the headlights behind them started dropping back.

'Good,' Dekker muttered. 'Now, if they'll just stay out of our way until we reach the Herky-bird, we should be OK.'

And then things seemed to happen in slow motion. As Richter glanced at the other Land Rover, only a few yards in front, its left-side front wheel bounced upwards, being deflected by a football-sized rock. That shouldn't have been a problem, but at almost the same moment the right-side wheel dropped down into a pothole.

The Pinky was already unbalanced, and this sudden lurch to the right completed the process. The Land Rover slewed inexorably sideways, the driver fighting for control. Then it toppled over, its right side smashing into the ground. Scattering men and equipment, it continued sliding several yards before impacting a massive boulder, then stopped dead.

Chapter Four

Kwon In-Ho, the *chung-wi*, or lieutenant, leading the patrol, had a real problem. They'd spotted the black-clad figure leaving the road and starting to cut across an adjacent field, which gave them an accurate reference point for their pursuit. The problem now was that, as they'd moved further away from the road, their search fan had of necessity become wider until, Kwon estimated, there were now gaps of fifty to seventy metres separating his soldiers. And that kind of spacing meant there was a good chance their quarry could elude them simply by taking cover somewhere, and then doubling back once they'd passed by. Or he could have moved right over to one side, well away from the searchers, and then carried on heading into the hills in front of them.

In short, having failed to find their man within the first few minutes, they were now probably just wasting their time. Reluctantly, Kwon called his troops to a halt, and made radio contact with his superior. The response was exactly as he'd expected: he was ordered to return his patrol immediately to T'ae'tan, and then report to the commanding officer. Within the North Korean military, there was no excuse for failure to achieve an objective: such failure was always considered to be either deliberate sabotage or dereliction of duty, no matter what the extenuating circumstances.

Meanwhile, at T'ae'tan, the unhappy lieutenant's immediate superior, Lee Chang-Ho, the *tab-wi* or captain, shut down his radio and gazed with foreboding at the secure telephone nearby. He could certainly put blame on Kwon for not capturing the spy, but he himself might also suffer, if it could be shown that his original orders to the lieutenant had in some way been inaccurate or insufficiently comprehensive. But, whatever the outcome of the night's activities, he knew he would have to pass on the unwelcome news to Pyongyang.

Lee reached for the telephone and dialled the number he'd scribbled on a notepad. When Pak Je-San himself answered, the captain explained briefly what had happened, stressing how the failure to capture the infiltrator was entirely due to the incompetence of Kwon and his men. When he finished speaking there was an ominous silence before Pak responded.

'I will discuss this fiasco with your commanding officer later today,' he hissed. 'Neither you nor the idiot you tasked are to leave the base until further notice.'

'Yes, sir.'

'Good. Now, thanks to your abysmal failure, we still have a South Korean spy at large within the area. Fortunately, I believe I know what his objective is, and there may still be time to retrieve the situation. Do you think you can find some men – more competent this time – who can carry out a series of simple instructions?'

'Of course.'

'Since this may be the only chance you'll get to salvage your career, you should listen carefully.'

For three minutes the captain jotted down sentences on his notepad. When the call ended, he sat for a few seconds reviewing what he'd written, then reached for the internal telephone.

Algeria

Dekker's driver immediately hit the brakes and slammed his own vehicle to a halt, headlights illuminating the wreckage of its comrade, and the SAS men swung smoothly into action. Two of them leapt out and raced over to the crashed Land Rover. Dekker stood up and looked all around behind them, checking on the positions of the pursuing vehicles, then also jumped out to help. Wallace remained in place and took careful aim with the Browning. Grabbing a 203, Richter climbed out of the Pinky, moved well over to one side of the crash site and took up a position beside a large boulder. If he got fired at, the last thing he wanted was bullets missing him but hitting the injured soldiers behind him. He aimed the weapon towards the path of the approaching vehicles, but held fire till the range reduced enough to allow for accuracy with the small-calibre assault rifle.

The Algerian jeeps were about two hundred yards away as Wallace started firing off bursts of three or four rounds at a time, the most efficient and accurate way to use the weapon, with the bonus of conserving ammunition. A headlight on the leading jeep was shot out immediately, and then the vehicle slammed to a halt. It seemed likely the Browning's bullets had done terminal damage to either the engine or the transmission.

The second jeep doused its lights and turned away, heading for cover over to the right. *Basic Infantry Tactics 101: Split your forces so as to deny the enemy the ability to concentrate all his firepower on a single area.* Unfortunately, Dekker's men couldn't do likewise.

The sky was brightening quickly, desert dawns being usually of short duration, and Richter could just make out the shapes of the soldiers climbing out of the crippled jeep. But, as he noted, they weren't running away but taking up positions to return fire. And seconds later the rattle of their Kalashnikovs became a distant counterpoint to Wallace's steady bursts of firing.

At that range their AK47s were hopelessly inaccurate, and Richter wondered why one of them hadn't stayed in the halted jeep to use the heavy machine-gun. Moments later, the same thought obviously occurred to one of the Algerians, who ran back and climbed into the abandoned vehicle.

'I see him,' Wallace called out, before Richter could speak. 'Take the Browning.'

Wallace grabbed his sniper rifle and stepped away from the Pinky. The Starlight scope and the heavier-calibre bullets – 7.62mm against the 203's 5.56mm – would make a huge difference. He dropped flat on the ground, spread the bipod legs and settled himself into the aiming position.

Richter grasped the Browning, pointed it at the jeep and fired a series of short bursts.

Then the machine-gun on the Algerian vehicle replied, tracer arcing towards them as the soldier corrected his aim. Bullets smashed into the nearby rocks, sending shards and splinters whizzing through the air. Kalashnikov bullets howled overhead, but it was the machine-gun that would kill them, if Wallace couldn't find his mark soon.

Richter glanced down as he heard a shot from the sniper rifle, and instantly the Algerian machine-gun fell silent. Looking ahead, he saw a bulky shape tumble backwards out of the jeep, and then shifted his aim from the vehicle to the muzzle flashes of the Kalashnikovs. He wasn't hopeful of actually hitting any of the Algerian soldiers, but if he could make them keep their heads down, and convince them that trying to get back behind the machine-gun was a really bad idea, it might be enough.

He looked around him. Dekker and four SAS troopers were struggling to free one of their comrades whose leg was trapped under the wreckage of the crashed Pinky, and beside them another soldier lay ominously still on the ground, his head at an unnatural angle to his body.

Then the second Algerian jeep drove back into view, the driver making for a group of rocks over to their right, with the clear intention of trying to outflank them. Richter swung the Browning around on its mount and fired a six-round burst, but the vehicle was too quick for him. It reached the shelter of the boulders and lurched to a halt, and he had no doubt that within a matter of seconds they'd be taking fire from two positions simultaneously. They had to start moving out, and quickly.

'Colin,' he called. 'We've got to get out of here.'

'We're ready,' Dekker gasped, as he and two other troopers lifted a wounded comrade into the Pinky. The soldier was obviously in great pain, his left leg below the knee a bloody mess, a section of bone protruding below the makeshift tourniquet someone had applied. Yet as soon as they'd got him seated, the man painfully reached for a 203 and brought it up to the ready position.

Dekker and his men went back to the wrecked Land Rover and returned moments later carrying another soldier, but this one was clearly beyond medical help. Silently, they laid the body in the rear section of the vehicle.

'Broken neck,' Dekker muttered shortly. 'Right, everyone, mount up. John, get us out of here.'

The driver climbed into his seat, jammed the Land Rover into gear, and gunned the engine. Wallace resumed his position at the Browning machine-gun, heedless of the bullets still spraying all around them, and fired a long burst that traversed from left to right, to include most of the positions where the Algerian soldiers might have taken cover. Two of the others followed his example with their assault rifles, while Richter and Dekker joined in by firing forty-millimetre grenades from a couple of the 203s.

Just thirty seconds after they took off, Richter heard an explosion close behind. The overturned Pinky had exploded in a ball of fire.

'High explosive and thermite?' he asked, above the din of the automatic-weapon fire.

'You got it,' Dekker said, changing the magazine on his 203. 'No better way to sanitize that vehicle.'

North Korea

In the pale light of early morning, Yi Min-Ho watched silently as the searching soldiers paused in their advance and assembled in a field lying about three hundred metres below his vantage point. He at first presumed they were being briefed on new search tactics, but after a minute they turned and headed back towards the road where their lorry was parked.

It looked as if the pursuit had been called off, but Yi feared that it might be a diversionary tactic, encouraging him to stand up and resume his journey. They could easily have left a couple of men behind, hidden in the undergrowth, waiting for him to move, so for ten minutes he lay there motionless, scanning the fields below with his binoculars. But there was no sign of life and he was certain the army lorry had definitely left the area, having watched it drive away down the road leading to the east, the sound of its exhaust gradually fading into silence.

Yi carefully checked the land lying above him, identifying the next available cover. He eased up into a low crouch, backed away from his hiding place and moved slowly up the hill. When he reached another clump of bushes, he slid in behind it and again studied the land below through his binoculars. Still nothing moved.

Cautiously, he stood upright for just five seconds, then ducked down again. No shots were fired, and the hillside remained empty and innocent-looking. They must have gone, he decided, whereupon he turned and ran quickly up the slope, stopping after a couple of hundred metres to check behind him again. He should be at least five hundred metres from where he'd last seen his pursuers, so unless some stay-behinds had somehow out-flanked him, he was already beyond effective range of their weapons.

He shrugged, and strode on, now making for a gap in the Kungnak-san range of hills that rose in front of him. His objective, T'ae'tan Air Base, lay directly to the east, but his aim was to get himself to the north side of the runway, so he chose a longer, north-eastern route.

Algeria

The Pinky was now overloaded by any standards. Designed to carry only four or five, it currently had nine on board, one of them dead and another badly injured. The rest hung on as best they could as the driver pushed the vehicle to its limits, the Land Rover bouncing and jolting alarmingly over the rough surface.

But hanging on was the least of their worries. About five hundred yards behind them, and gaining steadily, was the remaining Algerian jeep. Its driver clearly knew the terrain, and was currently following a parallel route across the desert that looked a lot smoother. His machine-gunner would fire occasional bursts after the fleeing Land Rover, with almost no chance of finding his mark in those conditions and at that range.

Half a mile further behind, two other sets of head-lights bored through the morning twilight. The three-ton trucks had not given up the chase.

'Foxtrot November, Alpha One,' said Dekker into his radio microphone, almost having to shout over the roar of the turbo-charged diesel and the rattling of equipment. 'We're heading back, with hostiles in pursuit. We're now in one vehicle only. I say again, one vehicle only. Our estimate is minutes zero six. Get those engines started, and drop the ramp.'

'Alpha One, roger. Call when you're thirty seconds out, and we'll hit the lights and start rolling.'

The Algerian jeep had closed to less than three hundred yards, and its machine-gun started up again, bullets striking the rocks around them, uncomfortably close. Though none actually hit the Land Rover, Richter guessed it was only a matter of time.

'We're not going to make it unless we stop those bastards,' Dekker called out.

'Fucking risky. If we slow down they'll be all over us.'

'Yes, but if we don't they'll catch us before we get to the plane. John, next big clump of rocks you see, dive behind it and stop. Then kill the lights.'

'Got it, boss.'

Two minutes later the headlights picked out a handful of large boulders off to the right of their path.

'That'll do,' Dekker called, and the Pinky changed course slightly to make towards them. 'We'll try to discourage them a bit, so use grenades.'

Richter, Dekker and two of the troopers began loading forty-millimetre grenades into their 203s. Then, on Dekker's command, they fired them back towards the vehicle in pursuit. There was no chance of hitting it, but this sudden display of firepower might make the Algerians back off.

The driver braked hard – the vehicle had no rear lights, so the pursuers wouldn't notice it slowing down – and slewed the Pinky around in a circle behind the rocks. He switched off the headlights as he came to a halt.

'Dave, you take the Browning. Everyone else, spread out. Don't fire until I give the order.'

Richter checked the magazine on his 203, found he had only four rounds left. He paused to change it, then ran over to a boulder looming by itself. He aimed the assault rifle towards the approaching jeep and waited.

The Algerian vehicle had already slowed down, and it suddenly veered off, heading away from their location. Somebody on board must have noticed that their quarry's lights had vanished, and guessed they could be driving into a trap.

'Fuck, these guys are good,' Dekker muttered. 'Dave, hit them with the Browning. Everyone else, get back in the Pinky. John, take us out of here – no lights.'

Wallace fired off several short bursts from the machine-gun, but the enemy jeep was already virtually invisible behind a rocky outcrop.

'Grenades, go,' Dekker ordered, and the night air filled with the sound of explosions as the Land Rover accelerated away.

They'd covered only about a quarter of a mile when Richter spotted the jeep behind them again, with its headlights switched off. The sky was lightening almost by the minute, and the Algerians had obviously seen the Land Rover get moving again. And now the visibility was good enough to enable fast driving without any lights at all.

'How far to the Herky-bird?' Richter inquired.

Dekker checked his GPS. 'Around a mile and a half.' Just then the machine-gun mounted on the pursuing jeep began firing again.

Wallace immediately stood up, grasped the Browning,

and began returning fire. Meanwhile, two of the SAS soldiers loosed off with their 203s. As before, the Pinky kept bouncing around too much for accurate shooting, but their onslaught might help keep the Algerians at a suitable distance.

'Foxtrot November, Alpha One. We're approaching one mile. Are you ready for us?'

'Affirmative, Alpha One. We're turning and burning, ramp down, lights off.'

Dekker looked back to check the position of the Algerian jeep, then focused forward, searching for the C-130. 'There it is.' He tapped the driver on the shoulder and pointed.

'I see it now.'

The Land Rover swerved slightly so as to approach the Hercules from directly behind.

'Foxtrot November, thirty seconds.'

'Roger.'

In front of them, the cargo-bay lights of the transport aircraft suddenly flared into life, so they could see the steel ramp clearly now. They could also see the four Allison turbo-prop engines, with their propellers spinning ever faster as the pilot opened the throttles to start the seventy-ton aircraft moving across the rock-strewn surface of the desert.

Behind them, the Algerian soldiers had obviously also spotted the aircraft, and their jeep now began closing the gap. Wallace quit firing in controlled bursts and let loose an almost continuous stream of bullets at their pursuers. One or two seemed to hit the jeep, but it didn't slow down, and still the Algerian machine-gunner kept shooting at them. More in hope than expectation, Richter aimed another three grenades at the vehicle, following those with a couple of bursts of 5.56-millimetre bullets.

'Foxtrot November, twenty seconds,' Dekker estimated. 'John, better get this right or else.'

The Hercules was already accelerating away from them, its speed rising steadily. They were now looking straight at the lowered ramp, the two loadmasters standing either side of it at the top, carefully watching their approach.

'Ten seconds.'

A long burst of fire from the pursuing vehicle raised clouds of dust just to the left of the Land Rover. The driver flinched, twitching the wheel momentarily to the right before resuming his course.

'Five seconds.'

The Hercules was accelerating through forty knots as the Pinky hit the ramp at fifty miles an hour. Its front wheels bounced, and for a sickening moment Richter feared that the vehicle might lose so much momentum that it wouldn't make it. But as their driver kept his foot flat on the accelerator, the four-wheel drive kicked in and the Land Rover lurched safely into the cavernous hold, slewing sideways as he hit the brakes.

Almost before it had halted, Richter could hear the whine as one of the loadmasters pressed a button to raise the ramp behind them. The aircraft instantly began accelerating faster, blowing clouds of desert dust and sand behind it.

The Algerian jeep stopped a couple of hundred yards away, to allow the machine-gunner a stable platform. He took careful aim and fired one long continuous burst straight at the rear of the departing aircraft's fuselage.

The first bullets impacted as the ramp slammed shut, punching easily through the thin aluminium and ricocheting off anything solid in their way.

'Get down,' Dekker yelled, and the SAS men tumbled out of the Land Rover and threw themselves flat on the floor of the hold. The two loadmasters moved to follow their example, but one of them got caught in the leg by a couple of the bullets and screamed in agony.

Then the Hercules bounced twice and lifted into the air. Climbing swiftly away, it turned south-west, heading for the safety of the Moroccan border.

T'ae'tan Air Base, North Korea

Yi Min-Ho crouched low on the rocky ledge he'd selected as his observation point, having checked that it wasn't easily visible from either above or below. It was hardly a comfortable location, but offered an unrivalled view of the air base below him, essential to allow him to complete his mission.

He glanced down the slope at the single east–west runway traversing the bottom of the valley, about fifteen hundred metres below him, then nodded in satisfaction. The OP was a rocky perch near the top of a ridge that dominated the landscape just to the north of the airfield, and he needed to be on this side so that he could see right into the hangars.

Like most North Korean airfields, T'ae'tan appeared to consist of a runway and not much else. Again, like most military airfields in this country, it was built close to a mountainside – or, in this case, a rocky hillside bordering the north side of the narrow valley. The reason for this was simple enough. The North Koreans always tried to construct hardened shelters for their air assets and command centres, and natural rock offered much better protection than concrete. Invariably expecting any attack to come from the south, they almost always began their excavations on the northern slope of the hill or mountain. Locating a hangar's entrance, its most vulnerable part, to the north ensured that the bulk of the rock obstructed any assault from the south.

Satellite photographs of T'ae'tan had revealed it possessed a long, straight taxiway, big enough to use as a secondary runway in an emergency. It bordered the runway itself on its south side, and extended some distance beyond it. There a spur ran off, splitting into two, and appeared to terminate in the hills fringing the south side of the narrow valley. In fact, these two sections of the taxiway led to the hangars excavated into the hillside, and it was those that Yi Min-Ho was now watching from his current perch on the opposite ridge.

The instructions he'd been given by his superior officer at Naegok-dong were clear and simple: he was to observe this airfield and assess its current activity. Specifically, he was to identify and report on the type, numbers and possible tasking of any unusual aircraft he spotted. His secondary task was to confirm the exact numbers of Chinese-built Shenyang F-5 single-seat jet interceptors – an old aircraft design based on the Russian MiG-17 – and also whatever Ilyushin Il-28 bombers the base had operational.

The Ilyushins had arrived at T'ae'tan back in October 1995, as part of a major redeployment of North Korean air assets that saw more than one hundred aircraft moved to forward bases close to the DMZ or Demilitarized Zone. South Korean experts calculated that the Il-28s could reach Seoul within as little as ten minutes, should hostilities break out.

By late morning, he'd already filled a couple of pages of his notebook with observations. His country's National Intelligence Service is technically advanced, but for counting aircraft Yi Min-Ho needed no more than a pair of binoculars and a pencil and paper. Of the three squadrons of F-5 aircraft known to be based at T'ae'tan, he'd counted only five different planes, and just three of those had so far got airborne. He'd watched the other two being moved from their hardened shelters and parked outside. Either all the remaining aircraft belonging to the squadrons were currently in deep maintenance, Yi surmised, or they'd been moved somewhere else entirely. And so far he hadn't seen a single Ilyushin.

Four of the six hangar doors he was watching were obviously newly constructed, which meant the North Koreans had recently dug some additional space into the hillside opposite. Yi had already estimated the likely number of aircraft these new shelters could accommodate, from careful observation with his binoculars of the old hangars through their open doors. He'd also noted that the single runway had been extended eastwards, as evidenced by new concrete a different shade to the original surface. This was another vital indication that the airfield's operational capability was being augmented.

After another scan with his binoculars to confirm nothing new was happening below him, Yi Min-Ho decided he might as well take an early lunch. He had to keep his strength up, but the prospect of consuming another MRE 'delicacy' was less than enthralling. He pulled the haversack towards him and picked through its packets to make a selection. As he swallowed the first tasteless mouthful, he comforted himself with the prospect of stimulating his palate with a chocolate bar afterwards.

On the south side of the airfield below the hidden observer, Pak Je-San's instructions were being followed to the letter. Twenty hand-picked soldiers, wearing camouflage clothing and equipped with powerful tripod-mounted binoculars, were spaced along the airfield perimeter, invisible from more than a few metres away, each studying their designated section of the hillside opposite.

The moment he learnt about a possible infiltrator, Pak had guessed the agent's objective would be T'ae'tan, simply because there was nothing else of military significance to South Korea in that sparsely inhabited region. The sighting of an intruder near Ugom had confirmed his suspicion that the unknown agent would be here trying to observe aircraft movements. Because the hangars all lay along the south side, he had deduced that the spy would be watching from the hills to the north.

And Pak was before long proved correct. When Yi Min-Ho raised his binoculars to check the airfield immediately before pausing to eat, their lenses had flashed briefly in the sun. That distant glint had been spotted by one of the watching soldiers, who had noted the spot carefully, then focused his binoculars and waited. Next he'd seen some sort of movement, though too indistinct to make out. That was when he decided to alert his superior officer.

Within five minutes, all the camouflaged soldiers were studying exactly the same location on the hillside opposite. Meanwhile, a six-man armed patrol, on standby since early that morning, was being rapidly tasked with an intercept mission.

Hercules Mark 5 C-130J, callsign Foxtrot November, over Morocco

'Was it really worth it?' Colin Dekker wondered, gazing across the cargo bay at the body of his Regiment soldier. In front of the battered Pinky, now securely lashed down to prevent it shifting, four of his men were administering whatever medical assistance they could to the soldier with the broken leg and to the injured loadmaster. The pain-killing injections would certainly help, but one of the bullets striking the loadmaster had severed an artery and, despite the tourniquet and the strapped-on compresses, Dekker realized the man's life was now hanging in the balance.

'Worth it? Buggered if I know,' Richter echoed him, after a moment.

'What was in that hangar, anyway?'

'You wouldn't believe me if I told you.'

'Try me.'

'Fuck-all.'

Dekker looked blank. 'What do you mean?'

'Nothing. *Nada. Rien.* I said you wouldn't believe me.' Richter sighed. 'The hangar was completely empty, or as good as. Just a cherry-picker and a couple of tractors.'

He pulled out the digital camera and selected 'view'. The first image appeared on the small screen, and Dekker studied it closely. Taken from above, it showed a considerable section of the interior of the hangar, but all he could see was a large expanse of empty concrete, and part of the cradle of a cherry-picker. He flicked to the next frame, and then the next.

'That doesn't make any sense,' he concluded. 'Are you sure that was the right hangar?'

'It was not only the one Six told me to investigate,' Richter replied, 'but it also had the largest number of sentries guarding it.'

'But why would the Algerians be guarding an empty hangar?'

'That's easy. Something's obviously missing, either lost or stolen, and I presume the guards are there to preserve the integrity of the scene. The difficult bit will be working out exactly what's been mislaid, but my own guess is they've lost an aircraft.'

Chapter Five

Anatoli Yershenko stood just inside the hangar and stared at the two massive grey interceptors in front of him, then glanced down at the paperwork he'd been given.

That was both the problem and the strength of a no-notice inspection. Because the base staff had no idea they were going to receive a visit, they had neither the chance to conceal their errors or omissions, nor the opportunity to ensure that their normal documentation was correct. What Lieutenant-Colonel Yershenko now had to decide was whether he was looking at sloppy paperwork or something much more serious.

He had no queries about the two interceptors. All the documentation the 524 IAP squadron staff had supplied for these aircraft was in order, as far as Yershenko could tell. The problem was that there should be *four* aircraft in this hangar, and so far nobody he had talked to was able to explain exactly where the two missing MiG-25s were.

According to squadron records, the two Foxbats had flown to the Zaporizhia state aviation maintenance plant in the Ukraine some two months earlier, which was certainly plausible. But when Yershenko had contacted Zaporizhia by telephone, nobody there could confirm the

75

date when the interceptors had arrived there or, more worrying, even if they had arrived at all. In fact, the administrative officer Yershenko talked to could find no trace of the side-numbers of the two MiGs anywhere in his records for the last six months.

But the two aircraft had certainly taken off from Letneozerskiy, so they must have landed *somewhere*, and Yershenko was determined to find out where.

What paper trail there was started with the air traffic control records in the tower nearby. As were all aircraft movements, the departure of the two interceptors had been logged, and their recorded destination was Zaporizhia. It was then things started getting foggy. ATC didn't record the names of the pilots, and the squadron records revealed that neither man had subsequently returned to Letneozerskiy. Both had been approaching the ends of their tours with 524 IAP, so had apparently proceeded to join their new squadrons once they'd delivered the Foxbats to the maintenance facility. Yershenko had already initiated a search to identify the current location of each pilot, but that was of secondary importance to finding the aircraft themselves.

One advantage in conducting such no-notice inspections was that the man in command of the team had the authority to compel officers of a much more senior rank to obey his instructions. He had scheduled a second interview with the station commander in a little over an hour, and the man should have found some satisfactory answers by then, or else Yershenko had the power to remove him from his post pending a full on-site investigation into the missing aircraft.

FOXBAT

T'ae'tan Air Base, North Korea

When he'd polished off the homogenous mush that served as his lunch, Yi Min-Ho resumed his scrutiny of the airfield spread out below him.

Though he wasn't sure if it had any significance, he had earlier noticed that only two of the six aircraft shelters he was studying appeared to be in use, and the doors of the four new ones had remained firmly closed the whole time he'd been watching. At first he'd assumed they might be empty, until he noticed a two-man patrol was guarding each one of them, a level of security not evident outside any other buildings on the base. That had to suggest there were items of some importance inside them.

One other thing also puzzled him. In the foothills beyond the new hangar entrances, and a short distance from the few administrative buildings, a three-storey structure had recently been erected. With curtained windows on all three floors, it looked residential, but that didn't make sense because people didn't normally live on an active airfield. Perhaps it was accommodation for the guards, but the building itself seemed far too big for that. He noted this down in his book as another oddity.

One set of the older hangar doors opened suddenly and a tractor backed out, towing another F-5 which Yi hadn't recorded before. He looked carefully at the fighter's side number and scribbled it in his notebook, together with the current time. The tractor halted and the driver unhitched the F-5, then drove back to the hangar. Two ground engineers appeared, pulling a low cart that maybe held tools, and stopped next to the fighter. One of them lifted an inspection panel on the fuselage below the cockpit, and both men got to work on the aircraft. Yi watched them with vague interest, simply because there was nothing else to do.

On the hillside about five hundred metres above and behind the lone NIS agent's observation point, a North Korean lieutenant stood staring down the slope. He could just see his quarry, or rather the man's head and his hands, holding a pair of binoculars, as he studied the airfield.

The patrol leader now had to ensure that the spy's focus remained fixed on the scene below, while he and his men attempted to make their approach unnoticed. The orders received from the official in Pyongyang might help them achieve that, so he raised the radio to his mouth and murmured a brief report, informing his superior officer that they were ready in position. Then he hand-signalled for his men to begin their approach. They'd already been briefed to halt a hundred metres away from the spy's position and await the lieutenant's command to move in for the kill.

Yi Min-Ho suddenly tensed and shifted his gaze. Three uniformed men had emerged from one of the few administration buildings and were heading briskly along the taxiway towards the four mystery hangars that were so carefully guarded. As they approached the nearest one, the two sentries outside it snapped to attention and saluted, then led them towards a side door.

Perhaps, Yi wondered, they would now open the main doors and he'd finally discover what the North Koreans had stored inside. And moments later his unspoken wish seemed about to come true, as the two massive hangar doors began to slide slowly apart.

The lieutenant had halted his men behind a low rise, gesturing them to keep out of sight while he himself moved forward to a position where he could more clearly overlook the spy's observation point. He too could see the airfield below, and he watched just as carefully as the officers approached the hangar. Everything was going as planned.

He paused another minute until the main doors began to open, then slid back down the slope and ordered his men forward, as quietly as possible. Though he was certain the South Korean's full attention was directed at the activity below, there was still the possibility that, despite outnumbering him six-to-one, if he heard them coming he could somehow escape down the hillside. The lieutenant's orders were specific: the man must be taken alive if possible, or else killed. His escape would not be tolerated. So they readied their weapons and moved carefully down the slope towards him.

Yi Min-Ho hadn't taken his eyes off the hangar since he'd watched the officers approach it, and at last both the doors were wide open. The problem was that he still couldn't discern what was inside because the interior lay in deep shadow. But that might not be a problem, because a towing tractor was now approaching the building. So Yi watched and waited.

On reaching the hangar, the tractor drove straight inside. For a couple of minutes there was no further movement, then the tail of an aircraft began to appear, which the tractor was clearly pushing. But the aircraft Yi now saw emerging from the hangar was completely unanticipated.

He had expected an F-5, which is a fairly small aircraft with a distinctive single rudder carrying horizontal stabilizers, but instead found himself staring at two enormous jet exhausts, topped by massive twin rudders. For a few seconds he had no idea what this huge aircraft might be, then, as realization dawned, he reached for his Kyocera satellite telephone. This news couldn't wait for his formal debriefing, so he switched it on, punched in a number, and waited for the connection to be completed.

Yi's dedication and focus often received favourable comment at headquarters, but unfortunately this time he had become rather *too* focused. So, as the North Korean soldiers approached his hiding place, all his attention was fixed on the open hangar door and the slowly emerging aircraft.

Just then a T'ae'tan soldier stepped silently onto the ledge beside him and pressed the muzzle of a Kalashnikov AK47 into the middle of his back. Yi reacted instantly. He dropped the phone and binoculars, and twisted away, knocking aside the barrel of the assault rifle as he simultaneously reached for his pistol. The guard stepped back, momentarily taken by surprise.

This brief moment was enough for the South Korean

agent. He grabbed up the satellite phone and vaulted off the ledge, running for his life down the slope towards the airfield, all the time dodging and diving from side to side.

The lieutenant shouted immediate orders, and within seconds the air was alive with Kalashnikov bullets. But shooting downhill isn't easy because of the perspective, and most of the shots went wide, smashing into the ground all around the fugitive.

As he ran, Yi Min-Ho heard the tinny voice of his controller issuing from the earpiece of the Kyocera. He dropped flat to the ground and rolled over so that he could face back up the slope. Then he pulled out the CZ75 and let loose half a dozen rounds at his pursuers, even as he tried to gasp out his story.

'They have new aircraft,' he yelled. 'I've seen a—'

At that moment three shells from one of the Kalashnikovs found him. The first tore through his left hand, severing two fingers and ripping the Kyocera from his grasp. Maybe fortunately, his agony lasted well under a second. The next round entered the top of his skull, ploughing through his brain and killing him instantly. Yi Min-Ho didn't even feel the third bullet.

Hammersmith, London

'I originally assumed it was just another cock-up by Vauxhall Cross,' Richard Simpson grumbled. 'Telling you to look in the wrong hangar, or even sending you off to the wrong airfield. But now it looks like they were probably right.'

Simpson had a famously low opinion of the professional abilities of the Secret Intelligence Service, commonly known as 'Six', and was always happy to share his prejudices with anyone who'd listen.

Richter had got back to the Hammersmith office fifteen minutes earlier, after spending what felt like a week bouncing around in the back of the 'Fat Albert'. The Hercules had stopped at Meknes for a refuel, but had taken off immediately afterwards, heading straight for Gibraltar and the Royal Naval Air Station, HMS *Rooke*. There they'd off-loaded the injured loadmaster, fearing he would not survive the flight back to the UK. The wounded man had lost so much blood that Richter personally doubted he'd last the day, but at least at *Rooke* he'd get proper medical care.

The C-130 filled its tanks again and got airborne, routed around Spanish airspace and headed north, landing at RAF Northolt to off-load Richter, the dead soldier and the injured SAS trooper – he had a badly broken leg, but the injury wasn't life-threatening – before continuing to RAF Lyneham in Wiltshire, where transport was waiting for the SAS team.

Simpson had sent a car to meet Richter, with a man from Vauxhall Cross in the back seat to collect the camera and receive a verbal debrief on what was seen at Aïn Oussera. The moment Richter opened his office door at Hammersmith, the direct line had begun ringing.

'So how come you think they were right?' Richter asked, wearily.

'Because of what's happened since you left for your away-day in Algeria. The troops that pursued you – they weren't regular army?'

'I doubt it. Most Third-World armed forces run a mile the moment they come up against any kind of competent opposition, but these guys didn't. They didn't back off and they used good tactics. They were definitely some kind of elite troops, and they bloody nearly had us.'

'And what are your conclusions about the empty hangar?' Simpson probed.

'My best guess is they've lost a valuable aircraft – or somebody's stolen one. The guards are probably just there to protect the scene of the crime while they continue to investigate it. So what else has happened in my absence that suggests Six have got something right for once?'

'Two things have arisen,' Simpson replied. 'Firstly, Algeria might not be the only nation to be having problems with its fighter inventory. The NSA claims to have intercepted signals in Iran that suggest the country may be missing a pair of interceptors. But then the Americans add that the traffic was "ambiguous", whatever the hell that means.'

'And second?' Richter prompted.

'And secondly we've had a surprise request from the Russians for assistance in tracking certain military aircraft movements. Their own military aircraft movements, to be exact. I've said you'll go to Moscow and help them out.'

'Why me? I was hoping for a bit of a break. Can't someone else go?'

'No, because the request from Moscow asked for you specifically.'

'Who's behind that?'

'Viktor Bykov – and he's now a senior general in the

GRU. Despite what you did to him in France, I think he trusts you – maybe more than I do. Anyway, it's your name on the ticket, and there's a diplomatic passport waiting for you now in the Documents Section. You're booked on tomorrow's British Airways flight, and Bykov or one of his staff will be meeting you at Sheremetievo.' He paused to check his notes, then continued.

'The Registry staff are preparing a laptop for you. It'll contain pictures from the US Keyhole birds that cover the specific dates and times the Russians have requested – suitably sanitized, of course. They've highlighted possible radar contacts that could be the aircraft the Russians are interested in, with their estimated points of departure and possible destinations. We've also arranged for a photo interpreter from N-PIC to be standing by in Washington and another one at JARIC in case you need further analysis, or additional frames to be sent.'

'What about a personal weapon?'

'Certainly not. You're going to Moscow to help the GRU track down some missing aircraft. It's merely a joint investigation into an anomaly, so what the hell do you want a gun for? And, Richter, I know that your concept of diplomacy is to break someone's leg and then say "Lean on me", but we're supposed to be working *with* the Russians on this, not against them. So try not to kill too many people while you're over there.'

Letneozerskiy interceptor base, Karelia, Russia

'I assure you, Colonel, that my staff correctly completed all the documentation before the two MiG-25 interceptors left this station. You've seen it, all of it. If any mistakes were made, they must have occurred at Zaporizhia. I've never trusted that maintenance facility. This isn't the first time their record-keeping has proved less than adequate.'

Anatoli Yershenko looked across the desk at the officer commanding 524 IAP. Colonel Grigor Adashev hadn't actually obstructed his inspection team, but he certainly hadn't helped much. And the colonel was now sweating slightly, which might be due to the heat pumping out of two large radiators – rusty and wheezing but undeniably effective – bolted to the walls either side of his desk. Or might there be another reason?

'So you say, Colonel, so you say. *My* problem is that I've talked to Zaporizhia, and the officer I spoke to insists there's no record of either aircraft in their database over the last six months. *Your* problem is that your recorded squadron strength isn't matched by the aircraft currently parked in your hangars, and you don't need me to tell you how serious that could be.'

'It's just a paperwork problem,' Adashev blustered, returning to the tune he'd been playing since this interview began. 'The fault lies at Zaporizhia, and if you do your job properly that's where you'll go next.'

Yershenko shrugged. Ultimately, it wasn't his problem anyway. He'd simply write up his report of the inspection, highlight the discrepancy and pass the buck to Moscow. But he would certainly visit the maintenance facility. The colonel might be right and, if only for the sake of completeness, the inspection team would have to investigate his claim.

'We'll be flying straight to Zaporizhia when we leave here.'

Adashev nodded. 'You might like to send a preliminary report through our communication facilities?'

'No thank you. Until we locate those two missing aircraft, it would be premature to contact Moscow. I'll file a complete inspection report once we've checked the records at Zaporizhia.' And he could have added: I'll file my report when there's no possibility of it being altered or delayed. In fact, he'd already telephoned his superior in Moscow with a brief outline of what had been discovered at Letneozerskiy.

Adashev stood up and extended his hand across the desk. 'I probably won't be seeing you again, Colonel, so I'll say goodbye now.'

After a moment's hesitation, Yershenko shook it, then turned and left the office.

The moment the door closed behind him, Adashev made a three-minute phone call to a trusted subordinate.

Seoul, South Korea

In a third-floor conference room at the National Intelligence Service headquarters at Naegok-dong, two men in shirtsleeves sat either side of a long table. Between them was a professional-quality reel-to-reel tape recorder hitched to an external amplifier and a pair of small speakers. A cassette player would have been far more convenient, but Bae Chang-Su – the autocratic head of the NIS – had insisted on the best possible audio quality, and that meant using the original tape and the Revox.

They'd played the recording four times already, and Bae knew they'd soon have to make a decision about what to tell the Americans.

'What did his previous reports contain?' he asked.

Kang Jang-Ho was Bae's direct subordinate and also Yi Min-Ho's briefing officer, since the infiltration of the NIS agent into North Korea had been sanctioned at the highest level. He now referred to his notes.

'He only made two brief calls, and there was nothing particularly significant in either. Yi contacted us once to confirm that he'd landed, and again after he had established his observation point overlooking the airfield. His only concern was that he'd almost been caught by an army patrol near Ugom, and he had the feeling they were deliberately waiting for him. Their truck had been parked on the road without lights and drove straight towards him as he came into view.'

'Do you give any credence to his suggestion that they knew in advance?'

'No, sir, I don't. There's always a heavy military presence in that area, so I think he just ran into a regular patrol that spotted someone suspicious and gave chase. The other possibility is that North Korean radar detected the inflatable heading for the coast, but I think that's unlikely.'

'Perhaps,' Bae grunted. 'What's your assessment of the situation now? Is Yi still alive?'

'Probably not. His last message' – Kang gestured at the tape recorder – 'suggests that he's been captured at the very least.'

He referred to his notes again. 'I've had the recording analysed by our technical staff. First, it's definitely Yi's voice: the voice-print analysis is unambiguous. Second, he's shouting and there are traces of panic in his voice, as he's clearly desperate to pass on a message to us. That could mean he was on the run. Third, there are the six shots heard at the beginning of the tape. Because of the volume of these explosions, the technicians believe the weapon was fired close to the Kyocera, meaning they were fired from Yi's own pistol, at whoever was pursuing him.' Kang glanced at his superior before continuing.

'And, at the very end you can hear the sound of other, more distant, shots, immediately before Yi's transmission ends. They must have been fired by his pursuers, and we have to assume that one of the bullets damaged the satellite phone, because the signal disappears immediately afterwards. We tried calling the unit several times over the next hour, but each time the system reported the Kyocera unavailable. It was then, following COMSEC procedures, recorded as destroyed and the number barred. So we believe Yi must have seen something so important that he ignored standard operating procedure by breaking communications silence in an attempt to call us.'

'And what about the message he tried to pass on?' Bae demanded.

Kang lifted his hands in a gesture of helplessness. 'All he says is that the North Koreans have new aircraft – then he was cut off. We don't know exactly what he meant by that, but must assume he saw something sufficiently unusual to risk calling us immediately.'

For a few moments Bae stared at the Revox as if willing it to supply the answer. Then he shifted his gaze back to his subordinate.

'I'm not prepared to risk sending another agent across the border, so I think it's time to involve the Americans formally. We'll just report what little we have, and see what they can do with their technical assets. Perhaps one of their satellites will be able to identify whatever aircraft Yi observed at T'ae'tan, and then we'll have a better idea what we're up against.'

Perm, Russia

There are a lot of bars in the city of Perm, catering for everyone from the habitual drunk to the purely social drinkers who have a need to be seen in the right place, at the right time, and with the right people. The Bar Sputnik fell somewhere between these two extremes. It was located down by the Kama river, identified by an illuminated sign showing a silver ball with four trailing antennae – representing the first-ever Earth-orbiting satellite – and with its tinted windows further darkened by years of tobacco smoke. Most of its clientele were working men, but with a sprinkling of young professionals: administrators, accountants and lawyers in the main.

Stools topped with faded red leather faced the long wooden bar, booths with fixed wooden tables lining the walls opposite, and a handful of tables and chairs occupied the open space just to the left of the street door.

At one of these tables, four men sat talking and drinking. One was young, maybe twenty-five years of age, slim, with fair hair and blue eyes. Two of his companions were late middle-aged and, more typical of most of the population in the area, had dark hair, brown eyes, flat, almost Slavic, features and bulky physiques. The fourth man, short, thin and somewhat older, looked almost oriental by comparison.

To any interested observer, the elderly man would have seemed the dominant personality. His name was Ryu Chang-Ho and he'd arrived in Perm just over two weeks earlier. When he spoke, he was listened to in respectful silence, and was clearly used to conducting life on his own terms.

For the most part, their discussion appeared amicable, though when Ryu made a suggestion, the other three quickly nodded agreement. But then the atmosphere at the table suddenly changed. Ryu leant forward and addressed the young man in a low, determined voice, and for the first time Georgi Lenkov showed signs of dissent.

He shook his head firmly. 'I will not do that,' he replied in Russian. 'I am not a traitor.'

Ryu leant even closer. 'I'm not asking you to do anything that would compromise your country,' he insisted. 'All I'm doing is offering you a substantial reward in exchange for your professional services.'

Lenkov shook his head again. 'No,' he said loudly. 'It's more than that, and you know it.'

Some of the other drinkers in the bar had turned at the sound of Lenkov's raised voice and were now looking towards the four men.

Ryu registered their interest, and motioned towards the door. 'We'll continue this outside,' he said, then stood up and walked out of the bar, with the other three following.

They crossed the street to the embankment skirting

the south side of the river. Ryu there produced a sheet of paper from his pocket and showed it to Lenkov. There were a number of figures scribbled on it, each prefixed by a US dollar sign, but no indication of what these sums were for.

'That,' Ryu said, pointing to a figure towards the bottom of the page, 'is what I'm willing to pay if you agree to join us.'

Lenkov hesitated for a moment. The amount the man was suggesting equated to about five years' salary for him but there was, the young Russian had already deduced, far more to this than just cash. For one thing, he had no guarantee of ever receiving the money. It's one thing to be told what you're going to be paid, but until the sum appears, it's all just talk. And even if this odd little man did deliver on his promises, Lenkov could foresee other obstacles to prevent him ever spending it, like getting a bullet in the head once his usefulness was over.

There were too many risks involved here, so he shook his head again, decision made. 'No, I won't do it,' he said firmly. 'And I'll have to report this to my superiors.'

Ryu's eyes glittered dangerously in the fading daylight. 'If you know what's good for you, you won't do that,' he hissed.

'I'm not taking any orders from you,' Lenkov snapped, then turned and strode away.

The other two men looked at Ryu, awaiting instructions. 'Follow him,' he ordered. 'I'll go get the car.'

Fifty yards away, Lenkov glanced behind him. The two other Russians were following him, one on either side of the road, as if ready to anticipate any turn that he made, while Ryu was walking briskly away in the opposite direction. For the first time a feeling of real apprehension crossed the young man's mind.

He began walking faster towards the centre of the city and away from the relative darkness of the embankment. But his pursuers merely speeded up as well, easily keeping pace with him.

Behind him, he heard a car engine start, its headlights shining across his back as the vehicle turned towards him. Perhaps he could thumb a lift, he considered briefly.

He looked back again but, as the vehicle headed towards him, it passed under a streetlight, and he recognized the sallow features of Ryu Chang-Ho in the driver's seat.

It was then Lenkov started running, his feet pounding loudly on the pavement as he desperately sought sanctuary. When the lights of another bar beckoned, he skipped across the road, pushed open the door and rushed inside.

But even as he strode across the room, he heard the street door slam open behind him, and a rough voice called out 'Police! Stay where you are.'

Lenkov turned to see the same two Russians advancing towards him. One of them was holding up a shield that looked remarkably like the double-headed golden eagle of the MVD, the Russian police.

'Those aren't cops,' he shouted desperately, as he backed away towards the smoky rear of the bar. But nobody was listening to him, as the sight of two men claiming to be MVD officers was quite sufficient incentive for them to all mind their own business.

They were on him in a moment, one man pinning him against the polished wood of the bar counter while the other pulled his hands behind his back and snapped a pair of handcuffs around his wrists.

Lenkov kept shouting for help as they hustled him towards the door, but nobody in the bar so much as looked at him. Outside, the car waited, Ryu still in the driver's seat, the engine idling and the rear door already open. The two Russians pushed Lenkov inside, then climbed in after him. The moment the door closed, the car drove away from the kerb.

'Where are you taking me?' Lenkov demanded in panic, but none of the three men replied.

As they began heading out of Perm, Lenkov started yelling at the top of his voice and kicking out at the men imprisoning him.

'Shut him up,' Ryu instructed briefly. One of the two burly Russians pulled a cosh out of his pocket, as his companion forced the captive's head forwards.

The cosh swung down in a short, vicious arc, smashing into the back of his skull. It wasn't sufficient to knock him out, but after the second blow Lenkov collapsed forward, unconscious, into the footwell.

Fifteen minutes later Ryu pulled the car to a halt by some thick woodland on the outskirts of the city. 'Bring him,' he instructed, and led the way between the trees.

As they dropped him to the ground, Lenkov was beginning to regain consciousness. The first thing he was aware of was rough hands emptying his pockets, taking his wallet, keys and loose change, and then unstrapping the watch from his wrist. He opened his eyes to see Ryu staring down at him, a semi-automatic pistol in his right hand. The two Russian thugs stood by, watching with disinterest.

'Wait,' Lenkov said, desperation in his voice. 'We can talk. I'll do what you want.'

Ryu stepped close to him and looked down. 'The time for talking is over, *comrade*. You should have taken what we were offering at the time.'

Lenkov lapsed into shocked silence as Ryu cocked his pistol.

The bullet smashed into the young man's face, just below his right eye, and he toppled backwards, killed instantly. The sound of the shot was shockingly loud in the silence of the wood, and birds flew out of the trees in panic, their wings beating an ironic applause to the execution, while somewhere deeper in the wood a dog started barking.

Ryu stepped forward, rolled the body onto its side and removed the handcuffs from the wrists, then the three men walked away without a backwards glance.

Seventy metres behind them, a middle-aged Russian peered cautiously from behind a tree, a dog lead clutched in his hand. He'd heard, but not seen, the shot being fired, and the sight of the three men walking away had immediately caught his attention. He looped the lead around a branch to stop his trembling dog from follow-ing him, then quickly made his way to the edge of the wood. Moments before he got there, he heard a car engine start, so he paused for a few seconds. Then he heard a vehicle moving off, and began to run.

Some fifty metres in front of him, a grey saloon car was driving away, bouncing over the rutted track as it headed towards the main road, but he couldn't make out the digits on its number plate. As he walked back into the wood to fetch his dog, almost the first thing he came across was the crumpled body of Georgi Lenkov.

Letneozerskiy interceptor base, Karelia, Russia

Yershenko was getting progressively more irritated with the staff at Letneozerskiy. He and his team had been ready to leave for almost two hours, but their aircraft – an Antonov An-28 – still wasn't ready. The delay, according to their pilot, who seemed almost as frustrated as his passengers, was because of a problem during refuelling.

One of the tanks wasn't filling properly, and the ground engineers had elected to carry out a visual inspection of its interior and to check the associated fuel lines for blockages and contamination. That had required specialized equipment and a fibre-optic viewing device, and simply assembling this had taken them over an hour. The process, as far as Yershenko could tell, would then take a further thirty minutes, and only then, assuming they found nothing wrong, would they be able to fill the tank.

It was nearly three hours after his inspection team had assembled in the squadron office, their bags beside them, that the Antonov was finally towed out of the maintenance hangar and chocked on the hardstanding in front of them.

'At last,' Yershenko muttered, as he watched the fuel bowser approach.

Fifteen minutes later, he strapped himself into his seat at the front of the cabin and opened his briefcase. His inspection report was far from finished, and he proposed to use this long flight to continue drafting the final document. And it wouldn't just be a single hop: the Antonov was a slow aircraft with a very limited range, so would have to land and refuel at least three times before reaching the Ukraine.

The aircraft levelled at ten thousand feet and the pilot relaxed, trimmed the Antonov for straight and level flight, and then picked up an en-route chart to work out an updated estimate for the next military airfield they'd be landing at to replenish their tanks.

In the passenger cabin behind him, Yershenko continued with his report while most of his team opened the packs of sandwiches they'd been given on departing Letneozerskiy. The Antonov didn't run to a galley – even the chemical toilet was very much an afterthought – so any food and drink had to be carried on board.

Twenty minutes after reaching its cruising altitude, there was a muted thud somewhere near the main radio set. It sounded almost like a bird-strike, so at first the pilot was relatively unconcerned. Just as a precaution, he tried calling the Letneozerskiy radar controller, but found the set was dead.

Loss of the main radio was an irritation rather than a serious problem, but it still remained a matter of concern. Thirty seconds later concern changed to worry when the pilot realized that the standby radio was also non-functioning. There were emergency procedures for this kind of situation, and obviously they would have to land as soon as possible to get the radios fixed. The pilot consulted his en-route chart, calculating times and distances, then selected cabin broadcast to tell his passengers what had happened, and explain what he intended to do.

But the words never formed, for at that instant there

was a colossal explosion somewhere in the lower section of the fuselage. The cabin floor erupted upwards, the detonation peeling the aircraft apart, twisting and severing pipes and wires, and scattering seats, boxes, cases and aluminium panels alike. Most of the team had removed their seatbelts and were now catapulted instantly from the falling wreckage. Mercifully for them, most were killed or knocked unconscious by the force of the explosion. The pilot was flung forward through the windscreen and was dead even before he started falling.

But Yershenko remained conscious all the way down and, in the last moments of his life, understood exactly why there'd been such a delay in refuelling at Letneozerskiy.

It doesn't take long to plummet ten thousand feet, and in just over a minute what was left of the An-28 and its human cargo impacted the frozen and unyielding ground at around two hundred miles an hour.

Back in the air traffic control room at Letneozerskiy, a senior officer advised the station commander that the Antonov had disappeared from the radar screen, with its pilot no longer responding to radio calls. The commanding officer ordered him to initiate a search and rescue operation immediately, then phoned each of the squadron commanders in turn to brief them on the apparent loss of an aircraft.

However deeply concerned the 524 IAP colonel sounded, he had already begun preparing himself for a long and completely unauthorized journey of his own that would take him first to a private bank in Austria, and eventually to somewhere agreeable in southern Europe, perhaps on the Mediterranean coast of Spain.

Chapter Six

Tuesday
Dobric Air Base, Bulgaria

Dobric Air Base near Varna had been 'inactive' since the millennium, but there are degrees of inactivity and, despite the fact that no aircraft flew to or from the base, there were always armed guards on duty there. This was because Dobric had become one of Bulgaria's largest repositories of reserve planes, aircraft stores and munitions.

Deliveries and collections were frequent, but these were always carefully pre-notified to ensure that sufficient staff were on hand to assist with the loading and unloading. So when a trio of unmarked three-ton trucks pulled up outside the locked main gates, the guard in the concrete security post at first more or less ignored them because no such movements had been scheduled for that day.

He watched with greater interest though when two men wearing Bulgarian Air Force uniforms climbed down from the lead vehicle and walked over to the security post, arguing loudly. Reassured by the sight of the familiar uniforms, the guard didn't think to pick up the assault rifle leaning against the wall beside him. Behind him, a small and cheap TV set blared out a current pop song, while professional dancers writhed unenthusiastically on the black-and-white screen.

One of the arrivals, who was using the name Draco, nodded to the guard and slid a folded sheet of paper through the slot under the window. The Bulgarian took it, expecting to find the address or location they were looking for but, on unfolding it, found it completely blank. He looked up in puzzled surprise to see the man smiling slightly.

The next thing he registered was the muzzle of a silenced pistol levelled at him through the slot. Before the guard could react, there came a sound like a cough, and he fell backwards, shot directly through the heart.

Immediately, the second man jogged over to the main gates and studied them carefully. Even if not electrified, some kind of an alarm system might have been expected, but he saw nothing there to cause him concern. That meant all they had to do now was find the key and get inside.

Typical of military establishments the world over, each gate comprised a ten-foot steel frame with cross-braces, and diamond-pattern wire mesh secured to it. He could have easily cut through this, but it was just as quick to climb over.

Grasping the wire with his gloved hands, he pulled himself up, jamming the toes of his boots periodically into the mesh, feeling for the firmer frame and cross-braces behind it. In less than ten seconds he was astride the gate, and fifteen seconds after that was standing outside the door of the security post, trying the handle.

As expected, the door was locked, so he reached down to his equipment belt and removed a crowbar from one loop. Then he forced the end of it into the gap around the door and pulled hard. The wood splintered, but held, so he changed position slightly and levered again. This time the door creaked loudly, then flew open. He stepped inside.

Ignoring the sprawled body of the dead guard, the intruder strode across to the open key safe bolted to the wall. Inside, there were probably a couple of dozen sets of keys hanging on labelled hooks, but he knew exactly which ones he needed. He chose two sets and headed back to the main gates. Inserting one key in the lock, he pulled the double gates open wide.

The moment he did so, the three trucks started up and drove inside the base. At this point he stepped up to the leading vehicle and handed over the second set of keys to Draco, who'd meanwhile returned to his cab. After that he closed and relocked the main gates. As the three-tonners drove away towards the storage buildings, the first intruder started a perfunctory clean-up operation in the security post, by dragging the guard's corpse out of sight of the window.

Deep inside the Dobric complex, the three trucks stopped outside a likely-looking building while the driver checked the number painted on its wall. He shook his head and they drove to the next one. There he swung the truck in a wide turn so that he could reverse close up to the doors.

Draco climbed down and jogged across to a sliding steel door, the second set of keys ready in one hand. The door was secured by a single lock, but before he tackled this he used another key from the same set to disable an alarm bolted to the adjacent wall. Once the tell-tale light changed from red to green, he inserted the key for the loading door itself. Thirty seconds later the two men were inside the building, the door left wide open and fluorescent lights blazing overhead.

They were joined by another four, all similarly wearing Bulgarian Air Force uniforms. They spread out quickly, systematically scanning the steel racks and piles of boxes for those they wanted. Within a couple of minutes one man called out, and the others gathered round to check that he'd found what they were looking for. In front of them rose a pile of some fifty wooden boxes, each over twenty feet long and bearing the stencilled marking 'R-40T'.

Draco nodded in satisfaction and began to issue crisp instructions. In one corner he had already noticed a forklift truck, specially modified to handle the awkwardly shaped boxes that were neatly piled against the walls or on rows of steel shelving. One of his men drove the forklift over to the boxes they had located and expertly plucked the top one off the pile. He manoeuvred it carefully down the aisle between the racks and deposited it neatly into the back of one of the three-ton trucks.

They'd already loaded ten of these boxes when a challenge rang out. Four Bulgarian Air Force guards stood in the open doorway, Kalashnikovs aimed directly at the intruders.

Sheremetievo Airport, Moscow

'We meet again, Mr Richter.'

Viktor Bykov looked pretty much the same as Richter

remembered – tall and thin with sharp, almost predatory, features. And he looked suspiciously pleased to see him.

'Hullo, Viktor,' Richter said, and shook hands.

Bykov snapped his fingers and a junior officer scurried forward to take the Englishman's suitcase. He extended a hand for the briefcase as well, but Richter shook his head. 'I'll carry this, thanks. I've had to sign for the laptop inside it, and I'll be in all sorts of trouble if I lose it.'

'Follow me. I have a car outside,' Bykov said, leading the way through the arrivals hall. Outside the terminal building a black Mercedes saloon stood idling beside the kerb, the driver leaning against the door. The number on the boot lid was 630 SEL, which meant nothing to Richter, who'd never been a fan of overpriced, overweight and frankly vulgar German machinery, but he did notice the registration plate: 'MOC 65'. Those three letters immediately identified it as a Russian diplomatic vehicle.

'You have diplomatic status?' he asked Bykov curiously, but the Russian shook his head.

'Thankfully, no. But having that plate makes things a lot easier, as it saves arguing with those idiots.' He gestured towards a number of traffic police who were eyeing the Mercedes in a somewhat hostile manner.

The junior officer put Richter's suitcase in the boot, then went to sit in the front beside the chauffeur. Bykov opened the rear door for their visitor, then slid in beside him.

'We've booked you into the Rossyia,' he announced, as the Mercedes pulled out into the flow of traffic. 'You may be interested to know that Muscovites refer to it as "The Box", so we thought you'd feel at home there.'

'The Box' was one of the nicknames of the Security Service, MI5, from its original postal address of 'Box 500, London'.

'Kind thought, Viktor, but you know I don't work for Five. In fact, I don't even work for Six, except indirectly.'

And that was the truth. Richter worked for the Foreign Operations Executive, a covert – and unacknowledged except when things went wrong – organization subordinate to the Secret Intelligence Service. Basically, FOE performed any dirty little jobs that Six itself didn't want to get involved with.

'Yes, we're aware that your employment arrangements are quite unusual. We did some checking on you through our London *rezident* before we extended this invitation. Despite what happened in France, I believe we can trust you to do the right thing.'

Richter inclined his head in acknowledgement. It was coming to something, he mused, when a senior Russian military intelligence officer seemed more inclined to trust you than your own boss did.

'So what's the story, Viktor?'

'If you don't mind, I'd rather wait until we get to the hotel. Then we can talk freely and in comfort.' As he said these words, Bykov gestured briefly towards the front seats of the Mercedes, and Richter understood perfectly. The GRU officer had borrowed the car only as a matter of convenience, but either its driver or the escort might well be reporting to a different master.

Careless talk could still cost lives, even in today's relaxed, post-glasnost, pro-capitalist Russia.

Dobric Air Base, Bulgaria

'Stop what you're doing right now,' the senior Bulgarian Air Force guard ordered, and strode into the warehouse. The other three members of his patrol followed him, their Kalashnikov assault rifles held ready. 'You.' He gestured with the muzzle of his weapon. 'Get out of the fork-lift.'

The man at the vehicle's controls climbed down and stood alongside his five companions, as they stared silently at the new arrivals.

Looking irritated by the interruption, Draco stepped forward. 'What's the problem?' he snapped.

'The problem,' the patrol leader explained, 'is that we have no collections or deliveries scheduled for today.'

'I don't understand. We have our orders.'

'Let me see them, then.'

Draco strode over towards the patrol commander, reached into his tunic pocket and pulled out a sheaf of papers that he handed over. The Bulgarian guard shouldered his weapon and flicked through them, then looked up, puzzled.

'These are blank,' he said.

'Oh, sorry, I must have given you the wrong ones. Here.' Draco reached inside his tunic again, pulled out a silenced semi-automatic pistol and fired a single shot. The Bulgarian fell backwards, his forehead sprouting a third eye, as a spray of blood and brains flew towards his companions.

'Now,' Draco yelled, jumping to one side, out of the line of fire. He brought his pistol to bear on another of the startled patrol members, fired again and watched the second man fall. To his left, three of his men had now produced their pistols but, despite the shock of the sudden attack, the two remaining patrol members reacted immediately, by splitting up and running outside the warehouse to raise the alarm.

'Find those two and kill them,' Draco ordered, and a couple of his men picked up the Kalashnikovs belonging to the two dead men, and followed the escaping Bulgarians out of the door. 'The rest of you, shift these bodies, then finish the loading.'

Outside, the two Bulgarian guards were running for their lives. They might have survived if they'd only used the buildings as cover, but in their panic both of them had decided that they must get back to the guardroom where the telephones were located. So they set off in a more or less straight line.

The first of their pursuers rounded a corner and spotted the two running side by side only about seventy yards in front of him. He knelt down, aimed the Kalashnikov and fired two rapid bursts of perhaps six rounds each. The result was immediate: both his targets fell clumsily to the ground, their weapons spinning uselessly from their hands. He stood up and watched their collapsed figures for a few seconds, then ran towards them.

One was clearly dead – two rounds had ripped through his back, emerging messily near his sternum – but the other was still alive. He'd been hit once in the lower back, the bullet cutting through his spine, and was now trying desperately to drag himself to where his Kalashnikov lay a couple of feet away. His assassin walked calmly across to the writhing figure, kicked the assault rifle well out of reach, then fired two rounds into the man's skull.

He next picked up the AK47s and slung them over his shoulder – the team being armed only with pistols, the Kalashnikovs might prove useful once they'd left Dobric. After searching the corpses for spare magazines and ammunition, he headed back to the warehouse.

Ninety minutes later, they'd loaded all three trucks with a total of forty-eight of the long, heavy boxes, sixteen to each vehicle. Draco checked their loads carefully to ensure that the weight was evenly distributed and properly lashed down. Finally he gave the order to drive off, but only after they had dragged the dead men out of the warehouse and dumped them out on the roadway near their two companions. That way, there'd be no immediate pointer to the munitions they'd stolen, though the theft was bound to be discovered within days or even hours.

The trucks stopped just outside the main entrance while the seventh member of the group locked the gates behind them. Then he carefully returned both sets of keys to the safe and climbed back over the gates to rejoin his companions. Before they moved off, they all discarded the Air Force uniforms they'd been wearing and replaced them with blue workmen's overalls.

Draco waved briefly from the cab of the leading truck, whereupon they turned out onto the road and headed south. Varna was only a short drive, about thirty-five miles, and Draco knew a cargo ship with Panamanian registry was waiting there for their precious load. Once they'd delivered it, this group of men would disperse, and probably never see each other again. They'd been recruited individually from the Bulgarian underworld for this single operation, for which they had all been very well paid. None had any idea what was contained in the boxes or of their importance to their recruiter, a middle-aged man of Chinese appearance who spoke their language only haltingly.

As the trucks bounced and rattled on down the road, only the drivers themselves were visible in the cabs. In the back of each vehicle the other men were completing their penultimate task by carefully pasting pre-prepared shipping labels over the stencilled 'R-40T' markings.

Rossyia Hotel, Moscow

The Rossyia is vast: twelve floors containing three thousand two hundred rooms; nine restaurants, two of which can each accommodate a thousand diners; six bars; fifteen snack bars, and the world's biggest ballroom. It also possesses a huge cinema, the Zaryadye, that can hold three thousand people. Publicity material relating to the hotel dubs it 'The Palace' but, as the black Mercedes approached the vast structure squatting beside the Moskva river, Richter could see why it had attracted that other, less complimentary, epithet, 'The Box'.

Bykov had booked him a room on the sixth floor, and the GRU officer suggested they adjourn to a bar, once Richter had deposited his bag there.

'We checked the room thoroughly for bugs yesterday,' he explained, 'but in Moscow you never really know who's listening to you. That's why I'd feel more comfortable in the bar. I regret to say that your presence here has not been met with universal approval, and I've been instructed that you should not to be allowed to visit my office or any other building used by the GRU or SVR.'

'Hotels and bars are fine with me,' Richter assured him.

They found a booth at the back, ordered drinks and waited till they were placed on the table in front of them.

'Right, Viktor, I'm all ears.'

Despite his fairly fluent English, for a moment Bykov looked confused – he hadn't heard that expression before – but then his face cleared. 'Very well. Let me start at the beginning. Since the break-up of the Soviet Union our armed forces have remained in a state of flux. For a long time it wasn't always clear exactly what weapons or aircraft were located at what bases, nor who had control of those assets. Salaries weren't being paid, officers and men weren't getting relieved at the ends of their tours of duty, all that kind of thing. It was a total mess, an administrative nightmare.'

Richter nodded. 'The West was very concerned about what was going on. But now you seem to have got everything sorted out, yes?'

'Yes, we have – or most of it, anyway. But as Moscow re-established positive control of all branches of the armed forces, and as a matter of routine began comparing listed inventories with the assets that could actually be located and identified, some accounting discrepancies were discovered.'

'"Accounting discrepancies"?'

'That's what Moscow called them, yes. At some of the more remote, less well-supervised military bases, it became apparent that some officers had been supplementing their salaries by disposing of certain equipment they decided was surplus to requirements. Basically, they would write off a few cases of AK47s, say, on the grounds that they had been damaged by immersion in water, and then sell them to anyone who wanted them. Once this came to light, Moscow finally understood why the Chechen rebels seemed so well-armed – they'd obtained most of their weapons and ammunition direct from Russian regular forces.'

'You didn't bring me all the way out here to talk about a few black-market Kalashnikovs, Viktor. What else went missing?'

A look of embarrassment flitted across Bykov's face. 'You're quite right. Missing small arms are a matter of concern, obviously, but we soon discovered that some larger and more expensive pieces of military equipment also couldn't be accounted for. In particular, we seemed to be missing a few aircraft.'

'What aircraft, precisely?'

'The Russian Air Force reported that it couldn't locate fourteen of its Mikoyan-Gurevich MiG-25 interceptors: the aircraft NATO has code-named the Foxbat.'

Richter stared at him. 'Jesus, Viktor, you can't misplace something that size, and certainly not fourteen of them.'

'I agree. Yesterday,' Bykov added, looking even more unhappy, 'that number went up to sixteen. An inspection team sent to the Letneozerskiy interceptor base – you might know it as Obozerskiy Southeast – in Karelia, near the Finnish border, couldn't account for two MiG-25s that were supposed to be on the strength of 524 IAP. What's even more disturbing is that all the members of the inspection team were killed outright when their aircraft crashed shortly after leaving the same base. An initial inspection of the wreckage suggests that it exploded in mid-air. We only know about the missing MiGs because the team leader telephoned Moscow two days earlier to explain that he'd have to go in person and check if they were currently at a maintenance facility in the Ukraine before he rendered his final report. I've since checked with Zaporizhia, the facility in question, and the MiGs definitely aren't there.'

For a few moments Richter was silent, then he spoke slowly. 'I can see your problem, Viktor. What I'm not sure about is how you think I can help you solve it.'

Bykov raised a hand to the waiter and requested another round.

'As you well know, we have adequate technical intelligence resources – satellites, phased-array radars and the like. Our problem is that our satellites carry out surveillance only of countries we consider to be hostile or potentially hostile to Russia. Likewise, our radars look outwards, across our borders, into China, Scandinavia and all the other countries that surround us. What we don't have is much satellite coverage of activity here *inside* Russia, and before we can work out where the MiG-25s have gone, we need to get access to the take from whatever satellites the Americans had within range when those aircraft went missing. So I supplied whatever dates and locations I could deduce to your section, and requested that you brought the images with you.'

'I've got them right here,' Richter said, touching his briefcase, 'together with our analysts' best guesses about the aircraft they've spotted on the films. I've also got

JARIC and N-PIC analysts standing by to talk to your people if necessary.'

'Thank you.'

'But first I have a question. In fact, I've got two. If somebody's buying or stealing Foxbats, that's only half the equation. Without munitions, spares, maintenance people and, obviously, pilots, the aircraft's just a thirty-ton paperweight. Are you missing any pilots or maintainers as well?'

Bykov nodded. 'I don't have exact figures, but I understand that a number of qualified Air Force personnel cannot currently be located. And your other question?'

'Why are you bothered? So what if some nation wants to beg, borrow or steal a handful of obsolete interceptors? Remember, the MiG-25's a forty-year-old design. If somebody had walked off with a dozen of your latest air-superiority fighters I could understand your concern. After all, you sell fighter aircraft around the world, and you've supplied that aircraft to a lot of countries – off the top of my head Algeria, Iraq and Syria to name but three – so what's so special about these sixteen antiquated Foxbats?'

'Let me ask *you* a question,' Bykov responded. 'Why did we build the MiG-25?'

For a few moments Richter just stared at the Russian. 'I don't see where you're going with this, Viktor.'

'It's crucial. When you know why we built the aircraft, you'll know why we're so worried about who's got them now.'

Richter nodded. 'OK, I'll play the game. We believe you originally designed the Foxbat to counter the American XB-70 Valkyrie Mach three bomber.'

'That wasn't in fact the case, but even if it was, the XB-70 project was cancelled well before the first prototype MiG-25 flew. We knew that the Americans had no other supersonic bombers planned, so why did we continue developing the aircraft?'

'Probably to counter the SR-71A Blackbird spy-plane. To catch it you'd have needed a Mach three interceptor.'

'Wrong again,' Viktor Bykov said. 'The Blackbird was never a real threat to us. That aircraft carried no weapons: all it could do was take pictures, obtain radar images and measure radiation.'

'So why *did* you build the Foxbat?' Richter demanded.

'Let me ask you another question,' Bykov said, clearly determined to spin this out. 'In September 1976 a renegade pilot called Viktor Belenko defected to the West from our airfield at Chuguyevka in a MiG-25 and landed it at Hakodate airport in Japan. The American Central Intelligence Agency and the Foreign Technology Division at Wright-Patterson took the aircraft totally to pieces before giving it back to us. You heard about that, no doubt?'

'It was before my time, but I've read some reports,' Richter replied cautiously.

'Do you remember what those reports said about the avionics and radar fit?'

Richter shook his head. 'Not in any detail.'

'Let me refresh your memory, then, though I didn't read the same reports that you did.'

'I'm certainly glad to hear that,' Richter murmured grimly.

Bykov smiled, then continued. 'The reports probably highlighted the lack of solid-state electronics in the avionics. Everything was old-style, with valve-driven circuits and equipment, and a massively powerful radar. I'm sure there was a certain amount of self-satisfied chuckling in the corridors of Whitehall and the Pentagon at the poor old Russians and their old-fashioned fighter.'

Richter shifted slightly in his seat. What Bykov was saying was indeed a fairly accurate paraphrasing of the classified analyses that had circulated in Western intelligence services following the examination of the misappropriated Foxbat by American technical experts.

'It apparently never occurred to anybody to ask *why*. *Why had we used valves* instead of printed-circuit boards and transistors? After all, in our other fighter aircraft we used similar technology to the latest American fighters. In fact,' Bykov added with a chuckle, 'some of the avionics we used were actually stolen from the Americans.

'Long before we built the MiG-25, we'd perfected solid-state electronics, and we had off-the-shelf components that we could have used in the aircraft, but we didn't. We took a step backwards and fitted valves, and all that other old-fashioned equipment. So I ask you again – why?'

'Viktor, I have no idea. The Foxbat was your front-line interceptor and—'

'Exactly,' Bykov interrupted. 'But *what* was it intended to intercept? That's the crucial question.'

'American bombers? B-1s and B-52s, I suppose?'

Bykov shook his head. 'To intercept those lumbering giants we would hardly have needed a Mach three fighter, and certainly not a fighter that can reach a ceiling of over thirty thousand metres. Let me give you a clue – EMP.'

'EMP? You mean electromagnetic pulse?' Richter frowned.

'Exactly. Add EMP to valve-based avionics and a Mach three interceptor with a thirty-kilometre ceiling, and what do you get?'

For a moment, Richter said nothing, his mind making connections that looked less and less attractive the more he thought about them. Then he looked back at Bykov.

'Oh, shit,' he said.

'"Oh, shit" is right,' Bykov agreed. 'The Foxbat was built for one role only. It was designed to intercept intercontinental ballistic missiles in their terminal phase – that's why it's so fast and flies so high – after detonation of one or more nuclear weapons. The EMP from a nuclear blast will fry solid-state electronics, but it has no effect on valve-based systems, and that's precisely why we fitted them. The Foxbat was designed as a post-nuclear exchange *survivor*. So the obvious conclusion is—'

'The obvious conclusion,' Richter interrupted, 'is that whoever's got your aircraft is planning on an exchange of nuclear weapons, and is intending to survive that exchange by using your Foxbats to take out the inevitable retaliatory nuclear strike in its terminal phase.'

Chapter Seven

'Is this all he had on him?' Pak Je-San demanded, staring down at the collection of objects arranged on a wooden table in front of him. He'd already looked with displeasure at Yi Min-Ho's bullet-riddled body in the mortuary next door.

'Yes, sir. We thoroughly checked the ledge he was using as an observation point, and there was nothing else there. We also surveyed the entire surrounding area, including the spot where the spy was killed, and found nothing further.'

Pak picked up the notebook and read the entries carefully: all related to a handful of F-5 fighters. That was exactly what he'd expected, for as soon as he'd heard about the possible landing of a spy near Suri-bong he'd ordered all operations involving the MiG-25 interceptors to cease. Opening the hangar doors to attract the South Korean agent's attention while the patrol ambushed him had been, he thought, a master-stroke. But he hadn't anticipated the Kyocera satellite phone, and that was a worry because it meant that the spy might possibly have disclosed what he'd seen emerging from the secure hangar.

But Pak doubted if the intruder had enough time.

He'd spoken to the *chung-wi* who'd led the patrol, and then to all of his men individually, about the exact sequence of events, and the timing didn't seem to work. He knew exactly when the hangar doors had opened, and when the lieutenant had ordered his men forward. There would then have been a short delay while the tractor was hitched to the aircraft, and another before any part of the MiG-25 could have been visible from the hillside opposite. Then the spy would have had to first identify what he was seeing, switch on the Kyocera, wait until it had locked on to a satellite, enter the number, and then wait for his contact in South Korea to answer.

As far as Pak could estimate, all that would take an absolute minimum of two minutes, but the *chung-wi* had assured him that two minutes after the hangar doors had slid open the spy was already dead. At worst, he might have got through to his contact in South Korea, but he'd certainly had no time to pass on a detailed report.

But whatever had happened, there was nothing else he could do about it now. The spy was dead and whatever knowledge he had gathered had died with him. Pak had obviously reprimanded the lieutenant for resorting to killing the man – if taken alive they could have used a variety of sophisticated techniques to loosen his tongue – but at least he hadn't escaped, and now the final stages of their operation could begin.

The North Korean Air Force was still flying the antiquated Shenyang F-5 at T'ae'tan but, as Yi Min-Ho had discovered, only a few of the old fighter planes now remained there. All the Ilyushins had already been redeployed to the forward bases at Nuchonri and Kuupri, located on the west and east coasts respectively, just north of the DMZ.

Pak wondered if the South Korean spy had noticed the lack of aircraft movements. In fact the F-5s were there simply as camouflage, something to park on the hard-standings whenever one of the American spy satellites was due to pass overhead.

The real activity at T'ae'tan centred on the four newer, closely guarded aircraft shelters where Pak had so far assembled twenty-four MiG-25 interceptors, mostly from Russia, but two from Iraq, one from Algeria, another from Iran, and the remaining four from India. And it wasn't just the aircraft themselves. Over the last three years he and his most trusted associates had bribed, suborned or blackmailed air force officers and NCOs from a number of foreign nations, and he now had a full maintenance team living in the curtained rooms of the new building almost adjacent to the hangars, as well as armourers and pilots. It also housed a virtually full inventory of spares and enough munitions to make the secret squadron of Foxbats a viable force.

The personnel enlisted had all been very well rewarded to change their allegiance – though not as handsomely as they believed because of the number of 'superdollars' included in their handouts of cash – and had all been promised substantial bonuses upon suc-cessful completion. Pak well knew that his government had no intention of honouring such a commitment. A bullet in the back of the head was a lot cheaper than a bonus of any size. The risk of loose talk was why all these foreign military personnel were accommodated here in the remote airfield at T'ae'tan rather than in Ugom or any other town.

Pak was now awaiting only the final two aircraft, and imminent delivery of the remaining munitions – the forty-eight R-40T air-to-air missiles which would bring his total arsenal up to one hundred and sixty-three. Known to NATO as the AA-6 Acrid, this is an essential component of the Foxbat's high-level interception system: a Mach 4.5 missile with a thirty-kilometre range and carrying a seventy-kilogram high-explosive fragmentation warhead. Coupled with the Foxbat's high-level capability and its immensely powerful Saphir-25 radar – NATO reporting name Fox Fire – it proves a highly effective weapon against high-flying, high-speed targets.

The Acrids were currently travelling by sea from Varna in Bulgaria, and would route through the Suez Canal to Bandar Abbas in Iran – the former Shah's premier naval base – and from there they'd be flown direct to T'ae'tan itself. And once those had arrived, everything needed would be in place.

Office of the Associate Deputy Director of the Central Intelligence Agency, Langley, Virginia

Following the events of 11 September 2001, there was a major shake-up in the American intelligence organization, a community still reeling from shock at the destruction of the Twin Towers and the attack on the Pentagon. And more so from what many perceived to be a series of inexcusable failures of intelligence collection and analysis.

One of the major changes was the creation of an entire new bureaucracy: the Office of the Director of National Intelligence. Its function was to integrate and analyse all intelligence – domestic, foreign and military – and assess its impact on both homeland security and American interests abroad. With the creation of the ODNI, the post of DCI or Director of Central Intelligence – the head of the CIA and the most senior intelligence community post in the United States – had ceased to exist.

This was a pity, because Walter Hicks would probably have made a very good DCI. He'd been the Director of Operations (Clandestine Services), and acting DCI, when a crisis had arisen that took America to the brink of thermonuclear war. His handling of the emergency had impressed the President. When the previous incumbent had retired for genuine health reasons as opposed to Washington-speak 'health reasons' – a euphemism for either sexual misconduct or some form of financial irregularity – Hicks had indeed been promoted, but not to the post of DNI. That job had gone to a career diplomat, probably because the White House didn't trust a professional spook to regulate or represent the interests of other professional spooks.

Instead, he'd become the new Associate Deputy Director of the CIA, and he wasn't much enjoying it. Hicks had always been a hands-on, let's-kick-some-ass kind of guy, and his enhanced salary didn't entirely compensate for having to be politically correct at all times and talk nicely to time-serving politicians demanding information that he personally didn't think they had any right or need to know.

Since his appointment, his already sparse fair hair had begun receding to the point where he was seriously considering shaving his head completely. He had even sold his forty-five-foot catamaran because he no longer had any spare time to sail her.

So it was with a certain sense of relief that he noted Richard Muldoon's name showing up in the appointments diary on his computer. He knew Muldoon well enough to realize that the gangling Head of the Directorate of Science and Technology – nobody had suggested changing the name of that particular section of the Agency – wouldn't bother him with anything trivial.

'Take a pew, and grab a coffee, Richard. What've you got?'

Muldoon put the file he carried on the conference table and helped himself from the coffee pot – he sometimes thought Hicks should simply take his caffeine intravenously and save all that messing around with cups and beans and percolators – then sat down opposite the ADD.

'We've received Flash traffic direct from National Intelligence Service headquarters at Naegok-dong in Seoul. The request came from Kang Jang-Ho – who's number two to Bae Chang-Su – but Bae himself countersigned it.'

'I'm pretty busy and you've read this file, so just give me the short version.'

Muldoon was used to dealing with Hicks, and had anticipated him. 'It's pretty simple. For the last few months the NIS has been picking up whispers about unusual air activity in and around the south-west corner of North Korea. Unfamiliar aircraft seen flying over the land and occasionally over the Yellow Sea, even the occasional sonic boom, that kind of thing. They sent out surveillance vessels, mainly commandeered fishing boats to allow an element of plausible deniability if they were intercepted, but their observers didn't spot anything they weren't expecting.

'The only military airfield in that whole area is T'ae'tan, located right here.' Muldoon pulled a map out of his file and opened it on the table. 'It's one of the closest North Korean airfields to Seoul, so the NIS has always tried to keep an eye on any new developments there.'

Hicks looked at the chart where Muldoon was pointing. 'Yes, got it. Carry on.'

'T'ae'tan is known to operate Ilyushin Il-28 bombers and Shenyang F-5 fighters, but what some witnesses reported seeing was nothing like either aircraft. The problem for the NIS was that those witnesses weren't exactly qualified in aircraft recognition, most of them being fishermen. But they kept getting so many reports they finally decided they needed to check on T'ae'tan and find out exactly what was going on there.

'So yesterday – Monday – they landed one of their agents just about here.' Muldoon pointed again to the map. 'His instructions were to trek across country to T'ae'tan and set up an observation point. Then he was to count the number of F-5 fighters and Il-28 bombers he saw and identify any unusual aircraft. He was using a satellite phone to call in reports, and they received his third and last one this morning. It started with the sound of gunfire, then he yelled "They have new aircraft. I've seen a—" And then his satellite phone simply went dead, and it's been off air ever since.'

'That's it?'

'That's it.'

'And they want us to do what, exactly?'

'The next time one of our Keyhole birds passes near T'ae'tan, they'd like us to tinker with the orbit so it's a bit out of sequence, then take a bunch of pictures to see if we can figure out what's going on.'

'And will we do that?'

Muldoon nodded. 'We don't have a lot of options, as Oplan 5027 commits us to lending our support to South Korea, and this request falls well within the parameters. So I've already confirmed the tasking – and I'd quite like to know what's going on over there myself.'

Yongbyon, North Korea

Yongbyon is a small and unremarkable town located about one hundred kilometres north of Pyongyang. In the mid-1960s the North Koreans established a large-scale nuclear research facility there, and ten years later they began construction of a nuclear reactor on the site. Within a further ten years they'd also erected a repro-cessing facility that would allow them to extract plu-tonium from nuclear fuel, and a separate research reactor rated at five megawatts. The DPRK built other reactors, including a two-hundred-megawatt installation at Taechon, but it was the Yongbyon complex that wor-ried everyone most.

Estimates prepared by South Korea, America and

Japan, based upon an IAEA calculation of the radioactive isotope content of nuclear waste unloaded from the five-megawatt reactor, suggested that by the end of 2004 the North Koreans could have extracted between twelve and twenty-four kilograms of plutonium.

In fact, they'd extracted rather more than even the most optimistic – or pessimistic, depending on point of view – of the estimates, but hardly any plutonium now remained in the lead-lined subterranean storage room at Yongbyon.

A modern twenty-kiloton nuclear warhead contains eight kilograms of fissionable material, so most assessments suggested that the DPRK might have enough plutonium to construct two or three nuclear weapons of this size. That assumed the North Korean scientists were constructing a weapon of modern design, using shaped charges known as lenses to initiate the detonation sequence. But no matter what method they were using to trigger the device, they certainly had enough plutonium to build at least one weapon, even if it was the size of a truck, as one Western scientist had sneered.

There are several problems associated with the production of nuclear weapons, but one of the most intractable is size.

The 'Little Boy' bomb that the USAF dropped on Hiroshima was about three metres long and weighed almost four thousand kilograms. It contained sixty-four kilograms of uranium 235, but the so-called 'gun' design was so primitive and ineffective that a mere 0.7 kilograms of the material underwent nuclear fission. But it still had a yield approaching fifteen kilotons and killed about one hundred and fifty thousand people.

The 'Fat Man' weapon dropped three days later on Nagasaki was even bigger and a lot heavier, with a slightly higher yield, and employed shaped charges to compress a core of plutonium into a critical mass. Plutonium is slightly easier to produce than uranium 235, and is the favoured material for regimes that are taking the first steps towards becoming full members of the 'nuclear club'.

The most important point about the first two American atomic weapons is that they were massive, and that was the problem the North Korean nuclear scientists had been struggling with. They could build such a weapon – since the October 2006 nuclear test in Hamgyeong province in North Korea that hadn't been in dispute – but constructing a weapon that was light and small enough to be carried by one of the regime's ballistic missiles was another story entirely. Nevertheless they'd succeeded, and the warhead they'd produced was designed to fit inside the nose cone of every missile in the North Korean inventory, from the old and basic Scud to the three-stage Taep'o-dong 2. They'd fabricated three ten-kiloton nuclear warheads using eighteen kilograms of fissionable material, and these had all been sent to the Chiha-ri missile site located a short distance north of the DMZ.

Just over a year earlier, the Yongbyon scientists had been given the most explicit instructions from Pyongyang – by Kim Yong-Su himself, in fact – to use a further twelve kilograms of plutonium in fabricating a twenty-kiloton weapon and detonation system for a highly classified project. That all made sense, but what didn't make sense were the additional orders. They were also to prepare four standard-size warhead casings, but fill them with scrap metal.

In a totalitarian regime like North Korea, survival usually comes down to quietly doing what you're told, so that's exactly what the scientists did.

Six weeks previously, a truck guarded by a troop of heavily armed soldiers had appeared in Yongbyon. The officer in charge had handed the commanding officer a set of orders signed by the highest authority in Pyongyang, and instructed his men to load the genuine nuclear weapon, stored inside a wooden crate, onto the lorry. As soon as it was loaded, the convoy set off again, its destination now the dockyard at Wonsan. The fake warheads were put into a storeroom, and then the scientists got on with their other work.

That afternoon, another convoy appeared at Yongbyon, this one in the charge of a *so-jang* – major-general – and within an hour the first of the four fake warheads had been loaded into one of the waiting trucks. From the outside, these specially designed vehicles looked pretty much like regular army three-axle five-ton trucks, albeit with solid sides. Somebody who knew about goods vehicles might have spotted the heavy-duty springs and uprated shock absorbers on the rear axles, but that was about the only indication that in each one of them most of the rear compartment was occupied by a lead-lined safe.

In fact, calling the structure a safe was to misstate the case. It comprised a fixed base and two long sides, formed from half-inch steel plates lined with lead on the inside. The two ends were made of the same material and hinged at the base, but were so heavy that closing them required the use of hydraulic rams powered by the truck's diesel engine. The top was even heavier, hinged on its long side and supported by a double set of rams. There were no locks, as the sheer weight of the plates made them superfluous.

Inside the box was a shaped cradle, and the entire structure had been designed for one purpose only: to carry the North Korean standard-size nuclear warhead. The design would allow the weapon to be lifted directly into the truck and then lowered into the safe.

Loading the trucks took the rest of the afternoon, and it was early evening before the vehicles were ready to leave. The Yongbyon commanding officer asked the *so-jang* if his men would like to eat at the facility before they left, but his offer was curtly rejected. They were, the major-general informed him, running on a very tight schedule, and rations had already been provided.

Five hours after the first of the trucks had entered the Yongbyon complex, the convoy was back on the road, heading east. But almost as soon as the vehicles had cleared the outskirts of Yongbyon they scattered, each of the trucks driving its scrap-filled 'warhead' to a different destination, escort vehicles full of armed soldiers positioned in front and behind.

They were each heading for a missile site on the east coast of North Korea, following orders from Pyongyang that were eminently clear, but which made little sense to any of the men, not even to the officer in command.

Rossyia Hotel, Moscow

'You didn't give us a hell of a lot to work with, Viktor,' Richter said as he opened up the laptop. They'd moved to a corner of one of the snack-bars that was temporarily closed – Richter presumed Bykov had organized that – so that nobody could overhear them or see the computer screen.

'I know, but getting any kind of information out of the airfields and squadrons was very difficult. Eventually I had my staff comb the local air traffic control records for the aircraft side-numbers, and simply noted the date and time of their last known take-off. I also asked for tracing action for the missing aircraft at all military airfields within the CIS. Sometimes that helped, but more often it didn't.'

Richter was silent for a few moments as he plugged in the computer and switched it on. Simpson hadn't given him any definite instructions about the information he could provide, but his recent experience in Aïn Oussera was quite probably relevant to the problem the Russians had uncovered.

'It may not just be *your* Foxbats that are going missing, Viktor,' he said, then outlined what he and the SAS team had discovered in Algeria. 'According to our trans-atlantic cousins, or more specifically the NSA, the Iranians may have lost an aircraft as well.'

'This problem could be bigger than we thought, then,' Bykov murmured as he produced a red-bound notebook from an inside pocket of his jacket. He opened it at a page that listed dates, times and sets of coordinates. Once the Dell's operating system had loaded, Richter double-clicked an icon that represented a map, and waited while the graphics program started.

The screen changed and an aerial photograph was displayed. It looked as if it covered about a ten-mile-square block of territory, and in the top left-hand corner was indicated an airfield.

'The centre of this image is the first set of coordinates you gave us,' Richter said. 'What our techies have done is provide a series of overlays so that idiots like me can understand what the pictures show. We can zoom in to see the details better, but this scale is probably best for what we want. The analysts have already worked on each picture and identified all the aircraft, ignoring everything except the MiG-25s.'

He manoeuvred the cursor over a symbol at the top of the screen and clicked the left-hand button below the touchpad. Instantly a grid overlay appeared, letters running horizontally and numbers vertically.

'According to my briefing, there's an aircraft contact in square delta five,' Richter said.

Bykov looked carefully at the screen. 'Yes, I can see something.'

Richter chose another icon, and a tiny red circle appeared more or less in the centre of the grid square. Inside this was a small silver dart.

'Right, that's the aircraft. Now, the satellite took several pictures of this specific area, but we've only been able to identify the same aircraft in three of them. That's just because of the high relative speed of the bird in its polar orbit. Rather than look at each picture individually, the techies have plotted the other two images of the aircraft onto this frame, so it's easier to see where it's heading.'

Richter clicked another icon twice, and two more small red circles appeared, a tiny silver object in each, tracking south-east. He clicked another button and a blue dotted line appeared on the screen, one end terminating at the airfield runway, the other extending beyond the third image of the aircraft itself.

'That's the Foxbat's apparent track. The problem is that we don't know if it continued heading south-east, or changed direction some time after the satellite's pass. And that, really, is the problem with all these pictures. At best, the satellite photographed the aircraft in four frames. Usually it was only two or three frames, and for several of the coordinates there were no birds within range at the time you specified.'

Richter leant back in his seat. 'I can show you the rest of the images if you'd like, but we've already done an analysis. In most cases the aircraft were detected heading south or south-east. Extrapolating the tracks doesn't really help, because there are so few coordinates, but about all we can be sure of is that the aircraft weren't making for Western Europe or the North Pole. Almost anywhere else is a possibility, though.

'The other obvious problem is the Foxbat's range, which is pretty short. There's no way these aircraft could have been flown out of Russia even with full tanks, so you're either looking at several refuelling stops or possibly the MiG being loaded into a transport aircraft or onto a ship, and then delivered somewhere as a piece of cargo.

'For what it's worth, our intelligence people have prepared a shortlist of likely client states. We've assumed that these aircraft have been obtained by a nation rather than some power-crazed individual. We're suggesting you should look at Afghanistan, China, India, Iran, North Korea, Pakistan and Taiwan.'

Bykov nodded slowly. 'Your analysis matches our

opinions. But we don't think India or Pakistan are likely customers, simply because both nations could have bought the aircraft legitimately from us if they'd wanted to. Afghanistan is too closely watched by the Americans for anyone to have flown either individual interceptors or a large transport aircraft into an airfield there without being detected. Taiwan seems unlikely, so that leaves China, Iran or North Korea.'

'But if the NSA is right,' Richter pointed out, 'Iran itself might be missing a MiG-25.'

Bykov nodded again. 'So that suggests China or North Korea. We've always feared China's intentions towards us. It's possible the sleeping giant is awakening and flexing its muscles, but our relations with Beijing have been fairly cordial lately. Not,' he added, 'that that means very much these days.'

As Richter reached out to close the lid of the laptop, Bykov's mobile phone rang. He stood up, pulled it from his pocket and moved out of earshot before answering the call. Then he closed the phone and walked back.

'We may have a lead,' he said, and Richter looked interested. 'A young man's body has been found in the woods outside Perm. He was murdered, a single bullet through the head, and apparently robbed.'

'So?' Richter asked. 'Why has the GRU been informed about a murder in the middle of Russia?'

'Patience, Paul, and I'll tell you. Perm lies at the southern end of the Ural mountains, more or less on the edge of Siberia. The closest airfield is Bolshoye Savino, a mixed-use military and civilian airfield. One of the squadrons there flies the MiG-31, the development of the MiG-25 that you call the Foxhound, and there are half a dozen Foxbats based there as well. The GRU's been informed because the murder victim, Georgi Lenkov, was a front-line MiG-31 pilot. Perhaps he was approached to steal an aircraft and refused, which means that whoever's orchestrating these thefts had him killed to stop him talking.

'More importantly,' Bykov went on, 'as far as I'm aware, no MiG-25s or MiG-31s have been reported missing from Bolshoye Savino, so perhaps the thieves are still in the area, looking for another pilot who *will* accept their offer. I think, my friend, we should take a trip to Perm.'

T'ae'tan Air Base, North Korea

Every time any nation on Earth launches a satellite, the American Space Command organization, co-located with NORAD at Cheyenne Mountain in Colorado, starts tracking it, and will continue to track it until it falls back to Earth. In fact, Space Command constantly monitors around ten thousand objects in orbit around the planet, ranging in size from fully operational communications, broadcast television and surveillance satellites down to space debris: bits and pieces of failed or damaged satellites, some as small as half an inch across.

The purpose of the monitoring is twofold. First, and most important, a launch from somewhere in Asia could simply be a nation using a redundant Soviet rocket to boost its latest scientific satellite into orbit. Or it could be a renegade Russian general with a chip on his shoulder and access to a bunch of rail-mounted ICBMs, trying to start World War Three. In either case, NORAD staff have about two minutes to decide whether or not this launch shows hostile intent and, if it does, what they should do about it apart from blowing the whistle and closing the blast doors inside the mountain.

The second reason for the monitoring process is that space craft are fragile, and the consequences of, say, the Space Shuttle hitting a one-inch bolt travelling at a couple of thousand miles an hour would be catastrophic. So before every launch, the Cheyenne Mountain people check their records to ensure that the flight-path of the launch vehicle is as danger-free as possible.

A spin-off from the monitoring system is that the paths of surveillance satellites of all nations are well known. By their nature, these vehicles behave unlike almost all other satellites because of their need to overfly as much of the surface of the planet as possible. They travel in polar, rather than equatorial, orbits at fairly low altitudes – typically between about one hundred and two hundred miles up – and move very quickly. In late evening you can sometimes see one, a fast-moving white dot illuminated by the rays of the setting sun.

The armed forces of most nations know these routes, and the times that these satellites are due overhead, and take extreme care to ensure that nothing sensitive can be observed by these silent and watchful 'eyes in the sky'. Submarines, for example, will avoid being on or near the surface when a satellite may pass overhead.

Originally, overhead times for the satellites were listed in tables that – depending on the country of origin – varied in security classification from 'Restricted' up to 'Secret', but these days simple computer programs provide the same information in a much more accessible form that is infinitely easier to understand.

T'ae'tan Air Base had such a program, and Pak Je-San was scrupulous in ensuring that none of his MiG-25s were ever outside their hangars when a pass was due. He was slightly less concerned about aircraft actually in the air, because surveillance satellite optics are optimized for surface surveillance, not fast-moving airborne contacts.

But, as with all computer programs, the information that comes out can only ever be as good as the data that goes in, and Pak Je-San was unaware that the Americans had been asked by the South Korean National Intelligence Service to ensure that a satellite passed directly over T'ae'tan as soon as possible. Because of the extreme sensitivity regarding the Korean Peninsula, the Americans had complied almost at once. They'd used the manoeuvring engines to make a slight change to the orbit of a KH-12 bird that had just started its northbound track from Antarctica, with the result that the satellite passed directly over T'ae'tan when otherwise its programmed orbit would have taken it north up the Yellow Sea and straight over China, avoiding North Korean territory altogether.

So the Foxbat that was being returned to the hangar by the ground crew wasn't quite inside the building when the satellite moved within range, currently one hundred and thirty-five miles above the surface. The first image recorded by its cameras was taken from a slightly oblique angle, while the huge twin rudders and jet exhausts of the MiG-25 were still visible outside the hangar, but by the time the second picture was taken the aircraft had vanished.

JAMES BARRINGTON

Directorate of Science and Technology, Central Intelligence Agency Headquarters, Langley, Virginia

Unlike its more primitive forebears, the KH-12 doesn't use any form of photographic plate or medium: it automatically converts the images into digital form and then transmits the data to one of several communications satellites in geostationary orbit above it. The data is then either transmitted directly, or possibly via another communications bird, to the Mission Ground Site at Fort Belvoir, near Washington, DC. From the Ground Site, the images are sent to the National Photographic Interpretation Centre – N-PIC – located in Building 213 in the Washington Navy Yard. This technology means that the data is available in near real-time, within minutes of the picture being taken.

Seventy-five minutes after the Keyhole had overflown T'ae'tan, Richard Muldoon was looking at the first of six images on the twenty-one-inch flat-panel monitor of his desktop computer, sent by secure electronic transfer direct from Building 213. Muldoon's Priority One instructions had ensured that an initial analysis had been undertaken the moment the N-PIC staff received the pictures.

Not that too much analysis was needed. Muldoon took one look at the distinctive tail-end of the aircraft sticking out of the hangar, and muttered 'Fuck me, they've got a Foxbat.'

Chapter Eight

Wednesday
Perm, Russia

'I don't care who you are or what branch of the military you represent. You can't just walk in here and expect to take over a murder investigation.' The Perm chief of police was a short, fat, red-faced man, his complexion growing angrier and more choleric by the minute. So far Bykov hadn't been getting anywhere with him.

The previous evening, he and Richter had flown in to Perm, a city about seven hundred miles east of Moscow, arriving too late to achieve anything useful that day. Bykov had left his card at the main police station, with a demand that the police chief make himself available for a meeting first thing next morning. The somewhat peremptory tone the GRU officer had used, Richter guessed, was probably the main reason why Kolya Wanov was so clearly unwilling to cooperate.

'Superintendent Wanov,' Bykov tried again, 'we're not here to either investigate the murder or impede your inquiries in any way. We just want answers to some questions. We understand that Georgi Lenkov's wallet had been stolen, so why are you so certain he wasn't killed in the course of a routine mugging that escalated out of control?'

Wanov shrugged. 'There's not much doubt about

that,' he replied grudgingly. Despite his belligerence, he knew he had little real choice here. Pissing off a senior GRU general would achieve nothing career-enhancing. 'First, at some point that evening Lenkov's wrists had been shackled with handcuffs. There were abrasions round his wrists consistent with restraints like regular police cuffs. If he'd been handcuffed, there would have been no need for a mugger to kill him. That's the first thing.

'We've received a couple of reports that a man answering to Lenkov's description was arrested by two police officers in a bar near the river on Monday evening. The problem,' the superintendent said with a mirthless smile, 'is that no police officers were anywhere near that location at the time, and there have been no arrest reports subsequently filed. Muggers don't usually work in pairs, impersonating police officers, and they certainly aren't likely to chase their quarry into a bar where anyone seeing their faces could later identify them.

'Third, the pathologist wasn't absolutely certain because of the extensive damage to the skull caused by the bullet, but he thinks Lenkov received at least one violent blow to the back of his head, probably administered with a cosh or club.

'And, finally, the body was found in woodland outside the city, and we know for sure he was killed there. The forensic evidence is overwhelming, even if we didn't have a witness who actually heard the shot. Anyway, muggers normally look for their prey in city streets. It was a deliberate act of murder, no mistake.'

Bykov nodded. It looked as if the Perm police had done their work thoroughly. 'That's clear enough for us,

Superintendent. But we believe the killing of this young Air Force officer may have wider implications affecting national security. We suspect the perpetrators are still here in Perm, and all we're asking is that the local police extend us a little cooperation.'

'What kind of cooperation?' Wanov asked.

'We'd like as little publicity as possible. Have you released details of Lenkov's name and profession?'

'Not yet.' The police officer shook his head. 'His parents live in Moscow, but they're away somewhere at the moment. We can't release details of the identity of the victim until they've been informed.'

'So who knows about the murder here in Perm?'

'It was reported in the local newspaper.'

'What exactly was said?'

'Just that the body of an unidentified young man had been found apparently murdered in the woods outside the city.'

'How did you eventually identify him?'

'A small stroke of luck. Whoever killed him took away his wallet, and emptied it, then discarded it. However, they overlooked an internal pocket where Lenkov kept his identity card. We compared the photograph with what was left of his face, and that was that.'

'So who exactly knows he was an Air Force pilot?'

'Just ourselves, and Lenkov's commanding officer at Bolshoye Savino. Probably no one else.'

'Can you keep it that way for a couple of days?' Bykov asked.

'If you can explain why, yes.'

'Superintendent Wanov, my investigation is classified at a very high level, well above Top Secret. My colleague here' – he gestured to Richter, who hadn't said a word since they'd entered the room – 'is an intelligence officer representing the government of Great Britain.' That was news to Richter, but he said nothing.

Wanov looked at him uncertainly, apparently torn between his desire to find out just what the hell Bykov was talking about, and his discomfort at having an identified Western intelligence agent sitting there studying him silently.

'Nothing I'm about to tell you is to leave this room, or is to be discussed with anyone else, at any level, at any time.'

Wanov nodded, then found his voice. 'I understand.'

Bykov continued. 'We believe that Lenkov was approached by agents of a foreign power and asked to steal a Mikoyan-Gurevich interceptor, one of the aircraft based at Bolshoye Savino. We assume he refused to carry out this act of treachery, and was killed because of that. We also believe those same agents are still here somewhere in Perm, and that they'll be currently trying to suborn another officer from the airfield. It's essential that we find out who these agents are, and who they represent. That means catching them in the act, and to achieve that we need your assistance and that of your officers.'

'How are you going to do it?'

Bykov smiled. 'At this precise moment, I've no idea. A lot will depend on what we can learn from the dead man's commanding officer and from his fellow pilots. If we're right, and he was approached by foreign agents, we're hoping he might have talked to someone else about it. That way, we might even be able to get a lead of some kind. That's our first job, but if we do manage to locate these agents, we'll need you to provide enough men to ensure that they don't slip through our fingers.'

Wanov nodded slowly. 'That won't be a problem, but make sure you give me as much notice as you can.'

Bykov stood up. 'Right. Now,' he said, 'we must get to the airfield. We have an appointment there in just under thirty minutes.'

Office of the Associate Deputy Director of the Central Intelligence Agency, Langley, Virginia

'So the Democratic People's Republic of Korea has got itself a Foxbat. So what?' Walter Hicks leant back in his seat, pulled out a stubby cigar and – in complete defiance of Langley's rigid no-smoking-anywhere-in-the-building rule, imposed by William Webster in September 1990 – lit it. 'So what?' he repeated.

And that was, Muldoon had to concede, a good question. Why should the CIA – or anyone else, for that matter – care in the least if the North Koreans had obtained a forty-year-old supersonic interceptor? But he suspected there had to be more to it than that.

'If it was just one Foxbat, I wouldn't care either, Walter,' Muldoon replied, 'but after seeing that picture from N-PIC I did some investigating, and I don't like what I found. We only got this image because of the request from the South Koreans. Now, I think it's significant that the first and only unplanned reconnaissance pass over T'ae'tan for the last two years should reveal the presence of a Foxbat. It appears the NKs have been timing their operations to coincide with periods when none of our birds have been in range. Yet, if they're just upgrading their air force with MiG-25s, why would they bother?'

'I suppose the North Koreans might consider re-equipping with Foxbats as an upgrade,' Hicks mused, 'but those aircraft are old and not that easy to fly. I'd have thought they'd be better advised to try stealing a few more Floggers or Fishbeds – or maybe even Fulcrums if they were feeling ambitious.'

Both the MiG-21 Fishbed and the MiG-23 Flogger are now obsolete, but are still being operated by North Korea. The MiG-29 Fulcrum was designed by the Russians as a direct competitor to the F-15 and F-16 interceptors, and is perhaps the most manoeuvrable fighter aircraft in the world, apart from the Harrier. With Mach 2 performance, it's a formidable adversary.

'Maybe they couldn't source any other aircraft type. Don't forget, their principal arms supplier now is China, not Russia. And if the NKs did manage to get their hands on some Fulcrums, keeping them in the air might prove a nightmare. Where would they find the spares? Do they even have maintainers skilled enough to work on them? The Foxbat, however, is an old and tested design with no fancy electronics.'

Hicks nodded. 'Yes . . . maybe they just thought they needed something quicker than a Shenyang F-5, and located a source that could supply MiG-25s instead. Perhaps it really is that simple.'

'I doubt it. I went back to check the Keyhole imagery for T'ae'tan for the last couple of years. You remember that in October of ninety-five the NKs relocated twenty-odd Ilyushin Il-28 bombers to that same airfield?'

Hicks nodded. 'Caused some jitters in the South when they realized that put them within ten minutes' flying time of Seoul.'

'Exactly,' Muldoon nodded. 'And they still had the F-5 fighters based there. Well, according to the N-PIC analysts, they haven't seen a single Ilyushin at T'ae'tan for the last eighteen months, and they've only been able to identify ten individual F-5s. That's way short of the number we believed was based there.'

'Perhaps they've kicked the bombers somewhere else. Maybe they thought having them so close to the DMZ was too provocative. As I recall, Seoul did complain about them.'

'Maybe they did,' Muldoon nodded, 'but there are other things that worry me, like the new constructions we're seeing there. T'ae'tan was never a major base, just a single runway and a couple of hangars dug into the hillside on the south side of the field, but the NKs have done a lot of work there recently. It's difficult to tell from the satellite pictures, because of the overhanging rock, but it looks like they may have excavated four new hangars, and they've certainly built what looks like a new administration block close by.'

'Maybe they're updating it. Perhaps they've got plans to expand the airfield, add a new runway or lengthen the existing one,' Hicks suggested.

'A new runway's not likely, Walter. T'ae'tan sits at the bottom of a fairly narrow valley running east–west, with hills enclosing it at the western end, rising to about six hundred feet. The land to the east is more level, but you're right – they *have* extended the runway in that direction. It was originally about a mile and a half long, and they've added enough concrete to now make it nearly three miles. That was already picked up by N-PIC when the NKs started construction work, but it didn't seem particularly significant just then.'

'Well, they'd need all of that length to handle Foxbats – those mothers don't exactly stop on a dime.'

'But do you really think the DPRK would go to the expense of nearly doubling the length of the runway at T'ae'tan just to accommodate one Foxbat? The only scenario making sense is that they've now got several of them.

'Now, I can't confirm that,' Muldoon continued, warming to his theme, 'because absolutely the only photographic evidence we have is the picture of the rear end of a MiG-25 that N-PIC sent over yesterday. All that proves is that there's at least one Foxbat at T'ae'tan. We know it's not a mock-up, because the Keyhole's thermal imaging sensors recorded that both the engine exhausts were still hot. It had either been recently flying or doing a ground run, but what the cameras picked up was part of a real aircraft.

'Meanwhile, there are a few other pointers, like the lengthened runway and the hangars. Every time the N-PIC analysts have spotted an aircraft on the ground, it's been parked close to one of the original hangars, not the new ones. When an aircraft's pulled out of a hangar to fly or do a ground run or whatever, it's normally left outside that hangar. That suggests the F-5s are in the two original structures, and there's something different kept in the new hangars.'

'Have they ever spotted anything in or near them?' Hicks asked.

'Not so far. Occasionally one of the birds might get a picture when one of the doors is open, but the hangars are built into the rock on the south side of the airfield, so the interior's always in shadow. The pass made yesterday was the first time they've seen anything significant. And the other thing is that those four hangars invariably have guards stationed outside them, almost always two-man patrols. So my tentative analysis is that there are several MiG-25s based at T'ae'tan, maybe as many as a squadron. But that raises more questions, like where did they come from? We're talking more freely to the Kremlin these days, and as far as I know they haven't sold much to the North Koreans over the last five years.'

'OK, Richard, let's assume for the moment that you're right, and that there's a squadron, or at least a significant number, of Foxbats at T'ae'tan. If the Russians didn't sell the MiGs to the DPRK, where did they come from?'

Muldoon smiled slightly. 'That, Walter is the big question, but it's always possible they stole them.'

'You're kidding.'

'No, I'm not. A couple of days ago the NSA detected some traffic on a military net in Iran that might have been referring to a missing aircraft. They're not certain, because it's possible the two people overheard were talking about a crashed aircraft – the context was ambiguous. But it could also be that some pilot's been bribed to fly his MiG out of Iran for a few pieces of silver.

'And then there's Aïn Oussera. We asked the Brits to go in there and take a look inside a heavily guarded hangar. They did, and found the building was empty, so the British SIS reckons the Algerians have also lost one or two aircraft, and the guards were simply there to preserve the scene while it's investigated. That sounds far-fetched, I know, but I'm inclined to agree with them. Aïn Oussera's known to be a Foxbat base, so if they have lost any aircraft, most likely they're MiG-25s. And subsequently the Brits fielded a request from the GRU for assistance in tracing certain aircraft movements inside Russia, and N-PIC supplied some satellite pictures for them. I gather the SIS has a man working with the GRU in Moscow right now.'

Bolshoye Savino Air Base, Russia

In fact Richter was, at that moment, a long way from Moscow. After leaving police headquarters, they'd gone straight out to the airfield at Bolshoye Savino, and fifteen minutes later they were sitting in the 764 IAP commander's office.

Lavrenti Oustenka was a full colonel, and looked it. He was one of those people who, no matter how they were dressed, where they were or what they were doing, just looked like a senior military officer. His hair was cropped to within a millimetre of his scalp, his chin bore not the slightest sign of stubble, and even sitting in the chair behind his wide desk he appeared to be fully at attention. He also didn't appear to show any particular aversion to having a Western intelligence officer involved in the operation to track down the men who'd recently killed one of his young pilots.

What he did appear to harbour doubts over was how successful that operation might be. 'Perm is a big city, you know, with well over a million inhabitants. It won't be easy to find these men, even assuming that they're still here and didn't leave straight after the killing.'

'My guess, Colonel,' Bykov said, 'is that they're still here. I won't insult you by pointing out that this information is classified, but I can tell you that we're unable to account for sixteen MiG-25 interceptors, from a variety of bases throughout Russia. We suspect that agents of a foreign power have been approaching MiG-25 pilots and inducing them to defect. And some of those pilots have been taking their aircraft with them.'

Oustenka shook his head. 'With respect, General, I find that difficult to believe. We keep meticulous records of all our aircraft. If a pilot did decide to defect, like Belenko did back in the nineteen seventies, it would be immediately obvious. A plane takes off and doesn't return – the station would soon know and Moscow would be informed. And there's also the question of range. The MiG-25 has a ferry range of about two thousand five hundred kilometres with full tanks, and it doesn't possess an in-flight refuelling capability. How could an aircraft stolen from here, say, possibly get as far as China or North Korea? It would run out of fuel hundreds or even thousands of kilometres before reaching its destination.'

Bykov nodded. This was ground that he and Richter had covered at length on their flight from Moscow.

'We're looking at something a little more subtle than some pilot climbing into a jet, heading east and hoping for the best. We believe that some senior officers have been paid off, and have been actively assisting with these thefts. That solves both the paperwork problem and the actual defection. When the MiG flies away from an airfield, everyone involved knows it won't be returning. The squadron commander will just instruct that the aircraft is being transferred to another squadron, or going off for deep maintenance, or is surplus to requirements and is being scrapped.

'That fabrication serves to keep the documentation correct, and also means that there's no problem over the aircraft's range. The air traffic control or operations people will just schedule the aircraft for refuelling at appropriate airfields along whatever route they've already chosen to get it out of Russia. This isn't some casual thieving, Colonel. Whoever's doing this is highly organized and very efficient. We've only just found out that our Air Force is missing sixteen aircraft, perhaps even more, yet until now nobody in Moscow had any suspicion that something was wrong.'

Oustenka now looked a little less doubtful. 'I can assure you, General, that all *my* aircraft are accounted for.'

'I don't doubt it,' Bykov replied dryly. 'Now, the scenario we envisage is that these foreign agents first find a pilot who's willing to participate. Then it's up to the pilot to identify those senior officers whose cooperation would be essential, and who in turn would be approached with the offer of a bribe. Only when everyone who needs to be involved has been suborned would the theft go ahead, as the appropriate documentation is prepared.'

'And you think Lenkov was approached?'

'Yes – and the fact that he's dead means he wasn't prepared to go along with them.'

'But why would he even have talked to them?' Oustenka asked.

'We don't know,' Richter said, 'but we presume their pitch would have been credible, and obviously unrelated to their real objective. For example, perhaps they told him they were making a documentary film about the Russian Air Force and would need some shots of MiG-25s engaged in practice air combat. Or they were trying to recruit current front-line pilots for instructor duties with a Third-World air force. Something like that.'

Oustenka nodded, and Bykov leant forward. 'Yes, Colonel?' he said.

'When I heard that Lenkov had been killed, I interviewed each squadron member individually and asked them if they had any idea who might have wished to harm him. One officer, Pavel Bardin, told me he'd been with Lenkov in a bar in the city one evening when three men approached them. They claimed to be looking for qualified MiG-25 pilots to join the air force of one of the Gulf States. Bardin took their contact number, though he wasn't really interested in taking such a step, but he said that Lenkov seemed more enthusiastic.'

Bykov looked triumphant. 'Where is this Bardin? Can we see him?'

Oustenka stood up and walked to the door of his office. He barked an order, then returned to his seat. 'He'll be here in a couple of minutes.'

Office of the Associate Deputy Director of the Central Intelligence Agency, Langley, Virginia

'Okay, Richard,' said Walter Hicks, 'you've almost convinced me about the "what". Based on your investigations,

I think it's at least possible that the DPRK has acquired a squadron of Foxbats. But what I still don't see is the reason. Why would the North Koreans go to all this trouble to get their hands on some forty-year-old obsolete interceptors?'

'I have no idea,' Muldoon shrugged. 'If they'd got their grubby little hands on a squadron of any new-generation air-superiority fighters, I'd be a lot more worried, because that could indicate they're planning an invasion against the South. You're quite right, the Foxbat *is* obsolete. It's not as agile as anything we're flying today, although it's still the world's fastest interceptor. But sheer speed doesn't count for a lot. Success in air combat is determined by agility, avionics, radar performance, missile technology and all the rest, and the Foxbat scores pretty damn poorly on most counts. But there must be a reason. They must want the aircraft for *something* and we have to figure out what.'

'How?' Hicks asked.

'Right now, I don't exactly know,' Muldoon admitted. 'We've got no sources we can tap inside the DPRK itself, and I doubt if Bae Chang-Su would be willing to risk infiltrating another of his agents north of the Demilitarized Zone. The NSA already monitors what signal and voice traffic there is in North Korea, and obviously they've not picked up anything of interest, or they'd have told us. So I guess the only avenue we have left is technical intelligence. I'll mark T'ae'tan and that entire area of North Korea a Priority One target for N-PIC, and suggest they modify the orbits of the Keyhole birds so that the NKs won't anticipate when they're overhead. That way we might actually get to see whatever the hell they're doing with those aircraft.'

Bolshoye Savino Air Base, Russia

Pavel Bardin was about six feet tall, with dark hair and eyes and a stocky build. He looked uncomfortable as he walked into Oustenka's office, and even more uncomfortable when the colonel introduced his visitors.

'Lieutenant Bardin,' Bykov began, 'let me assure you we have no interest in your reasons for engaging in conversation with these three men we've heard about. But we believe they were directly responsible for Georgi Lenkov's death, and we want to trace them as soon as possible. Now, I have a question for you. Colonel Oustenka told us they gave you a telephone number to contact them if you changed your mind about their offer. Do you still have that number?'

Bardin nodded, still unwilling to speak, and reached into the pocket of his uniform jacket. He pulled out a piece of folded paper and passed it to Bykov.

'It's a mobile number,' the GRU officer said, studying the first few digits. 'That means we can trace it and find out who the phone is registered to.'

Richter broke in. 'That'll give you a name and an address, probably both false, but it won't actually help us to find these men. I've got a better idea. Why don't we just ask Lieutenant Bardin here to call them and set up a meeting for tonight?'

The three of them stared at the young lieutenant, who was already shaking his head.

'Excellent idea,' Oustenka boomed, 'and I'm sure Lieutenant Bardin will be only too pleased to help avenge the death of his comrade.'

Reluctantly, Bardin turned the head shake into a nod and looked even more unhappy than before.

'Don't worry,' Richter assured him. 'You won't be meeting them just by yourself. We'll organize a full police presence and I'll be there too.'

'You?' Bykov and Oustenka blurted simultaneously, their surprise obvious.

'Damn right,' Richter said, turning to Bykov and switching back to English. 'Ever since I arrived in Moscow I've done nothing but tag along behind you, Viktor, like a spare prick at a wedding.'

'A what?' Bykov demanded.

'I'll explain it later. No offence, but I'm bored rigid. It's time I did something to justify my presence over here.'

He looked across at Bardin, whose unhappiness seemed to have deepened still further at Richter's lapse into a language he didn't understand.

'Don't worry, Pavel,' Richter said, once again speaking Russian. 'This kind of thing – it's what I do best.'

Chapter Nine

Wednesday
Pyongyang, North Korea

Pak Je-San sat stiffly upright on a hard wooden chair at the end of the long table, a notebook lying open in front of him. He was nervous and trying not to show it: the hierarchy of the North Korean government thrived on fear, using it to keep the population in line, and Pak sincerely believed they could actually smell any trace of it. For sure they – or more specifically Kim Yong-Su, sitting in an armchair at the head of the table – would pounce on any sign of weakness from him.

'And when do you expect the last of the interceptors to arrive?'

'Quite soon, I hope,' Pak replied. 'Ryu Chang-Ho reported that his first approach was turned down, but he has another possibility. If his offer is accepted this time, and the other officers can be bribed, the aircraft could be ready to leave the base within forty-eight hours. So the last two fighters could arrive in Pyongyang within four or five days.'

There was a grunt from one of the other four men. 'When you say his offer was "turned down", I assume Ryu ensured his target was not left in a position to reveal what had been discussed?'

Four pairs of eyes bored into Pak as he replied. 'Yes,

Ryu eliminated the target, as was done with every other unsuccessful approach.'

'Good,' Kim murmured, looking down at his notes.

Pak had been reporting to him at first on a monthly, then on a weekly, basis ever since this operation had started. And during every meeting he had hated looking into the man's dead, black eyes, which seemed capable of stripping the very flesh from his bones. And at every such meeting he had dreaded having to admit even the most trifling error or delay.

Now Kim Yong-Su was eyeing him directly again, his face expressionless. 'Exactly how many interceptors do you have now, Pak?'

'Twenty-four.'

'If Ryu fails to obtain another two aircraft, will your twenty-four be enough to complete the operation?'

Pak appeared to give the question serious consideration before answering, but there was no way he was going to say anything other than 'Yes'. Given a choice, he would have preferred a hundred MiG-25s, simply because there's safety – and reliability – in numbers.

At present, the aircraft maintainers at T'ae'tan were achieving about seventy-five per cent serviceability, which meant three out of every four Foxbats being able to get airborne at any one time. That proportion, he'd been assured by a couple of the Russian mercenary pilots, was pretty good for an aircraft as old as the MiG-25, especially as they didn't possess a full inventory of spare parts. But it also meant that one out of every four of the aircraft could *not* fly, so his squadron of nominally twenty-four planes was actually a force of only eighteen at best. But he wasn't going to tell Kim that. As it was, he just gazed straight down the table, not quite meeting Kim's eyes, and said, 'Yes.'

'And the missiles, what of them?'

'We have one hundred and fifteen at present, and another forty-eight currently en route from Bulgaria to Iran. When they arrive here in a few days' time, that will give us an arsenal of one hundred and sixty-three. A full warload for each MiG-25 is technically four missiles, but some of the pilots have suggested that two might be preferable, simply to allow the aircraft higher speed, better agility at altitude and greater endurance. My inclination is to arm each aircraft fully, but our decision will ultimately depend upon the tactical situation when we need to launch.'

Kim nodded slowly, but he wasn't yet satisfied. 'Pak, let us consider the worst-case scenario,' he said. 'Assume that Ryu Chang-Ho fails in his mission, or that the arrival of the last two interceptors is so delayed that the aircraft will not reach us in time to be deployed. Assume also that our enemies by some means discover that the ship travelling between Varna and Bandar Abbas is carrying the missiles and that they then intercept the vessel and seize the cargo.'

Pak didn't respond, just stared up the long table, waiting.

'Now, with that scenario, with two of your interceptors unavailable, and with almost thirty per cent of your arsenal of missiles seized, could your squadron of mercenaries still achieve the task we will be setting them?'

There was a long silence in the room, and Pak Je-San wasn't the only man present who had noted Kim Yong-Su's repeated use of the word 'your'. If this venture should end in failure, Kim was making it absolutely clear that the entire responsibility would fall on Pak's shoulders.

Again Pak considered his options, such as they were. If, on the one hand, he said his force would be able to cope, Kim might simply advance the schedule. But alternatively, if he said they wouldn't, then his own life might be forfeit. He swallowed twice, and opted for the middle ground.

'I believe the squadron would be able to achieve its tasking, but I would be very reluctant to commit our forces until we've made every effort to obtain those additional aircraft and missiles. Once the operation begins, there will almost certainly be no chance of organizing any resupply, and it would be unfortunate if the missiles were all ready to be flown in to T'ae'tan only to be stopped in transit by an air embargo.'

Pak thought for a moment he'd gone too far. Kim's eyes stared at him unblinkingly, and for a very long thirty seconds he did not respond. 'You should not, Pak Je-San, concern yourself with the government's overall strategy or operational timing. I am merely seeking an assessment of the ability of the forces you already control to carry out our bidding. That answer *you* have now supplied. *We* will decide when the operation should begin.'

'I understand that,' Pak said hastily. It looked as if he'd survived, for the moment, but he knew there was something else he had to say. Kim Yong-Su was a Party animal in the Communist sense and had, as far as Pak knew, absolutely no military experience or knowledge. If the operation was to succeed, there were some essential measures that must be taken in advance.

'If I may, there is also the matter of the tactical deployment of my' – he thought he might as well acknowledge that the squadron, and by implication its success or failure, belonged to him – 'assets prior to the start of the operation.'

'Explain.'

'At present, for logistical reasons all the MiG-25s are based at T'ae'tan. That is where we constructed the accommodation for the pilots and the maintenance staff, and where we have stored the spares and weapons. Before the operation begins, I intend to split the force into four, leaving one quarter of the aircraft and weapons at T'ae'tan, and sending the remainder to Nuchonri, Kuupri and Wonsan.

'That will give our enemies four different targets to engage, and also gives us greater geographical flexibility in our response to threats. By dividing our MiG-25 force between these airfields, we will be better able to respond to attacks from any direction.'

Kim looked at him, then nodded. 'That is sensible, Pak Je-San. I will ensure that you are told the moment we decide to commence our operation.'

Pak inclined his head in thanks.

The Party leader continued staring at him in silence for a few seconds more, then looked at the other men sitting at the table. 'Any other matters?' he asked softly, and was rewarded only by shaking heads.

Ten minutes later, Pak Je-San walked out of the building and, as always, sucked in a deep breath the moment he stepped outside – like a drowning man coming up for air.

Hammersmith, London

The Intelligence Director knocked on Simpson's door, waited for his response and then entered. Carrying a red file in his hand, he looked worried, but that was nothing new. The man normally looked worried, and not for the first time Simpson wondered why he hadn't taken up a less stressful career, like teaching. Though, he had to admit, getting thrown into a classroom full of the aggressive little bastards that were today's schoolchildren was hardly conducive to a quiet life.

'What is it?' Simpson almost snapped, as the ID sat down in front of his desk.

'An interesting though unconfirmed report from Vauxhall Cross. It's classified Secret and categorized as Grade Three intelligence that's come from an asset in Sofia, and it relates to a possible theft of munitions that might impinge upon Richter's current tasking.'

Simpson counted to three, very slowly. He had considerable respect for the ID's breadth of knowledge, and his dedication to the service, and the fact that his suits and shirts were always clean and neatly pressed, his shoes polished, and that his tie always displayed a perfect Windsor knot, but the man's slow and pedantic delivery of information never ceased to irritate him.

'I'm busy,' he snapped, 'so skip the caveats and just tell me what the fuck the man said.'

As usual, the ID looked faintly shocked at Simpson's language. 'Well, as I said, it's not been confirmed yet, but it looks as if there was a major theft of missiles from Dobric in Bulgaria yesterday.'

'Dobric? Never heard of it.'

'It's a disused airfield just over thirty miles north of the Black Sea port of Varna. Though it's been closed since the year 2000, the Bulgarians still have a lot of equipment stored there. Everything from torch batteries to moth-balled aircraft, from what I can gather. According to our source, yesterday some of the locals heard what sounded like small-arms fire coming from inside the base, and late yesterday afternoon a group of Bulgarian Air Force personnel turned up to investigate, heavily armed. According to an eyewitness, they had to force the main gate to get inside, and he claimed to have seen body-bags later being taken out of the base.'

'And this has what, exactly, to do with Richter?' Simpson was thinking the ID had strayed somewhat from the point.

'Dobric holds a large stock of Russian-manufactured AA-6 missiles, NATO reporting name Acrid. They're the ideal weapon for the MiG-25, and I understand that quite a few nations, including Russia, seem to have mislaid the odd Foxbat recently. The source's witness reported seeing three trucks leaving Dobric yesterday afternoon, loaded with long wooden crates, each about the right size to hold an Acrid. So perhaps someone, somewhere, is intending to marry the aircraft to the missile.'

Simpson nodded and held out his hand for the file. 'Leave it with me. I'll make sure Richter's informed as soon as possible.'

Perm, Russia

The Bar Moskva stood on the Kama Boulevard, on the south side of the river, and the meeting was set for seven. They'd spent a good deal of time after lunch discussing what options they had, but in the end it came down to Pavel Bardin dialling a mobile phone number and telling the man who answered that he might, after all, be interested in moving to the Gulf. The call took place at just after five.

Once the rendezvous was set up, Richter and Bykov were able to make their own arrangements. In Richter's case, that didn't take long. Bykov found him a shoulder holster from somewhere, and Oustenka then offered him a choice of either a Makarov PMM or a Yarygin PYa to carry in it. Richter would have preferred something manufactured well to the west of Moscow, but nothing like that was on offer.

The Makarov is loosely based on the Walther PP and was the standard Soviet Army sidearm until the end of the twentieth century. It fires a non-standard 9x18mm cartridge, and has a relatively small magazine capacity of twelve rounds. But the Yarygin replaced it in 2003, and that was much more to Richter's taste. It's chambered for the familiar 9mm Luger/Parabellum, and the magazine holds seventeen rounds – in Richter's opinion, the more bullets the better, *always*.

The Bolshoye Savino Air Base, like almost all military establishments in every country, possessed a pistol range, and Richter spent about forty minutes getting to know his borrowed weapon and firing a box of ammunition. At the end of it, he reckoned he stood a fighting chance of hitting most things he was likely to want to aim at, as long as the target didn't move too quickly and also stayed within about twenty-five yards of him.

Bykov went back into Perm and talked Superintendent Wanov into providing a hidden cordon around the bar. The men were not to move into position until Bykov, who would be sitting in a car parked a short distance down the road, instructed them to. Till then the police officers would wait in closed vans strategically located in adjacent streets, and all of them would be armed.

At six-twenty Paul Richter pushed open the door of the Bar Moskva and walked inside. He ordered an orange juice and a glass of water, and took the drinks over to a high stool situated at one end of the bar. From that position, he could easily see the door, the tables close to it, and anyone who happened to come in.

He'd been there for less than two minutes when his mobile rang. He looked at the number, recognizing it as Simpson's private line, but checked his watch to ensure that he had time in hand, and only then answered the call.

'Richter,' he announced briefly

'Are you in a secure location?' his superior demanded, without preamble.

'More or less. I'm sitting by myself in a Russian bar. Why?'

'Taken to drink at last, have you?'

'Not yet, but I'm working on it. I'm also in a hurry here, so what do you want?'

'A possibly related matter.' Simpson then outlined what FOE had learned about the robbery in Dobric. 'We don't know for sure that these Acrids were taken by whatever group has been acquiring the Foxbats, but being the missile of choice for the MiG-25, that's at least likely. Where are you? What progress are you making?'

'Not a lot so far, but I might have something concrete later this evening. I'm currently about seven hundred miles east of Moscow, in Perm, waiting for a couple of bad guys to meet with a MiG pilot from the local air base. If anything comes of it, I'll brief the duty officer tonight. Anything else you need to know?'

'No, that's it. Just keep in touch.'

Five minutes after Richter had ended the call, Pavel Bardin walked through the door. He ordered a vodka, and knocked it back in one as soon as the bartender had placed it in front of him. Then he ordered another, carried it across to a table beside the door, pulled out a newspaper and began reading. Or, at least, appearing to read, for every time the door opened, he looked up to scan the faces of the new arrivals.

The Russian was, Richter realized, both amateurish and terrified, which wasn't the best combination when about to encounter people who had killed at least once during the past week. But it was too late to do anything about that now, and what could he do anyway, because Bardin was the only one who might recognize the three men who had almost certainly killed Georgi Lenkov.

Seven came and went, and the door opened regularly to admit new arrivals, or to allow customers to leave. On each occasion, Bardin glanced at Richter across the bar and shook his head. The man was being about as subtle as a flying brick, and Richter knew the expected agents would twig what was up the instant they stepped through the door. The idiot would have to be warned.

He stood up to do so, and had taken no more than a couple of steps towards Bardin's table when the street door suddenly opened again, and two men entered. The pilot looked up at them, then turned towards Richter and nodded. He might just as well have waved a banner over his head carrying the words 'This is a trap.'

The men stopped dead, then turned round, yanked open the door and hurried outside. Richter muttered a curse and followed them.

He'd expected them to turn either left or right, making for wherever they'd left their car. But instead they sprinted straight across the road, towards the river. Off to his left, Richter saw the brief flash of headlamps, the signal agreed with Bykov to indicate that he'd radioed for the police cordon to be set up. But that now seemed rather academic, because Richter had realized there was a huge hole in their plan. If the bad guys had a boat waiting for them on the river, the police cordon became irrelevant. They'd covered all the surrounding streets, but not the water.

So Richter ran. But he'd barely left the bar when one of the running men looked back, then stopped and turned, tugging open his jacket. The moment Richter recognized the weapon, he dropped flat on the tarmac surface of the road. Because, in the uncertain light of the street lamps, he'd seen the unmistakable outline of a Skorpion machine-pistol and, with only the Yarygin, he was hopelessly outgunned.

The man in front of him squeezed the trigger, sending a stream of nine-millimetre bullets screaming over Richter's head to smash into the wall and windows of the bar behind him. As glass shattered, he heard shouts of alarm intermingled with cries of pain. Sighting down the barrel of the Yarygin, he loosed off two snap shots, barely aiming, just wanting to discourage the barrage of fire.

Both his shots missed, but the two men began running again, then abruptly disappeared from view as they reached the far edge of Kama Boulevard, and ran on down a flight of stone steps leading towards the river.

Richter jumped to his feet and chased after them, but slowed to a walk as he approached the top of the steps. That was just as well, because the moment he raised his head over the low parapet bordering the pavement, the guy with the Skorpion opened up again, a hail of copper-jacketed slugs knocking lethal chips of stone out of the wall as Richter dropped back down. A couple of the flying shards hit him in the face, opening up a long but shallow cut across his forehead.

He raised his right hand over the top of the parapet and fired two shots in the general direction of his quarry, then slid sideways until he was lying right beside the gap in the wall at the top of the steps. Behind him he could hear the sound of running footsteps. Glancing to his left, he saw Bykov approaching, pistol in hand, and gestured for him to keep back.

Cautiously he peered around the solid stone, ready to draw back at once. But there seemed no immediate danger as the two men had by now moved to the water's edge, where a third figure was waiting in a boat with a hefty outboard motor attached to the stern. Even as Richter watched, the boat swung away from the jetty and began accelerating fast towards the opposite bank of the river.

'Shit,' Richter muttered, realizing there almost certainly wasn't enough time to get the Perm police to arrange a reception committee on the other side. He stood up and hurtled down the steps, the Yarygin ready in his hand.

At the water's edge he stopped, feet apart, and raised the pistol to take careful aim, supporting his right hand with his left to steady the weapon. The boat was probably thirty yards away as he fired his first shot. It was bobbing and bouncing on the water as it gathered speed, its three occupants crouching low.

The moment his shot rang out, one of the figures turned, and seconds later the Skorpion began to return fire. But a bouncing boat is too unstable a platform from which to shoot accurately, and although Richter flinched when a couple of rounds struck the jetty a few feet away, he knew it would be a miracle if any of the bullets hit him.

His advantage was to be standing on solid ground, so he concentrated on making each shot count. His second shot also missed, but the third scored a hit. One of the men gave a yell of pain and slumped forward, while the boat suddenly veered to the left. But it was Richter's fourth bullet that did the real damage.

It hit the outboard motor's fuel tank, sending a spray of petrol right across the open cockpit. The man armed with the Skorpion was still firing, and whether it was due to muzzle flash from the machine-pistol or a spark from one of Richter's bullets ricocheting off something metallic he'd never know, but with a sudden roar the vessel erupted in a ball of flame.

Richter lowered his pistol, the weapon instantly irrelevant, and just watched the conflagration. The petrol-soaked clothing of the fugitives caught fire immediately.

Illuminated by the burning fuel, their three indistinct figures gyrated in violent, panicky movements as they frantically tried to beat out the spreading flames with their bare hands.

It was never going to work, and almost simultaneously they reached the same conclusion and leapt overboard. The water doused the flames straight away, but the boat was still fully ablaze and only a madman would attempt to climb back on board. Richter guessed that the three men would try to swim for the opposite bank of the river.

'I had hoped to question them.' Bykov was panting slightly as he stopped beside Richter and looked out at the ball of flames where the powerboat was now drifting slowly on the current.

'We might still be able to, if any of them manage to reach the shore.'

'I've asked Wanov to send some of his men over to the other side, and to organize a couple of boats to recover the wreck, but they'll take a while to arrive and it'll be dark soon. This is *his* town, and he really should have arranged something to cover the river.'

'We should have thought about it ourselves, Viktor. With hindsight it's an obvious escape route. You can't blame Wanov – he did exactly what we asked him to.'

Bykov shrugged. 'You're right, but it's too late now. Maybe we'll find some clue on whatever's left of that boat. It has to be registered to somebody.'

Pyongyang, North Korea

Kim Yong-Su sat in his office in the centre of Pyongyang and checked everything one last time. When Pak Je-San had first explained his plan back in the autumn of 2003, Kim had realized two things.

First, the timing was absolutely crucial: they had to make their move when the nearest American aircraft carrier was at least forty-eight hours sailing time distant, and no Aegis cruisers were in the vicinity of the Korean Peninsula. In its final phase, the plan would only work if they could achieve some measure of air superiority – though he knew they could never achieve total control, because the South Korean aircraft were much more up-to-date than those of the DPRK. That meant having no American carriers around, with squadrons of F/A-18 Super Hornets embarked.

Second, and equally important, they had to maintain an appearance of normality until the last possible moment. That involved two operation orders. The first, 'Silver Spring', had been prepared for public dissemination: just another routine, no-notice exercise to check the operational readiness of the North Korean forces to respond if faced with an unprovoked assault from south of the DMZ. He'd sent copies to Seoul so that South Korea would be pre-warned about this exercise, and had also alerted Moscow and Beijing. All nations advise their neighbours whenever they plan to run military exercises, just to ensure that such operations are not mistaken for anything else.

And following this convention, Kim believed, was his master-stroke, because while the South Koreans and their

American lackeys were carefully watching the 'Silver Spring' manoeuvres, the preparations for 'Golden Dawn' – his hidden plan for the occupation of South Korea – could continue undetected. And once it was executed, the results would be as devastating as they were unexpected.

Kim nodded in satisfaction, then instructed his aides to send the preparation signal for 'Silver Spring', as an unclassified message, while simultaneously dispatching a Top Secret signal to begin the initial phase of 'Golden Dawn'.

T'ae'tan Air Base, North Korea

Less than two hours after arriving back at T'ae'tan, Pak Je-San was called to the station commander's office to take an urgent telephone call from Pyongyang. He ran up the stairs and into the room, and snatched up the receiver. The commander was still sitting behind his desk, so Pak dismissed him with a curt gesture, and waited until the man had left the room before he spoke.

'This is Pak Je-San.'

'I have been waiting to speak to you for almost five minutes,' barked the unmistakable voice of Kim Yong-Su. 'We have begun the countdown. Begin the dispersal of your assets.' And the line went dead.

For a few seconds, Pak still held the receiver to his ear, listening to an echoing silence. Then he slowly lowered the handset to its cradle, and turned to go. Outside the door, the station commander was waiting to regain possession of his office. The expression on Pak's face instantly told him that the call from the capital had been important.

'They've started the countdown?' he asked.

'Yes,' Pak agreed, 'the clock's running.' Then he headed briskly for the stairs. There was a lot to do and very little time to do it. The Dobric missiles might arrive before Kim gave the final order, but Pak knew there was now almost no chance of getting those last two MiG-25s.

Chapter Ten

The lights had burned in the hangars throughout the night as maintainers struggled to get every Foxbat ready and, as the sky next lightened with the dawn, twenty out of the twenty-four aircraft were ready to fly, a better result than Pak Je-San had expected.

He hadn't slept at all. He had been too busy working out the logistics of the dispersal of the interceptors and, equally important, of the personnel, stores and supplies that would need to be transported by road, and it had still taken him most of the night just to get everything in place.

One of his biggest headaches was the regular over-flight of surveillance satellites, and this wasn't just a matter of the orbiting American vehicles. Pak knew that relations were much improved between the West and the Confederation of Independent States, formerly known as the USSR, so he also had to avoid Russian platforms, and even the Japanese had four orbiting spy satellites, specifi-cally intended to provide surveillance of the Korean Peninsula. Yes, the Japanese were continually worried about what the North Koreans might get up to – as well they should be, Pak reflected, with a grim smile.

A handful of passing satellites obviously wouldn't

stop the operation, but it still made sense to avoid alerting Japan or the West unnecessarily. Pak wanted, therefore, to get the road convoys away from T'ae'tan while
all those spies in the sky were well out of range. And
equally he wanted the MiG-25s to taxi out of the hangars
and launch within that same brief window.

He'd already decided to send five of his precious Foxbats to Nuchonri, the closest military base to Seoul, and
the same number to the airfields at Kuupri and Wonsan,
on the east coast, facing the Sea of Japan. That would
leave him with just five serviceable MiG-25s at T'ae'tan,
and a further four being worked on. The aircraft maintainers had estimated that they might get one or even two
of the remaining aircraft operational within forty-eight
hours, which might be time enough.

Pak checked his computer once again, studying the
list of satellite transit times. For this he was using, with
some amusement, a program called Orbitron that he'd
downloaded from a Polish website. Despite being free-
ware, it was a very powerful and comprehensive program with a database containing over twenty thousand
satellites. For obvious reasons, it didn't include all the
classified surveillance birds, but Pak had already added
those manually, and he reckoned this database was now
about as accurate as any others available.

What he did not know was that the CIA had now
altered the orbits of two of the Keyhole satellites, so the
tracks the Orbitron program displayed were substantially inaccurate.

That was why, when the first five Foxbats, bound for
Wonsan, taxied out of the hardened shelter and headed
for the runway, one Keyhole bird was only ten minutes

from reaching a point almost directly above the airfield. And when this satellite passed overhead, travelling at a little over seven kilometres a second, its cameras were able to record all five aircraft – one airborne and tracking north-east, one rolling down the runway and the other three lined up waiting to enter it.

Perm, Russia

Viktor Bykov had been right: the boat was registered to someone. Irritated by the failure of his force to capture the three fugitives the previous evening, Superintendent Wanov ordered the remains of the boat to be thoroughly checked as soon as his men had hauled the wreckage ashore.

Screwed to the transom was a registration plate and, after cleaning off a deposit of soot and other muck, they'd identified its owner as a small company in Perm itself that owned a dozen similar craft. The moment they opened their doors for business that morning, Wanov had appeared in person, demanding to inspect all their hire records. This produced the address of a hotel on the outskirts of Perm, so just after ten that morning Bykov and Richter found themselves standing in one of the rooms that three guests had been occupying for the last two weeks.

All around them, police officers and forensic scientists were prodding and poking, taking pictures or lifting prints to try matching against the fingertips of the burnt corpses recovered from the river that morning. Unsurprisingly, given the circumstances, all three men had drowned, and the routine autopsies would be carried out later that same day.

So far, nothing significant had turned up in any of the hotel rooms. The three had been travelling light: the closets held few clothes, and most of the drawers were empty. Everything they had found so far would have fitted easily into three airline carry-on bags – which was presumably the point.

In one room, however, they'd found a locked brief-case, which had yielded easily enough to the point of a screwdriver. Inside were almost fifty thousand American dollars in medium-denomination notes – doubtless a residue of the funds used for bribing senior officers at military bases – and two boxes of nine-millimetre Parabellum ammunition. One of these boxes was full, the other held about twenty rounds, and the rest of its contents were probably now lying at the bottom of the river along with a Samopal 68 Skorpion machine-pistol and whatever other weapons the mystery men had been carrying.

But of personal documents there was not a sign, or anything else that could identify them, where they came from, or what they wanted here.

Feeling defeated, Richter walked out of the hotel room and found Bykov in the corridor. The Russian smiled and held up his mobile phone. 'We may have something here,' he said. 'The mortuary staff have recovered a note-book from one of the corpses. It's waterlogged, but we may find something useful inside it, once it's dried out. The car's waiting for us outside. Let's go.'

**Office of the Associate Deputy Director of the Central
Intelligence Agency, Langley, Virginia**

'You were right,' Walter Hicks said, looking down at the
photographs Muldoon had placed on his desk. Both men
had arrived at work much earlier than usual, precisely to
check on any overnight images that the surveillance birds
might have obtained.

The pictures were the raw 'take' from the Keyhole
satellite, flashed to N-PIC via a ComSat bird over the
Pacific Ocean, and forwarded from there direct to Langley. The fully annotated photographs would follow as
soon as the N-PIC staff had completed their interpretation. But what these pictures showed was quite obvious,
even to untrained eyes. Four aircraft were clearly visible,
three waiting on the taxiway and one on the runway
itself. And a fifth had just taken off and was opening to
the north-east, away from T'ae'tan.

'They're all Foxbats,' Muldoon said. 'The only other
aircraft they could possibly be is the MiG-31 Foxhound,
but the 'hound's twin jet pipes are a different shape, and
it's got fairings at the leading edge of the wing root,
so I'm satisfied these are Foxbats. We'll have to wait for
N-PIC to confirm it, but I'd bet my pension against
them being anything else.'

'Where are they going, and what were they doing at
T'ae'tan?'

Muldoon shrugged. 'My guess – and that's all it is at
the moment – is that the North Koreans have converted
T'ae'tan into a maintenance or holding facility, and
they've been storing the Foxbats there. I don't think these
aircraft we see are just getting ready to do a few circuits

and bumps. They've probably been repaired or serviced or something, and are returning to whatever base they came from.'

'Which is?'

'Take your pick. If that aircraft opening to the north-east is already on track, it could be heading for the Air Command headquarters at Chunghwa, or else to the coastal airfields at Kuupri and Wonsan. Or maybe even the Third Air Combat Command base at Hwangju. If the North Koreans now have a squadron or two of Foxbats based anywhere, it means they've been very clever at evading the Keyhole overflights. We only got these shots because we'd already modified the orbit of a *second* bird. If it had still been on its original track, these aircraft' – Muldoon tapped one of the pictures with his index finger – 'would have been long gone before it got within range of the base.'

'OK, Richard, we now know that the North Koreans have obtained at least five Foxbats. What we still don't know is what they plan on doing with them, and I can't think of an easy way to find out. So what's your recommendation?'

'We kick this upstairs to the ODNI right now. Something's going on over there, and deciding what to do about it is way above my pay scale, and probably yours too.'

North Korea

North Korea is a country somewhat smaller than the state of Mississippi, has a population of a little over twenty-two million, and a Gross Domestic Product of about twenty-three billion dollars US. Over thirty per cent of that GDP goes straight into the military budget, and almost one in every four North Koreans is either on active service or a reservist.

Facing them on the southern side of the Demilitarized Zone is about the same number of troops. The South Koreans have around three-quarters of a million active-service personnel – including some forty thousand American forces stationed in the country – and four and a half million in the reserves. But the North Koreans have the advantage in armour and artillery pieces. Only in combat aircraft are the numbers more equal, both forces being able to field about eight hundred, but here the advantage lies very definitely with South Korea. Not only does that country enjoy a slight numerical superiority but, far more important, North Korea's aircraft are older, slower and a lot less capable.

Instructions for the 'Silver Spring' exercise had been prepared and dispatched months earlier, but the 'Golden Dawn' orders had been sent only three weeks ago, sealed in envelopes with explicit written instructions that they were to be opened only when Pyongyang so ordered. In military bases, strung like beads on a string all along the northern perimeter of the Demilitarized Zone, active service troops now began preparing for the coming exercise and – though they didn't know it – the invasion of South Korea.

Vehicle maintenance was given the highest priority – when the order was finally given by Pyongyang, everything had to work perfectly – so extreme care was being taken to ensure that all tanks and artillery pieces were ready for action. Communication systems were checked, and then checked again, because a battle could be lost if command and control functions didn't work properly. Further down the line, foot soldiers were given extra practice on the rifle ranges. Reserve troops were called up and issued with equipment and ammunition, but not yet weapons. Those would be handed out at the last moment, as Kim Yong-Su didn't relish the thought of having four and a half million armed men roaming the country, even if they were official reservists.

There had been a succession of exercises leading up to 'Silver Spring'. Those had admittedly been just paper exercises, partly because the country didn't have the fuel or resources to squander on real-life manoeuvres, but mainly to avoid the American spy satellites detecting their activities. As in all invasions throughout history, secrecy and surprise were essential.

Each such exercise had followed the same basic scenario: a blitzkrieg offensive followed by a rapid advance using overwhelming force. A pounding artillery assault to destroy and demoralize the enemy, then wave upon wave of tanks, followed by the infantry, because a war on the Korean Peninsula would be won or lost on the ground.

Overhead, the North Korean Air Force would engage and try to neutralize the opposition fighters, though the best they could have realistically hoped for was a draw. But that, of course, was before Pak Je-San had devised the radical concept behind 'Golden Dawn', and then secured his secret force of MiG-25s.

The Foxbat is the fastest interceptor ever manufactured, able to outrun any fighter or bomber, and it carries a formidable array of weaponry. That, plus the fact that, as far as Kim knew, neither the South Koreans nor the Americans had any idea these squadrons existed, should give them all the edge they would need. In one sense, everything now rested on Pak Je-San's shoulders.

And the new instructions from Pyongyang were highly specific: each commander was to open his copy of the sealed 'Golden Dawn' operation orders, prepare his troops, and await the executive command.

But what none of them yet knew was the secret, hidden component of Pak Je-San's plan that might ensure the invasion would be a walkover.

Perm, Russia

Mortuaries have a particular smell. No matter what air-conditioning or ventilation system they possess, there's always the pervading odour of formaldehyde overlaid with faint olfactory echoes of urine, faeces and partially digested food. The Perm mortuary was no exception, and Richter could detect that same smell even before Bykov pushed through the double doors and they entered the building.

The Russian flipped open a leather wallet to show his identification, which the white-coated receptionist studied carefully, then gestured for them to follow him through another set of double doors and down a corridor. At the end was a small seating area, with half a dozen armchairs and a low table, brightened by a vase of wilting flowers. The receptionist pressed a button on the wall, invited them to sit, and retraced his steps.

Richter sat down immediately. He had spent long enough in the Royal Navy to subscribe to the philosophy that there's no point in standing if you can sit. Or, for that matter, being awake if you can be asleep. Bykov stood or, to be accurate, paced.

A couple of minutes later a short, red-faced, cheerful-looking man pushed through the door to one side, drying his hands on a paper towel.

'General Bykov? My name is Marshek, and I'm the pathologist.' He extended his right hand and Bykov shook it readily. Richter remained seated, his hands firmly in his pockets. He guessed that Marshek had washed his hands properly after rooting through the intestines of some corpse, but didn't feel like risking physical contact just for the sake of politeness.

'You've found a notebook, I understand?' Bykov began.

'Indeed, as I informed the police earlier. It was inside a buttoned trouser pocket on one of the dead men. All his other pockets were empty, apart from the obvious stuff like handkerchiefs and combs. We found nothing else on any of their clothing, not even manufacturers' labels. Do you want to see the bodies now?'

'Not unless we need to. How did they die?'

'All three of them drowned, but they'd already suffered severe burns before they entered the water, and one had also received a bullet wound. But it was the temperature that really killed them. Cold shock,' he added, by way of explanation.

'You mean hypothermia?'

'No. I mean cold-shock reflex. They didn't survive long enough for hypothermia to be a problem. If you enter water that's significantly colder than your normal body temperature, there's a natural reflex action and you gasp for air. If that gasp occurs under the surface, the lungs will fill with water, and that's pretty much it. Even if you survive the immersion, extremely cold water will chill the body rapidly, and the river temperature last night was around five degrees centigrade. You become unconscious once your core temperature drops to about thirty degrees, and you'll be dead when it reaches twenty-five. Hypothermia is only a factor to consider if you survive the initial immersion and the rapid cooling.'

'The notebook?' Richter prompted, in Russian. He wasn't there to listen to a lecture on cold-water survival criteria.

The pathologist looked at him as if seeing him for the first time. 'Just a moment,' he said, and pushed his way back through the door. He returned in a few moments holding a plastic bag inside which there was a small note-book with a blue cover.

'We dried it out as best we could. Some of the pages are still stuck together, but most can now be separated. Its owner used a ball-point pen rather than ink, so what's there is fairly legible.'

He handed the bag to Bykov, who looked at it questioningly.

Marshek shook his head. 'It's already been checked, and there aren't any fingerprints. I would be amazed if there had been, after immersion in the river overnight. When you've finished looking at it, please leave it with the receptionist on your way out.'

Bykov merely nodded, then pulled the notebook out of the bag and opened it on the table in front of Richter.

Only the first dozen or so pages had been used, and most of what was recorded there was not in either the Roman or Cyrillic alphabets. Instead, the notes used some form of pictogram, interspersed with the occasional word in Russian.

'Do you recognize it?' Bykov asked.

Richter shook his head. 'If it isn't a pictorial code of some kind, it has to be one of the Oriental languages – like Chinese or maybe Japanese – but I don't know enough to even recognize which. You must have people on your staff who could identify it?'

'Of course. The trouble is, they're back at headquarters, not out here in Perm. I'll need to scan these pages and email them to Moscow.'

'What about the words written in Cyrillic? Do any of those mean anything to you?'

Bykov flipped through the pages rapidly, shaking his head occasionally. 'No, nothing here. These are just the names of towns and cities, perhaps where they'd developed contacts. It was probably easier to use the Russian name instead of trying to transcribe it into the other language they used. Look here. That's "Moscow", then "Letneozerskiy" – where two MiG-25s went missing, and so on.' His voice died away as he stared at two words on the last page.

'What does it say?' Richter asked.

'Slavgorod North,' Bykov said, clearly puzzled. 'But I've not been notified of anything happening there, and they don't even operate MiG-25s as far as I recall.'

'Where is it, exactly?'

'It's a military airfield lying about sixteen hundred kilometres east of here.'

'That falls well within the cruising range of a MiG-25, so if they'd managed to persuade Lenkov to steal one, maybe they were intending to refuel it there before flying it out of the country. We need to go there immediately, Viktor.'

'I agree.' Bykov nodded. 'We can't handle something this sensitive over the telephone. I'll get the jet warmed up.'

That, Richter reflected as the Russian general pulled a mobile phone from his pocket and began dialling a number, sounded more impressive than it was in reality.

They'd flown to Perm in a Russian Air Force Antonov An-72 transport aircraft, confusingly painted in Aeroflot livery. Known to the West by the NATO reporting name 'Coaler', it wasn't exactly an executive jet, having been designed as a small, general-purpose STOL transport capable of carrying either cargo or up to thirty-two passengers on drop-down seats attached along the sides of the cabin. Powered by two Lotarev turbofan engines, mounted above and in front of the wings, which gave the aircraft a peculiarly hunched appearance, it was reasonably fast and had a range of well over two thousand miles.

Their journey out from Moscow had been very noisy and relatively uncomfortable, but a lot faster than trying to get seats on a commercial aircraft. And anyway it was, Richter guessed, the only aircraft Bykov had been able to commandeer at such short notice. As the Russian general headed for the door, Richter again wished he'd had the foresight to bring earplugs.

FOXBAT

T'ae'tan Air Base, North Korea

By late morning, the last of the departing MiG-25s had lifted into the air and roared away from T'ae'tan, heading for Wonsan. It was the final departure Pak Je-San had scheduled. This particular Foxbat had originally been one of the first flights planned, but it had gone unserviceable on engine start. Fortunately, it involved a relatively minor problem that the maintainers had rectified within a couple of hours, so the only subsequent delay was having to wait for a clear window between the regular surveillance satellite overflights. Once Pak felt confident none was within range, he had ordered the aircraft to be towed out of the hangar and started up. Just five minutes later it had accelerated down the runway.

Arranging the road convoys had presented far less of a problem, and considerably less of a security headache. There had been no mechanical problems at all with the trucks, and he was now merely waiting for final confirmation that they'd arrived safely at their destinations. That, however, would not take place before early evening at the soonest.

Chapter Eleven

The Antonov An-72 transport aircraft touched down smoothly, the powerful brakes and reverse thrust stopping it within a remarkably short distance. This aircraft had been designed specifically for short-field operations.

As the Coaler turned off the runway, Richter glanced out of the window and noticed a hulking shape on the far side of the airfield.

'That's interesting.' He raised his voice over the noise of the engines. 'There's a Condor parked over there.'

'A what?'

'A Condor – an Antonov An-124.'

Even bigger than the massive American C-5 Galaxy, the Condor, which the Russians call a 'Ruslan', is the world's biggest aircraft. It was originally designed by the Antonov Bureau to transport a complete SS-20 intercontinental ballistic missile system. It has an enormous payload of one hundred and fifty thousand kilograms – nearly one hundred and fifty tons – and has an eighty-eight-seat passenger cabin located behind the wing. It's able to transport almost anything, including main battle tanks and helicopters. And, as it immediately occurred to Richter, fighter aircraft.

'That could be the link we're looking for,' he said.

'Maybe the Foxbats aren't being flown out of Russia. Maybe these comedians have organized heavy transport aircraft to take them to their ultimate destination. You might be able to get one inside that Antonov.'

Bykov crossed the cabin and looked out. 'The MiG-25's bigger than you think, Paul. Unless you took the wings and rudders off, it simply wouldn't fit in there. And disassembling the MiG is a major job. Trust me, it would be much easier to fly it out of the country.'

Slavgorod North's commanding officer, a Russian Air Force colonel named Denikin, didn't look pleased to see them. Bykov had called him from the An-72 shortly after they took off from Bolshoye Savino, and clearly the prospect of a GRU general with an unnamed but obviously non-Russian 'assistant' poking around his airfield didn't appeal to him.

'We'll need to speak to the crew of that Ruslan you've got parked on the airfield,' Bykov informed him, 'but first I want to check all your transit and aircraft movement orders.'

'Very well,' Denikin said stiffly, and gestured for them to follow him. He led the way into the Operations Room, a large square space with staff working at benches along the walls, and across to a plotting table. There he pulled two loose-leaf binders from a shelf and opened them. 'This folder contains all the movement orders we've received during the last two months, and these ones here are the transit orders for the same period. May I ask what you're looking for?'

'Yes,' Bykov said, bending over to study the binders. 'We're investigating unusual aircraft movements. Has

Slavgorod North been involved in any deployment of fighters or interceptors heading east?'

'Of course.' Denikin nodded immediately. 'This is a staging airfield. We're regularly refuelling aircraft in transit.' He reached for the transit orders binder, flicked through the pages until he found what he was looking for, and pointed. 'Here, for example: five days ago one Sukhoi Su-27 and two Su-24s staged through here. And this order is for two MiG-25s that arrived from Bobrovka two weeks ago. They were refuelled, and the pilots stayed here overnight, then they left the following morning.'

'Where's Bobrovka?' Richter asked, 'and where were they going when they left here?'

Denikin glanced questioningly at Bykov, who gave a slight nod. 'Bobrovka's near Kinel, in Samarskaya, and from here the two interceptors were going on to Domna,' Denikin replied, after glancing down at the page in the binder. Richter still looked blank, so the colonel walked across to a wall map showing the entire extent of the Asian landmass and picked up a wooden pointer.

'That route took the aircraft in a more or less straight line across Russia from west to east,' he said, indicating each base in turn.

'What was their ultimate destination?' Bykov asked.

'Chuguyevka. We weren't informed of their original airfield of departure, only that they were routing to us from Bobrovka. From here, they flew to Domna, then Komsomolsk-na-Amur and on to Chuguyevka.' Denikin's pointer traced the remainder of the route across the continent.

'That's one of our easternmost MiG-25 bases,' Bykov

explained for Richter's benefit. 'It's not far from Vladivostok, sandwiched between China and the Sea of Japan. I think it's usually indicated on American charts as Bulyga-Fadeyevo.'

'I know where it is,' Richter confirmed. 'We talked earlier about Viktor Belenko, if you recall.'

A look of pain flashed across Denikin's face at mention of the renegade Foxbat pilot's name. Clearly that defection was still something of a sore point in the Russian Air Force, even forty years later.

'Have there been any other movements of MiG-25s through Slavgorod?'

Denikin flicked back through the binder and found transit orders for three more pairs of Foxbats, all following broadly the same route across the CIS, and all with Chuguyevka listed as their ultimate destination.

'How many MiG-25s should there be in total at Chuguyevka?'

'The resident squadron is 530 IAP,' Denikin said, 'and they fly a mixture of MiG-25s and MiG-31s. I don't know what their normal strength is, but probably around thirty-five to forty aircraft.'

'Very well,' Bykov said. 'We'll need copies of all the movement and transit orders relating specifically to MiG-25s for the last six months. Please organize that immediately.'

Denikin saluted briskly, called one of the operations staff over to the plotting table and began briefing him. Bykov motioned Richter to one side of the room, out of earshot.

'Those documents look authentic to me, which probably means something's going on in Moscow that I don't know about. I'll need to check the audit trail of each order and find out who issued the original instruction, and that's going to take time. It looks like whoever's stealing our aircraft has a very senior officer working for them, probably at Arbat Square.'

He was referring to the location of the Russian Ministry of Defence in downtown Moscow.

Richter gazed at him thoughtfully. 'You're probably right. And as all the MiG-25s we've seen any details of are ending up at Chuguyevka, their final destination has to be North Korea. Nothing else makes sense. If they were going to China, they'd track east or south-east from Domna, and certainly wouldn't go anywhere near Komsomolsk or Chuguyevka. Both Japan and South Korea are American allies, and if they wanted fighter aircraft they'd buy something made by Northrop or McDonnell Douglas, not old-fashioned MiGs. North Korea's the only destination that makes any sense.' He paused, then continued. 'And there's something else.'

Bykov nodded, following his train of thought. 'The North Koreans have a nuclear capability. Their possession of atomic weapons, plus these MiG-25s, and their rocky relationship with South Korea, make a very worrying combination. Investigating the mechanics of how they organized this will have to wait. You'd better talk to your people back home, and I must go straight back to Moscow.'

'Is there anything else, General?' Denikin asked, walking over towards them.

Bykov shook his head, but Richter had one more question. 'We're going to have to leave here shortly, Colonel, so we won't have time to talk to the crew of the Ruslan. What's that aircraft doing here?'

'Just like most of the aircraft we handle, it's staging through. It's a regular run, carrying spares and replacement parts.'

'Spares for what exactly, Colonel? And where's its destination?'

Denikin smiled slightly. 'Chuguyevka, as a matter of fact, and its cargo is MiG-25 and MiG-31 parts for 530 IAP.'

'Thank you, Colonel.' Richter turned and followed Bykov out of the Operations Room. 'Cheeky bastards,' he muttered, as they headed down the corridor together. 'My bet is that most of the MiG-25 stuff on that Ruslan will be smuggled straight out of Chuguyevka, down to Vladivostok, loaded onto a ship and taken down the coast to Ch'ŏngjin or some other North Korean port. This has been altogether a really slick operation.'

While Bykov found an internal telephone to order a car to take them back to the Antonov, Richter pulled out his Enigma mobile phone, checked the signal, then dialled Hammersmith. The T-301 offers military-level encryption to both parties of a conversation, as long as they're both using Enigmas or something compatible, but it looks pretty much like any other mobile.

When the Duty Officer answered, Richter gave him a brief summary of what he'd discovered so far.

'Wait one.'

Thirty seconds later Simpson was on the line. 'Are you sure about this, Richter?'

'Depends what you mean by "this". I'm certain that the Russian Air Force has lost a bunch of Foxbats, yes.

The route we've been tracking across Russia suggests that the client state is North Korea. What I don't know is what the men in Pyongyang intend to do with their new toys, but they wouldn't have gone to all this trouble just to stand around and admire them. I'm also worried about those truckloads of Acrids stolen in Bulgaria. I'd lay money that, no matter where they are now, the ultimate destination of those missiles is North Korea.'

'I tend to agree. The question is, what do we do about it? Is this just the North Koreans upgrading their air force with a bunch of old Russian interceptors, or is it something more than that?'

'It has to be more devious. If they wanted newer aircraft than they've got already, they could have bought them openly. Plenty of nations are happy to deal with Pyongyang if there's a decent profit involved. And why choose Foxbats, which are old and difficult to fly and, according to Bykov, were designed from the start to intercept ICBMs? I'm thinking that might suggest North Korea is preparing to get involved in a nuclear exchange, and they've acquired those MiGs as a last-ditch defence against nuclear retaliation.'

'But against who?' Simpson was openly sceptical. 'The South Koreans don't have any nukes, and I really don't see even those idiots at Pyongyang trying to take on either China or Russia. And, no matter what missiles they use, most of America is well out of range.'

'Agreed, but if the North Koreans invaded the South, the American cavalry would have to come galloping to the rescue – and *they've* got plenty of buckets of instant sunshine.'

'Don't be flippant, Richter. I don't believe the Yanks

would initiate a nuclear exchange. They'd rely on conventional forces.'

'I know,' Richter agreed. 'But suppose the South Korean forces get pushed back further down the peninsula by an initial advance from the north. That's always been acknowledged as a possibility because of the sheer size of the DPRK armed forces. Oplan 5027 – that's the basic warplan the American and South Korean combined forces would follow to counter an invasion – admits that, if the North Koreans use blitzkrieg tactics, they could overwhelm the Southerners' defences.

'But conventional wisdom suggests that even if the NKs managed to advance a long way into the South, they haven't got the resources available to consolidate any territory they'd capture. The Americans would send reinforcements and those, combined with the South Korean forces, would push the invaders back to the north of the DMZ.'

Richter paused for a few moments, still working things out. 'But what if the North Koreans have a different agenda? What if, once they've established themselves in the South, they threaten to nuke any US reinforcements being shipped in, or any build-up of local forces that might oppose them? That would cause a stalemate, and if the Americans couldn't send back-up forces to South Korea safely, they'd be left with only two options. They could simply abandon South Korea, which isn't really an option at all. Or they'd need to escalate the conflict with surgical nuclear strikes on North Korea's army, its airfields, or even Pyongyang itself. So *that* could be the nuclear exchange the DPRK is anticipating.'

'I still don't believe the Americans would resort to the

use of nuclear weapons – but you do make a persuasive case, Richter.'

'A lot depends on what the Yanks have got in the area already. I've no clue about US force dispositions, but you should be able to find that out from Washington. If the nearest American carrier battle group is off the Korean Peninsula, I don't think there'd be a problem. If it's parked in Pearl Harbor, there might be.'

'I'll check, and get the wheels turning across the pond.'

'What do you want me to do? Come back to London?'

Simpson didn't respond for a few moments. 'No,' he said finally. 'It might be useful to have you there on the scene, so to speak. Get yourself out to Seoul and make your number with the National Intelligence Service people. I'll . . . Wait.'

The phone was put down in Hammersmith and Richter heard a faint swishing sound that was probably a mouse rolling over its mat and then a few clicks as Simpson pressed buttons. Then he heard a muttered curse and what sounded like an exceptionally angry click. Richter's superior had been a late and very reluctant convert to computers, and so there had been a PC terminal in his office for only about three months. He still wasn't very good with it.

'Here it is,' Simpson said, picking up the phone again. 'The man in charge is named Bae Chang-Su. I've never met him, but by reputation he's something of a martinet – even worse than me. I thought I'd save *you* the trouble of pointing that out, Richter,' Simpson added waspishly. 'His number two is Kang Jang-Ho. I'll contact Bae and tell him you're on your way. Let us know when you get there.'

'Right.' Richter ended the call and walked over to where Viktor Bykov was waiting for him beside a dark blue car, flicking through copies of the movement orders. In the distance, he could hear the sound of the Coaler's engines spooling up.

Office of the Associate Deputy Director of the Central Intelligence Agency, Langley, Virginia

Richard Muldoon sat down at the conference table and opened a red folder. 'Our second rescheduled Keyhole bird has taken some more pictures,' he began, and passed a sheaf of photographs across the table to Walter Hicks.

'Talk me through them, Richard.'

'N-PIC have sent over a dozen pictures, fully annotated. There are five aircraft on the taxiway, heading for the end of the runway, presumably preparing to leave T'ae'tan for some other base. From the paint jobs and markings we've confirmed that these aren't the same ones we saw in the first set of images, so that means the DPRK has at least ten of these aircraft.'

'Right,' Hicks said, scanning the pictures. 'And how many could they have in total?'

'Frankly, we've no idea, as we don't know the size of the new hangars they built at T'ae'tan. If they excavated deep enough into the hillside, each could hold maybe ten or fifteen aircraft the size of a Foxbat, but it's a flexible feast. They've still got some F-5 fighters there at the airfield, and they're parked in hangars as well. So the numbers could range from the ten we already know about up to maybe forty or fifty maximum.'

'Any way we can refine that?'

'Not unless they happen to move more of the aircraft while one of our birds is overhead. We've no assets on the ground that I know of, and I don't think flying a reconnaissance aircraft over North Korea would be too smart an idea. Even if we pulled a U-2 and flew that, I doubt we'd gather any useful data. The hangar doors are probably kept closed except when they're manoeuvring aircraft, and even if they were open there's a limit to what we'd be able to see because of the overhang of the hillside.'

Hicks pulled out a pack of small cigars and put them on the table beside him. 'What about sending in a Predator?' he asked.

'The same arguments, really. Unless we had one flying right past the hangar doors just when they opened them, the same limitations would apply. The Eighth Army already has several Shadow UAVs operating over the Demilitarized Zone. They're pure reconnaissance drones, and their main task is monitoring North Korean activity close to the DMZ. They've overflown nuclear sites and airfields, but only occasionally, and as far as I know they've never detected anything particularly useful. It's also worth stating the obvious, that if we *did* fly a Predator over T'ae'tan at low level, the North Koreans would probably shoot it down, and then they'd know for certain we were on to them.'

'Yeah, I see what you mean. So the short version is that we know the DPRK has a minimum of ten Foxbats, and maybe as many as fifty, but we still don't know *why* they've got them. Did the N-PIC analysis of the pictures identify anything else?'

'Yes.' Muldoon nodded. 'There's a road convoy of eight trucks leaving T'ae'tan, all about three tons. They look like standard army lorries. Obviously we can't be certain what they're carrying, but we can guess because N-PIC knows exactly where they're heading.'

'How come?' Hicks asked, selecting a cigar and carefully lighting it.

'Two subsequent Keyhole passes showed the same vehicles heading for Nuchonri. If the North Koreans are planning some kind of action against the South, dispersal of those Foxbats to several different airfields makes sense. In which case, logic suggests the trucks are probably carrying spares and munitions for the same aircraft.'

Hicks stared down at the images for a minute or so, drawing slowly on his cigar, then he gathered the photographs together and passed them back across the table.

'Forget the hard evidence. What's your gut feeling about this, Richard? What do you think the North Koreans are planning?'

'I really don't know, but I don't like it. I don't, too, like the fact that they've got hold of an unknown number of Foxbats, and I particularly don't like knowing that they managed to sneak them into the country without being detected – by us or by anyone else. But I think what worries me most is the truck convoy. That suggests T'ae'tan might have been used as the base for training and so on, but now the assets are being dispersed because the North Koreans are almost ready to launch whatever plan they've been hatching.'

Hicks nodded slowly, stood up and walked across to

his desk. He picked up the internal phone and ordered coffee for two, then came and sat down again at the conference table.

'What did the DNI think?' Muldoon asked.

'The Director of National Intelligence is a diplomat, not an intelligence professional, and it doesn't help, either, that he's an idiot,' Hicks said, now treading familiar ground. 'In fact, he knows as much about intelligence analysis as I know about the dark side of the moon. He thinks we're overreacting, and it's just a coincidence that the DPRK has bought itself a bunch of Foxbats. He actually believes Pyongyang is just re-equipping its armed forces.'

'That's it?'

'That's it,' Hicks confirmed.

Muldoon opened his mouth to reply, then closed it on hearing a double knock on the door. A young blonde girl walked in carrying a tray of coffee. She placed it on the conference table, smiled at them both, and left.

Hicks reached over and pulled the tray towards him. 'So what's your recommendation?'

'If the DNI won't do anything, we won't be able to pass it up the line to the White House or across to the Pentagon – or not officially, anyway. I mean, I can make some calls, give some people a heads-up on what we've seen, but that's about all. But I do think we should watch the situation, and it wouldn't hurt to find out what assets we have located in the area. I know what military forces we have in South Korea, but I'd like to know what the Navy's got thereabouts, and what other battle groups could get there inside a week.'

'That's not really within our terms of reference,

Richard, but if this does blow up in our faces, some wise-
ass is bound to ask why we didn't know, and it would be
nice to have our answer ready. I'll make a couple of calls
to the Pentagon, try to shake a few trees over there.'

Rossyia Hotel, Moscow

The An-72 Coaler landed at Chkalovsky military airfield late that evening. Hidden away amidst woods in
the eastern suburbs of Moscow, Chkalovsky, designated
Scheikovo on most aeronautical charts, is the training
centre for Russian cosmonauts, and is better known as
'Star City'.

Once they'd deplaned, Bykov organized transport to
take Richter back to the Rossyia, then himself climbed
into a car with a uniformed driver for the journey to his
office at Khodinka airfield.

At the Rossyia, Richter deposited his bags in his hotel
room, then headed downstairs to grab a late dinner.
Returning to his room, he set up the laptop and logged
on to the internet, first checking flight times, with prices
and availability. What he saw made him whistle softly,
but he printed the relevant page on his portable ink-jet,
then locked his room and walked out of the hotel.

Clear of earshot, he used the Enigma to dial the Duty
Officer's number at Hammersmith.

'Richter,' he announced.

'Are you in Seoul yet?'

'You've got to be bloody joking. About the only places
in Russia where I can get a flight to South Korea are

Moscow and Vladivostok and, when I worked out that I was a lot closer to Moscow, I came back here.'

'So when's your flight?'

'The earliest is about seven-thirty tomorrow morning – but I won't be on that.'

'Why not?'

'Because, for reasons that don't make any sense to me, all the morning and afternoon departures out of Moscow head *west* to get to South Korea, not east as you might expect. They then all change in Frankfurt, Amsterdam or Paris, which bumps the flight time up to fifteen or twenty hours. I've no intention of sitting around in some antique Aeroflot heap for that length of time.'

'So?' The man sounded bored.

'So I'm taking an evening flight. The Aeroflot five seven three leaves here at eighteen-twenty tomorrow. It's still a twelve-and-a-half-hour flight, because it routes via Beijing, but that's a hell of a lot better than twenty hours. It reaches Seoul about noon the following day, so can you pass that information on to Simpson?'

'Is that it?'

'No. I've just checked the ticket prices, and the econ-omy-class single fare is a couple of thousand dollars American. Tell Simpson I'm booking a Business Class seat, which I hope will mean the stewardess looks like a woman instead of an all-in wrestler, and I'm not sur-rounded by goats and Russian peasants. That'll cost him about three or four thousand dollars, so he'd better make sure the credit card he gave me is good to cover it. If the card maxes out I'll be using the return half of the ticket I've already got to come back to Heathrow. OK?'

'OK. Have a good flight – whichever one you catch.'

Chapter Twelve

Pak Je-San was getting worried. When he'd sent his emissaries over to the Russian Federation to source aircraft, spares and munitions, he had imposed a rigid communications schedule. All of them were expected to contact him by telephone at least once every twenty-four hours, though he never specified precise times.

Of all his agents, Ryu Chang-Ho was probably the most reliable, and Pak now hadn't heard from him since Wednesday afternoon. Ryu had been in Perm that evening, and Pak had been expecting his call, even if only to hear that his second approach had been turned down.

But no call had come through, and since Wednesday Pak himself had barely drawn breath as the plan moved inexorably towards completion. He'd been totally committed to organizing the dispersal of the aircraft and stores, and with trying to achieve all that whilst still avoiding detection by the American spy satellites. But at the back of his mind he'd been getting more and more concerned about Ryu, and he now realized he could wait no longer.

He picked up his desk phone and dialled the number of Ryu's mobile, but all he heard was a recorded message.

That meant the phone itself was either switched off or currently outside the range of the nearest cell.

Pak depressed the receiver and dialled the other number Ryu had given him, for a landline in Perm. It rang six times, then a deep male voice answered with a single Russian word: '*Da*?' – 'Yes?' Pak immediately ended the call since the voice definitely wasn't Ryu's.

Clearly something had gone wrong and, if Ryu had been rumbled, it meant that the Russians probably now knew that their missing aircraft were in North Korea. If he was already dead, it was possible the authorities in Perm had fitted call-tracing equipment, which was exactly why Pak had ended the call so abruptly. In the few seconds he'd been connected, his precise location couldn't have been traced, but they might still have been able to identify which country he was calling from.

But now, with Operation 'Golden Dawn' already under way, what the Russians knew or didn't know would hardly matter.

Office of the Associate Deputy Director of the Central Intelligence Agency, Langley, Virginia

It's one thing to schedule aircraft movements so as to avoid them being spotted by surveillance satellites, though even that's extremely difficult because of the sheer number of orbiting vehicles currently scanning the planet's surface. But it is quite a different matter when massed troop movements are involved. For these simply cannot be hidden from view, and as soon as the first phase of 'Silver Spring' began, successive passes by

KH-12 birds, recording images every five seconds, started detecting everything from the heat blooms of tank and truck engines to the numbers of individual soldiers.

The moment the N-PIC analysts saw these pictures, they flashed them straight to Langley. The CIA duty staff immediately called in Richard Muldoon, and after a brief glance at the images he telephoned Walter Hicks.

'What's your take on this, Richard?'

'I don't think we need too much analysis here, Walter,' Muldoon replied, spreading a selection of photographs across the table. 'Starting from the west side of the Korean Peninsula, we've got the 815th Mechanized Corps moving south-east from Kobuldong towards the DMZ. The 820th Armoured Corps is doing the same from Songwŏlni, and over to the east the 9th Mechanized Corps is heading south from Kosan.

'At all the southern airfields there are clear indications of increased activity, loads of aircraft parked on hardstandings with fuel bowsers and armament trolleys alongside them. The southerly missile bases are also very active, and so are those on the east coast – Hochon, Nodong, Mayang and Ok'pyong in particular.

'The North Koreans have made us aware of a scheduled no-notice exercise.' Muldoon opened a folder and extracted a single sheet of paper. 'It's called "Silver Spring" and it's the usual scenario: faced with an unprovoked assault from the capitalist lackeys in Seoul, the brave North Korean forces will fight to the last man to repel the evil invaders.

'Two things worry me about this, though. First, the DPRK forces usually busy themselves conducting paper exercises, not real-world stuff. Second, while all these troop movements could be entirely innocent, if they *are* planning an invasion, deployment of these forces is just what you'd expect. My concern is that what we're looking at now is the implementation of a secret movement order from Pyongyang, under the cover of this "Silver Spring" exercise, and that when the moment's right they'll head south across the border, catching everyone wrong-footed. In that case, we're watching the DPRK transitioning to war – and there are no prizes for guessing which country will be under attack.'

'There's no chance that they really are just conducting an exercise?'

'I wouldn't put any money on it. Don't forget the Foxbats. N-PIC have identified the munitions on the trolleys beside them as R-40 air-to-air missiles – AA-6 Acrids – and probably the T variant. They're loading the 'bats with warshots, and that means they expect to use them.'

'OK,' Hicks said, 'I'll take this evidence to the DNI and see if he still thinks the North Koreans are just undertaking a service upgrade. I already checked with the Pentagon about our force dispositions, and we've nothing local to the Korean Peninsula. Our closest maritime support – that's the *Enterprise* Carrier Battle Group – is about three days away in the north Pacific Ocean. We've got a couple of frigates off Busan in South Korea, and a hunter-killer submarine about a thousand miles south of the peninsula.'

'That's all?'

'Yup, that's all. The only other Western naval asset anywhere close is the British Royal Navy's carrier *Illustrious*, heading for home. It's currently off the south-east coast of Japan, en route from Tokyo to Manila. The ship has seven Harriers on board, plus there are three other warships – frigates, I think – and four supply ships in company.'

Muldoon laughed briefly. 'Seven Harriers? The North Koreans have got, what, eight hundred plus combat aircraft? I know every little helps, but that's just ridiculous.'

'Yes, I know. The DNI won't be able to ignore these,' he tapped the photographs, 'so, exercise or no exercise, the Joint Chiefs will at the very least hike the DEFCON state. There's not a hell of a lot more we can do here at Langley, but my guess is the White House will kick the military into gear. They'll get the *Enterprise* moving as fast as possible, and warm up the B-52s and the Minutemen. They'll try and talk to the North Koreans as well, but at present we don't have any direct diplomatic contact with Pyongyang, and I doubt if a few stern words from our current National Security Adviser would cut much ice with them anyway.'

Muldoon nodded. 'I can't argue with any of that, but one thing bothers me – apart from the US getting dragged into yet another shooting war. Pyongyang knows our commitment to South Korea, and their leaders must realize that we'll oppose them once they cross the DMZ. OK, they may have timed this action so that we don't have any naval forces in the immediate area, but they sure as hell know we'd send some real fast. Every analysis I've seen confirms that the North Koreans can start a war, but they don't have the resources to win one, or even consolidate any territorial gains they might make. So why are they doing this?'

'Maybe their "divine leader" is a lot more stupid than anyone's giving him credit for.'

'Maybe . . . or maybe he's a lot smarter than we thought, and he's discovered a wrinkle that he thinks might make this work. And there's something else. We had a request from the British SIS yesterday, asking for our present force dispositions relative to the Korean Peninsula. I told you they've got this man in Russia looking into the missing Foxbats and according to their source the MiG-25 was built specifically to counter incoming ICBMs. Maybe Pyongyang has stolen the aircraft to defend the country against any retaliation from us using missiles. And the Foxbats wouldn't have any trouble carving up our B-52s as well.'

'Shit,' Hicks muttered.

'That's about the size of it,' Muldoon agreed. 'If I'm right, it's a real high-risk strategy, but just because it's high-risk doesn't mean it won't work.'

National Military Command Center, the Pentagon, Washington, DC

Walter Hicks gazed around him as he walked into the NMCC at the Pentagon. It was pretty much as he remembered it from the last time he'd been there, another occasion on which America was confronted with a nuclear exchange, only then the threat had been much closer to home.

The National Military Command Center is a suite of offices situated on the third floor of the Pentagon. One office processes the raw data, making it a very noisy environment because of the rows of clattering telex machines that print reports and information from sources around the world. A battery of clocks shows a selection of world time zones, and there's a permanent map display to indicate the location of America's strategic assets and the principal troop dispositions of all other major national armed forces. The Emergency Conference Room is next door, and by comparison extremely quiet.

The ECR comprises two different levels. The Battle Staff, the NMCC's duty officers, sit on either side of the 'leg' of a huge T-shaped table and collate data. Positioned along the bar of the 'T' are four Emergency Action officers, each at a specialized console equipped with an awesome array of communication links allowing them to contact American forces almost anywhere in the world.

The Joint Chiefs of Staff, essentially the American President's War Cabinet, have seats on a raised platform above and to the left of the Battle Staff table. Opposite them are six huge colour television screens that can display maps of any part of the world, plus charts, plans, surveillance photographs, troop concentration data and other types of graphic or text that might help to clarify a particular situation.

The NMCC forms part of a single vast command structure that includes the White House Situation Room and the hardened facilities at Cheyenne Mountain; at Offutt, the location of the Underground Complex; and at Raven Rock. All these sites are linked by telephones, faxes, telex machines, radios, computers and high-speed secure data links. The briefing would be delivered in the

Pentagon, but the duty staff at the other sites would also be able to hear every word that was said.

Walter Hicks listened with a sense of déjà vu as the Senior Duty Battle Staff Officer introduced him. It wasn't the first time he'd briefed the Joint Chiefs but, unlike on the previous occasion, the substance of this briefing would be largely conjecture. He began almost every sentence with a qualifier – 'We think'; 'Analysis suggests'; 'It is possible' and so on – and he didn't like resorting to that at all. The Joint Chiefs didn't like it either, and said so, repeatedly.

'The CIA has been informed, I hope,' a senior USAF general interrupted almost immediately, 'that the North Koreans have a no-notice exercise called "Silver Spring" planned sometime in the next month or so?'

'Yes, General, the Agency is well aware of that. Our concern, however, is that Pyongyang may have scheduled this exercise simply to allow them to mobilize their forces for an invasion of South Korea without attracting unwelcome international attention until it's already too late.'

'What proof have you that what's going on right now in North Korea is anything more than such an exercise?'

'Absolute proof is probably impossible to find, because we have no HUMINT resources north of the DMZ, so we're entirely dependent upon our interpretation of the technical intelligence obtained. The NSA has intercepted a much higher than normal level of signal traffic in North Korea, primarily from Chunghwa, their Air Command headquarters, and Hwangju, the headquarters of the Third Air Combat Command. They haven't managed to decode many of these messages, because it looks as if the North Korean military are using new encryption routines, but nothing Fort Meade has deciphered so far indicates that this is more than just an exercise.

'Despite that, we're very concerned on two counts. First, most North Korean military exercises we've been made aware of in the past have been paper or tabletop routines. But this time the satellite imagery shows deployments of major forces along a very broad front, all ultimately heading towards the Demilitarized Zone. These movements include large numbers of troops as well as armoured divisions. We've also detected increased activity at various airfields in the south of the country and at missile launch sites. That might be explained as part of the exercise, but only if we accept a fundamental change in the way the North Koreans normally do things. We could easily discuss the implications of these movements all day without reaching a consensus.

'The second factor is more compelling. Why have the North Koreans secretly acquired at least ten MiG-25s? We're concerned that they've obtained these Foxbats to counter the more advanced aircraft employed in the South Korean Air Force.'

'That won't wash, Mr Hicks,' the general interrupted again. 'The Foxbat is an obsolete design. Yes it's fast, but it's not agile. The MiG-25 is *old* technology and there's no way it could survive in air combat against modern warbirds like the F-15 or F-16.'

'That's your field of expertise, General, not mine,' Hicks replied equably, 'and I don't entirely disagree with you. But there is another possibility that's more worrying. The British SIS has obtained information from the Russians that the Foxbat was specifically designed to intercept ICBMs in the terminal stages of flight. So maybe the North Koreans want them as a last-ditch defence against a missile attack.'

This statement was followed by a long silence. The possibility that the MiG-25 was anything more than just an old, fast interceptor had clearly not occurred to the assembled officers.

'A missile attack from where?'

'From us. From a Minuteman in a silo in Montana, or from one of our boomers. As I understand it, our nearest surface group is at least two or three days' sailing time away from the peninsula, so if North Korean forces do head south, across the Demilitarized Zone, the only viable counter to such an invasion might be the missiles in our silos or submarines.'

'The President would never authorize a first strike against North Korea, Mr Hicks,' another general pointed out, 'and there would be no need for us to take the nuclear option. We've got bombers at Andersen Air Base on Guam as a deterrent against exactly this kind of incursion. They're B1-Bs, B-2s and B-52s, and they're more than capable of flattening any advance the North Koreans could achieve. And whether it took us a few days or even a few weeks, we could easily land enough forces on the peninsula to push them back using conventional weapons and tactics.'

'I know,' Hicks nodded. 'What concerns the Agency is the other side of the coin, if you like. *We* may not resort to the use of nuclear weapons, but the fact that the North Koreans have obtained these aircraft suggests to us that *they* might be intending to do so. We believe they could be planning a blitzkrieg assault across the DMZ, and then would attempt to stop any counter-attack by threatening to target their nuclear arsenal on any assets we might send in support. As a viable threat, that would stalemate the situation. And knowing the regime in Pyongyang, we shouldn't doubt they would carry out this threat if they had to. If this operation goes the way we think it might, we could easily lose South Korea totally.'

The Gold Room, the Pentagon, Washington, DC

Despite its official name, the Emergency Conference Room had not been designed for conferences, only briefings, so as soon as Walter Hicks had finished delivering the Agency's assessment of the current situation, the Joint Chiefs left the ECR and moved along the corridor into the 'Gold Room' conference suite, also on the third floor of the Pentagon.

Thirty minutes after Hicks had departed, the Joint Chiefs of Staff decided that the situation in North Korea was sufficiently serious to merit an upgrade in the alert status of US forces worldwide, and the most senior general present recommended this precaution to the President in a lengthy telephone conference call that included the Secretary of Defense.

Fifteen minutes after that, the American alert state was upgraded to DEFCON Four, and alerting signals were dispatched to all units and formations, worldwide. At the same time, most specific orders were flashed to the USS *Enterprise* in the North Pacific Ocean, but for the eyes of the captain only.

The President then instructed the Secretary of Defense and his National Security Adviser to contact Pyongyang to obtain clarification of North Korea's intentions, and to request an emergency session of the United Nations Security Council to discuss the ongoing situation. That, the President said, would probably turn out to be just another goddamned waste of everyone's time, but after the Iraq fiasco he thought they should at the very least go through the motions.

Base Communication Center, RAF Mildenhall, Suffolk

In a scene repeated in communications centres around the world, the warning bell, to indicate receipt of a signal classified 'Secret' or above, sounded as the teleprinter began clattering. The Duty Communications Officer walked briskly over and scanned the lines of text as they were printed out.

FLASH OVERRIDE
FROM: JCS WASHINGTON DC/ /J3 NMCC/ /
TO: AIG 931
SECRET
(S)   SECRETARY OF DEFENSE HAS DECLARED STEP UP IN DEFENSE READINESS CONDITIONS (DEFCON) FROM DEFCON 5 FOR US FORCES WORLDWIDE TO DEFCON 4. COMMANDERS WILL TAKE APPROPRIATE ACTIONS TO ASSURE INCREASED READINESS.

'Oh, fuck,' he muttered, tore the signal out of the machine, rapidly entered the Date-Time Group and the originator in the log, then left the Center at a run.

The Gold Room, the Pentagon, Washington, DC

Two hours later, highly detailed orders, classified Top Secret and prepared on the specific instructions of the President, were sent with Military Flash precedence from the Pentagon to the United States Strategic Command (USStratCom) Center at Offutt Air Force Base in Omaha, Nebraska.

Office of Commander-In-Chief Fleet (CINCFLEET), Northwood, Middlesex

The briefing had been arranged with under thirty minutes' notice for all participants, and was classified Top Secret. The lowest-ranking officer inside the locked room was a Royal Navy commander, and he was there only to change the hastily prepared vu-graphs and slides, and point at things on the screen.

A four-ring captain stood beside the podium. He'd already run through the substance of the raft of signals they'd received from both the Americans and the Chief of the Defence Staff in London, and he'd just finished the operational appreciation and tactical situation.

'In your opinion, how much of this is pure speculation on the Americans' part?' CINCFLEET demanded.

'Frankly, sir, I think most of it. All they know for sure is that there are troop movements taking place north of the Korean Demilitarized Zone that could be interpreted as the prelude to an invasion, though they're also consistent with the pre-planned exercise designated "Silver Spring". They also know that the North Koreans have obtained a minimum of ten MiG-25 interceptors. But in the overall scheme of things, I don't believe a dozen Foxbats will make any significant difference, bearing in mind that our intelligence suggests that the North Koreans can already field over eight hundred combat aircraft.'

'What's your analysis of the Americans' suggestion that those MiG-25s are intended to intercept incoming ballistic missiles?'

'I believe it's fanciful at best, sir. I understand the Russians have confirmed it was specially designed for that tasking, but I personally doubt if any aircraft would be capable of achieving this. The speeds involved would be just too great, and the intercept calculations too complex. I also don't myself believe that the North Koreans are planning to invade the South, so I think the Americans are reading far more into this situation than the evidence warrants.'

'Noted,' the admiral said. 'Very well, we've been instructed to assist, so what assets do we have in that area?'

The captain stepped across to the large-scale dropdown chart he'd been using to show North Korean troop movements, and indicated an area towards the south of the peninsula. 'About here, sir, off the southern tip of Japan, is the *Illustrious* group, returning home after a deployment to Australia, and presently en route between Tokyo and Manila. As well as the carrier, which has seven Harriers embarked, the group includes the Type 42 destroyer *Edinburgh* and two frigates: HMS *Cornwall*, a Type 22, and the Type 23 HMS *Portland*.'

'Support?'

'They have four Royal Fleet Auxiliaries in company –

the tankers *Oakleaf* and *Grey Rover*, and two of the Fort-class solid-stores vessels, namely *Fort George* and *Fort Austin.'*

'What assets have the Americans got, apart from their troops in South Korea?'

The captain pulled down a larger-scale map and pointed to a spot in the northern Pacific Ocean. 'The USS *Enterprise* Carrier Battle Group is currently about here. According to Washington, it's en route towards North Korea but realistically they don't expect it to reach the area for at least two or three days. Their best forecast is fifty hours, but there's a tropical storm brewing to the north-east of the Korean Peninsula, and the CBG's arrival time will depend on how the weather system develops, and whether or not the ships have to detour around it.'

The admiral made the only decision possible, his instructions from Downing Street and the CDS having been most specific. 'Very well,' he said. 'Signal *Illustrious* and tell her and her escorts to take on fuel to their maximum capacity. Then the group is to split. *Illustrious* and *Cornwall* are to proceed north into the Yellow Sea, while *Oakleaf* and *Fort George* are to follow and catch up as quickly as they can.

'*Edinburgh* and *Portland* are to move into the Sea of Japan and the two remaining RFAs are to follow. Once there, this group is to hold position off the east coast of the Korean Peninsula, keeping well clear of territorial waters, and then monitor shore and air activity north of the DMZ.

'*Illustrious* is to report passing abeam the southern tip of the peninsula, and is then to hold position southwest of Inchon, outside Korean territorial waters, pending diplomatic clearance from Seoul to move closer.

'The Air Group is to prepare for both offensive and defensive operations, including Combat Air Patrol and ground attack, and all ships are to ensure that they carry sufficient warshots to conduct autonomous real-world operations for a minimum period of three days, pending the arrival of the auxiliaries. Detailed tasking instructions will follow. Any questions?'

The captain shook his head. 'No, sir.'

'Finally,' CINCFLEET added, addressing the assembled officers, 'I've received further instructions regarding our independent nuclear deterrent. Downing Street has instructed the CDS to retask our patrolling submarine until this crisis is resolved. I will be issuing separate orders to HMS *Victorious* in due course.'

Rossyia Hotel, Moscow

Paul Richter closed his laptop, disconnected the power cable and tucked everything away in the leather carrying case. His small suitcase was already packed and sitting beside the door of his hotel room. Three minutes later he walked out of the building and climbed into the taxi he'd ordered. He had nearly three hours before his flight to Seoul was due to leave Moscow, which even by Russian standards should be time enough.

HMS *Victorious*, Barents Sea

Commander-In-Chief Fleet exercises operational control of Britain's Trident boats, which provide the independent nuclear deterrent. Unlike surface ships, which can both send and receive detailed messages via satellite wherever they are in the world, communicating with submarines is difficult. The deeper the boat submerges, the more difficult communications become. The standard operating procedure is for submarines to deploy a short aerial designed to receive Extremely Low Frequency signals. ELF is very slow, so it's only possible to send a very small number of characters in a given time period – normally between two and four characters a minute. Passing a complete operational message by this means would clearly be impossible, so ELF is only used to transmit a coded warning to a submarine.

This type of message is a repeated sequence of a few characters. The acronym, when decoded, will advise the submarine that an operational message is going to be transmitted, the time it will be sent and the transmission method. At the specified time, the submarine will reduce its depth and either trail a long aerial reaching up to just below the surface, or else extend a vertical aerial above the water from the sail. The former is slow but relatively secure, while the above-surface aerial allows reception of high-speed transmissions but naturally carries a greater risk of detection.

Just over an hour after the briefing finished at Northwood, a Group Warning Signal was transmitted to HMS *Victorious*, the single 'boomer' on patrol, from the ELF radio relay station situated near Rugby in Warwickshire. Twenty-five minutes afterwards, a Military Flash Operational Tasking Signal was relayed by communications satellite to the submarine. Five minutes after this signal had been received, the boat was again submerged at its normal operating depth.

Chapter Thirteen

In some ways, the programmed troop movements were overkill, but Pak Je-San knew that they'd only have this one chance and he was determined to get it right.

Even before any reservists were called up, or a single vehicle or aircraft started its engine, the regular forces of North Korea were already able to unleash a devastating attack on their southern neighbour. Because of Seoul's proximity to the DMZ, the South Korean capital was within range of some five hundred North Korean artillery pieces, including the 170-millimetre Koksan gun, and over two hundred 240-millimetre multiple-rocket launchers. It has been assessed by Western intelligence agencies that the North Korean forces could, without any significant troop or artillery movements, unleash a barrage of up to half a million rounds per hour against Seoul and other strategic targets in the north of the country, and could sustain that level of assault for several hours.

North Korea's one million or so soldiers are organized into 170 brigades and divisions that include special operations groups, artillery, tank and infantry units, and about sixty of these are permanently located south of a line running between Pyongyang and Wonsan. The country has deployed well over half of its forces close to the DMZ, and about seventy per cent of its front-line troops – some 700,000 men, 2,000 tanks and 8,000 artillery pieces – are permanently based within a hundred miles of the Demilitarized Zone. Many of these units are located in underground or hardened facilities, almost a North Korean trademark, of which there are more than four thousand close to the DMZ.

And it's not just troops on the ground. The North Korean Navy, a significant force in its own right, has positioned the majority of its surface vessels and submarines in forward bases on both coastlines of the peninsula, near to the DMZ. Forty per cent of the country's 800 fighter aircraft are also based very close to the border. Without repositioning a single soldier, vehicle or aircraft, the DPRK is capable of launching a major attack on South Korea within a matter of hours.

But Pak Je-San had no intention of doing any such thing: his plan was a good deal more subtle, and should, he hoped, take the Americans and the South Koreans completely by surprise and negate their carefully constructed defensive strategy. Details of the constantly evolving Oplan 5027 have been known within Pyongyang and the country at large for well over a decade. In fact, news statements in the North Korean media frequently refer to it by name.

The mountainous terrain of the Korean Peninsula would largely dictate the way any invasion must be conducted, as was equally obvious to the planners in Washington and Seoul. The advance towards Seoul by ground forces would have to proceed down the Chorwon, Kaesong-Munsan and Kumwa corridors, crossing the Imjin or Han rivers, and the troops would then be facing well-prepared defences, including the South Barrier Fence, manned by South Korean and American troops of the Combined Forces Command.

Standard battle tactics decree that any attack across the DMZ would be preceded by a major artillery barrage, possibly by special forces' raids against highly specific strategic targets, and even by missile- or artillery projectile-delivered chemical and biological weapons designed to kill or incapacitate the defenders.

The Combined Forces Command perception is that any invasion of South Korea would be conducted in three phases. In the first, the ground forces would smash through the CFC defences and destroy their ability to counter-attack. In the second phase, Seoul itself would be isolated and captured. This would be the prime objective, because nearly half of the population of South Korea lives within forty miles of the nation's capital. The third phase would be essentially mopping-up exercises, before the occupation of the entire peninsula.

To counter this, Oplan 5027 postulates that substantial numbers of American troops – nearly 700,000 men – and armour would be landed in the south of the peninsula and that these assets, supported by aerial bombardment, should be able to push the DPRK forces back north of the DMZ. Amphibious assaults into North Korea would isolate and surround the enemy, and air power would help destroy their land forces in the narrow passes through which they'd have to travel. The ultimate intention of the Oplan, since its 1998 revision, is to continue the advance north to capture Pyongyang, eliminate the DPRK leadership there, and thus place the whole of the peninsula under South Korean control.

And all that, of course, was also known to Pak Je-San, which was exactly why he'd devised 'Golden Dawn'.

Seoul, South Korea

The flight to Seoul was nothing like as bad as Richter had expected, Aeroflot having come a long way since the last time he'd flown with the airline, but it was still a hell of a long haul from Moscow to Korea.

He had never been comfortable sleeping on an aircraft unless he was absolutely exhausted, and he was far from tired as he boarded the flight. Despite reading distractedly for a couple of hours, and then lying with the seat reclined as far as it would go, sleep still eluded him.

The first thing he did on departing Kimpo International Airport was to switch on his Enigma mobile. Less than thirty seconds after it reported good signal strength, he stepped away from the group of Asian businessmen standing waiting for taxis in front of him to answer it.

'Richter,' he announced.

'You've taken your time. I've been trying to get hold of you for ages.'

'I've been on an aircraft for the last twelve hours, Simpson. In case you didn't know, you're supposed to switch off your mobile while you're in the air.'

That wasn't strictly true, but Richter had left his phone turned off deliberately, on the off-chance that he might get some sleep.

'Things have been developing since you left Moscow,' Simpson continued regardless, and he then explained

Washington's concern about the DPRK troop movements their satellites had detected north of the Korean Demilitarized Zone.

'So what are they doing about it?' Richter asked.

'Pretty much as you'd expect,' Simpson sighed. 'They've asked for an emergency session of the United Nations so that Pyongyang can have a chance to explain exactly what they're doing.'

'They'll insist it's just an exercise,' Richter interrupted.

'They already have. So then Washington broke protocol and contacted the North Koreans direct. They claimed it's a routine exercise called "Silver Spring", but nobody believes them. The Americans will continue with the usual diplomacy, but I don't think they seriously expect anything useful to come of it, so they're now also looking at military options. Their nearest surface group, the *Enterprise* CBG, is currently in the north Pacific and still a couple of days away from Korea. So they've now hiked the alert state to DEFCON Four.'

'That's not good news.'

'No.' Simpson's tone was uncharacteristically subdued. 'We're not fully in the loop here, but the Intelligence Director thinks the Yanks will probably target North Korean airfields and military bases with their ICBMs, silo- and sub-launched, and inform Pyongyang that they've done so, just to try to make them back down. Or, in case they really *are* conducting this "Silver Spring" thing, to make sure that it stays just an exercise.'

'What do you want me to do?'

'First, make your number with the NIS, then request them to fly you down to Kunsan as soon as possible.'

'Which is where, exactly? And what do I do when I get there?'

'It's an air base on the west coast of South Korea. Let me know your likely arrival time as soon as you've worked it out, so I can coordinate things from here.'

'What things, exactly?'

'You're going back to sea, Richter. The *Illustrious* has been retasked by their Lordships at the Admiralty, and she's lurking around somewhere off the Korean Peninsula right now, ready to help repel boarders. I'll ask them to send a chopper for you. I want you to get on board and brief the captain on what you found out in Russia, and what you think the North Koreans are likely to do next.'

'Terrific,' Richter replied, with a marked lack of enthusiasm.

'I *thought* you'd like that,' Simpson rang off abruptly.

As Richter slipped the mobile phone back into his jacket pocket, a smartly dressed Korean approached him somewhat diffidently.

'Mr Richter?' he asked, and received a nod.

Looking relieved, the man pulled out a wallet to show an identification badge comprising an eight-pointed gold star inside a blue circle, with the words 'National Intelligence Service' inscribed around the lower half of the circle, and what was presumably the same legend in Korean around the top half. On the opposite side of the wallet was a plastic card with the man's name, photograph and personal details.

The badge meant nothing at all to Richter, who'd never before seen a National Intelligence Service ID. Since nobody, apart from Simpson and presumably now the NIS hierarchy, knew he was due to arrive in Seoul, he guessed the guy was probably genuine. But Richter would never take anything at face value, so before he went anywhere he intended to run a check.

'The car is over here, sir,' the man said, leading the way towards a Mercedes saloon.

'How did you recognize me?' Richter asked, as he put his two cases in the boot.

'Your Mr Simpson' – the name came out more like 'Thimthon' – 'sent us a description and a photograph.'

'Most considerate of him,' Richter murmured dryly. 'Two questions first. Where are we going? And what's the name of the head of your organization?'

The man smiled as he opened the rear door of the car. 'To our new headquarters building at Naegok-dong, and that's where Bae Chang-Su, the Director-General of the NIS, is waiting to meet you.'

'Good enough,' Richter said, and climbed into the back seat.

United States Strategic Command (USStratCom)
Command Center
The Underground Complex, Offutt Air Force Base,
Omaha, Nebraska

The foundation of America's national strategy of deterrence is called the Triad. Nothing to do with Hong Kong street gangs, the Triad comprises the three strategic elements of the American military machine: long-range bombers, land-based ICBMs and ballistic missile-carrying submarines.

Each component of the Triad provides America with a different strength and capability, and presents an enemy with three entirely different threats to counter. Of the three, the submarines, the SSBNs, are arguably the most lethal, offering a unique combination of mobility, colossal firepower, invisibility and hence survivability, while at the same time providing American leaders with a global strike capacity with the highly successful Trident missile.

There are usually between five and fifteen SSBNs constantly at sea, manoeuvring within designated patrol areas that each extend to around one million square miles, ready at all times to react to coded instructions to launch one or all of their twenty-four Trident missiles.

All US nuclear-powered submarines are assigned to either the Pacific or the Atlantic Fleets, but control over their strategic assets, meaning the missiles, is vested in the United States Strategic Command. The USStratCom Command Center is the locus of this organization and its primary function is to transmit National Command Authority directives to the strategic arsenal of all three legs of the Triad, under the ultimate authority of the President of the United States of America himself.

The USStratCom Command Center is a purpose-built, two-level, fourteen-thousand-square-foot concrete and steel section of the Underground Command Complex, which also houses the Force Status Readiness Center, the Intelligence Operations Center and various other strategically vital offices. Like Cheyenne Mountain, the complex can be sealed in times of tension or war, and is able to operate independently for prolonged periods of time. Critical command and control communications equipment is specially shielded against the effects of the electromagnetic pulse which follows a nuclear explosion, and allows the Commander In Chief of USStratCom to control forces worldwide both before and during a nuclear war.

As soon as the Joint Chiefs of Staff increased the readiness state for US forces globally to DEFCON Four, CINCSTRAT ordered the complex to be sealed, then summoned his senior staff for a high-level restricted-access command briefing.

'Gentlemen,' General Mark Winchester began, 'the CIA has obtained technical intelligence that shows North Korean forces assembling north of the Demilitarized Zone. Pyongyang is claiming that these manoeuvres are part of an exercise called "Silver Spring", but the fear in Washington is that they're actually the prelude to an invasion of South Korea.

'The White House, in consultation with the Joint Chiefs, has taken this threat sufficiently seriously to go to DEFCON Four, and our forces will remain in this state, or in a higher state of readiness, until either the threat is dismissed as a false alarm or an invasion attempt is actually made by the DPRK.'

Winchester paused and glanced around the long oblong table. Nobody spoke, or reacted in any way, which is precisely what he had expected. All of his senior staff had been fully aware of the situation for at least one day, and most of them had moved into the complex even before CINCSTRAT. The briefing he was giving would, essentially, tell them nothing they didn't already know, but it would summarize the latest intelligence and, more importantly, lay out the options available and the actions then to be taken.

'The first task is to ensure the integrity of our C^3I assets,' General Winchester said. He pronounced it 'cee cubed eye' and the acronym stood for command, control, communication and intelligence. 'I want continuous checking routines to be run on all our landline, radio, microwave and satellite systems with immediate effect, starting with the Red Phone system and JANET.'

The 'Red Phone' is the slang term applied to the Primary Alerting System, a network of dedicated telephone circuits that allows USStratCom controllers to communicate directly with over two hundred operational centres worldwide, including individual intercontinental ballistic missile silos and missile-launch control centres.

'JANET' is the Joint Chiefs of Staff Alerting Network, which comprises direct lines to the National Military Command Center in the Pentagon and to all other principal command headquarters. The system permits CINCSTRAT to communicate immediately with the two National Command Authorities – the President of the United States and the Secretary of Defense – and with the Chairman of the Joint Chiefs of Staff and other military commanders.

The Command Center also has access to a vast range of radio networks, operating in every available frequency band. These networks, in conjunction with relay and communications satellites, allow direct contact with aircraft in flight in any part of the world, and allow the transmission of National Command Authority orders to American military assets worldwide.

'The North Korean threat, assuming this is not just an

exercise, isn't directed ostensibly against the United States, but I want to ensure that we're ready in all respects should the situation deteriorate and involve a direct threat to the homeland. The longest-range missile the North Koreans are known to be working on currently is the Taep'o-dong 2, and the latest intelligence assessments suggest it probably can't reach any part of the continental US except Alaska, which doesn't really count.'

Winchester got the smiles he expected. 'But intelligence has been wrong before, so within the next four hours I want to see two additional E-6B Cover All aircraft holding at Tinker Air Force Base in Oklahoma at Alert Thirty and Sixty, and another National Airborne Operations Center E-4B at Alert Thirty here at Offutt.'

Originally, the Strategic Air Command's airborne command post was an EC-135, code-named Looking Glass. When this platform was retired from service, the upgraded E-6B TACAMO aircraft assumed the mission, and the revised code-name Cover All.

'Finally, I want the Ground Mobile Headquarters deployed immediately, and to be fully operational no later than twelve noon tomorrow. Send it somewhere central – Colorado or Kansas, say – and ensure that communications with it are kept to an absolute minimum to avoid compromising its location.'

In the circumstances, what Winchester was ordering was overkill, but he'd never seen any point in having assets if they weren't being used, and the Ground Mobile Headquarters was USStratCom's last-ditch asset. An entirely self-sufficient mobile unit, it can set up operations anywhere inside the United States and there duplicate all the control functions of the Command

Center itself. By virtue of its mobility, its location cannot be known far enough in advance to get programmed into enemy missile-guidance systems, so it is effectively invulnerable to an enemy strike.

'Any questions?' Winchester asked, but nobody spoke. 'OK, command briefing complete. Let's get to it.'

NIS Headquarters, Naegok-dong, Seoul, South Korea

Richter was escorted to a conference room located on the top floor of the National Intelligence Service headquarters in southern Seoul. The white five-storey structure had a square central entrance hall, topped with a dome, but the bulk of the building consisted of two curving arms of offices that embraced the approach road. As 'spook central' buildings go, it was more attractive than most.

'Mr Richter.' A short, stocky man stood up from his seat at the end of the long table and walked towards him, extending his hand. 'My name is Kang Jang-Ho, and I'm the deputy director of this facility. Bae Chang-Su, the director, will be here shortly. You've had a long flight, I understand. Can I offer you some refreshment?'

Richter shook Kang's hand. 'Yes,' he then replied, realizing that he felt pretty hungry: even business-class meals on Aeroflot were not too appealing. 'That would be very welcome.'

'Coffee and sandwiches – something like that?' Kang suggested, picked up a telephone and held a brief conversation.

As he put the instrument down, another man entered

the room, taller and slimmer and with a thin moustache. From the way Kang straightened up, Richter guessed this must be the 'autocratic' Bae Chang-Su, as proved the case when the newcomer introduced himself.

They sat down at one end of the long table, equipped with chairs for over a dozen people, Bae taking his seat at the end.

'You have some information for us, I understand,' he began.

Richter nodded and explained what he and Bykov had found out in Russia, and the assumed destination of the missing MiG-25s. The South Koreans had already known some of it, but the probability that Foxbats had also been stolen from Algeria was news to them.

'According to General Bykov, at least sixteen have gone missing from Russian air bases, and we think maybe two from Aïn Oussera in Algeria, totalling a minimum of eighteen. Because of the fragmented state of the military in Russia, and the possibility that somebody high up in the Defence Ministry is facilitating these thefts, there could be a lot more aircraft unaccounted for. My own guess is that there must now be at least twenty MiG-25s north of the DMZ.'

Bae didn't appear surprised by this. 'What I can't understand is why the North Koreans would want these aircraft. All their combat planes are old and no match for ours, so I would expect them to go after more modern fighters.'

At that moment there was a knock on the door, and a young man entered carrying a tray of refreshments. Richter waited until he'd left the room before responding.

'According to my source in Moscow, the North Koreans may have picked on the MiG-25 because it was specifically designed to intercept ICBMs in the terminal stage of their flight. More importantly, the Foxbat is about the only aircraft likely to be left flying after the first nuclear explosion, because the EMP – the electromagnetic pulse – will fry the electronics of pretty much everything else, either in the air or on the ground.'

'You're suggesting the North Koreans intend to launch a nuclear attack?' Bae asked tightly.

'I honestly don't know,' Richter replied, 'but what concerns London is exactly the point you've already made. Why would they choose the MiG-25 unless they had a very good reason? And its survivability after a nuclear exchange is about the only explanation we've come up with. Our main concern is that, even if the West doesn't resort to nuclear weapons, the North Koreans would, just to eliminate the opposition and give them immediate control of the skies. They could keep their fighters and bombers secure in hardened shelters, detonate a nuke over the joint South Korean and American forces, then fly these Foxbats to intercept any missiles the Americans launched. That would soon eliminate most of the opposition on land, and could give them air superiority because the only aircraft left flying would be North Korean, allowing them to consolidate an advance towards Seoul.'

For a few moments neither Bae nor Kang responded, just stared across the table at each other as Richter began another sandwich.

'You don't paint an attractive picture,' Bae Chang-Su said eventually, 'but it may interest you to know that, in our last discussion, Washington outlined a remarkably similar scenario.'

'So what's your government doing about it?'

'I can't be specific about our military response, because I don't know precisely what orders have been given, but you can assume our armed forces have escalated the alert state. The government has already made representations to Pyongyang, and we've sought assistance from the Americans under the terms of Operation Plan 5027. Meanwhile, until our neighbours in the north make some kind of move, that's about all we can do.'

The sound of an approaching helicopter became audible, and Bae glanced out of the window. 'Excellent,' he murmured. 'Your taxi's arrived on time, Mr Richter. London asked us to provide you with transportation as far as Kunsan, and I understand your Royal Navy will be sending an aircraft to meet you there.'

Six minutes later Richter was gazing out through the side window of the Bell helicopter. Kunsan Air Base lay about a hundred and twenty miles almost due south, and his flight would take a little over an hour.

Only forty-eight hours earlier he'd been climbing into the rear of the Antonov An-72 transport aircraft at Slavgorod North for the flight back to Moscow, and since then he seemed to have spent most of his time either busy on the phone or in the air. As the helicopter lifted off, he stared at the white shape of the NIS headquarters receding below him, and wondered what the *next* forty-eight hours might bring.

Chapter Fourteen

Saturday
Kunsan Air Base, South Korea

Seventy-five minutes after lifting off from Naegok-dong, the Bell touched down at Kunsan Air Base. As the rotors slowed to a stop, the crewman slid the side door open but gestured to Richter to remain in his seat. A refuelling bowser was waiting to one side of the landing pad, and beyond it Richter could see the familiar shape of a Royal Navy Merlin ASW helicopter ground-taxying slowly towards the Bell he was waiting in.

The crewman gave a thumbs-up, then gestured towards the open door. Richter picked up his two bags and stepped out onto the discoloured concrete. He moved briskly away from the Bell before stopping beside the marshaller who was waiting for the Merlin, wands crossed below his waist. The Merlin parked some twenty yards away, its nose dipping as the pilot applied the brakes.

The engines and spinning rotors of the Royal Navy helicopter combined to create a noise that was deafening. Richter gestured to the marshaller that he was the passenger for this aircraft. The South Korean lifted one of his wands to attract the Merlin's pilot's attention and pointed the other one at Richter, then waved for him to go forward.

Richter ducked involuntarily as he moved under the rotor disk, and headed for the open side door. The aircrewman gave him a grin as he stepped into the rear compartment, and handed him a passenger helmet, based on that worn by British Army tank drivers. He then gestured to the instructor's seat on the mission console. Directly behind the aircrewman's seat, it lies on the starboard side of the Merlin and faces aft.

The moment Richter secured his seatbelt, he heard the aircrewman confirming that their passenger was on board. Moments later, the Merlin began moving forwards. This aircraft's downwash is so powerful that it's capable of wrecking any smaller helicopter nearby, so it continued ground-taxying until it was well clear of the Bell.

A minute later, as the helicopter finally reached the taxiway, its engine note rose to a shrill scream audible even through the muffling effect of the headset. The Merlin lifted straight up into the air, then adopted a nose-down attitude as it began climbing and accelerating, heading west away from the airfield.

In minutes they were 'feet-wet' – over the sea – and established at five hundred feet and, Richter guessed, travelling at around a hundred and twenty knots, a ground-speed of nearly one hundred and forty miles an hour.

'How far to Mother?' Richter asked.

'About fifty miles,' responded the pilot, Lieutenant Craig Howe. 'We'll be there in around thirty minutes. So you're Royal Navy, I gather? No civilian would say "Mother".'

'Ex,' Richter confirmed. 'I used to fly Sea Harriers for the Queen.'

'Oh, God, not another fucking stovie,' Howe muttered.

Richter merely grinned at that, leant back in the seat and closed his eyes.

United States Strategic Command (USStratCom) Command Center
The Underground Complex, Offutt Air Force Base, Omaha, Nebraska

General Winchester glanced around the Senior Battle Staff Area situated on the lowest level of the Command Center. Each senior officer sat at a workstation console which provided him or her with access to state-of-the-art data management systems and integrated secure and non-secure voice communication facilities. Video monitors located at each console displayed mission-critical information that allowed the proper control and management of the command's missile and aircraft assets.

Lower-ranking staff officers were working simultaneously in the Support Battle Staff Area on the upper floor. These terminals differed from those of the senior staff in displaying more detailed data, rather than the global picture necessary for overall situation assessment.

The principal system used for storing and processing information is the Automated Command Control System, which stores data regarding everything from the current and forecast weather to tactical information about force movements and submarine, aircraft and missile status and availability.

Like the NORAD complex located inside Cheyenne Mountain, the USStratCom Command Center taps into a number of different surveillance systems designed to detect the launch and subsequent trajectory of both ICBMs and SLBMs.

Data is simultaneously transmitted to USStratCom, NORAD, the NMCC in the Pentagon and the Alternate National Military Command Center in Pennsylvania. At USStratCom, the data collected is fed into a high-speed computer for processing, and is then displayed on the Command Center's eight large wall screens at the same time as it's shown on video monitors positioned in front of CINCSTRAT, the senior battle staff and the Warning Systems Controller.

Data on the trajectory and predicted target area undergo a one-minute 'confidence rating' check, and once it's clear that the missile is real – that is, not resulting from some form of computer-induced glitch or bad data – CINCSTRAT can launch additional aircraft for national survival and pass on advisory and preparatory information to his strategic assets. The order to retaliate with a strategic nuclear strike has to be issued by the President himself, to be relayed then by USStratCom. CINCSTRAT alone cannot make that decision.

'OK, everything looks fine from here.' General Winchester returned his gaze to his console, while speaking into his headset microphone. 'Senior Controller, call the roll.'

For the third time that afternoon, Lieutenant-General Virgil Neuberger moved the trackball and sent the cursor spinning across the screen. He selected 'Strategic Assets', clicked 'OK' and began to read the figures into the command group intercom.

'Submarines, first. We have eleven SSBNs on patrol, with two more preparing to sail within the next twelve hours – one from Kings Bay, Georgia, the other from Bangor, Washington. All have been passed coordinates for their targets in North Korea if this thing does turn to rat-shit. The other five SSBNs are in maintenance or deep refit, and so can't be deployed within the time available.

'Land-based missile forces are fully briefed and their alert status has been increased from ninety minutes' notice to sixty minutes' for launch. Of the five hundred Minuteman Three missiles, only twenty-three have been reported as unserviceable. Eighteen of these have minor software or other faults, which have been assessed as capable of rectification within six hours. Five have major faults, which would take over thirty hours to fix.'

'That's not a bad turnout,' Winchester interrupted. 'Where are those missiles with major faults located?'

Neuberger paused for barely a second before replying. 'One each at F E Warren and Minot, and three at Malmstrom in Montana. Interestingly,' he added, 'the minor faults are similarly spread – three at F E Warren, five at Minot and the other ten at Malmstrom.'

'OK, we'll make a note of that. It sounds like somebody at Malmstrom's falling down on the job, so maybe I'll send a few no-notice inspection teams over to Montana once this party's over. What about the bombers?'

'Barksdale is reporting four per cent of their B-52s unserviceable, and Minot has three per cent out of action. Whiteman reports only one B-2 unserviceable. On Guam, which is probably where our immediate response would originate if the North Koreans do decide to cross the line, Andersen reports all aircraft serviceable.'

'So, in summary, we're in pretty good shape,' Winchester concluded. 'Let's hope we don't have to take this all the way to the wire.'

MV *Kang San 3*, North Pacific Ocean

It had been, by any standards, an unusual voyage.

The two three-thousand-ton cargo ships – the *Kang San 5* was in company – had sailed from Wonsan over a month earlier. They'd each had their normal complement embarked, but both were additionally crewed by ten soldiers, all under the command of a *chung-yong*, or lieutenant-colonel, on the *Kang San 3*. All the military personnel had been armed, and the ships' captains had been visited at Wonsan by a senior government official and been instructed to obey their orders without question.

A week before the ships sailed, an armed convoy had appeared at the Wonsan dockyard and a large crate had been loaded into the forward hold of the *Kang San 3*. The hold had then been locked, and a relay of soldiers posted on guard outside.

The ships had headed south into the East China Sea, passed east of the island of Taiwan, and continued south to Legaspi in the Philippines. They'd taken on maximum fuel and off-loaded most of their cargo of cement, embarked several hundred bales of cloth destined for merchants in Papua New Guinea, and sailed again.

Their next port of call had been Lae, on the east coast

of that island. Once the cloth had been unloaded and they'd again filled their bunkers, the two ships had set off without embarking any fresh cargo. They'd steamed north-east through Micronesia, past the Marshall Islands and on across the open expanse of the Pacific Ocean to Honolulu. After refuelling, they sailed again, heading east-north-east in the general direction of Los Angeles. They kept well clear of all the main shipping routes, because that was the way the planners in Pyongyang wanted it.

When they reached a position about fifteen hundred nautical miles north-east of Hawaii, the captain of the *Kang San 3* was handed a sealed envelope by the *chung-yong*.

'I don't understand,' he said, as he read the orders a second time.

'You don't have to, captain,' *chung-yong* Lee Kyung-Soon replied. 'All you have to do is obey. Do you have any questions about your instructions?'

'No, but—'

Lee shook his head. 'Then we understand each other. Order your crew to prepare to abandon ship immediately.' Through the bridge window he pointed at the *Kang San 5*, a quarter of a mile off the starboard bow, which was visibly slowing down in preparation to receive the crew of her sister ship. 'I will join you myself once I've completed my final tasks on board.'

As the captain made a broadcast to alert the crew for action, Lee headed down the companionway from the bridge and made his way to the forward hold. The two soldiers on guard outside saluted him as he approached, and unlocked the watertight steel door. Inside the hold, he headed across to a wooden crate that was the only thing the cargo space now contained, loosened six turn-buckles that held one of its sides in place, and dropped the panel to the floor.

In the crate was a bulky spherical object trailing wires and cables, with a basic control panel partially obscur-ing it, apparently inactive, since none of the lights was illuminated. On the floor of the crate were two large dry-cell batteries, terminals already connected, with a series-fitted master-switch screwed to the side of the crate.

Lee reached inside and turned the switch. Immedi-ately the control panel sprang to life, lights illuminating and dials registering. He checked the instrumentation against a printed list clipped below the panel, then began running through a series of actions to ensure that all the circuits were fully functional.

Satisfied that the instrumentation was registering cor-rectly, he moved to the second and final phase of his task. He turned his attention to a small alphanumeric key-board located directly below a ten-inch TFT panel and fed in a six-digit code that he'd been instructed to mem-orize at his last briefing in Pyongyang. The panel lit up and a menu appeared that Lee methodically worked his way down.

The penultimate item on the list was a communication check, and Lee simply selected 'radio' and checked that the built-in receiver was getting a signal from the *Kang San 5*, where the lieutenant had been instructed to broad-cast music on a specific frequency. The tiny speaker immediately began emitting sounds definitely not to Lee's taste, but that didn't matter.

He keyed the frequency he'd been instructed to use,

and checked twice to ensure that he'd got it right. That done, he made a final visual check of the entire apparatus before he turned away and walked out.

On deck, he opened his briefcase and extracted a satellite telephone and GPS receiver. He noted the position the GPS was recording, then made a thirty-second telephone call, before making his way towards the waiting lifeboat.

Forty minutes later, the *Kang San 5* began a slow turn to the west, towards the distant Midway Islands, and began picking up speed, leaving her deserted sister ship now dead and silent, wallowing in the long swell.

HMS *Illustrious*, Yellow Sea

The flight deck of the *Illustrious* was a scene of noisy, but clearly organized, chaos. Without ear defenders, the roar of jet engines was deafening, and Richter's nostrils immediately filled with the unmistakable smell of burning kerosene. Two Sea Harriers were waiting at the aft end of the deck, their Pegasus engines running, and both still with telebrief lines connected, so Richter guessed their pilots were getting last-minute instructions from the Operations Room. On the deck in front of them, the Merlin that had served as his personal taxi was shutting down, rotors folding into the fully aft position preparatory to the helicopter being towed over to the starboard side of the deck, close to the island, to clear the carrier's runway for the Harriers. Meanwhile, right forward, on zero spot just to the right of the ramp, another Merlin was waiting to lift off.

Waiting for him at the bulkhead door in the island –

the steel structure containing the bridge, Flyco and other offices on the starboard side of the deck – was a lieutenant wearing 3J rig, a dark blue 'woolly-pully' over a white shirt. He led Richter up to Flyco, on the port side rear of the bridge. In fact, Richter knew the way blindfolded, as he'd spent around four years at sea on all three of the CVS carriers when he was a squadron pilot, and on numerous occasions had been required to report to either Commander (Air) or Lieutenant Commander (Flying) and, during Sea Harrier operations, both officers were to be found in Flyco.

'Mr Richter, sir,' the lieutenant announced, and a bulky man with a heavy beard, sitting in the right-hand chair, swung round, the three rings on his shoulder epaulettes glinting in the sun. In front of him, the ship's Lieutenant Commander (Flying) was sitting in another black swivel chair, controlling flight-deck operations.

'Welcome back, Spook,' said Roger Black. 'I wondered if the "Mr Richter" we had been asked to collect from Kunsan would turn out to be you.'

Richter smiled and extended his hand. 'Congratulations on your promotion, Blackie.' When he'd last seen Black – during a spot of continuation training in the eastern Med that had turned into rather more than the routine two weeks – he'd been Lieutenant Commander (Flying) on board the *Invincible*.

'So what kind of trouble are we in this time?' Black asked. 'Whenever you're around, uncivilized things seem to happen. There were a few bodies lying about on Crete after you left the island, I understand.'

'They weren't *all* my fault, Blackie, and this time *none* of it's my fault.'

'It seems you know this gentleman?' a voice interrupted. Black stood up and Richter turned round to face the captain, a tall, slim, fair-haired man with thin lips and a nose that even an ancient Roman might have considered excessively aquiline.

'Yes, sir, we met on board the *Invincible* when I was Little F.'

'Welcome aboard, Mr Richter. I'm Alexander Davidson.' The captain extended his hand. 'I gather you've some information for us about what's going on north of the border.'

Richter nodded, with a glance round Flyco before replying. As well as the three senior officers, a naval airman was sitting waiting to execute Little F's instructions and control the deck lights, and just beyond Flyco, on the left-hand side of the bridge wing, a lookout was standing with binoculars hung around his neck. From past experience Richter knew that rumours spread on warships at almost the speed of light, and what he had to tell the captain now probably shouldn't be allowed too wide a distribution.

'Could we perhaps adjourn to the Bridge Mess, Captain?'

Davidson raised his eyebrows slightly, but nodded. He walked back onto the bridge to inform the Officer of the Watch where he'd be, then returned to Flyco and led the way down one deck. Richter and Black followed him into the Mess and the commander slid the door closed.

'Well, Mr Richter?'

'I probably don't know a great deal more than you do because I've spent most of the last two days in the air.'

'Where were you two days ago?' Black asked.

'Pretty much in the middle of Russia at a place called Slavgorod North. I was with a GRU general trying to find out who'd stolen about half a squadron of MiG-25 Foxbat interceptors from the Russian Air Force.'

'And did you?'

'I think so, yes. We believe Pyongyang coordinated the thefts and that the aircraft are now somewhere in North Korea, probably sitting in hardened shelters close to the DMZ. We also think a theft of around fifty AA-6 Acrid air-to-air missiles from a depot in Dobric, Bulgaria, was orchestrated by the same people. Bolt the Acrids to the underwing pylons of the Foxbats and you've got a very potent weapon system.'

'Agreed,' Black observed, 'but even if the North Koreans have, what, twenty Foxbats loaded for bear, as the Americans would say, that's still only a tiny number of aircraft in relation to their known air assets. I don't see why the Foxbats would pose too much of a threat, simply because of the aircraft the South Koreans can operate. So why are you here, and why is everyone so worked up about this business?'

'I'm here,' Richter said, 'because this is where my boss wants me to be, and I don't have too much say in the matter. But the worry shared by SIS and the Americans is that possession of those Foxbats might encourage the North Koreans to escalate this into a nuclear conflict. And the reason we think that is simple – EMP, electromagnetic pulse.'

Briefly, he explained the design of the MiG-25. Then Davidson asked him almost exactly the same question as Bae Chang-Su had done in Seoul, and Richter gave him virtually the same answer.

'Are you seriously suggesting the North Koreans will use nuclear weapons?'

'I really don't know, but it's difficult to come up with any other valid reason for them stealing the Foxbats. The aircraft is old – even obsolete – but it's the only interceptor in the Korean Peninsula that could survive the EMP after a nuclear detonation, and still function. And that's what's worrying both London and Washington.'

Ok'pyong missile base, North Korea

The Taep'o-dong 2 missile sitting on the launch pad at Ok'pyong had taken the North Koreans almost a year to prepare.

Like its predecessor, the Taep'o-dong 1, its first two stages were liquid-fuelled, but the third stage was powered by a solid-fuel motor. That also contained the payload, and designing that was what had taken the most time. The device sitting at the top of the forty-six-metre-high ballistic missile was special in every way, and designed for a single purpose. As far as the North Korean scientists were aware, it was the first, and quite probably the last, such 'warhead' ever constructed.

Alongside the launch pad a servicing gantry had been erected, and white-coated technicians swarmed over it, checking that everything was properly secured and ready for the launch. The final procedure, before the countdown began, was to load the fuel tanks of the first two stages, and for that manoeuvre everybody left the pad apart from the fire crews and a mere handful of other essential personnel.

Four hours later, the Taep'o-dong 2 sat ready. The pad was now deserted apart from the armed guards posted to ensure nobody approached it, and the countdown began in a blast-proof concrete bunker half a mile from the site.

T'ae'tan Air Base, North Korea

Pak Je-San gazed around the hangar with some small satisfaction. The maintainers had by now got two of the unserviceable Foxbats into flying condition, which was a better result than he'd secretly hoped. He now had seven MiG-25s operational here at T'ae'tan and twenty-two in total, including the aircraft he'd dispersed to the other three airfields.

Even better news was that the forty-eight R-40T missiles his agents had stolen from Dobric had arrived the previous day at the port of Bandar Abbas in Iran, and would be flown from there direct to T'ae'tan. They were scheduled to arrive within hours, before being distributed to the other airfields. That would give them a combined arsenal of over one hundred and sixty missiles and that, Pak Je-San felt confident, was more than enough. If they then ran out of munitions, the war would already be lost.

Oval Office, White House, 1600 Pennsylvania Avenue, Washington, DC

'Not exactly a surprise, then?'

'No, Mr President,' agreed the Secretary of Defense,

walking across the Oval Office and placing a sheaf of papers on the supreme commander's mahogany desk. He'd just flown back from an emergency session of the United Nations' Security Council in New York. The President had known the Secretary of Defense for years and trusted his judgement more than almost anyone else in his own administration.

'What did they say, exactly?'

'Just what the CIA expected. That all the manoeuvres the NKs are currently carrying out are part of this exercise they claim to be running.'

The President leant back in his seat and steepled his fingers, then abruptly sat forward again. 'Are we reading more into this than we should? Could it really be just a routine exercise?'

The Secretary of Defense shook his head decisively. 'I suppose there's about a one per cent chance that we're mistaken, but I believe the evidence is unambiguous. North Korea is gearing up for a push south across the DMZ.'

'I've been briefed by the Joint Chiefs already, but what's *your* take on this? If the Agency *is* right, what can we do to stop them? Do we have enough forces in South Korea to counter an outright invasion?'

The Secretary of Defense shook his head. 'There's no way of stopping a North Korean advance, because they outnumber the South in armour, battlefield artillery and also men. That's always been acknowledged as a virtual certainty. What they lack is support and supply chains in depth, so they could certainly get their forces some way into South Korea, but they wouldn't be able to sustain their advance or consolidate their positions, and eventually we'd be able to push them back across the DMZ. The one-liner here is that the North Koreans can start a war, but they can't finish one.'

'I don't want them to *start* a war. We've got enough problems in the Middle East as it is.'

'If they did cross the DMZ it would give us the excuse we need to take out the leadership in Pyongyang.'

The President shook his head. 'I know, but the timing's not right and we're stretched thinly enough as it is. Right, let's review the evidence that the North Koreans are planning something.'

'I do believe it's convincing, Mr President. The satellite imagery shows definite manoeuvres by their troops, and the Eighth Army is now operating several Shadow 200 unmanned aerial vehicles over the DMZ. They fly at between ten and fourteen thousand feet and they're pretty much invisible at that altitude. They've now been redeployed to cover areas further north and the data they've collected support the satellite pictures. We've also flown them over the nuclear plant at Yongbyon and other sensitive sites, and we've been using Guardrail Common Sensor systems close to the DMZ.'

'Guardrail?'

'It's an airborne communications and signals intelligence system – COMINT and SIGINT – developed by the NSA, and it's recorded a marked increase in radio and signal traffic in the area. Now, none of this conclusively proves that the North Koreans are planning an invasion, but collectively it certainly suggests they're planning *something*.

'As you know, sir, we've normally no direct contact with Pyongyang, so we've used the strongest diplomatic language we could at the UN, and told them we'd retaliate if any of their troops moved across the DMZ. We just got a bunch of blank stares from the delegation and a repeat of the *It's all an exercise* bullshit. They said if their troops did cross into or through the DMZ it would only be because of navigation errors in the heat of the exercise, and therefore they urged that no retaliation be considered.'

'Great,' the President muttered. 'So now they want us to sit back and do nothing while they head straight for Seoul. Well, we're not going to do that. You clearly told them we'd be prepared to use all our military assets, including missiles, to defend our allies?'

'Yes, and they insisted it was just an exercise. And then warned that any attack by us or South Korea would be vigorously repulsed.'

The President stood up and paced back and forth behind his huge desk for a minute or so. He sometimes found that walking helped clarity of thought.

'Let me just summarize the information I've already been given. The North Koreans could invade the South and there wouldn't be a hell of a lot we could do to stop them. But they don't have the resources to consolidate their advance, and we'd be able to land enough troops and armour to drive them back within a few weeks. Is that a fair assessment?'

'Yes, Mr President.'

'And presumably they know this as well as we do?'

'I can't speak for the leadership in Pyongyang, but I think their senior military officers will be aware of the limitations in their supply system, yes.'

'So let me ask the obvious question. Why would they

do it? Why would North Korea consider mounting an invasion that they know must ultimately fail? What's their objective? And would they use nuclear weapons to achieve it?'

The Secretary of Defense, faced with not one but four 'obvious questions', guessed that the one the President really wanted an answer to was the last of them.

'Frankly, Mr President, I'm not convinced, for several reasons. We know the North Koreans have developed nuclear weapons, because of the underground test they carried out in the fall of 2006. But detonating a small atomic device in some kind of test rig isn't the same as bolting one to a bus on the top of a missile and dropping a cone over it. The miniaturization process is difficult and complicated, and I still think it's beyond the North Koreans' technical competence. The CIA believes they've been in contact with Iranian scientists, but it's not clear who's advising who, and I still say it's significant that neither nation has so far demonstrated that they have a long-range nuclear delivery capability.'

'But you do accept that they possess the raw material to manufacture nuclear weapons?'

The Secretary of Defense nodded. 'Yes, obviously. All our analyses suggest that the Yongbyon reprocessing plant has been producing weapons-grade fissionable material for some time. We don't know how much they have, but the IAEA calculated a maximum of about thirty-five kilograms. A twenty-kiloton weapon needs eight kilograms of plutonium, so that suggests they could have manufactured four fairly low-yield devices at the most. They obviously used some of it for the Hamgyeong province tests, so our best guess is they've got no more than three functioning devices, and that's not enough to make a credible threat against South Korea – or anywhere else, for that matter.'

The President sat down again. 'I hear what you say, and I don't disagree with your conclusions, but the facts remain. North Korea appears to be planning an incursion across the border. Unless the leadership in Pyongyang has completely flipped, they must have a good reason for doing it, and also be confident they can get away with it. So we'll work on that premise. First, let's call the roll. What have we got in South Korea right now?'

The Secretary of Defense settled back in his chair. 'Militarily, the two countries are unevenly matched in almost every sector.' And he outlined the discrepancies in their inventories. 'You should also be aware, sir, that defeating North Korea by military means, if it comes to that, is not going to be an easy option. Before you make any decisions, you need to be fully informed of the likely consequences.

'The public perception is that North Korea is a grindingly poor country with a starving and dissatisfied population ruled by two psychopaths, one of them now dead.'

This is literally true. Kim Il Sung – the 'Eternal Leader' – died in 1994 but is still the official ruler and has, since his death, made no decisions worse than he did during his live tenure. The functional head of state is the 'Dear Leader', his son. This scenario led the CIA to describe North Korea's system of government as the 'CFC Gambit' – the acronym standing for 'crippled, fearsome and crazy'.

'The reality,' the Secretary of Defense went on, 'is

somewhat different. The nation *is* a poor country by Western standards, but the vast majority of the people are unswervingly loyal to their leader, and would happily fight to defend him and their homeland. He almost certainly *is* a psychopath, and he's definitely deluded – he claimed not long ago that he'd shot five holes-in-one during a single round of golf, which would make anyone who's ever picked up a golf club doubt his sanity.'

The President laughed briefly.

'More seriously, the country's been in a state of siege ever since the nineteen-fifties, and the bulk of their GNP is spent annually on preparations for war. And, by any standards, they are very well prepared for conflict.

'Just to give you a few examples: most of their fighter and bomber aircraft aren't kept in hangars the way ours are. The North Koreans excavate deep into the northern slopes of the mountains, which are mainly granite, and there create huge underground spaces for their aircraft. They choose the north side because our bombs or missiles would have to be dropped or fired from the south, so the bulk of the mountain would be in the way. The rock above the tunnelled-out hangars is far too thick for bunker-busting bombs to penetrate. To be specific, our GBU-28 can cut through twenty feet of reinforced concrete: most of the North Korean bunkers are protected by around two hundred sixty feet of granite.

'According to the latest estimate, North Korea has well over eight thousand individual underground sites linked by three hundred fifty miles of tunnels. That's enough to shelter most of their air force from any attack we could launch using conventional weapons. There's also nothing we could do to cut their lines of communication or to try to decimate their military command structure, because they're underground as well. One report suggested that their bunkers hold over a million tons of food, one and a half million tons of fuel and nearly two million tons of ammunition and stores. In short, we could launch a massive bombardment of all known North Korean military facilities and achieve virtually nothing in terms of affecting their ability to wage war.

'Defeating the Iraqis was easy: they had low morale and faced overwhelming odds. The battles took place on almost ideal terrain for our forces – wide open deserts – and we achieved virtually immediate air superiority. North Korea, however, is mountainous, and even if we did gain control of the skies – which is by no means certain – that probably wouldn't help much. The battles there will be won or lost on the ground.

'I mentioned their superiority in numbers of tanks. The North Koreans not only have more tanks than our combined forces can field, but most analysts believe they're better vehicles as well. They're faster, with thicker armour and more powerful main guns. They've also developed tanks specifically for fighting in the hills and valleys of their country. They're designed to manage better on steep slopes, and they can ford the deepest rivers.

'And that's just one way in which the North Koreans have prepared for a war that they're actually expecting to fight. They've also got the biggest special force in the world – about one hundred twenty thousand men. They've got twelve thousand anti-aircraft guns, fifteen thousand shoulder-launched surface-to-air missiles, and about seven hundred high-speed patrol boats, most carrying surface-to-surface missiles, plus long-range anti-ship missiles.

'Their fighter aircraft are mainly old and slow, but North Korea's a very small country, and any air battles will be more like Second World War dogfights than the kind of combat our pilots are generally trained for. There just won't be the opportunities for our guys to engage targets at long and medium range, because the North Korean aircraft will pop up from behind a mountain, fire a salvo and drop down again. The air war will be messy and fought at very close quarters, which is exactly how their pilots have been trained to fight.

'The last point to remember is probably the most important: North Korea *expects* to fight a war. South Korea is seen as enemy territory, but is also regarded as merely a client state of America, and therefore of little real importance. America itself is and always has been North Korea's main enemy, so their leadership believes that the war will ultimately be a contest between these two countries. Pyongyang does not expect China or Russia or anyone else to intercede on its behalf, or to offer any kind of assistance, and all its preparations are directed towards a fight to the death between them and us. If we attempt to invade them, Pyongyang will respond with all the forces at its disposal, including whatever weapons of mass destruction its scientists have been able to fabricate. It will do its very best to destroy the United States and kill as many of our citizens as possible. *That* is their leader's philosophy, and *that*'s what really scares me.'

'You've done a pretty good job of scaring me too,' the President said. 'So what response do you suggest?'

'As you know, Mr President, we're committed to developing a defence shield between the two Koreas, and we've allocated an eleven-billion-dollar budget to achieve that. The problem is that we've done almost nothing so far. We've withdrawn a lot of our troops from the area immediately south of the DMZ simply to reduce possible tension. And we're also in the process of upgrading the Patriot missile systems we've positioned there from PAC-2 to PAC-3, but that's about all.

'What we can't now do is reinforce our troops there very quickly, because of the logistics involved. This situation has blown up really quickly. The Joint Chiefs anticipate it will take a minimum of a week to assemble the men and supplies we'd need, and probably another week to ship them to the peninsula. If the invasion starts within the next few days, South Korea simply won't have the ability to stop the advancing troops. The South can slow them up, but ultimately the North will just roll over the defenders.

'The other problem is that right now we don't have any surface assets that close. The *Enterprise* Carrier Battle Group is currently in the North Pacific, and they've been ordered to head towards Korea, but we're still talking days before they get within striking distance.

'The only options we'd then have would be to hit the attacking forces with bombs from our aircraft at Andersen on Guam, or use ICBMs from here in the States, or our boomers – missile-carrying nuclear submarines – but they wouldn't be able to stop a ground assault.'

'Why not?'

'Numbers, Mr President, numbers. As I've said, the North Koreans can field over a million front-line troops and almost five million reservists. Unless we carpet-bombed or nuked the entire front, we'd have no hope of stopping them, and anyway tactics like that are considered politically unacceptable in the current international climate. If we did get involved, we'd be expected to use smart munitions and carry out precision attacks. Using those tactics against the sort of forces the North Koreans can field would be like a mosquito biting an elephant.'

'So what's your own recommendation?'

'From what I witnessed at the United Nations, diplomacy isn't going to work here. I think we should carry on with what we're doing already. We prep Andersen and get the bombers moving, fly them towards the Korean Peninsula but hold them clear of territorial waters, just to let Pyongyang know we've got the capability to strike if they do launch an invasion. That's one threat. Against the possibility of North Korea escalating this to a nuclear conflict, keep the ICBMs and the boomers at a high alert state, so that we can respond real fast if we have to.'

'The missiles are holding at Alert Sixty now.'

'It's your decision, Mr President, but I suggest bringing them to Alert Thirty fairly soon, and I'll make sure Pyongyang knows that we've done so. It may not stop them, but it'll sure as hell make them stop and think.'

Chapter Fifteen

Saturday
Ok'pyong missile base, North Korea

They stopped the countdown at launch minus eight minutes, awaiting the executive order from Pyongyang that would either see the missile launched or force them to begin the complex process of reversing the actions they'd taken so far. Just under fifteen minutes later, the secure teleprinter spat out half a dozen lines of text, and almost immediately afterwards the direct line from Pyongyang rang. Two minutes after that, once the commanding officer was satisfied with the authenticity of the orders he'd been given, the countdown resumed.

A little after four-fifteen that afternoon, local time, those missile control staff who weren't manning consoles watched through six-inch-thick armoured glass as an explosion of flames and smoke enveloped the pad. The first stage of the Taep'o-dong ignited with a roar that could be heard miles away, and the bunker shook and vibrated. Slowly, so slowly that it seemed it must fall back to earth, the pointed nose of the missile rose above the conflagration and accelerated steadily into the clear blue sky.

There was a smattering of applause once it became clear that the first stage was performing faultlessly, but the most critical part of the flight was still to come.

HMS *Illustrious*, Yellow Sea

'Flash, flash, flash. Homer, Whisky Charlie with flash traffic. Missile launch detected from the east coast of North Korea in the vicinity of Ok'pyong at sixteen seventeen local time, zero one seventeen Zulu. Stand by for initial trajectory estimate.'

'Whisky Charlie, roger.'

The lieutenant manning the Homer position immediately selected the group line.

'All positions, Homer. Flash traffic from AEW Sea King Whisky Charlie. Missile launch reported from the vicinity of Ok'pyong, waiting for initial trajectory data.'

There was a moment of dead silence while everyone who had access to a radar screen stared at it, watching the combined ship's radar and data-linked picture.

'Flash. Homer, Whisky Charlie. Missile trajectory looks like south-east. No immediate threat.'

On the Operations Room displays, the return was now beginning to open to the south-east. Then it seemed as if everyone started talking at once, before the Group Warfare Officer silenced them and made a broadcast on all group lines and the ship's main broadcast system.

'Action stations. Action stations. Air raid warning red. I say again. Action stations. Air raid warning red.'

Then he switched off the broadcast and opened the line to Flyco. 'Flyco, GWO. What's the circuit and deck state?'

'One Merlin on deck, turning and burning. Two Harriers in the range. One Merlin on recovery about half a mile astern. No scheduled movements apart from the Merlin turn-round.'

'Roger, expedite the recovery and call the moment he's secured. Shut down the other Merlin and clear all personnel off the deck as soon as possible.'

The GWO went back to the group line and ship's broadcast. 'All positions, GWO. Secure all external hatches and openings. Assume Damage Control and NBCD State One. Break. Homer, GWO. What's the endurance of our airborne assets?' In the background could be heard the muffled slamming of watertight doors being closed. Although the opening trajectory of the missile was away from the ship's position, it could always be turned around or, worse, it might just be the first launch of a salvo.

'Already checked. The two Harriers are twenty-eight minutes to start of recovery, the AEW Sea King and the two Merlins can stay up for a couple of hours.'

'Good. Keep them out there.'

'GWO, Flyco, the Merlin's on deck and secured.'

'Good. All positions, GWO. Release Goalkeeper to unrestricted operation. Engage full ECM. Advise the ships in company.'

Goalkeeper is a fully autonomous close-in weapon system manufactured by Thales Nederland, specifically designed to intercept incoming shells, and both ballistic and sea-skimming missiles. Its heart is a 30mm seven-barrel Gatling gun – the same weapon that's used as a 'tank-buster' on the American A-10 Thunderbolt II – firing four thousand two hundred rounds a minute, guided by an X-band search radar and a combined X-band and Ka-band monopulse Cassegrain engagement radar, backed up by an optical system.

Against a high-speed target like the Russian SS-N-22

Sunburn Mach 2 sea-skimming missile, it's designed to detect it at 1,500 metres and complete the kill at 300 metres, in just over five seconds. By any standards, it's a formidable weapon, and the *Illustrious*, like her sister ship *Invincible*, was equipped with three of them – one on the bow, the second amidships on the starboard side, and the third on the port side aft, just below the Flight Deck on a custom-designed platform.

In less than three minutes, *Illustrious* was fully secured, the gas-tight citadel in place, and positive air pressure established – a basic but very effective defence against chemical or biological attack – and the captain had just okayed the Military Flash signal that would be sent by satellite to advise CINCFLEET of the missile launch.

HMS *Victorious*, 200 miles west of Novaya Zemlya, Barents Sea

The Barents Sea is not the deepest water in the world by a long way. Much of the sea floor, especially to the west and south-west of Novaya Zemlya and to the north-east of Murmanskiy Bereg, is under six hundred feet deep. The captains of ballistic missile-carrying nuclear submarines prefer to lurk in areas where they have more freedom to manoeuvre than such shallows allow, but the latest orders hadn't allowed Commander Richard Clare such latitude.

His redefined patrol area committed him to maintaining position about three hundred nautical miles to the north of the tip of Poluostrov Kanin, right on the edge of the deeper water of the central Barents Sea.

Clare hadn't left the control room of *Victorious* in almost fifteen hours, apart from visits to the Officers' Heads and a couple of trips to the Wardroom for sandwiches and coffee. No hot food had been prepared, or would be available, in the boat until it was secured from silent running, because cooking inevitably causes rattles and clangs as pots and pans are used. All off-watch crew members were confined to their bunk spaces, and all video and audio equipment had been switched off, apart from personal players using earphones only. The atmosphere in the boat was tense with anticipation, but very quiet.

Richard Clare was worried about on-board noise. He was also worried about seabed passive sonar arrays, ASW helicopters and hunter-killer submarines, like the small but silent and deadly Alphas.

But what worried him most was steaming around in the Russians' back garden. The problem was, he couldn't see any alternative to this.

The operational range of each Trident II D-5 SLBM carried by the *Victorious* was around five thousand miles. This meant that, from the boat's current location, each of the eight MIRVs contained within the Trident's warhead could easily strike a target anywhere inside the Confederation of Independent States – the territories of the old Soviet Union.

They could also, if the missiles' navigation computers were reprogrammed, strike any target in the United States located to the east of a line drawn from Miami straight up to Minneapolis. Or, looking south and east rather than west, any target in China, Japan, the countries of the western Pacific Rim or Africa. In fact, about the only nations *Victorious*'s missiles couldn't hit were Australia, New Zealand and South America.

He would have much preferred to be patrolling the wide, safe and, above all, *deep* waters of the North Atlantic, but in order to hit the targets he'd been given in North Korea, he had no option but to stay in the Barents Sea. The signal from CINCFLEET had made it perfectly clear that time was of the essence: to reposition the boat in the North Atlantic would have taken too long and, for most of the transit, North Korea would have been beyond the range of the Tridents, and that was unacceptable.

It made good tactical sense, but that didn't mean Clare had to like it.

North American Aerospace Defense Command, Cheyenne Mountain, Colorado

For the last thirty years of the twentieth century, and well into the twenty-first, America's anti-missile defences have relied upon DSP (Defense Support Program) surveillance satellites located in geosynchronous orbit some twenty-two thousand two hundred and fifty miles above the surface of the Earth.

The replacement system – SBIRS (Space Based Infrared System) – met substantial delays, but the new SBIRS Mission Control Station at Buckley Air Force Base in Aurora, Colorado, was commissioned more or less on time at the end of 2001, and now controlled the orbiting DSP satellites as well as operating the ALERT tactical warning centre.

The three front-line DSP birds were located over Central America, above the Indian Ocean and more or less over the middle of the Pacific Ocean. Two other spacecraft were available as orbiting spares, ready to take over when one of the satellites reached the end of its useful life.

Their sole purpose was to detect missile launches anywhere in the vast area under surveillance, using a huge infrared telescope designed to identify the heat flare of the missile's rocket engine almost immediately after launch. The only thing that could delay detection was adverse weather, because thick cloud would prevent the infrared radiation reaching the telescope until the missile had cleared the cloud tops.

Over the Korean Peninsula, the weather was clear, and the Pacific Ocean DSP bird located the launch six seconds after the first-stage motor of the Taep'o-dong fired. Eleven seconds after that, the on-board computers had identified Ok'pyong as the launch site and calculated the missile's initial trajectory.

Immediately, the DSP satellite transmitted the data to Buckley, where high-speed computers assessed the calculated trajectory to determine if the missile was on a 'threat fan': meaning if the flight-path could conceivably end in the United States or any allied nation. The initial data showed that the North Korean missile was heading east-south-east, which meant it couldn't hit mainland America – but the Hawaiian Islands or even Mexico remained possible, though unlikely, targets.

Simultaneously, Buckley's data links flashed details of the launch to NORAD. Moments later, a klaxon sounded, a light flashed, and a computerized voice announced

'Missile alert! Missile alert!' One of the huge vision screens displayed the warning 'MISSILE EVENT' in red in the top left-hand corner. In the top centre was the word 'SECRET' and below that, occupying most of the screen, was an outline map of the Pacific Rim, with the Korean Peninsula on the left-hand side.

Dominating this display was a large red dot positioned over Ok'pyong, indicating the launch point, and a line pointing east-south-east, showing the missile's initial trajectory. At the end of the line was a quadrilateral shape, narrow where it joined the line but widening out from that point. This showed the threat fan: the computer system's assessment of the area within which the missile could land, which was updated every second or two as additional data was processed.

Automated instructions were sent to the Pave Paws phased-array radar control room at Beale Air Force Base in California, and the new X-band radar base on Kwajalein Atoll in the western Pacific, listing the launch and trajectory coordinates and instructing the radars to begin tracking the missile.

The moment the launch data had been confirmed by an automated back-check to Buckley, officers began broadcasting verbal confirmation to supplement the automatic threat warning systems.

'All stations, this is Brass Hat. Ballistic missile launch detected from Ok'pyong in North Korea. Initial trajectory one two seven degrees true, flight-time is – on my mark – two minutes and fifty-five seconds. Stand by for calculated impact point. This is *not* a drill.'

FOXBAT

North Pacific Ocean

One hundred and eighteen seconds after lift-off, and well out over the Pacific Ocean, the first stage of the Taep'o-dong dropped away, its fuel expended, and the second stage immediately ignited. That was scheduled to burn for a further one hundred and five seconds before the third, solid-fuel, stage would fire.

Two hundred and twenty-three seconds after launch, the second stage of the Taep'o-dong disengaged from the missile and began a long uncontrolled tumble to the sea below, and the third-stage motor flared into life. The programmed burn time was one hundred and two seconds, but the fuel was actually expended in ninety-eight seconds. Not that it made any difference.

Three seconds after the sensors had confirmed the engine was dead, six explosive bolts fired on the third-stage/payload junction, and the now-empty tube fell away, taking with it the telemetry transmitter. Now that the third-stage burn was complete, there wasn't anything the scientists and technicians at Ok'pyong could do to direct the weapon, because the nose-cone hadn't been designed to be steerable. All they wanted was extreme range, and they'd know the result of the test-flight soon enough.

The warhead on this missile wasn't a nuclear device or a chemical weapon or anything of that sort. In fact, about all the aerodynamic tip of the Taep'o-dong contained was a dozen hollow metal objects designed as radar reflectors, and a small explosive charge to rupture the nose-cone before re-entry. The cone itself was made from fibreglass with a heat-resistant ceramic coating to be as light as possible, and the weight and shape of the 'warhead' had been carefully calculated to ensure reasonable directional stability whilst still achieving maximum range.

The final component was a small transmitter inside a protective heat-resistant canister, locked onto a single frequency, and a radio altimeter that would send it an electronic signal when the canister reached a predetermined height above the ocean. The transmitter would then begin sending out a repeated signal and that, the missile designers had calculated, would be sufficient to achieve the desired result.

Ok'pyong missile base, North Korea

One after the other, the telemetry screens ranged in front of the North Korean technicians went blank. Though they all knew in advance that was exactly what was supposed to happen, some of them still looked slightly nervous, as if they might somehow be blamed for the ensuing loss of data from the Taep'o-dong.

Only the commanding officer looked pleased as he picked up the secure telephone to tell Pyongyang that the missile had functioned precisely as they'd planned.

North American Aerospace Defense Command, Cheyenne Mountain, Colorado

'Say again,' General Wayne Harmon demanded.

'We've lost contact with the missile, sir, just after third-stage burnout at around three hundred twenty seconds, and the DSP birds are no longer holding it. I've run diagnostics and everything's in the green. The Pacific Ocean satellite is still tracking residual heat from the burnt-out second and third stages. When we lost it, the missile had reached just over two hundred miles altitude, seven hundred miles down-range and a speed of thirteen thousand miles an hour.'

'OK,' Harmon said, 'so that's the end of the boost phase and it's up in the thermosphere. The Pave Paws at Beale should still be tracking it, and we'll get their feed momentarily. And if Beale can't locate it, Kwajalein Atoll will pick it up. Project the trajectory, see where the DSP birds think it's heading.'

On the display screen, a green line appeared, running straight through the quadrilateral and finishing in the North Pacific Ocean about midway between Hawaii and the west coast of Mexico.

'This reminds me of the Taep'o-dong type 1 they fired back in ninety-eight,' Harmon observed, 'except that the trajectory is different and this one looks like it's going a hell of a lot further. Unless they've incorporated some kind of mid-course guidance, it's no threat to us. This looks in fact like a pretty standard missile test. Keep checking the track and let me know when the DSP birds detect re-entry.'

A few seconds later the first data from the Pave Paws radar was overlaid on the screen, supplemented moments afterwards by the feed from Kwajalein Atoll. The two radars were displaying good solid contacts, and the predict vectors fairly closely matched the track suggested by the DSP satellites.

'All stations, Brass Hat. DSP missile tracking confirmed by radar. Predicted impact point is between Hawaii and the west coast of Mexico. Trajectory calculations suggest no threat to the US or any allied territory. Initial analysis supports routine test of a three-stage missile, probably a Taep'o-dong type 2.'

The predicted impact point was necessarily vague, depending on a number of different factors, including the missile's speed, the maximum altitude it would reach before gravity started pulling it back to Earth, and its aerodynamics and ability to withstand the heat generated by atmospheric friction during re-entry. The longer the radars tracked the missile, the more accurate the prediction would become.

'All stations, Brass Hat. Radar data indicates the missile has just passed the apogee. Refined calculations suggest the impact point will be approximately one four zero degrees west, thirty-five degrees north.'

And then something unexpected happened.

'Sir, the Kwajalein Atoll radar shows the warhead breaking up.'

'What altitude?'

'Around three hundred and twenty miles.'

'It's not atmospheric friction, then. Maybe they've developed a system of decoys that they're trying out. Or even an MIRV.'

A Multiple Independently-targeted Re-entry Vehicle is a way of combining several weapons inside a single missile. Typically, the nose-cone is ejected simultaneously with first-stage burnout, to reveal the MIRV 'bus' – the device that carries the individual warheads. After passing the apogee, the 'bus' manoeuvres using small rockets controlled by an inertial guidance and GPS system to alter its trajectory to match that of the first weapon. Once established, it releases the free-falling nuclear device, manoeuvres again to the trajectory of the second weapon, and repeats the process. Defending against this type of attack is extremely difficult, and such missiles frequently include decoys, with a radar signature similar to the warheads, and chaff – the last being thin strips of aluminium designed to swamp radars. If the MIRV warheads are released soon after apogee, meaning the top of the missile's trajectory, the spread can be very large.

Ever since the alert began, General Harmon had been in direct communication with both the Pentagon and the White House.

'Mr President, we're detecting about a dozen returns, spreading out in a fan. It now looks like a test of decoys, not a MIRV, because the trajectories are fairly close together and the release occurred simultaneously.'

'And the impact point?' The President had asked this same question four times since the three-way conversation had started, and each time Harmon had given the same answer.

'In the Pacific, sir, somewhere north-east of Hawaii.'

'So you're sure none of the warheads, or whatever this fucking thing is carrying, could reach American soil?'

'No, sir. The laws of physics are absolute. The contents of the North Korean warhead are headed straight down towards the surface of the ocean, and there's not the slightest possibility any of them could hit even Hawaii, let alone the continental US.'

MV *Kang San 5*, North Pacific Ocean

Standing at the stern of the *Kang San 5*, Lee Kyung-Soon saw the flash and checked his watch. Right on time. Moments later he saw a compelling and utterly distinctive shape climbing above the horizon, and a few seconds after that heard the echoing thunder of the detonation.

This ship was, he knew, a safe distance away from the explosion on board the *Kang San 3*, but despite that he walked briskly back to the accommodation section and climbed up to the bridge. There he made a broadcast forbidding all crew members to venture out onto the upper decks for at least the next two hours. He knew that radiation could pass through steel, but at that distance there was realistically very little danger from fall-out, and the blast wave would dissipate long before it could reach them.

North American Aerospace Defense Command, Cheyenne Mountain, Colorado

The klaxon sounded again, startlingly loud in the vast operations room.

'Nuclear detonation! Nuclear detonation! Stand by for location.'

General Harmon looked up at the display screens, his eyes confirming what he was hearing through his headset. 'Whereabouts, for fuck's sake?'

'North Pacific Ocean. Approximately fifteen hundred miles north-east of Hawaii. It now looks like the North Korean missile was a live one.'

'Mr President,' Harmon said, his voice high with tension, 'I repeat there's no danger to us or anyone else, but we've just detected a nuclear detonation in the North Pacific. One of the devices deployed from the North Korean missile was obviously a functioning nuclear weapon.' The silence on the line was so long that for a moment Harmon thought the communication link must have failed. 'Mr President?'

'Still here, General. What's the location of the explosion?'

'Roughly fifteen hundred miles north-east of Hawaii, sir. And that means—'

'I know what it means, General. It means the fucking North Koreans can now deliver a nuclear payload to the west coast of mainland America.'

Office of the Associate Deputy Director of the Central Intelligence Agency, Langley, Virginia

'I don't believe it,' Walter Hicks said. In front of him lay a series of photographs of the aftermath of the nuclear detonation in the Pacific, taken from surveillance satellites, and a hastily prepared schematic showing the path the North Korean missile had followed. This did, Hicks had to admit, suggest that the warhead had been responsible for the detonation.

But if that hypothesis was correct, it left a whole raft of unanswered questions, starting with *how* and finishing with *why*.

'What have we got from Ok'pyong?' he asked.

Richard Muldoon leant forward and placed three

more photographs on Hicks's desk. 'These,' he said, 'are from the pass immediately before the North Koreans hit the starter button. They show a large, probably three-stage, missile on one of the pads at Ok'pyong. Based on the shadow and the angle of the sun, and making an allowance for the thickness of the launch platform, N-PIC has calculated the height at between one hundred forty and one hundred fifty feet, with a diameter of just over six feet. That means it's a lot bigger than a Scud or a Taep'o-dong 1, so their analysis is that it was almost certainly a Taep'o-dong 2. It had probably been fitted with an elongated nose-cone, as the one they launched back in July zero six from Musudan-ri was only about one hundred twenty-four feet tall.'

'Do you believe North Korea's developed a missile-capable nuclear weapon, and that's what they've just test-fired?'

'I don't know, but it *is* the logical conclusion. There's no doubt that they fired a missile, and there's also no doubt a nuclear weapon was detonated at about the time and at the same place the missile landed. I'm just not certain the two events are linked, not least because all our previous estimates suggested that the Taep'o-dong 2 had a likely maximum range of about four thousand miles. The distance this missile travelled was closer to six thousand. That's a hell of a jump – a massive improvement if it was carrying a nuclear warhead as well. Empty, maybe it could have made the distance – with a weapon on board, I doubt it.'

'How big was the nuke?'

'Think Hiroshima. Ten, maybe fifteen, kilotons, an

absolute maximum of twenty. We'll have a better idea when we get the results of the atmospheric sampling.'

'An air-burst?'

'N-PIC doesn't think so. The Keyhole birds recorded two small merchant ships in the area shortly before the launch from Ok'pyong. Early images showed them sailing south-east in company, but a few hours before the explosion one of them turned north-west towards Polynesia, and the other stopped moving altogether. If the missile was the real deal, the stationary ship probably had a homing device on it – the Taep'o-dong is very inaccurate – and the second vessel then embarked the crew and sailed out of the danger area. Personally, I think we're looking at a redundant merchantman with a bomb in the hold triggered by a timing device. N-PIC's tracking the second ship, and we'll confirm its identity pretty soon, but it looks as if both were flying North Korean flags.'

Hicks leant back in his chair and laced his fingers behind his head. 'This is fucking serious, Richard. If the North Koreans *have* developed a missile that can travel six thousand miles, that puts a hefty chunk of mainland America within range. Whatever the truth about the missile, we now know for sure that Pyongyang's capable of detonating a nuclear weapon outside a hole in the ground in North Korea, and that significantly alters the balance of power in the region.

'It also alters things here in the States. We haven't got an effective anti-missile shield working yet, so if the North Koreans did decide to launch a nuclear attack, there wouldn't be a lot we could do to stop them. I know we could easily turn their country into a radioactive wasteland – and I'm sure Washington would be happy to do just that – but we'd also be looking at a serious death toll over here. Meanwhile, I know the Pentagon has just hiked the DEFCON state to Three, but is there anything else we can do?'

Chapter Sixteen

Sunday
HMS *Illustrious*, Yellow Sea

'What are you going to do now?' Roger Black asked Richter.

They were sitting over the remains of a late breakfast in the Wardroom dining room. During the night, the *Illustrious* had moved further north, and deeper into the Yellow Sea. The Air Group was still flying continuous sorties, the Harriers carrying out Combat Air Patrols with live weapons, and the Merlin squadron doing ASW operations – for real. The North Koreans possessed nearly a hundred submarines, ranging from Yugo midget subs to twenty or so Romeo-class patrol boats, locally constructed vessels based on a 1950s Russian submarine. Most of them were armed with torpedo tubes, and just because the Romeos were of an old design, that didn't mean they weren't a threat.

The ship had secured from Action Stations when it became clear that the missile launch from Ok'pyong was an isolated occurrence, but it was still operating at Yellow Alert, the second-highest state, as a precaution. Moving around was difficult, as most of the watertight bulkhead doors in the main fore-and-aft port and starboard passageways were currently being kept closed.

'Frankly, Blackie, I don't know,' Richter replied. 'My

boss sent me here to brief the captain, which I've done, and that's the limit of my instructions at the moment. There's no point in flying me back to Seoul, because there's nothing useful I can do there. Anyway, if the North Koreans do launch an invasion attempt, South Korea's one place I definitely don't want to be.'

There was a roar from above as a Sea Harrier accelerated along the flight deck, followed a few seconds later by the second aircraft of the pair.

'But I can take a turn in a Harrier, if that would be any help. If the squadron's going to be flying CAP sorties round the clock, you're going to need all the pilots you can get. I'm still technically in the Royal Naval Reserve, and I've got about four hundred hours on FA2s, so I think I can probably drive a GR9.'

Roger Black stared at him across the table. 'The trappers would have a field day with that! But these are exceptional circumstances, and it might be useful,' he said. 'The squadron's a man short already, after one of the junior pilots went down with a stomach bug. An extra driver would be no bad thing in the meantime, so I'll talk to the CO, see if he'll bend the rules and have you.'

As the two men stood up, the Tannoy burst into life. 'Commander (Air) and Lieutenant Commander Richter are requested to report to the bridge.'

'They're playing our tune,' Black remarked.

'Yeah,' Richter concurred. 'I'm just not sure I want to stay for the dance.'

FOXBAT

Intercontinental Ballistic Missile (ICBM) Complex, Malmstrom Air Force Base, Great Falls, Cascade County, Montana

The missile control compound was a three-acre fenced-off area out on the perimeter of Malmstrom Air Force Base, but the casual visitor might be forgiven for assuming that he'd been sent to the wrong location.

The entire area was virtually featureless scrubland, surrounded by an eight-foot-high chain-link fence, within which were a handful of pole-mounted floodlights, two wooden huts and six vehicles. On the fence next to the gates was a sign that read 'US Government Property: No Trespassing. Use of Deadly Force Authorized', and beside that a single telephone handset labelled 'Security'.

After approaching the compound at a steady twenty-five miles an hour, the Ford compact braked to a halt. Captain Dave Fredericks climbed out, strode over to the gate and picked up the telephone. He identified himself, quoted his official number, and waited until the electric lock buzzed and the gate swung open. Then he got back into the Ford and drove through the gates towards the first of the two huts. Behind him, the gate swung shut and its lock clicked home.

As Fredericks and his passenger, Major Richard Whitman, entered the wooden hut, they were greeted by two armed guards who then checked their identification cards with extreme thoroughness, despite the fact that both men were known to the guards almost as well as their own families. The two officers were finally ushered towards a small elevator, whose control panel contained two unmarked buttons. After Whitman pressed the lower one, the lift door closed and the elevator descended just over fifty feet.

When the door slid open again, they were facing a short corridor, at the far end of which was a four-ton blast door that could be opened only from the other side. That meant from within the missile control capsule itself. Whitman and Fredericks stood together in front of a closed-circuit television camera, permitting the staff inside the capsule to identify them visually while Fredericks read out their military identification numbers into another telephone handset. A warning bell sounded and the blast door slowly swung open.

The first ICBM silo complexes, constructed in the tense and uncertain years immediately following the end of the Second World War, were fairly small and self-contained, and almost inevitably subterranean. Most of these complexes comprised three launch silos, where the missiles resided vertically below solid concrete half-moon doors, a control centre, living area, and utility sections. Each launch silo contained an ICBM, usually an Atlas, with an equipment and maintenance room to one side and the propellant store on the other. The Atlas was a liquid-fuelled rocket, and the transition from an inactive state to firing readiness was a prolonged and hazardous process, due to the highly volatile fuel.

And there were other dangers, too. The Atlas was an excellent delivery vehicle when it worked, but during an extensive series of test-firings carried out in the early 1960s, launch failures had been both common and spectacular. A missile that detonated its fuel load in or close to its silo was quite capable of destroying the entire launch complex. The introduction of the Minuteman, with its solid-fuel motor, had considerably reduced the inherent risks. As a result, five hundred units of this missile, now in its Minuteman III version, provided the backbone of the American ICBM force.

Unlike the early silos, the current Minuteman launch complexes are huge. Radiating from the central missile control capsule, like the spokes of an immense wheel, are narrow tunnels through which run the communication links to ten Minuteman silos in all. Each is separated from its neighbouring missile, and from the control capsule itself, by a distance of at least three miles, and the hardened silos themselves extend ninety feet deep and are constructed of reinforced concrete designed to withstand the blast effects of a nearby nuclear detonation.

Inside each silo a single LGM-30 Minuteman Three sits on huge coiled springs designed to act as shock absorbers in the event of a nuclear strike. A one-hundred-ton concrete hatch protects each missile from above, and this lid is blown off the silo immediately prior to launch. Sixty feet tall and weighing well over thirty tons, the missile is accelerated by its three-stage solid-fuelled motor to a velocity at burnout of fifteen thousand miles an hour, about Mach 23 at altitude, has a ceiling of around seven hundred miles, and a maximum range that's still classified but is in excess of eight thousand miles. It normally carries three W62, W78 or W87 warheads, each inside a Mark 12A re-entry vehicle contained within the nose-cone, giving a total yield of between one and two megatons, or between sixty times and one hundred and twenty times the explosive power of the Hiroshima weapon.

Usually, the change-over of watch in the control capsule is the occasion for light-hearted banter. All the officers know each other, and frequently meet socially as well as professionally. But not this time. They'd all now been briefed on the detonation of the North Korean nuclear weapon in the Pacific and were well aware that a shooting war was at the very least a strong possibility.

'What's the state of play, Jim?' Whitman asked the outgoing senior officer, Major James Keeble.

'Pretty much what you'd expect. We've been ordered to retarget all missiles at coordinates north of the Demilitarized Zone. Most of the targets are airfields, known missile sites and command centres, but a couple of missiles are aimed at Pyongyang itself. We've run operational readiness and diagnostic checks on all the Minutemen, and the numbers are in the green. We completed that about ten minutes ago.'

'The message folder's over there beside the teletype machine,' Keeble completed his handover briefing. 'Good luck, and look sharp. Today could be real bad news.'

USS *Enterprise*, North Pacific Ocean

CVN-65, the USS *Enterprise* – often referred to as the 'Big E', 'Mobile Chernobyl', or even 'Starship' or 'Starbase' because it shares the name of the spacecraft in the *Star Trek* television series – is the longest naval vessel in the world, at eleven hundred and twenty-three feet. Commissioned in November 1961, it was the first nuclear-powered aircraft carrier, equipped with eight reactors, four propellers and four rudders, and even today, nearly half a century after the vessel was launched, it's still an impressive sight. Displacing nearly ninety-four thousand tons, but still capable of speeds in excess of thirty knots, the ship has a flight deck that extends over almost four and a half acres, and it carries ten squadrons of aircraft that are launched from four steam catapults. The ship's company numbers three and a half thousand, and the air wing adds an additional fifteen hundred personnel. The ship is, by any standards, a massively impressive expression of American military might.

The *Enterprise* was the capital ship of Carrier Strike Group Twelve, and in company with her were the guided-missile frigate USS *Nicholas*, the two Aegis-system guided-missile destroyers USS *Leyte* and USS *McFaul*, and the Fast Combat Support Ship USNS *Supply*. Somewhere in the same stretch of ocean, but invisible to all, was the last vessel in the group, the USS *Alexandria*, a Los Angeles-class nuclear-powered hunter-killer that, like all submarines, remained completely unaffected by the weather on the surface.

The problem faced by the *Enterprise*'s captain was simple enough. He'd been ordered by his controlling authority to divert to the Korean Peninsula, but currently between the ship's position and his destination was a large tropical storm that showed no particular inclination to move anywhere in a hurry.

Steaming right through the middle of this weather system wasn't an option. No competent mariner in his right mind would venture anywhere near a tropical storm, irrespective of the size and power of his vessel, and William 'Buck' Rodgers was extremely competent, for the small handful of naval officers selected to command America's capital ships are the absolute cream of their profession. And even if Rodgers had been prepared to risk such a dangerous passage with the *Enterprise*, there was no way he would expose the other, much smaller, Group Twelve vessels to the same danger. One way or another, they would have to go around it.

He'd summoned his senior meteorological officer and instructed him to calculate the storm's likely track and speed and, once he had the met man's best guess to hand, he had then spent twenty minutes discussing the problem with his ops officer, and deciding the optimum course for the battle group to take.

Only now, twelve hours later, did Rodgers finally leave the bridge and head for his cabin. On his way down, he stuck his head into the met office and congratulated the staff there for their judgement, because they'd been right. The senior met officer had predicted that the depression causing the storm would deepen and head south-east, a movement that would take the worst of the weather away from the *Enterprise*'s direct track towards the Korean Peninsula. And the picture on the weather radar now showed that trend clearly.

The group would just clip the northern edge of the storm, and the sea was already rough, with white horses everywhere and a long swell running. The navigator had told Rodgers that they would be clear of the storm within about five hours, and then they could turn south-west, crank up the engines and head straight for Korea.

They had a long way to go but, at least for the Super Hornets, they should be within flying distance of the peninsula within twenty-four hours.

FOXBAT

HMS *Illustrious*, Yellow Sea

When Richter and Black stepped onto the bridge, they found Alexander Davidson waiting for them. He took a last look through the windows, had a short word with the Officer of the Watch, then motioned for them to follow him down to the Bridge Mess.

'CINCFLEET has finally replied,' the captain announced, as Richter slid the door closed. 'Our American cousins are not entirely certain what happened to the missile launched from Ok'pyong yesterday, but they do know that a nuclear device with a yield between fifteen and twenty kilotons was detonated in the North Pacific ocean on that missile's extended flight-path. The obvious conclusions are that the North Koreans have manufactured a nuclear weapon small enough to be carried by a Taep'o-dong, and that this missile's range has been significantly increased by the addition of a bigger third stage. If those deductions are correct, about a third of mainland America is now under direct threat from the Pyongyang regime.

'And that, I suspect, is why CINCFLEET didn't get back to us sooner. They've been waiting for the Americans to confirm exactly what happened, but they still don't know for sure. Meanwhile, two North Korean merchant ships are known to have been in the area of the Pacific where the detonation occurred, so it's also possible that one of those was carrying the weapon, which was detonated using a timer or radio signal. But, whatever the truth, the Americans now know that Pyongyang definitely has a missile that can reach the US West Coast, and that they possess working nuclear weapons.'

'So what does CINCFLEET want us to do now?' Black asked.

'I've received no further tasking orders,' Davidson admitted, 'so we carry on. That means CAP and ASW patrols, and a permanent AEW Sea King presence. We stay for the moment at Yellow Alert and just hope this whole situation blows over.'

'Rather than blows up?' Black suggested.

'Quite.'

Intercontinental Ballistic Missile (ICBM) Complex, Malmstrom Air Force Base, Great Falls, Cascade County, Montana

'Jim was right,' Richard Whitman muttered, almost to himself. From the moment he'd pressed the button to swing the blast door shut behind the two off-watch officers, the capsule communication systems – comprising speakers, telephones and teletype machines – had remained ominously silent.

Then, twenty-six minutes after Keeble had left, the alarm bell sounded, indicating an Alert Command received from Offutt. Whitman and Fredericks immediately initiated the standard response procedure. Fredericks sealed the blast doors and switched the capsule to emergency air and power supplies, while Whitman, as the senior officer, picked up the red phone that was their link to USStratCom's Primary Alerting System. The voice at the Command Center sounded clipped and somewhat metallic.

'An Emergency Action Message has been received

from the National Command Authority. Standby for immediate retransmission. Out.'

The line went dead but, even before Whitman had replaced the telephone, the high-speed teletype began clattering, spitting out lines of text. Fredericks got to the teletype first, and scanned rapidly over the printed pages.

'This appears to be an authentic Emergency Action Message, sir,' he called out. He tore off the sheets and passed them to Whitman.

'Roger,' replied Whitman, then grabbed a pencil as the overhead speaker crackled into life.

'Stand by for authentication message. Prepare to copy. Message reads Oscar Tango Three Charlie Delta Seven Foxtrot November Papa Juliet Nine Sierra.'

Whitman's fingers flew across the paper, copying down the phonetic symbols that comprised the twelve-digit authentication message. The speaker crackled back into silence and, as Whitman reached for the current launch code, the teletype began printing again, repeating the same authentication as hard copy. Fredericks tore the latest sheet from the teletype and placed it in front of Whitman. Together, the two officers compared the three lines of symbols – the printed launch code, Whitman's hand-written digits and the sheet taken from the teletype.

'Authentication is correct, sir,' Fredericks announced.

'I concur,' Whitman replied. 'Open the box.'

There are two red padded chairs in the missile control capsule, positioned at right angles to each other and a regulation twelve feet apart, into which the duty officers strap themselves when an alert is called. Each chair faces an identical console, on which is displayed the current status of all ten Minuteman missiles, and which also contains the buttons and switches used to launch them.

Between the two chairs, on a wall shelf, is the so-called Red Box. Identical to the boxes found in the cockpits of B-52 and other nuclear-capable bombers and the command and control centres of ballistic missile-carrying submarines, the lid of the box is secured by two combination locks. For added security, each officer knows only one of these numbers. Inside the box is the Emergency War Order containing the Top Secret validation codes that are used to authenticate the Nuclear Control Order when it's issued, and the two silver keys required for missile launch.

The two officers reached up and spun the numbers on the combination locks, which clicked open almost simultaneously. Whitman reached inside the box and pulled out a sealed folder with a bright red cover, and the two firing keys. He passed one key to Fredericks, and put the other one on the console in front of his own chair.

Whitman unsealed the folder and laid it flat. Fredericks then passed him the hard copy of the Emergency Action Message, and the two officers carefully, letter by letter, compared the teletype message with the Top Secret code in the folder. If there was any discrepancy at all between the two, they were ordered to disregard the message and consider it invalid.

Whitman leaned back. 'The Emergency Action Message is verified,' he said, and there was no mistaking the slight tremor in his voice. They'd gone through this routine before, countless times in exercises and endless practise scenarios, but this was the first time, ever, they'd done it for real.

'I concur, sir,' Fredericks said.

'OK, we go to Alert Thirty, by the book. Strap in.'

Both officers moved to their red chairs, sat down and tightened the seatbelts which held them firmly in place.

'Insert keys,' Whitman ordered. 'On my mark, turn to the ready position. Three, two, one, rotate.'

Both keys turned smoothly in their locks, and the two men ran through the well-practised sequence of actions that gradually increased the readiness state of the missiles under their control.

'What now, Major?' Fredericks asked, leaning back in his chair and staring across at his superior officer.

'Now we wait,' Whitman said, 'and hope to Christ somebody out there sees sense before we turn those keys again and start World War Three.'

Pyongyang, North Korea

'Are you certain the Americans now believe we have the capability to strike them at will?'

For a few moments Kim Yong-Su didn't reply, choosing his words with care. 'I cannot guarantee that,' he said, 'but the operation devised by Pak Je-San went precisely as planned. Faced with unequivocal evidence of the missile launch, and the equally obvious detonation of the weapon, there must be only one logical conclusion they can draw.'

'And what of "Golden Dawn"?'

Kim shrugged his shoulders. 'It was always inevitable

that the Americans or the Japanese, and certainly the South Koreans, would become aware of our recent troop movements. I was never totally sure we would be able to allay any suspicions that "Silver Spring" was more than just an exercise. As you know, for "Golden Dawn" to work at all, it was essential we moved our ground forces into the correct positions. There was always the possibility that surveillance satellites would detect our new aircraft, and after the missile firing they'll now be quite certain we have something planned. But we are still not absolutely committed. If you wish it, we can stop "Golden Dawn" even at this stage, and just let the exercise run its course.'

The 'Dear Leader' – the North Korean media had recently stopped using that title, but Kim could think of him in no other terms – shook his head. 'No,' he said firmly, 'we will continue as planned. When will you issue the final order?'

'Today,' Kim replied, 'the moment I leave here, if that is still your wish.'

For a few moments the man said nothing, then nodded slowly. 'We will proceed as planned,' he said, and stood up, his diminutive five-feet-three-inch stature barely augmented by the three-inch platform heels he habitually wore. He then picked out a phrase he liked from one of the many British and American war films in his personal video collection.

'Make it so.'

FOXBAT

HMS *Illustrious*, Yellow Sea

The view along the flight deck was just as Richter remembered it. Beyond Cobra One, the black-painted 'runway' stretched out in front of his Harrier, the ski-jump at the end appearing disconcertingly vertical. Richter's aircraft was callsign Cobra Two. The other Harrier was being flown by a senior squadron pilot.

He'd received a full briefing on the GR9 earlier that morning, but it was essentially the same aircraft that he'd flown previously, the principal differences being the enhanced Pegasus Mark 107, which delivers an extra three thousand pounds of thrust, and the notable absence of the excellent Blue Vixen pulse Doppler radar. Richter thoroughly approved of the more powerful engine but, like every 800 Squadron pilot he'd talked to since he'd arrived on board, he thought the decision to remove the radar was simply crass stupidity. It had all the hallmarks of a political decision made by some elected idiot who wouldn't recognize a Harrier if he woke up inside one.

Richter glanced to his right. The telebrief lead had been removed a couple of minutes earlier, and all they were waiting for now was the green light from Flyco. The ship was swinging steadily to port and picking up speed, turning into the wind to achieve the proper flying course for the Harrier launch.

He felt more than saw the ship's turn slow, and then stop, and he switched his attention to the Flight Deck Officer, who was dividing his time between the two aircraft and the flight deck lights. As Richter watched, they changed from amber to green, and the FDO immediately acknowledged it.

Thirty seconds later, Cobra One accelerated rapidly along the deck, and lifted apparently effortlessly into the air over the ski jump. The moment the first Harrier had cleared the end of the runway, the marshaller directed Richter forward. He lined up his GR9 on the centreline, set the jet efflux nozzles to the correct angle, and waited expectantly.

Moments later, the FDO signalled him to launch, and he pushed the throttle fully forward, the noise of the Pegasus rising to a scream as the jet surged forward. He mounted the ski jump, the landing gear compressing below him as the Harrier instantly changed direction, and moments later he was airborne, the GR9 climbing rapidly away from the ship. Richter began easing the nozzles back into the fully aft position for normal flight, raised the gear and flaps, then pressed his transmit button.

'Homer, Cobra Two is airborne, heading zero six five, and passing four thousand in the climb.'

'Cobra Two, roger. Maintain heading and continue climb to Flight Level three two zero. Cobra One is left eleven o'clock, similar heading and passing seven thousand. Break, break. Cobra One and Two, go tactical.'

'Homer, roger. Break. Cobra Two from Cobra Leader, stud five, go.'

Richter clicked his transmit button in acknowledgement and changed frequency. The Homer position is normally manned by an air traffic controller, and is responsible for the launch and, more important, the recovery of fixed- and rotary-wing aircraft to the ship. But the patrol and combat phases of a flight are invariably conducted under the supervision of a fighter controller.

'Cobra Two.'

'Roger, Cobra One. Cobras, checking in.'

'Roger, Cobras. No trade for you at present,' the AEW Sea King bagman replied. 'Call level at three two zero and maintain heading. Pigeons Mother two four zero at twenty.'

Office of the Associate Deputy Director of the Central Intelligence Agency, Langley, Virginia

'Hi, Richard. You've got more pictures?' Walter Hicks asked.

Muldoon nodded. 'They're not a hell of a lot different from the previous imagery, and show pretty much the same stuff, troop and vehicle movements and so on. But N-PIC has done a more detailed analysis of the military activity as a whole, and I don't much like what they've found.'

He spread several large black-and-white pictures across the conference table. Each had been printed on a sheet of photographic paper that was much larger than the image, so the pictures could be more conveniently surrounded by numerous printed labels and lines pointing out features. All were stamped 'Top Secret/NOFORN' at both the top and bottom.

'I think we're all agreed now that the "Silver Spring" exercise is just a cover. North Korea's definitely gearing up for war. Apart from the troop movements, there's a lot of activity at some of their missile bases, and the only good news is that N-PIC has identified all the weapons on the pads as No-dong medium-range missiles. In other words, no Taep'o-dongs.' He took a pen from his pocket and pointed to one of the images. 'Look at the missile site preps. Getting Sangwon, Yangdok and Chiha-ri up to speed makes sense – those are the closest bases to the Demilitarized Zone – but at these sites we're not seeing missiles actually on the pads, just increased numbers of personnel, trucks and so on. What particularly bothers me is the activity on the east coast of the peninsula, at No-dong, Hochon, Mayang and Ok'pyong.'

'You might be reading too much into that, Richard. Those bases are within easy missile range of Seoul. If the North Koreans are planning an invasion, they might guess we'd take out their most southerly bases, and they're warming up these others as reinforcements.'

'I might agree with you, Walter, except for these pictures.' Muldoon sorted through the images on the table and selected two of them. 'This one is the launch pad at Mayang, and this is Ok'pyong. Notice anything odd about them?'

Hicks leant forward and pored over the images for a few seconds.

'Here,' Muldoon said, and proffered a three-inch magnifying glass.

'Thanks.' A couple of minutes later Hicks sat back in his chair. 'Nothing strikes me as significant there. In each frame I see a missile beside the launch tower but that's about it.'

Muldoon nodded. 'N-PIC has confirmed that they're both No-dong liquid-fuelled weapons. They're a tried and tested design with a range of about twelve hundred miles. What N-PIC is concerned about isn't the missile itself but the trucks parked near the pads in both pictures.'

'What? The five-tonners?'

'That's what they look like, but according to N-PIC those aren't standard trucks. Their sides are solid, probably steel, not canvas, which is unusual. They also have metal rear doors, which again is non-standard. And in one of the pictures the satellite got an oblique view of the interior of one of them, from which evidence N-PIC thinks there's a large metallic object inside it.'

'Which means what?'

'The analysts can't be certain, but there's a strong possibility that these trucks have been built specially to transport nuclear weapons, and their unusual metal structure actually serves as a kind of lead-lined box devised to hold them safely. The design isn't unlike those we ourselves have used in the past. And this picture' – Muldoon selected another one – 'shows what looks remarkably like a warhead being installed in the No-dong on the pad at Mayang.'

Hicks peered back at the images. 'So if the guys at N-PIC are right, the North Koreans may have shipped a couple of their nukes from wherever they store them to Mayang and Ok'pyong. What about the other sites?'

'N-PIC's looking into that right now. The analysts are running back-checks to see if they can trace the routes those trucks took to get to the missile bases. That might confirm, or at least indicate, their likely cargoes. But assuming our deduction *is* right, the question really is why would they be preparing nuclear-tipped missiles at two of their east coast bases?'

'What's the payload of the No-dong? Can it carry a nuke?'

'If you'd asked me that question a week ago, I'd have said "no". But, since the Taep'o-dong launch from Ok'py-ong, my best guess is "maybe". The payload's about one thousand kilograms, well over two thousand pounds. All our analysis to date suggests that if the DPRK has man-aged to fabricate any nuclear devices, they'll be fairly small, around a ten- to twenty-kiloton yield, which is exactly what we saw in the Pacific. And if a Taep'o-dong can carry one, it would probably also be within the No-dong's delivery capabilities.'

'And another aspect to this,' Hicks interrupted, 'is the size of the North Korean nuclear arsenal. How many weapons do they possess? What's the latest estimate?'

Muldoon shook his head. 'It depends who you're speaking to. Until yesterday, guesses could vary from none to about six. Today, some people are talking maybe a dozen or more. But if these pictures mean what we think, that suggests they've got available a minimum of two nukes. Which brings me to the location of those weapons. Why the east coast? They can't target US rein-forcement shipping or the *Enterprise* group because, without surveillance aircraft or satellites, they have no way of knowing where they are. Unless the Chinese are telling them, which is pretty unlikely in the current polit-ical climate. But, in any case, medium-range missiles like the No-dong aren't much use against mobile targets, because they're just not accurate enough. Interceptor-launched air-to-surface missiles are a much better solution.

'That implies their targets are more likely to be static

– downtown Seoul, for example – but the No-dong is really the wrong weapon for launching an attack on any part of South Korea, because it's got too long a range. And we've positioned Patriot batteries all the way along the southern edge of the Demilitarized Zone and around Seoul so their chances of prosecuting a successful attack aren't that good. I'm wondering therefore if they've got another target in mind.'

'You mean Japan?' Hicks looked up sharply. 'You think they'd launch a first strike at Japan?'

'I don't know. They might not need to,' Muldoon replied. 'The threat would probably be enough. Just suppose that is in fact Pyongyang's plan. Once they've got all their assets in position, they simply phone up Seoul, Tokyo and the White House and say they're going to cross the DMZ and occupy the entire peninsula. They've got the troops and armour to do it, easily. And add the scenario that if they meet any resistance from South Korean forces they'll nuke Japan. And, if we try to interfere, they'll do the same to the US west coast.'

'Jesus. Nuclear blackmail with a twist. So these missiles are aimed at Japan, but the real target's South Korea and the US of A.'

'Exactly. And knowing the reputation of that slant-eyed little bastard in Pyongyang, I've no doubt at all that he'd push the button if he had to, because he'd have nothing left to lose. Don't forget that Oplan 5027 includes plans to take control of the entire peninsula if North Korea does launch any kind of an invasion attempt. If he makes the threat and then loses the battle, he knows as well as we do that North Korea will cease to exist within a matter of weeks.'

Muldoon gathered up the photographs and replaced them in the red 'Top Secret' folder on the table.

'So what do we do about it?' Hicks asked, obviously a rhetorical question. 'This is a hell of a case to build on just a couple of satellite images that could easily be interpreted more than one way.'

'I don't know, Walter. I don't know if the N-PIC analysts are right and, if they are, I don't know what we should do about it. But whatever response is appropriate, the Agency certainly won't be involved. This must now be a purely military matter, so I'd suggest going back to the Joint Chiefs through the DNI and passing the buck to them.'

HMS *Illustrious*, Yellow Sea

The Admiralty's intention in sending *Illustrious* into the Yellow Sea had been to try to intimidate the North Koreans into not doing anything stupid, like crossing the DMZ, though just how successful one small carrier and a handful of aircraft would be was obviously a matter of opinion. Richter personally didn't think a nation possessing about the fourth-largest military machine in the world would take much notice, but nobody was ever going to ask his opinion.

His CAP sortie had been entirely uneventful, ninety minutes spent cruising at high level in bright sunshine, and had served really only to reacquaint him with the Harrier. But throughout the sortie he had remained supremely aware that, for the second time in his life, having been involved in the Falklands War as a Harrier pilot on board the *Invincible*, he was flying a fully-armed jet fighter in a potentially, if not actually, hostile environment.

Back on board, he changed and showered, had a meal in the Wardroom, and then went to bed. He was back in the flying programme in less than six hours, so was determined to snatch what sleep he could, when he could.

Pyongyang, North Korea

Kim Yong-Su sat in front of the computer monitor in his office and checked the operational readiness database.

Thirty minutes after he'd been given the order to execute 'Golden Dawn', he'd instructed all the units under his control to report their readiness, and he'd received confirmation from the last airfield, Haeju, just a few minutes before. As far as he knew, everything was now fully prepared for the operation but, as a precaution against incompetence or over-enthusiasm, or even treachery, at a lower level, he'd carefully recorded the name and rank of each officer who'd reported his unit ready in the database, together with the date-time group when that report was made. He'd also tape-recorded each telephone call, and placed every signal in his office safe. If heads rolled after this, Kim Yong-Su was determined that his wouldn't be among them.

He checked the listings yet again, making absolutely sure he'd missed nothing and that the North Korean war machine was in all respects ready for immediate combat, then he picked up the red telephone on the corner of his desk. Of all the instruments in his office, that was the one least used. It connected directly to the private office of the 'Dear Leader' himself.

Kim had no need to dial a number or press a button. Within five seconds a familiar voice spoke in his ear. 'Yes, Comrade Kim?'

'We are ready,' he said simply.

Chapter Seventeen

Sunday
Oval Office, White House, 1600 Pennsylvania Avenue,
Washington, DC

It was the first time Richard Muldoon had ever been inside the White House. Walter Hicks, on the other hand, was very familiar with the security and routine. His meeting with the DNI had been brief, and his discussion with the Chairman of the Joint Chiefs of Staff even briefer. Inside two hours, he and Muldoon had been sitting in the back of an unmarked Agency car heading for Pennsylvania Avenue.

The Oval Office wasn't designed for discussions involving a large number of participants, so only seven people had assembled there. The President and the Secretary of Defense, the Chairman and Deputy Chairman of the Joint Chiefs and the Director of National Intelligence were in attendance, as well as Hicks and Muldoon themselves.

'How *certain* are you of this?' the President demanded as his opening gambit.

'Right now, we're not certain of anything, Mr President. The photo interpreters at N-PIC believe the latest images show four nuclear weapon transport vehicles, and they've traced one of these back to the vicinity of the nuclear plant at Yongbyon. That proves a truck probably adapted to carry a nuclear warhead was driven to a missile launch site, but it doesn't prove the truck was ever at Yongbyon, nor that there was ever a missile warhead in it. It's inevitable that there are always gaps in our satellite surveillance programme, but one picture shot at Mayang does apparently show a warhead attached to the top of the No-dong located on the pad.'

'And what's your take on this, Don?'

General Donald Sterling shook his head. 'I don't know, Mr President. I don't doubt that the North Koreans are up to something, but I still find the idea of them threatening a first strike against Japan difficult to believe. And it wouldn't necessarily work anyway, since we've positioned Patriot PAC-3 missiles at Kadena Air Base on Okinawa, and those should be able to take out most incoming weapons.'

'"Most" isn't "all", General,' Walter Hicks pointed out.

'Agreed, though they'd probably take account of eighty to ninety per cent of any first strike. But my feeling is that a threat against Japan seems altogether too complex and convoluted. The North Koreans aren't interested in Japan: they want to grab control of the southern part of the peninsula. So why don't they just go ahead and invade?'

'Two reasons, General,' Muldoon broke in sharply. 'First, they know the contents of Oplan 5027 just as well as we do. They know that if they just mount up and head south, they'll easily smash through the DMZ and the defences behind it, and maybe even take Seoul. But they also know that we'll land reinforcements within a couple of weeks, and do our best to push them right back where they came from. And that then our intention will be to take Pyongyang and occupy *their* nation. That's indisputable, so if they do want to invade South Korea, and get to stay on there, they're going to have to be clever and sneaky about it.

'That's the first reason. The second is that if they do target Japan with nuclear weapons, the Japanese will scream so loudly under threat that we'll have no option but to back off, to save them from worse. The moment we do that, there's nothing at all to stop North Korea taking the South, and the missile threat will remain even after they've occupied the entire peninsula. If this plan comes off, we could lose South Korea *and* Japan without a shot being fired in anger, and without being able to do a single thing about it.'

'Of course we can do something about it,' Sterling snapped. He wasn't used to being lectured by a civilian – far less a civilian who worked for the fucking CIA – in front of the President of the United States of America. 'We could take out their missile sites, right now.'

'With what, General?' Hicks asked. 'If I recall correctly, the diplomatic moves that we tried earlier didn't get us anywhere, and the only definite response from Pyongyang was that if they were attacked either by the US or the South Koreans, they would consider it an act of war and respond accordingly. If you send in a strike force from south of the DMZ, or use our own silo-based missiles or bombers, that's most definitely an act of war against North Korea.

'Unless you can guarantee to eliminate every single missile and aircraft the DPRK owns, before the dust has settled Pyongyang will have launched whatever they've got left – nuclear, chemical, biological or otherwise –

straight at Seoul and killed half the population of South Korea. And in the eyes of the world it would be *our* fault for launching an unprovoked attack. We'd be censured by every nation on Earth, and the reparations we'd be forced to pay could bankrupt us.'

The silence that followed was broken finally by the President himself. 'Well, General? I think the Agency has made a valid point. Could you actually guarantee to destroy every single North Korean missile and aircraft?'

'Obviously not,' Sterling muttered, fuming.

'Right,' the President said crisply, 'so let's look at our other options. If a first strike is out, what can we do, apart from just standing by and watching? Mr Hicks?'

The ADD had expected this question, but hadn't anticipated that he himself would be the one it was directed at. 'I'm an intelligence professional, Mr President, not a military officer. Therefore I'm not the best-qualified person to answer you.'

'No, but I'd still be grateful for your input.'

Hicks ran through the options in his head. 'Well, I think we should maintain our present high state of alert. That means keeping the bombers in the air and the missiles at short notice for release, and we should tell Pyongyang that we're doing so. I think that's important because it will show them that we're not going to let them get away with any offensive actions. I'd also suggest sending a couple of Aegis cruisers to the Sea of Japan as soon as possible, to engage any missiles the North Koreans do decide to launch.'

Sterling interrupted him. 'The *Enterprise* Carrier Battle Group includes the *Leyte* and *McFaul*, both Aegis guided-missile destroyers. But the Japanese have four *Kongō-*

class destroyers, a modified version of our *Arleigh Burke* design with the same system on board, and they're currently a lot closer.'

The President shook his head. 'Sorry, Don, I've already talked to the Japanese Prime Minister, and he's not prepared to commit any of his own forces at the moment. He doesn't want to risk provoking Pyongyang, and he thinks stationing a couple of Japanese destroyers close enough to the east coast of North Korea to intercept missile launches would be seen as provocative. I might not agree with his position on this, but I can't argue with that reasoning. Anything else, Walter?'

'We'll also need the military ready to roll in case the North Koreans do decide to cross the DMZ. I presume you've already organized reinforcement troops, General?'

Sterling nodded. 'Of course, but the logistics of the situation mean it will still be several more days before the first ships are ready to sail, and then they obviously have to make a lengthy transit.'

'How long?' the President demanded. 'The last briefing I received suggested two weeks in total.'

'We can probably improve slightly on that, sir. The latest estimate is ten days from today to the first of our reinforcement troops landing in South Korea.'

'So if Pyongyang decided to mount a conventional invasion and troops crossed the DMZ tomorrow, say, there'd be *nothing* we could do to stop them, and we wouldn't have enough reinforcements on the peninsula to start pushing them back for nearly two weeks. We'd expect our subsequent campaign to occupy North Korea to last a minimum of a month, assuming, of course, that neither side resorted to the use of nuclear weapons or other WMD. And that's presuming we could manage to dig the North Korean forces out of their bunkers.'

'That's a fair summary, sir,' Sterling responded, 'though we could certainly use the bombers out of Andersen to slow their advance. The Korean terrain means that any war in the peninsula is going to be won or lost on the ground. Air superiority helps, obviously, but it's not the decisive factor that it would be in, say, a European or Middle Eastern conflict.

'The timescale for our campaign in response to an invasion is a real flexible feast because the question of WMD adds a different dimension. The use of these weapons could radically affect the outcome of any campaign in Korea. Whether or not the Agency's right in its belief' – Sterling's tone clearly suggested that he considered this a very remote possibility – 'that Pyongyang *is* trying to play some complicated game using nuclear blackmail to neutralize our likely response, we do already know that the country has the capability to detonate nuclear weapons.'

'We're not yet convinced,' Hicks interjected, 'that the missile they fired was actually carrying the weapon that exploded.'

'Nor am I,' Sterling agreed, 'but I don't believe we can dismiss the possibility. This is a difficult assessment, sir, but we do know the North Koreans have produced working chemical munitions small enough to be delivered by artillery pieces, so they clearly have some expertise in the field. And that's another factor. Their chemical agents include adamsite, phosgene, prussic acid, sarin, tabun and several variants of the mustard gas used back in the

First World War. We believe they've got at least five thousand tons of chemical munitions in storage, mainly in mountain tunnels that are invulnerable to attack except from something like a cruise missile. And we probably wouldn't want to hit them because of the risk of spreading the very agent we're trying to destroy.

'They've done less work on biological weapons because of the danger to their own population if they deployed them, but we do know they've developed weaponized strains of anthrax, bubonic plague, cholera, smallpox and yellow fever. Because we don't know exactly how they've engineered these bioweapons, we can't develop vaccines or inoculate our forces against them, so we'd have to rely on full NBCD suits and masks for protection. And that would make the physical fighting of this war a lot more difficult – the suits are effective, but they're very cumbersome, and the masks can cause problems with communication systems.'

'Are you really saying we might not win a war against them, if it came to that?' the President asked.

'No, sir. We have the technology and the resources to defeat them, that's not in doubt, but it won't be easy. The North Korean conventional forces are imposing enough. Add their probable willingness to scatter chemical and biological munitions over the battlefield, or even use nuclear weapons, especially if they're being forced to retreat, and you'll appreciate that we could face a long, bloody and very costly campaign. If we do end up fighting another war in Korea, my personal belief is that we should be thinking at least in terms of months, not weeks, before we could bring it to a conclusion. And it could very easily turn into another Vietnam.'

The last sentence clearly hadn't pleased the President. 'So what do you suggest?'

'I think we may have to consider the use of tactical nuclear weapons at an early stage in the conflict, preferably after the North Koreans have employed some kind of weapon of mass destruction, so that America will be seen as defending South Korea against an unprovoked attack, but we should also be prepared to use them in a first strike, as that should ensure the campaign will be finished quickly, with a minimum loss of American or South Korean lives.'

The President turned in his seat to look at the Secretary of Defense. 'Do you agree with that assessment?'

'I've no doubt the general's right about Pyongyang's chemical and biological arsenal, and I believe they'd resort to using any and all weapons at their disposal if they thought they were losing the war. I think we should be prepared to employ whatever force is necessary to stop a North Korean attack, and that should include tactical and possibly even strategic nuclear weapons.'

'What about the first strike option?'

The Secretary of Defense shook his head firmly. 'No, Mr President. On that subject I have to agree with the Agency's recommendation. If we initiate a conflict, America will be reviled and there would be the most severe international repercussions. My view is that we should certainly be prepared to use whatever weapons we have, but only in response to an attack initiated by Pyongyang.'

'So what do we do right now?'

'I suggest, Mr President,' said General Sterling, 'we continue with our plans to reinforce the troops we already have stationed in South Korea. I also think we should ensure that Pyongyang is fully informed that we're doing so. We should meanwhile keep our homeland ICBMs at a high alert state, and keep the bombers from Andersen airborne, with fighter support, and close enough to North Korea that they're painting on their surveillance radars. And then we wait for the gooks to either finish this exercise they're allegedly running, or begin whatever the hell else they've got in mind.'

Intercontinental Ballistic Missile (ICBM) Complex, Malmstrom Air Force Base, Great Falls, Cascade County, Montana

As the alarm bell rang again in the missile control capsule, Major Richard Whitman reached out for the red telephone with some trepidation. The keys were inserted and turned to the 'ready' position, and the Emergency Action Message had been authenticated. The next logical step would be the launch itself.

Known as the 'release' message, the Nuclear Control Order is the last instruction given before actual firing of the missile, but is subject to additional verification. A second missile control crew in one of the squadron's other four launch capsules must conduct the same sequence of checks on all the various messages received. Any crew in the squadron can thus delay the launch of a missile if they believe the order to be invalid.

This delay lasts only for a fairly short period, after which the veto is automatically cancelled, but it can be applied as many times as is desired, and a single crew could therefore effectively prevent the launch from taking place.

Finally, to release the missiles, the two officers have to turn their keys to the launch setting simultaneously and hold them there for at least five seconds. This is the reason for the wide separation of the two control positions, as the keys are simply too far apart for one man to turn them both at the same time.

'Stand by for Nuclear Control Order,' said the voice on the telephone. 'Prepare to copy. Nuclear Control Order is code Foxtrot Lima Charlie Two Six Two Seven. Read back.'

'Roger, Command,' Whitman said. 'I copy Nuclear Control Order code Foxtrot Lima Charlie Two Six Two Seven.'

'Affirmative.'

Dave Fredericks already had the Emergency War Order folder open, and was running a stubby finger down the list of Nuclear Control Order codes – the so-called 'Gold Codes' – all of which have seven digits.

'Here,' he said. 'Foxtrot Lima Charlie Two Six Two Seven decodes as "Bring all missiles to Alert Fifteen, and hold at fifteen minutes to launch". At least we're not at war yet,' he added.

'Not quite,' Whitman replied, 'but we're sure as hell getting closer. OK, you heard the man. Start bringing them to the boil.'

Oval Office, White House, 1600 Pennsylvania Avenue, Washington, DC

The Secretary of Defense replaced the telephone handset and turned round. 'Offutt reports our ICBMs are now at launch minus fifteen minutes, Mr President.'

'Let's hope they stay there, as I don't much like this,'

the President said, to nobody in particular. 'We seem to be waiting now on Pyongyang and, if the Agency's right, when they do decide to jump, there might not be a lot we can do about it.' He turned back to Walter Hicks, who was refilling his coffee cup from one of the silver pots the stewards had brought in fifteen minutes earlier. 'We've looked at a nuclear blackmail attempt before, Walter, so how credible do you think this threat is against Japan? Does the Agency feel sure the North Koreans could possess warheads small enough to be carried by their short-range missiles?'

'It's credible enough to take seriously, Mr President. They've been working on their atomic weapons programme for a long time now. Back in the fall of ninety-eight two nuclear weapons were tested at Ras Koh and Wazir Khan Koh in the Kharan Desert in Pakistan. At that time, Pakistan couldn't possibly have produced enough plutonium from its research reactor at Pinstech to create one nuclear device, let alone two. So we believe those tests were joint ventures between North Korea and Pakistan, with Pyongyang – or rather Yongbyon – supplying the fissionable material and most of the technology. That's why we believed they had a credible nuclear capability even before that Pacific explosion, and that's why we should take them seriously now.'

'And you think their intention is genuinely to target Japan?'

'I don't know, sir.' Hicks shook his head in a helpless gesture. 'All I can tell you is that we think they must certainly have a fairly small nuclear arsenal. If they were going to fire weapons across the DMZ into South Korea, we would expect them to use their southerly missile bases, and shorter-range weapons like the Scud B or Hwasong 5 and 6. All three of those can reach the southern tip of the Korean Peninsula, and they've got maybe seven or eight hundred altogether, easily enough to ensure some would get past our Patriot batteries. They'd probably launch non-nuclear missiles to overwhelm the Patriots, and then fire their missiles armed with nuclear warheads towards the end of the barrage. And, of course, there'd be no way of our telling what each missile was carrying until it detonated.

'Preparing to launch nuclear-tipped No-dong missiles from places like Mayang and Ok'pyong only makes sense if they're planning to fire them in an easterly or south-easterly direction. And the only target that's out there is Japan.'

'You seem to be forgetting something, Mr Hicks,' the Secretary of Defense interrupted. 'The No-dong has a fairly limited range, and the shortest straight-line distance from North Korea to Japan – or at least to Kyūshū, on Japan's south-west tip – is directly over the southern end of the Korean Peninsula. If Pyongyang was really trying to threaten Japan, they would be more likely to load the nuclear warheads on missiles at their southernmost bases, which lie just north of the DMZ.'

Hicks shook his head again. 'I disagree, Mr Secretary. As I've just said, if they fired their missiles directly over South Korea, the Patriot batteries would certainly be able to take out some of them. Pyongyang knows we've got Patriots there, even if they don't know their exact locations. To avoid that risk, if they are targeting Japan, launching their missiles on a south-easterly trajectory from bases well to the north of the DMZ is the only strategy that makes sense. That way they'd avoid the Patriots, and once they're in the air we've got nothing that can stop them. I don't have too much confidence in the effectiveness of the PAC-3 batteries on Okinawa, because the best time to intercept an ICBM is during the boost phase, not after the missile's re-entry.'

'And the reality of the situation is that if they *do* manage to detonate an atomic bomb, even a small one, on Japanese soil, we're probably going to get involved in a nuclear exchange,' the President said gloomily. 'After all, we can hardly stand by and let them nuke one of our most important allies in the area. So how effective do you think these Russian aircraft – those Foxbats that the North Koreans have stolen – would be at intercepting our incoming missiles?'

Before Hicks could answer, General Sterling chimed in. 'They wouldn't be a particularly viable defence, Mr President. I know the Russians claim the aircraft was designed for that role, but it's old, it doesn't have particularly good serviceability, and it's probably being flown by North Korean pilots with little real experience of either the aircraft or its weapon systems. They might score some successes against ICBMs, but those aircraft would be useless against nuclear-tipped cruise missiles or air-dropped weapons. If we deliver a nuclear strike, there's no way a handful of near-obsolete interceptors could stop it.'

'I quite agree, General,' Hicks said, 'but what worries the Agency is another aspect of the Foxbat's design: its survivability in a post-nuclear strike environment. If I was a betting man, I'd suggest that the MiG-25's alleged ability to intercept ICBMs is only half of the equation, and perhaps not even the most important half. I believe the main reason for them is because, if an airburst weapon is detonated over the Korean Peninsula, the Foxbat will remain operational because of its old-style valve technology. The EMP, or electromagnetic pulse, will fry everything else. That would give the North Koreans immediate and total air superiority, and don't forget that the MiG-25 is still the fastest interceptor ever built. In the right hands it's therefore a very potent weapon.'

'And that,' Richard Muldoon interjected, 'could indeed be a part of their overall strategy. Target Japan with No-dong missiles tipped with nuclear warheads, and then detonate another weapon over Seoul, say, if we or the South Koreans resist their southern advance. That would virtually eliminate any opposition to their invasion.'

'How dangerous is this EMP?'

'To human beings, Mr President,' Hicks replied, 'it's completely harmless. Obviously the detonation of any nuclear weapon could kill thousands as a result of the blast, burns and radiation, but the electromagnetic pulse just sends an instant power surge through all electronic equipment within range. That cooks solid-state circuitry, unless it's very well shielded, so that would include telephones, computers, radar sets, and most communication devices.

'Our pilots would find their aircraft impossible to fly, especially the new generation of air-superiority fighters. Even those that don't rely on flight-control computers would still find their radars burnt out and their weapon control systems inoperative. Missile radars and infrared homing devices wouldn't work. On the ground, most of our command and control systems would be destroyed, all the way down the line to the radios carried by individual soldiers. Vehicles with engine-management systems wouldn't start or run. Targeting computers in tanks wouldn't work. Even electronic devices like digital watches would fail.

'In short, we'd be reduced to fighting the kind of battle last seen in the First World War – with no smart weapons, very few working vehicles, and poor or non-existent communications. And, worse still, the only aircraft flying overhead would be those operated by the North Korean Air Force.

'It's also possible that, if Pyongyang scheduled the nuclear detonation precisely – I mean, if *they* decided when they were going to trigger it rather than react to a counter-attack by us – their armed forces could power down their own electronic equipment and get their vulnerable assets into underground shelters for the duration. That wouldn't guarantee everything would work when they hauled it out again, but almost certainly they'd be left with a better battlefield capability than we would.'

For a few moments the President sat in silence, sipping his coffee thoughtfully. Finally, he replaced his cup on the table and leant back in his chair. 'I hear the Secretary of Defense's opinion about the possible consequences of us initiating a first strike against North Korea, but I'm beginning to think that it might be the only way we could win this thing.'

'Mr President, I must strongly advise—'

'Hear me out, please. You people are my military and intelligence experts. What you've told me so far is that

North Korea probably has missile-deliverable nuclear weapons and is most likely to target them on Japan, and even the USA, as nuclear blackmail to stop us resisting their invasion of South Korea. If we counter-attack, they could detonate a nuclear air-burst over the peninsula that will cripple our conventional forces. The implication is that we won't be able to roll them back north of the DMZ the way Oplan 5027 envisages, and the only option we'll be left with is surgical nuclear strikes with cruise missiles and the like. And even if we do that, they could still launch a nuclear attack on Japan, and that would generate an international political shit-storm like we've never seen before. And it's still possible that we could lose South Korea to their invasion. Is that a fair summary?'

Heads nodded, but none of the men in the Oval Office responded verbally.

'OK, so it seems to me that the only way we can avoid getting royally shafted by that little bastard in Pyongyang is to hit him first. I know they could still launch a massive assault on Seoul, but if we can take out their long-range missile sites – the ones with the No-dong weapons – we could at least prevent an attack on Japan. That seems to me to be our first priority. If we can keep this conflict within the Korean Peninsula, we'll have a much better chance of coming out smiling. Anyone disagree with that?'

'With the principle, no, Mr President,' the Secretary of Defense said, 'but I'm still very unhappy with the idea of America launching a first strike – especially a nuclear first strike – on a country that, as far as the rest of the world is concerned, is apparently just conducting a military exercise. Whichever way you look at it, and however you try to justify it, that would still be accounted an act of war.'

'There might,' Richard Muldoon said tentatively, 'just might, be a way around that.'

'What?' the President demanded. 'How?'

So Muldoon told him.

Hammersmith, London

Richard Simpson wasn't normally to be found in his office at weekends, but the escalating crisis in Korea had changed all that. However, as it was a Sunday he'd forgone his usual grey pinstripe suit and Churchill brogues in favour of blue slacks, an open-neck shirt and loafers. He looked as if he should be out on a golf course somewhere, but nobody had the time or the inclination to point this out to him.

He was reading the overnight messages and signals when the Intelligence Director knocked on his door and walked in.

'The Americans,' the ID announced, 'have come up with a plan.'

This was one of the shortest sentences Simpson had ever heard him speak, and the slightly shocked expression on the man's face suggested that whatever scheme Washington or Langley had concocted might be the reason for that.

'Which is?' Simpson prompted.

'They want us, or rather the Royal Navy, to attack four North Korean bases and destroy missiles they believe could be carrying nuclear payloads and are aimed at Japan.'

'Do they, now? Let me see.'

The ID handed over the slim folder he was carrying and sank down into the chair facing Simpson's desk. 'It would amount to an act of war and an unprovoked assault, so it's absolutely out of the question.'

'Not necessarily,' Simpson argued, reading quickly through the four pages that the folder contained.

'You can't be serious, Director. We have no authority to instigate such an action, and I very much doubt if their Lordships at the Admiralty would look upon it with favour.'

'You're not keen on the idea?' Simpson stated the obvious.

'No, not at all.'

'Well I like it. The tricky bit's going to be selling it to the Navy, but if it's packaged right they might just go for it.'

'I cannot support this proposal, and you should be aware that I will have to put my objection in writing if you elect to proceed.'

'Objection noted. Now get out of here and organize me a car and driver. Then pre-warn Northwood that we'll want a conference with CINCFLEET staff as soon as we arrive.'

'Are you expecting me to accompany you?'

'Certainly not. You'd only depress everyone. So you can hold the fort here. I'll take whichever wheel I can raise at Legoland.'

The sniff as the ID stood up and headed for the door was more eloquent than anything he could have verbalized. Simpson stared after his retreating back for a moment, wondering if it would be worth while trying to find someone more amenable to replace him, then picked up the scrambled phone and dialled Vauxhall Cross.

Office of Commander-In-Chief Fleet (CINCFLEET), Northwood, Middlesex

'The admiral is extremely busy, gentlemen. As you'll appreciate, the crisis on the Korean Peninsula is occupying most of his time, and I very much doubt if he'll be able to see you.' The captain was clearly unimpressed by these two men – a senior Secret Intelligence Service officer, and the head of an outfit he'd never even heard of – demanding to see the Commander-In-Chief Fleet.

But Richard Simpson was not a man used to having obstacles thrown in his way. 'Listen to me, Captain, I hold a rank equivalent to an Air Vice Marshal and my colleague here is slightly more senior than that. We have information for your admiral that could significantly affect the outcome of the Korean crisis, and that he will definitely want to hear. If we don't get to see him within the next fifteen minutes, I'll be making two calls tomorrow morning and by the end of the week you'll be down at the Job Centre – that's if the admiral himself doesn't fire you first. Do I make myself clear?'

'Perfectly . . . sir.' The captain appeared unfazed, and the second word came as an obvious afterthought. 'But I still doubt if the admiral will find time to see you. However, it's his decision, not mine, so I'll convey the substance of your message to him.'

'Nice going, Richard,' Nicholas Ashton remarked as the captain left the room. 'Nothing like issuing a blatant threat or two to ensure we get all the willing cooperation we need.'

Ashton was P4 at SIS – his full title was Head of the Middle East Controllerate of the Directorate of

Requirements and Production – and he was the most senior officer Simpson had been able to rustle up at such short notice.

'Threats usually work, in my experience.' Simpson smiled nastily. 'You'll notice that at least he's now gone to ask.'

Five minutes later the captain returned and beckoned to them. 'If you'll follow me, please.'

He led them down several flights of stairs, descending well below ground-level into the semi-hardened operational headquarters, and finally pulled open a heavy steel door. The room beyond was vast, rising at least three storeys high, and expansive enough to accommodate over fifty people working at separate consoles arranged in rows. On the wall facing them was a huge screen currently displaying the Korean Peninsula in considerable detail, dotted with red marks indicating DPRK troop concentrations, airfields and missile sites. On the screen beside it, a larger-scale display showed the entire action area with Allied force dispositions. At first glance, this was noticeably less impressive, the principal symbols indicating the two halves of the *Illustrious* group in the Yellow Sea and the Sea of Japan respectively, and the *Enterprise* Carrier Battle Group still some distance out in the North Pacific.

Several senior Naval officers stood looking up at the screens. The captain led the way over to them, and made the necessary introductions.

'I understand you have some information relevant to the present crisis?' the admiral inquired.

'Not entirely,' Simpson replied first. Though, as the Head of an SIS Controllerate, Ashton was technically his senior, this was Simpson's ball and he fully intended to run with it. 'We have exactly the same information, but I know something about it that you don't.'

'I don't have time for riddles, Mr Simpson, so tell me what's on your mind.'

'You've had a request from Washington about undertaking a possible first strike against North Korean missile facilities? A strike, in fact, using the Harriers from *Illustrious*?' Simpson opened a notebook and read out a date-time group.

'Yes,' the admiral replied, 'we've received that signal, but I'm not sure the Americans entirely grasp the magnitude of what they're asking from us.'

'Actually, I think they have grasped it, and SIS believes such action might be the best response to whatever nasty little plan Pyongyang has cooked up.' The admiral opened his mouth to reply, but Simpson didn't give him the chance. 'As we see it, there are exactly two choices here. If we sit back and do nothing, and just wait for the North Koreans to push their way south across the DMZ, or launch a nuclear attack on Japan or whatever else they intend to do, we'll be forced to react *after* the event. If the Americans are right, the North Koreans' attempted nuclear blackmail might well work because, even if South Korea is occupied by the DPRK and Japan simultaneously held hostage, that's still a far better outcome than the probable alternative, meaning an exchange of nuclear weapons that would leave a million corpses rotting in Seoul and probably twice that number in Tokyo.

'The ace in the hole that Pyongyang holds is their possession of nuclear weapons, but they can't have that many so they've got to use them intelligently, hence their probable plan to strike at Japan. If they merely fired them into South Korea, the American Patriot batteries would hopefully take them out, and then the US war machine would roll the invading forces back across the DMZ, all the way to Pyongyang, which would be a military disaster for the North. So I think Washington is right in its thinking.

'The only ploy that makes sense is that North Korea should threaten an American client state, which describes Japan fairly accurately, and hope that by doing so it will keep the Yanks off the playing field. The second string to their bow involves their recent demonstration in the Pacific that clearly shows they have missiles able to reach mainland America. Pyongyang may be confident that those two threats will be enough to stop the US getting involved any further. Then they can cross the border in the reasonable certainty that the South Korean armed forces will offer them little or no resistance, simply because the government in Seoul will realize that the Americans won't be coming to bail them out.'

'You appear to be remarkably well informed, Mr Simpson.'

'I am, Admiral, because that's my job. Now, if we can eliminate the nuclear threat, taking out the No-dong missiles, Pyongyang's going to have to rethink all this. If they can't threaten Japan, they have one less lever to use in persuading the Americans not to interfere. And there are still a lot of unanswered questions about what happened out there in the Pacific. The CIA isn't convinced that missile was actually carrying the weapon. Instead, they think the nuclear device was positioned on the ship the North

Koreans allegedly used as a target, and that it was in fact detonated using either a timer or a radio signal. In short, they reckon it was a bluff that now the US might just call.

'I'm quite sure the North Koreans well know that if they do launch a conventional invasion, and they haven't already neutralized America, their country will then cease to exist as an independent state within about a month. So, if we manage to take out the nukes, we could well be stopping this whole operation in its tracks. No missiles could equal no invasion. It's as simple as that.'

'I don't dispute anything you've just said, but the reality remains that such an attack would constitute an act of war. That needs government approval and, after the mess in Iraq, your chances of persuading Downing Street to sanction this action are, I suspect, substantially less than zero. I exercise functional and operational control of that ship, but there's no way I can authorize HMS *Illustrious* to launch a first strike against North Korea.'

'No,' Simpson agreed, 'but I can.'

'What?' The astonishment in the admiral's voice was obvious, and the expressions on the faces of the other naval officers told the same story.

'In a manner of speaking, anyway.'

'You'd better explain that.'

'I've already got one of my men on board the *Illustrious*.'

The admiral looked keenly at Simpson. 'Are you telling me one of the ship's present company works for *you*?'

'No.' Simpson shook his head. 'He's been investigating a number of Foxbats that went missing in Russia, and seem to have since found their way to North Korea. So I sent him down to Seoul first, and then on to the ship to deliver a briefing to the captain and senior officers. He's still there now. His name's Paul Richter and he's a former naval officer and a qualified Harrier pilot, so he can take an aircraft and do the job solo.'

The admiral looked somewhat stunned. 'I presume you don't have any kind of a military background, because you clearly have no conception of the logistics involved in such an operation. Your man Richter can't simply climb into a Harrier, pop over to North Korea and destroy a handful of missiles. It's not like hiring a Ford Fiesta from Hertz.'

A polite titter passed round the assembled officers.

Simpson nodded patiently. 'Richter's very resourceful. I'm sure he'll find a way.'

His quiet confidence seemed to unsettle the admiral. 'Very well, let's assume he did manage to do it. How are you going to overcome the diplomatic problem that a pilot in a Harrier flown from a Royal Navy aircraft carrier has launched an unprovoked attack on North Korea?'

'Three things to mention. First, it isn't my intention to launch an unprovoked attack. If North Korea's actually entirely innocent and just playing war games to keep the population busy and take their minds off the dire state their country is in, fine. We can all go home and forget any of this ever happened. I'll only instruct Richter to execute this action if and when Pyongyang makes a hostile move, or else issues some kind of ultimatum.

'Second, if this plan works, the last thing anyone's going to worry about is which aircraft or pilot did the job. Third, Richter's now a civilian, and nothing to do with the Royal Navy. If push comes to shove, I'll concoct a story that he had a sudden brainstorm and pinched the jet.'

'You'll throw him to the wolves?' Ashton asked.

'No way,' Simpson shook his head decisively. 'He's far too valuable to me to lose. Whatever the outcome, I'll make sure he's protected.'

HMS *Illustrious*, Yellow Sea

The knocking on his cabin door was loud and sudden, and woke Richter immediately. He felt like he'd been asleep for only a matter of minutes, but from looking at his watch he saw that it was early evening.

'Coming,' he called, rolled out of the bunk and wrapped a towel around his waist. He slid the cabin door back and peered out. A communications rating stood in the corridor, a clipboard and a buff envelope in his hand.

'Sorry, Commander. We've received Secret Flash traffic for your eyes only.' He offered the clipboard. After Richter scrawled an approximation of his signature in the correct column, the rating handed him the envelope and walked away.

Richter sat on the edge of the bunk, ripped open the envelope and pulled out three sheets of paper covered in double-spaced printing in capital letters. He glanced at the originator – SIS via CINCFLEEET – and quickly read the text. Then he read it again.

'Fucking Simpson,' he muttered, stood up and began to get dressed.

Chapter Eighteen

Sunday
HMS *Illustrious*, Yellow Sea

Richter found Roger Black in Flyco, precisely where he'd expected him to be.

'Blackie, a word in private, if you can spare the time.'

Black looked down at his flying programme. Two Harriers had taken off ten minutes earlier, and they were now expecting the two aircraft they'd relieved to land-on shortly.

'Will this take long?' Black muttered distractedly.

Richter nodded. 'It might.'

'Right, just wait till we've recovered these two jets, then I'll be with you.'

At that moment the intercom buzzed from the Ops Room, and Lieutenant Commander (Flying) pressed the key to answer. The intercom was on speaker, and his voice echoed from it: 'Flyco.'

'Flyco, Homer. Cresta One and Two are on recovery, estimate minutes three. Request flying course.'

'Roger, Homer. Clear to the low wait. Call visual.'

Richter leant back against the bulkhead and watched. Numerous things had to happen now at more or less the same time, and the intricate process always fascinated him.

Little F pressed another intercom key. 'Bridge, Flyco. We have two Harriers on recovery, request DFC.'

The Officer of the Watch didn't use the intercom to reply, but instead appeared at the opening to the bridge.

'We're turning now, sir, and increasing speed. I'll call steady.'

'Thank you.' Little F selected the flight deck broadcast. 'Flight deck, Flyco. Stand by to recover two Sea Harriers, number three spot.'

On the deck below, the FDO raised one hand in acknowledgement.

'Flyco, Officer of the Watch. Steady on DFC of two four five.'

'Roger.'

'Homer, Flyco. DFC two four five.'

'Flyco, Homer, roger.'

'Flyco, Homer. Cresta are visual with the ship, coming to your frequency.'

'Roger that.'

And then a new voice, clipped and precise, broke in. 'Cresta Two.'

'Cresta One, loud and clear. Break, break. Flyco, Cresta One with Two in company, visual. At the slot.'

'Cresta, Flyco, roger. Wind down the deck at twenty-two, gusting twenty-five. No circuit traffic.'

'Copied. Landing order will be Two, then One.'

Richter heard the roar overhead as the two Harriers overflew the ship and turned to port to start their left-hand circuit, the distance between them opening sharply. The pilot of the second aircraft had to allow time for the first to come to a hover alongside, then land, and finally move off the spot before making his own final approach.

'Green deck fixed wing,' Lieutenant Commander (Flying) ordered.

The rating sitting at the control panel made the appropriate switch and echoed the order: 'Aye, aye, sir. Green deck fixed wing.'

Richter watched critically as the first aircraft began approaching the ship, speed dropping away as the pilot used vectored thrust to slow the Harrier until it was exactly matching the *Illustrious*'s forward speed of eighteen knots. The scream of the Pegasus was very audible even through Flyco's armoured glass. The pilot visually checked the deck, watched for the FDO's signals, then began transitioning to starboard.

Above three spot, the aircraft stopped and Richter, who had hundreds of hours' flying time in the same type, marvelled again at the sudden immobility in mid-air of the sleek fighter. Then the pilot reduced the thrust and the Harrier started descending. It hit the deck fairly hard – most Harrier vertical landings are best described as 'firm' – and then almost immediately taxied away towards the forward end of the flight deck, clearing the way for his wingman, who was already moving alongside the ship, to land.

The second landing was a mirror image of the first, and the moment the Harrier touched down Roger Black stood up. 'Good landings,' he said, touching Little F on the shoulder. 'Tell the Senior Pilot I said so, please.'

'Will do, sir.'

'That used to be the Royal Navy's definition of exceptional flying ability, if I remember rightly,' Richter said. 'The same number of take-offs as landings?'

'It still is,' Black replied. 'I'll be in the Bridge Mess,' he added to Little F, 'listening to Spook's bad news. It *is* bad news, I presume?'

'It is for someone,' Richter agreed, and followed Black out of Flyco and down the stairs.

Intercontinental Ballistic Missile (ICBM) Complex, Malmstrom Air Force Base, Great Falls, Cascade County, Montana

'Stand by for Nuclear Control Order. Prepare to copy. Nuclear Control Order is code Oscar Charlie Three Lima Nine Four Sierra. Read back.'

'Roger,' Whitman said, looking down at the paper in front of him. 'I copy Nuclear Control Order code Oscar Charlie Three Lima Nine Four Sierra.'

'That's affirmative.'

Whitman looked over at Fredericks, who had copied down the release code as Whitman read it back to USStratCom, and was checking the Emergency War Order folder.

'OK, we're still not launching anything,' he said, passing the folder over to Whitman for verification. 'Code Oscar Charlie Three Lima Nine Four Sierra decodes as "Bring all missiles to Alert Five, and hold at five minutes to launch". Looks like we're still in an escalating situation.'

'Roger that,' Whitman said, and glanced at the rows of tell-tales in front of him. The one labelled 'Strategic Alert' was illuminated, but all the others – 'Warhead Armed', 'Ready to Launch', 'Launch in Progress' and 'Missiles Away' – remained dark. And, as he began running through the familiar sequence of commands that would bring and then hold all missiles at five minutes' notice to launch, Richard Whitman fervently prayed that they'd stay that way.

HMS *Illustrious*, Yellow Sea

'Is it just me, or is this sheer fucking madness?' Roger Black asked. He was sitting at the small table in the Bridge Mess, and for the third time was reading the signal Richter had received earlier.

'It's not just you, Blackie.'

'And why am I reading this anyway? It says specifically it's for your eyes only.'

'I don't care about the distribution list. My boss has no clue about the way a warship works. He doesn't seem to realize there's no possible way I could do something like this without serious support from the ship.'

'It doesn't mention your section here. This signal was authored by somebody at SIS, following a request from the CIA.'

'That's what it says,' Richter agreed, 'but this smells like a typical Richard Simpson set-up. The Company may well have requested assistance from us because we're here and on the spot, but I'll bet the rest of this plan was concocted by Simpson himself.'

Black put the three sheets of paper down on the dining table. 'So what are you going to do?'

'First,' Richter said, 'I'm going to ask you formally if the ship will assist me. You're Commander (Air), so you own the Air Department. If you say "No", that's the end of it as far as I'm concerned. I can't do this without support.'

'What do *you* want me to say?'

Richter wearily rubbed a hand over his face. 'Frankly, I'd be quite happy if you told me to get lost. But I can't ignore this.' He pointed at the signal between them. 'I'm out of touch with the latest intelligence, obviously, but this looks to me as if it's come straight from the CIA, and I think their analysis – or what proportion of it I can deduce from this – is probably right. If it is, then what they're suggesting does make sense. More importantly, if we *don't* comply, we'll quite likely find ourselves in the middle of a shooting war that will include nukes from both sides. And however you slice it, that's really bad news.'

Black glanced down at the signal before replying. 'If you go ahead with this, we're going to be in a shooting war anyway.'

Richter nodded. 'I know, but it's probably the better of the two alternatives.'

'Right,' Black said. 'If you want my support, you've got it. I'll go and talk to the captain. I'm sure he'll be amenable.'

'He probably will be. He'll be out here safe in the Yellow Sea, in this steel war canoe bristling with close-in weapon systems and surrounded by frigates and Harriers on CAP. I'll be the one out in the bundu getting my arse shot at.'

Black grinned at him and stood up. 'That's true, but at least he'll be thinking of you.'

'Do you want me to tag along now?'

'Probably better not, but I'll take the signal, if you don't mind.'

'Be my guest.'

Roger Black returned to the Bridge Mess five minutes later and opened the door to let the captain enter first. Richter stood up but Davidson motioned him back to his seat, then sat down opposite. 'I'm not entirely happy about this, Mr Richter.'

'I'm not wild about it myself, sir. But from what I know of the situation it might actually be the most sensible course of action.'

'I don't dispute that. What I'm concerned about is the suggestion that you undertake this as a solo mission. I think you'll need help.'

Richter shook his head immediately. 'I can't ask anyone else to do this, sir. It's going to be hairy enough for me.'

Davidson turned to Black. 'What's your opinion, Wings?'

'I don't think you'll pull this off by yourself, Paul. I know you're a very competent pilot, and your record speaks for itself, but you've been away from regular flying for some time. You're not that familiar with the new weapons on the GR9, but even if you were, this is a highly dangerous mission into very hostile territory. At the very least you're going to need a wing-man to watch your back.'

'So what are you suggesting? You can't make this an official operation. This signal makes that quite clear.'

Black unfolded the sheets of paper and glanced down at them. 'I agree. The exact wording they've used here is "an illegal act by a renegade pilot".'

'That'll be me,' Richter said. 'And I think it would be a lot more difficult to explain it away as "illegal acts by a squadron of renegade pilots".'

'We're not talking about a squadron, Paul, or anything like it,' Black said. 'I'm thinking about one wing-man beside you, and one or two above to provide top cover. Or perhaps two pairs to hit two targets each. That's four aircraft maximum.'

Richter's gaze switched between the two men. 'I think we need to be absolutely clear about this,' he said. 'If you give me the go-ahead for this it will be an illegal act – an act of war, in fact – against a country that's expressed no hostile intent whatsoever towards the United Kingdom. If I don't make it back, the best outcome would be for me to go down with the aircraft. If I'm captured, I've no doubt I'll spend some time in a cellar somewhere having my fingernails pulled out and various bones messily broken before they finally stick what's left of me up against a wall and summon a firing squad. And the same will apply to any other pilot who goes in with me.

'That's one aspect of the situation. The other is that their Lordships at the Admiralty will probably not be entirely delighted if the captain and senior aviation officer on a Royal Navy capital ship are found to be conspiring with a civilian pilot to commit the said act of war. My guess is that the subsequent court martial would be the least of your worries. We could be talking of dismissal from the service, loss of pension rights and all the rest. Maybe even a charge of treason. This is serious stuff.'

Davidson smiled thinly. 'I have a substantial private income, Mr Richter. I'm in the Navy because I like it, not because I have to be. I'll make it clear that the final decision was mine, and I'll issue appropriate orders to all those involved. If this particular can of worms ever gets opened, I'll make sure I'm the one in the firing line.'

It was a somewhat mixed metaphor, but Black and Richter knew exactly what he meant.

'Obeying an order an officer knows to be illegal is also a courtmartial offence,' Richter pointed out. 'But if I handed you a copy of that signal with a few changes on page two, you wouldn't know the order hadn't come direct from CINCFLEET and, unless you went down to the CommCen to see the original, you'd never know that I'd made any alterations. That might provide a bit of protection.'

'True,' Davidson said, 'but that would put you right in the frame if this all goes wrong.'

'I'm used to that. About the only advantage in working for Richard Simpson is that he'll do whatever's necessary to protect his staff, as long as he thinks what they've done is justified. As this' – he pointed at the signal – 'is almost certainly his idea, he'll find it very difficult to do anything other than support me. So don't worry about my career, such as it is.'

'Right,' Davidson said. 'I think we have a broad agreement. I'll order our escorts to new positions, and move the ship closer to the North Korean coast. Wings, have a quiet word with a few of the more enthusiastic squadron pilots and ask them if they'd like to go along for the ride.'

'Aye, aye, sir.'

Davidson stood up and extended a hand. 'Good luck, Mr Richter. I hope to see you back on board when this is all over.'

FOXBAT

Pyongyang, North Korea

Kim Yong-Su was not surprised that he'd heard nothing further from the 'Dear Leader'. He was well aware of the significance of the action they were planning, yet despite all the time and preparation that had been involved, he still wasn't certain Pyongyang would actually go through with it.

But late that evening his direct telephone line rang, and the voice he heard sounded full of confidence as the 'Dear Leader' announced that 'Golden Dawn' would start at precisely 0530 local time the following morning, with the first troop movements at 0630.

HMS *Illustrious*, Yellow Sea

'You have three volunteers to go along with you,' Roger Black announced as he walked in and closed the door behind him. Richter was in the admiral's quarters at the stern of the ship, just forward of the Quarter Deck, maps of North Korea spread out over the dining table in front of him. 'They're the Senior Pilot, and two of the most experienced men on the squadron: Charlie Forbes and Roger Whittard. You'll make a good team.'

'I'm still not sure that it's such a good idea.'

'I disagree, and so does the captain. You've about a one per cent chance of pulling this off if you go in by yourself. With a four-aircraft group, the odds are maybe fifty per cent.'

'That good, eh?'

Black smiled at him. 'Well, maybe a *little* better than that.'

Richter picked up a large buff envelope, prominently marked 'Secret' at top and bottom and with a large red 'X' on each side. 'I've got the latest satellite imagery, but it only confirms what we already thought. The No-dongs that the Yanks think have nuclear payloads are located at Mayang and Ok'pyong, those being the two most southerly missile bases on the east coast, and at Hochon and No-dong.'

'Do they want you to hit all four of them?'

Richter nodded. 'Yes, they're desperate to knock out anything the North Koreans have got that can reach Japan. The east coast missiles *must* be destroyed. Everything else is of secondary importance.'

'And do they really think that having us carry out this mission will prevent a North Korean invasion?'

'It's a fine line. Because Pyongyang threatened that any attack by South Korea or the Americans would be considered an act of war, there's some chance that if we do it, the North Koreans might be confused and not react, or not react as violently. And that might work: after all, *I'm* confused, and I'm supposed to know what's going on. But if the Americans are right, and whatever plan Pyongyang has cooked up relies on these missiles and their warheads being available, taking them out will certainly fuck things up for them. If they don't have any nukes to threaten Japan, the invasion of the South might have to be called off. That's what the Americans are gambling on.'

'Is it worth while doing anything to sanitize the aircraft?' Black asked.

Richter considered the question for a few moments.

'If one does get shot down, a new paint job isn't going to fool anyone, and the whole point of this is that the attack aircraft must clearly not be American, so the "Royal Navy" logos and squadron markings should stay. That might tell any eyewitnesses that the aircraft are British, though I doubt if many North Koreans would be able to recognize a Harrier. And especially not one that's two hundred feet above the ground doing about five hundred knots. They'll hear it, but they probably won't ever see it.'

'You still think a low-level approach is best?'

'I don't think there's much choice, Blackie. If we go in at high or medium level, we'll get picked up by radar and every SAM battery and anti-aircraft gun emplacement within range will start shooting at us. Not to mention having to tangle with their Fishbeds and Floggers, and at high level a Foxbat would eat a Harrier for breakfast. At low level, the GR9 can outrun, or at least outmanoeuvre, anything they've got, I hope. A high-speed, low-level quick in-and-out is the only way this is going to work.'

Oval Office, White House, 1600 Pennsylvania Avenue, Washington, DC

'Welcome back, Walter. You've some news for us? Good news, I trust?'

'News, Mr President, yes,' Walter Hicks said, sitting down in front of the desk. 'But "good" isn't the word I'd use to describe it. It looks as if Pyongyang is moving additional troops closer to the northern edge of the Demilitarized Zone, and our satellites have detected activity at most North Korean airfields.

'Normally, they keep their aircraft in the hardened shelters dug into the mountains, but we're now seeing quite a few Ilyushin 28 bombers parked out on hardstandings, and some have begun running their engines – the heat blooms are unmistakable. Just as worrying is that there are also large numbers of fighters on the ramps, mainly Sukhoi Su-25s, MiG-19s, 21s, 23s and Shenyang F-5s. Those are all old and fairly obsolete types, but we've also counted twelve Foxbats.'

'And the implication is that they're gearing up for military action?'

'It's difficult to put any other interpretation on it, Mr President. Historically, the North Koreans have always been frugal in their use of aviation fuel, because they haven't got much of it, and their pilots carry out the minimum possible numbers of sorties per year as a result. We've *never* seen anything like this level of activity before. Nor do they seem concerned that we can clearly see what they're doing, yet they obviously know we have satellites overflying the peninsula, because in the past they've taken care to restrict their activities to those periods when none of our birds were within range.'

'Perhaps they know the preparations they must make are too extensive to be carried out between passes,' the President suggested.

'Perhaps,' Hicks agreed. 'The other, less attractive, explanation is that they *want* us to see that they're gearing up for war. They want us to be aware that they're serious. In that case, some kind of an ultimatum or demand might be on its way to us right now.

'But I do have one small piece of good news. The Agency's been contacted by the British SIS, and they've said that they will be able to launch an air raid into North Korea should it become necessary. They'll send a Harrier from the warship *Illustrious* and aim to hit the east-coast missile bases.'

'Just one aircraft? Will that be enough?'

'Apparently it took quite a lot of persuasion to get the Royal Navy to commit even one Harrier, sir. But it's a very capable aircraft, and it should be possible for the pilot to achieve his objective. For one thing he'll have surprise on his side. And the attack will obviously come from the east, from the Sea of Japan, while North Korea's defences are optimized for assaults from the south, across the Demilitarized Zone, so the DPRK forces should be looking the wrong way.'

'What about the North Korean fighters? They've got swarms of them.'

'Agreed, Mr President, but with the exception of the Foxbat they're all old and slow, and the Harrier should be able to avoid or outrun them.'

At that moment the door opened and the Secretary of Defense walked in, looking agitated and carrying a slim red folder. He nodded a greeting to Hicks, then turned to the President. 'I've just taken this off the teleprinter from Pyongyang. It's addressed personally to yourself, to the Prime Minister of Japan and to the President of South Korea.'

He passed the folder across the desk. The President

opened it and read the short printed message it contained. Then he looked over at Hicks.

'You'd better tell your contacts at SIS to get that Harrier warmed up,' he said. 'It's pretty much as you predicted. They say they hope we were watching the recent demonstration of their Taep'o-dong 2 missile's effectiveness, and they claim here it followed a homing beacon to land on an obsolete freighter they were using as a target.

'They've also released details of that successful flight, and the detonation of their nuclear weapon, to all the international news agencies. So this is going to be all over the papers tomorrow. They've also helpfully explained, just in case the editors are too stupid to get the point, that approximately one-third of the continental United States is now within range of their weapons. The talking heads are going to have a field day working out exactly which cities the gooks will be able to nuke if we piss them off in any way. The public backlash is going to be huge, and we're going to have to tread real careful.

'That's merely the preamble, if you like. The meat's in the second paragraph, and this stuff hasn't been given to the press for obvious reasons. They've targeted nuclear-tipped missiles on Japan, and are threatening to use them if our embedded forces oppose their "peaceful" incursion to "liberate" South Korea from its capitalist oppressors. And if we do interfere directly, the first target of their now fully-functioning Taep'o-dong type 2 ICBMs will be Los Angeles.'

FOXBAT

HMS *Illustrious*, Yellow Sea

Richter was still working with Roger Black in the admiral's quarters, studying maps of North Korea and trying to work out the optimum routes in and out – the tracks that would avoid as many of the known anti-aircraft defences as possible. Then suddenly the telephone rang.

Black answered it, then handed the receiver to Richter.

'Commander Richter? This is the CommCen, sir. We've just received a Flash signal for you, but it's only a single word.'

'Which is?'

'The word is "PROXIMATE", sir. Do you need me to spell that?'

'No,' Richter said, sounding resigned. 'I know what it means, thanks.'

'It's a go?' Black asked, as Richter replaced the phone.

'That was the code-word. It's a go. We need to get airborne at first light tomorrow morning.'

Chapter Nineteen

Monday
USS *Enterprise*, North Pacific Ocean

Captain William Rodgers woke up the moment the phone in his cabin began to ring. He'd always been a light sleeper, and whenever he was at sea he seemed preternaturally attuned to any unusual noise or motion, even a slight change in the direction the ship was steering.

'Yes?'

'Officer of the Watch, sir. You asked to be called when we reached six hundred miles from the peninsula. The satnav says that's where we are right now, and the Hawkeye's warming up.'

'Thanks, I'll be right there.'

A signals yeoman was also waiting on the bridge when Rodgers arrived, and handed him an envelope. The captain ripped it open, pulled out the signal and read it. The yeoman waited, signal pad and ballpoint pen in hand.

'No reply,' Rodgers said. 'No, wait a minute.'

There would, he knew, have to be some kind of a response to the signal, which had basically ordered him to hold the Carrier Battle Group well clear of North Korean territorial waters, and emphasized that neither the ship nor its air group were to participate in any acts of provocation. The latter instruction had merited a paragraph of its own, and had included a prohibition on any flights from the *Enterprise* except for purposes of pure self-defence, and that included surveillance and intelligence-gathering missions.

Rodgers was going to have to think more about that, but for the moment he'd already decided that the Hawkeye was going to be launched well before he had 'officially' read this signal. He'd also decided something else.

He turned to the signals yeoman. 'No reply to this, but contact the *Leyte* and *McFaul* and tell them to detach. They're to go to maximum speed and set up a picket line between the Korean Peninsula and Japan. On my authority, if any missile is launched from North Korea over the Sea of Japan, they're to engage it.'

Positioning the two Aegis guided-missile destroyers ahead of the carrier would provide an extra margin of safety.

Eight minutes later, the *Enterprise* altered course slightly to port to take advantage of what little wind there was and, moments after the ship steadied on its new heading, an E-2C airborne early-warning aircraft, using the callsign Alpha Three, was accelerated into the air by the starboard bow steam catapult. It climbed away from the ship and continued up to just over thirty thousand feet, heading south-west directly towards Korea.

Mayang Missile Base, North Korea

Pak Je-San had meticulously plotted each stage of the operation, and had provided Kim Yong-Su with both an outline plan and explicit details. Kim, in turn, was implementing it step by step, with the full approval of the government in Pyongyang. Because of the scope of the operation, a number of the actions Pak had specified would necessarily have to be carried out by junior officers who would certainly not be privy to the overall strategy.

An Air Force *tab-ryong*, equivalent to a colonel, at the Mayang missile base was one of these officers. He'd been puzzled when Pyongyang had instructed him to mount a No-dong missile in the launch gantry. His confusion stemmed not from the instruction itself, which was clear enough, but simply because of the actual missile he'd been told to prepare. Mounting the payload and fitting the nose-cone also didn't make sense to him, because he'd already been told that the 'warhead' was a fake, filled with scrap metal.

But when he read the last instruction from Pyongyang, he finally grasped the totality of the part of the operation in which he was personally involved, and its simplicity and elegance made him smile.

HMS *Illustrious*, Yellow Sea

Normally the main briefing room door was left open, but when Richter arrived at just before four that morning, the door was closed and a burly 800 Squadron chief petty officer was standing outside.

'Commander Richter? You're the last one, sir.' He opened the door and ushered Richter inside, then closed it behind him.

'Come in, Paul,' said Roger Black. He was standing at the front of the room, the three other pilots, all wearing flying overalls, sitting in the front row of seats directly facing him. Off to the right-hand side were several white-boards, and at the back of the room a flight planning desk with dedicated computers, none of which would be used during this briefing.

Usually Harrier pilots are briefed by an intel officer who would use a Powerpoint presentation delivered on a secret computer known as CSS. This is a remarkably useful system that enables secure planning, encrypted messaging, the storage and display of classified documents and mapping, combined with real-time intelligence information. But Richter had no idea how to use the system, and in any case the signal from Simpson had been absolutely specific: no details of any aspect of the mission were to be entered on any data storage device, and all planning materials were to be destroyed as soon as the briefing was completed.

'I've been explaining the substance of the mission to these three,' Black said, 'but despite that, they still seem keen to go with you.'

Richter nodded to them and sat down at the end of the row. 'I'm very grateful. I think you're all mad to volunteer, but I do appreciate it.'

'As you're all aware, this mission has not been authorized by our controlling authority,' Black began. 'The intention was that Paul Richter would carry out a solo sortie into North Korea, and we all know how futile that would probably have been. For this to work, we'll need a minimum of four aircraft – two pairs – on the mission. The captain is aware of what's going on, and has given it his full support, but nobody outside this room is to be told anything about this operation, whether it succeeds or fails. As far as the rest of the ship's company is concerned, you're going up as two pairs of CAP aircraft to practise one-on-one air combat under South Korean control.

'I've had a met brief, and the weather's going to continue pretty much the same as it's been for the last week. That means clear skies, light winds, and zero precipitation. Now, Paul's done all the mission-planning, so I'll hand over to him.'

As Black sat down in the front row, Richter walked over to the lectern, selected a map and switched on the overhead projector. On the screen behind him a detailed map of North Korea sprang to life. He turned to check that it was in focus, then back to face the men sitting in front of him.

'Good morning, gentlemen. This briefing is classified Top Secret and is extremely sensitive, to put it mildly. We're about to commit an act of war against a country that in no way threatens, or has ever threatened, the United Kingdom. We're acting as proxies for the Americans, much as we've already done in Iraq, but this time I personally think the action is justified.

'My first point is not directly connected with the mission, but needs emphasizing. You must be fully aware of the likely consequences if you get shot down. The North

Koreans' human rights record is dismal, to say the least. The best you can hope for is that they'll simply shoot you, but it's more likely you'll spend a considerable length of time in one of their concentration camps, and finally be killed in some kind of medical "experiment". The worst is probably Camp 22, up in the north-east corner of the country, near Haengyong. That establishment holds about fifty thousand prisoners, most of whom will end up gassed or poisoned in Pyongyang's experimental biological and chemical warfare programme. You need to be in absolutely no doubt about this. The North Koreans have pulled off a difficult trick: they've managed to make the Nazis' concentration camps look relatively humane.'

Richter paused and looked at the impassive faces staring back at him.

'All four of us will be carrying Walther PPK pistols with one full magazine. This weapon is not intended for you to fight your way out of North Korea. It's so you can put the barrel against the side of your head and pull the trigger, if you do end up on the ground. That, I assure you, may be your last resort but by far your best option. Do you all fully understand that?'

The three pilots nodded, and Richter shook his head.

'And you still want to go on this mission? Well, I think you're all certifiable.'

The Senior Pilot, Lieutenant-Commander Dick 'Shorty' Long, laughed briefly. 'If you go, we go,' he said. 'It's as simple as that, Paul, so stop trying to talk us out of it.'

'OK, it's your funeral – metaphorically speaking, I hope. Right, now, the mission.' Richter turned his attention back to the map and used a pen as a pointer. 'These are our targets. From the north: Hochon, No-dong, Mayang Island and Ok'pyong. The highest priority is Ok'pyong, partly because of statements made by a North Korean defector.

'In August nineteen ninety-three a thirty-year-old lieutenant named Im Young-Sun, who'd been employed in the North Korean Military Construction Bureau, defected to the South. He was extensively debriefed by the Americans and, amongst other things, claimed that missiles based at Ok'pyong were normally targeted at Japanese cities and US bases in Japan.

'According to the Americans, their satellites, mainly KH-12 birds, have detected an unusual kind of truck at Ok'pyong, a vehicle they believe has been specially modified for the carriage of nuclear weapons. From this they inferred that the No-dong missile now sitting on the launch pad at Ok'pyong is carrying a nuclear payload, and the reason we've been asked to hit the other three bases is because identical trucks have been spotted at them as well. And at Mayang, here, one satellite image actually shows a warhead being mounted on the missile.'

Richter paused for a few moments, studying the map showing the locations of those four missile bases. Something was nagging at him about this mission, something that wasn't quite right, but he couldn't put a finger on it. It would, he hoped, come to him eventually.

'OK, there are four targets and we have four aircraft and, as Wings has said, the optimum tactics are to fly as two pairs, and each pair will take out two targets. The geographical separation of the bases means that one pair will attack Hochon and No-dong, and the other two will hit Ok'pyong and Mayang. I'm volunteering myself for the two southerly bases, because Ok'pyong's the highest priority.'

Almost before he'd finished speaking, Dick Long turned slightly in his seat to address the other two pilots. 'I'll take Ok'pyong and Mayang with Paul. Your targets will be the other two.'

'The mission callsigns will be Cobra and Viper,' Richter said. 'Splot and I will be Cobra; you two are Viper. Now, the weapons. In an ideal world, we'd get airborne, climb to about ten grand, pop off a bunch of Storm Shadows, and land back on board in time for breakfast. Unfortunately, we don't have that particular missile available, for reasons we're all aware of – like the fact that it doesn't actually work with the GR9 – so we're left with Mavericks, Brimstone, CRV7 rockets, Sidewinders, and bombs various.

'I've been over this with both Dick and Wings. Our targets are No-dong missiles, actually waiting on the launch pads. These are highly dangerous but comparatively fragile and, more importantly, liquid-fuelled. The fuel is TM-185, which is basically a mixture of twenty per cent petrol and eighty per cent kerosene, plus an oxidizer known as AK-27I, making a highly explosive combination. The fact that satellite imagery shows them on the pads suggests that they've been fuelled already. Normal operating procedure is that the tanks would be left empty until the missile's mounted on the gantry, because moving a rocket full of liquid propellant is highly dangerous.'

Richter exchanged the map for a photograph of the missile base at Mayang and pointed out the gantry and No-dong standing on the pad, then he showed satellite images of the other three bases.

'There's no point in hitting these weapons with a Brimstone anti-tank missile because the warhead wouldn't detonate. But we do need to hit them hard and accurately, so the best option is probably the Maverick with a proximity fuse and electro-optical guidance. The maintainers have loaded one pair on each Harrier so we'll have two shots at each target. For the scatter-gun option, each aircraft also has two operational pods of CRV7s, so that's an additional thirty-eight rockets. If you hit one of the missiles and get its fuel to detonate, that will almost certainly destroy anything else above ground in the vicinity.'

'So once you've targeted the Maverick you need to watch out for the fallout from the explosion,' Dick Long said, turning in his seat to face Forbes and Whittard. 'Be prepared to haul off the moment the warhead detonates.'

Richter nodded agreement. 'For self-defence, we'll each be carrying two AIM-9L Sidewinders. We're having to compromise on this mission, because we also need a drop tank due to the long transit. Mother moved closer to the peninsula during the night, and is presently loitering about twenty miles off the South Korean coast due west of Seoul. The fastest way to reach our targets is to fly straight there, but that would mean crossing directly over North Korea, and that's not the brightest of ideas. The DPRK has one of the most comprehensive air-defence networks on the surface of the planet. It's got nearly ten thousand anti-aircraft guns, plus Russian SA-2, SA-3, SA-5, SA-7 and SA-16 surface-to-air missiles. Most of the SA-2 and SA-3 batteries are located near the coastal areas, and the SA-5s are close to the DMZ and Pyongyang itself.'

Richter replaced the photograph the OHP was displaying with an aeronautical chart of the Korean Peninsula on which he'd drawn the track he'd planned for their sortie.

'So we're going to avoid all that lot and take the pretty route. On take-off, we'll form into two pairs in loose formation and transit due east, overflying Seoul. We've already received diplomatic clearance, and I'll give you contact frequencies, callsigns, SSR codes and procedures for the en-route radar units at the end of this briefing. The peninsula's about a hundred miles wide, and to conserve fuel we'll transit at high level – I hope around thirty thousand feet, but it'll depend upon the clearance we get from Seoul.

'There's no point in trying to sneak across at low level because the North Koreans have really good radar coverage of the area south of the DMZ and they'd definitely see us, which would probably make them even more suspicious than they may already be. By transiting at high level I'm hoping they'll think it's just another border patrol.

'Once we go feet-wet over the Sea of Japan we'll turn south-east so that we're not perceived as a threat by North Korean air defence radars, and then start a cruise descent. By my calculations, and based on the route I've worked out, we should drop below the North Korean radar horizon when we get below five thousand feet. We'll continue descent to fifteen hundred feet and turn port onto a northerly heading, to keep us at least thirty miles clear of the coast.'

He replaced the aeronautical chart with a more

detailed version which showed the east side of the peninsula.

'When we reach here – one two nine degrees east, thirty-nine degrees north – we split into two pairs and turn towards our respective targets. Viper will track approximately zero one zero towards Hochon, and Cobra three four five for Mayang. Once established on track, both pairs will descend to five hundred feet, and jettison drop tanks at least two miles before reaching the coast.

'Vipers will hit Hochon first, then turn east for Nodong, as the two sites are very close together. When those attacks have been completed, your escape vector will be one four zero, giving you the shortest possible track to the coast. Then head south-east until you're clear of North Korean territorial waters, before turning west once you're south of the Demilitarized Zone. If you have to land in South Korea it shouldn't be a problem. The major airfields have been briefed that one or more British fighters may be carrying out practice diversions today. I'll give you contact frequencies and landing charts at the end of this briefing. And, *in extremis*, there are plenty of roads and hard surfaces you can land on.

'If your aircraft is damaged and you can't make it back, try to get over the Sea of Japan before ejecting. The water's fairly warm, and your survival time should be several hours. As you know, *Edinburgh* and *Portland* are operating to the east of the Korean Peninsula and, if you do ditch, their helicopters will be available to rescue you. That assumes, of course, that the sky isn't full of enemy fighters. If you eject over North Korean territory, you're on your own.'

He turned to Commander (Air). 'Where's the Sea King, Blackie?'

'It should be in position shortly,' Roger Black replied. 'We've sent an AEW Sea King east of the peninsula, and the bagman will call traffic on your discrete frequency, using callsign November Alpha. He'll use simple codes: Alpha for a clean picture; Bravo for single contacts and Charlie for multiple bandits. The King flew out there about an hour ago, and by now it should be refuelling from *Edinburgh* using HIFR. That's another possible rotary-wing rescue aircraft, but the crew's first priority is calling hostile contacts. The aircraft will only be available for SAR operations once the tactical phase of the mission is over.'

'Thanks,' Richter said. 'Now, Cobras – Splot and I – have drawn the short straw. Mayang is near the coast, and we should get there at about the same time as Vipers hit Hochon, so it will still be a surprise attack. Our problem is Ok'pyong. From Mayang we'll have to turn southwest and it's a seventy-odd-mile overland transit. It's certain that by the time we get there the NK defences will have been alerted and, frankly, our chances of getting through the anti-aircraft barrage they'll throw up will be fairly slim.'

Richter stopped talking and eyed the men sitting in front of him. None seemed particularly perturbed by anything he'd said so far, but he hadn't expected they would be. Harrier pilots are among the elite of the fast-jet world, used to handling a difficult aircraft under the most demanding conditions. And, as was comprehensively demonstrated in the Falklands War, the aircraft itself is enormously capable. In that conflict the Harrier was both outnumbered and outperformed by the aircraft flown by the Argentine Air Force, but despite this suffered no casualties in air combat and shot down twenty enemy jets. Richter wasn't worried about air combat – he thought the Harrier could hold its own against anything the North Koreans flew apart from the Foxbat – but the sheer number of SAMs scared him.

'Any questions?' Four heads were shaken in unison. 'Above all, remember to watch out for the SAMs.' Richter held up three envelopes. 'Right, these are data packs listing the frequencies, squawks and so on. They're classified Secret because of the information they contain on South Korean airfields, so remember to dispose of them correctly once you get back from this little excursion. The EMCON policy is unrestricted whilst we're under South Korean control, but keep communications on our discrete frequency to a minimum, as the last thing we want is to alert the North Koreans by unnecessary radio chatter.

'Now, if there's nothing else, I'll shred this lot here and meet you in the ACRB for a plate of low-cholesterol bacon butties in five minutes. We should aim to get airborne in about three quarters of an hour.'

Pyongyang, North Korea

Kim Yong-Su was awoken by the telephone ringing. Like most other North Korean senior officials, he'd taken to sleeping in his office so that he could be contacted immediately by the leadership.

'Kim Yong-Su,' he announced, glancing at the wall clock.

'It's Pak Je-San,' the caller replied.

'Yes?' Kim's voice was noticeably more abrupt now he realized he wasn't addressing the 'Dear Leader'. 'What do you want?'

'I'm not sure it's significant, but two of our radar units – the stations at Ongjin and Haeju – have detected the launch of four aircraft from the British warship that's been operating west of Seoul.'

'That ship has been flying aircraft regularly for the last two days.'

'I know, but all those flights have remained within patrol areas over the Yellow Sea. These aircraft have climbed to high level and headed into South Korea. None of the aircraft have done that before. Judging by their secondary radar returns, they're now being controlled by the radar unit at Seoul.'

Kim Yong-Su sat down at his desk and thought for a few seconds. 'You were right to call me, Pak. If the British were intending a pre-emptive strike against our missile bases, they'd probably cross into the Sea of Japan and then launch an attack from there.'

'But we have no quarrel with the British.'

'No,' Kim replied, 'but they're still the best friends the imperialist Yankees have. If Washington says "Jump", all the spineless British ever say is "How high?" It looks as if you were right, Pak. The only surprise is that the British are doing the Americans' dirty work for them. I must pass on this information at once. Ensure that all our southern radar stations are warned about these aircraft, then launch our interceptors and alert the missile bases.'

Kim put down the phone and reached out a hand for the red telephone. Before picking it up he looked again at the clock. It was *very* early, but he knew the information couldn't wait. The high command had to be informed. The next phase of the plan was about to be implemented.

E2-C, callsign 'Alpha Three', Sea of Japan

'Climax, this is Alpha Three.' 'Climax' was the USS *Enterprise*'s tactical voice radio callsign.

'Alpha Three, Climax. Go ahead.'

'Climax, we're feeding you data through the JTIDS and we're not seeing much we didn't expect north of the DMZ. But we've just picked up four contacts in the Yellow Sea, heading east towards Seoul and wearing South Korea-block squawks. It's subjective, but they looked to us like carrier-launched aircraft. We were briefed to expect one contact in that area sometime this morning, not four. Can you check with Intelligence and get an update?'

'Alpha Three, stand by.' There was a short pause while the radar operator in the Combat Information Center on the *Enterprise* consulted someone, then he replied. 'Nothing known by us or the JIC, Alpha Three. We understood *one* aircraft. We'll request a flash check with Homeland Intelligence.'

'Roger that.'

USS *Enterprise*, North Pacific Ocean

William Rodgers was, like the captains of all US Navy carriers, a highly experienced aviator. He had over three thousand hours in the F-14 Tomcat, an aircraft he'd been sad to see finally retire, though he had to acknowledge there were undeniable advantages to the new F/A-18 Super Hornet. And, though his craft now displaced ninety-four thousand tons, he still thought like a pilot.

The moment he heard the exchange between the Hawkeye and the radar operator he strode across the CIC and peered at the officer's display. It was linked to the E2-C's sensors through the JTIDS (Joint Tactical Information Distribution System) and the four contacts, now well into South Korea and still heading east, were clearly displayed.

'That's them?' he asked, bending forward to point at the returns on the radar screen.

'Yes, sir. The Hawkeye reported them first appearing over the Yellow Sea, pretty much where that little British carrier is supposed to be operating.'

'Those carriers may be small, Lieutenant,' Rodgers growled, 'but they still pack a serious punch.' For a few seconds he just stared in silence at the screen.

The signal that was still tucked in his hip pocket was absolutely unequivocal: he was to do nothing that might provoke or irritate the North Koreans, just in case they decided that hitting Los Angeles with a nuclear weapon was the most suitable response.

That was one factor.

The other factor was right there on the radar screen in front of him: the tiny, relatively slow-moving returns that he knew represented four British Harriers embarking on a mission that wasn't quite suicidal, but certainly came close. Four subsonic single-pilot aircraft trying to carry out strike missions – strike missions actually requested by Washington – and facing not only an air force on high alert that could field in excess of eight hundred fighters, but entering territory that was guarded by one of the highest concentrations of surface-to-air missile and gun systems in the world.

Rodgers knew what his orders were, knew that they were clear and concise and absolutely specific, and knew what the consequences were likely to be if he ignored them. But he couldn't forget his hours in the driving seat of a Tomcat, the feeling of loneliness and vulnerability when approaching a hostile environment, and knew that the four men in the Harriers would be feeling exactly the same.

He stood up straight, his decision made. It was, he hoped, the right one, but he'd accept the consequences later if it turned out he was wrong. He muttered something under his breath that sounded to the radar operator suspiciously like 'Fuck Washington', then issued his orders.

'OK, we were expecting a single contact to follow a similar track to that. My guess is that the Brits decided to fly more than one aircraft. Get the Prowlers and the Hornets warmed up in case they need any help. Advise me the moment they clear the coast and start to drop.'

Cobra and Viper formation, above South Korea

The Senior Pilot in Cobra One was to the right and ahead of Richter's GR9, Viper One and Two half a mile behind.

From just over thirty-five thousand feet, the mountain-ous countryside of the Korean Peninsula looked starkly beautiful, the early-morning sun casting enormous shadows that turned whole valleys into black pits. They were approaching the coastline about ten miles north of Kangnung, and preparing for descent.

They'd contacted Seoul as they approached the coast and received immediate clearance to climb and cross the peninsula. They'd also confirmed with the controllers that other Sea Harriers might be landing in South Korea during the morning, but obviously hadn't explained why.

'Cobra Two, Vipers, switch to tactical on stud four.'

Richter switched frequency and checked in. 'Cobra Two.'

'Viper One.'

'Viper Two.'

'Roger, Cobra Two, Vipers. Stand by for rate one right turn onto one four zero in thirty seconds.'

'Roger.'

'Cobras, Vipers, turn now, now, now.'

As the Senior Pilot finished the sentence, all four air-craft swung gently to the right – a rate one turn being comparatively slow – and steadied on their new heading.

'Cobras, Vipers, this is November Alpha.'

'November Alpha, Cobra One, you're loud and clear.'

'Roger, Cobra Lead. You're identified, Picture Alpha.'

Just under six minutes later the four Harriers throttled back and began a cruise descent. Passing twelve thou-sand feet, their Radar Warning Receivers showed the last of the North Korean surveillance radars beginning to lose contact, and by the time they reached eight thousand, the RAWs were silent.

'Cobras, Vipers, stand by for a hard port turn onto north. Turn now, now, now.'

The moment they steadied, and passed five thousand feet in descent, Long ordered them to accelerate. Their comparatively slow speed and turn away from North Korea might have fooled the DPRK radar controllers, but none of them felt like betting on it. Their best weapons now were speed and surprise.

USS *Enterprise*, North Pacific Ocean

In the CIC, the radar operator called out to the captain. 'Sir, those four contacts have cleared the east coast of South Korea, but they turned south-east and they've just started to descend.'

'Of course they're heading away from North Korea. They're not stupid. If they'd turned towards the north, every radar station above the DMZ would have been tracking them, and feeding their coordinates to their SAM sites. Just keep watching. When they're low enough, they'll head north.'

Pyongyang, North Korea

'Sir,' the voice of the radar supervisor at the coastal radar station sounded calm and controlled, 'those four aircraft are now heading away from us, and they've started descending. I suggest they're probably just on a regular patrol, and therefore no direct threat to us.'

'You could be right,' Kim Yong-Su replied, 'but your orders are perfectly clear. We still believe they may be planning an attack, so continue watching the areas out to the south and east, and inform me the moment you see any sign of them returning.'

USS *Enterprise*, North Pacific Ocean

'You're right, sir. They've turned north and increased speed. They're not squawking Mode Charlie, but the Hawkeye estimates they're down below two thousand feet.'

'Got that,' Rodgers said, and opened the intercom link to PriFly. 'CAG, this is the Captain. What's the state of play with the Hornets?'

'Ready to go, sir. I've eight interceptors fully prepped, plus four fitted with refuelling pods that I'll send off about forty minutes afterwards to pick them up on the way back.'

'And the Prowlers?'

'Two waiting on the bow catapults, sir, as you ordered.'

'Very good. Launch the Prowlers and get the Hornets ready to follow.'

The deck was a scene of frantic but organized activity. The deck of any aircraft carrier at launch or recovery is one of the busiest, and certainly one of the most dangerous, places in the world. The *Enterprise* has four steam catapults, two on the foredeck and the other two amidships, and each would be used twice in quick succession to get the eight Super Hornet interceptors airborne.

But first the flight deck crews were going to get the two Prowlers into the air. The EA-6B has been around since the early 1970s, and is still the American Navy's primary electronic attack aircraft, scheduled to be replaced in about 2010 by the EA-18G Growler, the electronic warfare version of the Super Hornet.

The *Enterprise* began a gentle turn as flight deck crew members checked that the Prowlers and their pilots were ready for launch. The moment the massive ship steadied, PriFly issued clearance to launch both aircraft. The blast deflector lifted behind the EA-6B on the starboard bow catapult and the pilot ran up the two Pratt and Whitney turbojets to full power. The J52 engines are non-afterburning, but are still powerful enough to give the Prowler a maximum speed of nearly six hundred miles an hour. The aircraft was heavy: although it wasn't carrying drop tanks, it had a maximum load of four AGM-88 HARM anti-radar missiles and a single ALQ-99 TJS external pod.

Once the Prowler pilot indicated he was at full power, the steam catapult was triggered and the EA-6B shot along the deck. Thirty seconds later the second Prowler launched from the port catapult. Both aircraft took up a south-westerly heading and began climbing to their pre-briefed altitude of thirty-two thousand feet.

'Climax, Zapper formation is switching to discrete.'

'Zapper, Climax. Roger.'

The Prowler crews switched frequencies simultaneously.

'Zapper Two.'

'Two from One, roger. Break, break. Alpha Three, this is Zapper formation in the climb to three two zero heading two three five and squawking mode three alpha code four three two one.'

'Zapper, Alpha Three, you're identified. Maintain heading and call level at three two zero. Squawk standby. No traffic at present.'

'Roger, Alpha Three.'

On launch, they were over five hundred miles from the Korean Peninsula, and at that height they were still well below the radar horizon of any DPRK surveillance sites.

The range/height calculation as it relates to radar coverage is simple enough: because of the curvature of the Earth, an aircraft at an altitude of five thousand feet will paint on a surveillance radar at a range of about fifty miles. To ensure the Prowlers stayed undetected, the Hawkeye would instruct them to begin descent before they reached the theoretical radar horizon, and set them up in a holding pattern at least one hundred miles from the east coast of the peninsula. From that point, they would be able to hit the first of the North Korean radar sites, assuming their assistance was needed, in less than twelve minutes.

Cobra and Viper formation, Sea of Japan

Flying in formation at well over four hundred miles an hour and less than five hundred feet above the surface of the sea, a pilot's concentration has to be absolute.

A split-second's inattention and the Harrier could plunge into the waves or plough into another aircraft, and the four GR9s had widened their formation slightly to provide an added margin of safety.

'Vipers, Cobra One. Stand by for split in thirty seconds.'

Richter took his eyes off the view through the windscreen for the bare few seconds it took to visually check his cockpit, then looked back.

'Split now, now, now. Good hunting, Vipers.'

But as the tracks of the two pairs of Harriers diverged, the AEW Sea King radar controller passed his first traffic information message, and it wasn't good news.

'Cobras, Vipers, November Alpha. Picture Charlie. Launches from the airfields at T'ae'tan, Nuchonri, Kuupri, Wonsan, Toksan and Ŏrang. Multiple bandits, all tracking towards the east coast of the peninsula. Stand by for numbers and locations.'

'Shit,' Richter muttered. 'That's all we needed.'

USS *Enterprise*, North Pacific Ocean

The first Hornet taxied to the starboard bow catapult, expertly directed by a marshaller, and stopped with its nosewheel in precisely the right spot. The holdback – a steel bar designed to stop the aircraft moving forwards when the engines were run up to full power prior to launch – was attached to the rear of the nosewheel landing gear, and the front hitched to the catapult itself. Steam swirled around the men carrying out these tasks, giving the scene a somewhat surreal appearance.

The blast deflector was raised behind the Hornet and the pilot ran up the two General Electric F414-GE-400 turbofans to full cold military power, then cut in the burners. The noise of the engines rose to a scream, and almost immediately the aircraft lurched forward as the catapult accelerated it down the deck. At the far end, the Hornet dipped down briefly towards the sea, then rose quickly and climbed away, but nobody except the officers in PriFly were watching it. Instead, they were busy preparing for the next launch, and the Hornet on the port bow catapult was already in place and spooling up its engines.

Five seconds later, the second Super Hornet was airborne, and in under three minutes all eight aircraft were in the air and climbing away from the *Enterprise*. They formed into two groups of four, climbed to thirty-five thousand feet and took up a south-westerly heading.

Mayang, North Korea

The *tab-ryong* was scanning the surveillance radar screens when a shout from one of his controllers drew his attention to two very fast-moving contacts approaching from the south-east. They were travelling at around five hundred miles an hour, and were heading straight towards the missile base.

'Excellent,' the colonel murmured, then picked up a microphone to make a broadcast.

'Air raid warning! Air raid warning! Two aircraft approaching from the south-east. All anti-aircraft crews stand by. Fire at will, but wait until you are certain of your targets.'

Outside the bunker, every surface-to-air missile battery and anti-aircraft gun position was fully manned, and the *tab-ryong* had also stationed an additional fifty soldiers armed with shoulder-launched missiles around the perimeter of the base. His orders had been most specific: the attacking aircraft were under no circumstances to be allowed to escape.

Next the colonel dialled a telephone number from memory, which connected him with the senior controller at Toksan, the closest interceptor base.

'This is Mayang,' he said. 'We have two fast-moving contacts approaching on bearing one five zero, range twenty miles.'

'Very good. We'll vector four of our interceptors towards you. Ensure your crews hold fire when our fighters approach. I'll advise you once they reach five miles from your boundary.'

'Understood,' the *tab-ryong* replied, then used his microphone to warn his gun and missile crews.

Cobra formation, Sea of Japan

Richter followed the Senior Pilot in a turn to port. When he'd steadied, he glanced briefly out to starboard to see the Vipers heading away to the north. He checked his weapon controls, making sure he knew exactly where the switches were, and almost immediately his Radar Warning Receiver sounded.

He studied the Zeus 'frying pan' display that surrounded the GR9's HUD. A single line was showing in the ten o'clock position, meaning his aircraft was being intermittently irradiated by the lowest lobes of a North Korean surveillance radar somewhere on the coast to the south-west. That wasn't a problem, but it was a definite attention-getter.

He checked the INGPS. They were seventeen miles from Mayang, their first target, and the coast of the Korean Peninsula was now clearly visible in front of them.

'Two from One. Master arm on.'

Richter clicked his press-to-transmit button in acknowledgement, and made the switch, arming his weapon systems. Fifteen miles to go. The RAW, part of the Marconi Zeus ECM system, was now detecting numerous radar transmissions, but only from surveillance radars. No SAM fire-control radars or fighter sets yet but, if the Sea King bagman was right, that was going to change very soon.

And then Richter suddenly realized what had been bugging him ever since he'd seen those first satellite pictures of the North Korean missile sites. And he now deduced the probable reason for the sudden flurry of aircraft take-offs from the North Korean airfields.

'All callsigns, Cobra Two. Abort! Abort! Abort! Vipers and Cobras abort. Haul off and reverse course. Cobras turn port, Vipers starboard. Opening heading south-east. Get the hell out of here, buster. Vipers acknowledge.'

And as he said the words Richter hauled his GR9 round in a tight turn to port.

'Vipers, all copied. Reversing course.'

'Cobra Two, Leader. What the fuck's going on?'

Richter didn't reply immediately, concentrating on getting his aircraft heading away from the hostile shore.

'We've been sold a pup. It's a trap. I suddenly realized what didn't make sense. The North Korean military does almost everything underground. They've got the facilities to prepare their missiles in hardened shelters, so why are there four missile launch pads with No-dongs sitting on them, right out in the open and close to the coast, so they're a really attractive target?'

'To persuade us or the Americans to attack them?'

'Exactly. And once we'd carried out the raid, and probably got our arses blown out of the sky in the process, Pyongyang would launch an attack across the DMZ and be able to claim they were acting in self-defence.'

Dick Long pulled alongside Richter's Harrier as the two aircraft headed south-east at better than five hundred miles an hour. Before Long could reply, the AEW Sea King bagman broke in.

'Cobra Two, November Alpha, all copied. Understand the hunt is off. Break, break. Vipers, Cobras right one o'clock range eight, similar heading. Call visual.'

'Vipers visual with Cobras.'

'So what now?' Dick Long asked.

'Right now,' Richter said, 'I don't know. Let's get south of the DMZ, just in case some of those aircraft November Alpha detected were Foxbats, out looking for an easy kill.'

Chapter Twenty

Monday
USS *Enterprise*, North Pacific Ocean

'Sir, the Hawkeye reports multiple aircraft contacts launching from the southerly airfields in North Korea, principally Kuupri, Nuchonri, Ŏrang, T'ae'tan, Toksan and Wonsan. Judging by their speed and rate of climb, they look like interceptors. And I'm – stand by. Sir, the four British fighters have turned back.'

Rodgers acknowledged the call and concentrated on the display in front of him, where the JTIDS was showing exactly that. Numerous new contacts were being displayed over the North Korean landmass, but Rodgers wasn't interested in those – at least, not for the present. Instead, he focused on the Harriers. The southerly pair had turned hard to port, and the other two to starboard, and all were now heading away from the east coast of North Korea at a speed the computer calculated at around five hundred miles an hour, clearly aiming to link up into a formation of four in a matter of minutes.

'What the hell happened?' the captain murmured. Then, louder. 'Did you detect any stand-off weapon release? Any sign that they've used long-range air-to-surface missiles?'

'Nothing showing on JTIDS, sir. Stand by, just checking with Alpha Three.' There was a short pause.

'Negative from the Hawkeye, sir. No weapon release seen. It looks like they just changed their minds and decided to go back home.'

Mayang, North Korea

The *tab-ryong* was staring in disbelief at the radar screen beside his desk. The aircraft he'd been told would be trying to attack his site had suddenly turned around, and were already over twenty miles away, all without a shot being fired or a single surface-to-air missile launched. What could have gone wrong?

The colonel had prepared the missile site exactly as Pyongyang had ordered, with an old and battered No-dong, previously used for engine tests and other development work, mounted in the firing gantry, and with the fake warhead inside the nose-cone. He'd been instructed to take as long as he could to mount the warhead, to make sure the American spy satellites got at least one good picture of it.

He'd done all that, and he guessed that officers in charge of other missile bases on the east coast of North Korea had probably received similar orders. The American aircraft – he assumed they were American – had clearly been flying on an attack vector, but had broken off at almost exactly twelve miles range.

He suddenly remembered that twelve miles was the international limit of territorial waters. Had the Americans been trying to provoke a response, probing close to the coast and then breaking off just before infringing North Korean territory? He shook his head. No, he didn't believe that. It was as if the pilots had suddenly been recalled, after being ordered to abort the raid.

Whatever the reason, he had to report this. And, he expected, the men in Pyongyang would not be happy with the news.

Cobra and Viper formation, Sea of Japan

'Cobra Leader, November Alpha. No hostiles in pursuit. Most of them appear to be recovering to their bases.'

'Roger that. Break. Cobra Two, Vipers, commence climb to thirty-five thousand feet.'

At low level the Harrier, like all high-performance jet aircraft, burned far more fuel than at altitude, where the engine worked much more efficiently. They'd dropped their external tanks less than ten minutes earlier, so conserving fuel wasn't a priority but, as they seemed safe from pursuit, gaining height was a prudent move.

Pyongyang, North Korea

'They must have noticed something,' Pak Je-San insisted. 'Something must have made those pilots realize it was a trap.'

'Very probably,' Kim Yong-Su agreed, 'but exactly what happened is irrelevant. The fact remains that the fighters – and they were British, not American – turned away and didn't continue their attack, which has put us in a very difficult position. We no longer have the justification we need to begin our operation against South Korea, and now we must decide what to do next.'

'I would proceed as planned,' Pak suggested. 'Everything is in place.'

'Fortunately, that is not your decision,' Kim hissed. 'I'm perfectly aware, as is the "Dear Leader", that this was your plan, but we've both reminded you before that your involvement is now purely practical. *We* will decide all matters of strategy.'

Kim put down the phone and sat in silence for a few moments. But Pak was right: everything *was* in place. The only difference was that by giving the go-ahead now, North Korea would clearly be labelled the aggressor, rather than a sovereign nation defending its territory against an unprovoked attack. But would that make any difference in the long run? If their plans succeeded, the opinion of any other nation or international body would probably be irrelevant, because Korea would at last be united.

But, ultimately, the decision wasn't his to make. He reached forward and picked up the red telephone.

Four minutes later Kim Yong-Su ended the call with a somewhat shocked expression on his face. He'd expected that the 'Dear Leader' would be disturbed by what he had to tell him, but he'd been completely unprepared for the screaming rage that had resulted.

He'd suggested caution, that the best option might be to try to entice the Americans or the British to carry out an attack somewhere else, or even for the North Koreans to fake an assault themselves, photographing the destruction of one of their airfields by missiles fired by their own military, and then claiming it was an act of aggression by the South Koreans. That would give them the excuse they needed to smash through the Demilitarized Zone.

The 'Dear Leader' had rejected this suggestion out of hand, and issued his own very specific instructions, and not for the first time Kim wondered at the man's sanity. But an order was an order, and despite his personal misgivings, he had no doubt at all what would happen to him if he disobeyed. He sat at his desk for a few moments, collecting his thoughts, then picked up the telephone. His first call was to Pak Je-San, and he simply told him to implement Phase Two of 'Golden Dawn', immediately.

Then he dialled the number that gave him direct access to the commanding officer at the Chiha-ri missile base.

North Korea

North Korea's planned assault strategy against its southern neighbour was simple, effective and comprehensive.

Western analysts believed the initial attack would probably be a form of electronic warfare, with highly trained North Korean hackers disrupting American computer-based communication links. That would be followed by assaults using the 120,000 North Korean special forces against specific American and South Korean military bases, airfields and the like. The main assault would follow, with sustained artillery barrages aimed at Seoul and other strategic targets lying close to the DMZ. And, whilst that was taking place, North

Korean troops would swarm across the Demilitarized Zone through pre-prepared tunnels, dug deep underground, and emerge *behind* the Combined Forces Command lines. Estimates suggest there may be as many as twenty such tunnels running under the DMZ at present, some of them capable of handling up to 15,000 troops per hour.

That was the conventional view, and it was the battle plan that the Americans and South Koreans had formulated their own strategies to counter. In fact, the allied Operational Plan was simple enough in concept: the CFC forces would retreat in the face of the North Korean attack, giving ground as slowly as possible, while American reinforcements would be deployed to the south of the peninsula, and would then advance northwards, driving the attackers back.

The North Korean leadership in Pyongyang had always recognized that the main obstacle to their conquest of the South was America's involvement. Despite their belligerent rhetoric, in a war with the United States, they knew North Korea would ultimately lose, simply because no small nation, no matter how dedicated and able its forces, can hope to defeat a superpower. The disparity in the sizes of their respective arsenals and military machines ensured this.

That was why Pak Je-San's plan called for the flight of the Taep'o-dong missile as an essential first step, because if they could convince the Americans that their involvement in the peninsula would lead to nuclear attacks on the superpower itself, there was a very good chance that the invasion of South Korea might succeed. American public opinion would surely force the government not to react?

But Pak Je-San had an additional string to his bow. When he'd explained his overall plan to the leadership in Pyongyang, he'd emphasized that the artillery bombardment of South Korea would ultimately be counter-productive. The ideal solution would be the elimination of a large proportion of the population of the South, but not the destruction of the country's infrastructure, and he'd therefore tailored his plan to achieve this objective.

It was to be a four-stage process. *First*, assemble the troops ready to cross the Demilitarized Zone, either on the ground, while supported by tanks and armour, or through the tunnels. *Second*, destroy the CFC's ability to repel the invasion. *Third*, launch an attack using short-duration chemical weapons targeted on the major centres of population in and around Seoul. *Finally*, send in the occupying force.

The troops were already in position, and the chemical weapons had been assembled and prepared for use. North Korea has always designed its chemical and biological weapons to be fired from howitzers and other artillery pieces, but inevitably these are relatively small and lightweight munitions. To ensure that Seoul suffered a devastating attack that would overwhelm the South Korean government and population, Pak Je-San had planned to use Scud missiles carrying the largest available chemical warheads. Six such weapons, he had calculated, would be enough, but these could only be launched once the North Koreans were certain the

American Patriot anti-missile batteries had been eliminated as a viable defence.

And that was now in the hands of the commanding
officer at Chiha-ri.

Oval Office, White House, 1600 Pennsylvania Avenue, Washington, DC

'Mr President, we've had a message from the *Enterprise*.
The captain reports that one of their Hawkeyes detected
a four-aircraft raid approaching the North Korean missile
bases.'

'Good,' the President nodded. 'It looks like the
Agency's idea worked, General.'

Donald Sterling shook his head. 'No, sir. The carrier
also reports that the raid turned away from the coast at
the last moment, apparently without releasing any
weapons.'

'That's a fucking disaster,' interrupted the Secretary of
Defense, his voice loud and angry. 'If those missiles are
still on the launch pads, Japan's at risk, and there's
nothing we can do about it.'

'We could still—' General Sterling began, but was
interrupted by the ringing of one of the telephones on the
President's desk.

'Just a moment, Don.' The President picked up the
phone and listened for a few seconds. 'OK, send them in.'

There was a brief double-tap on the door, and then
Walter Hicks and Richard Muldoon entered the Oval
Office.

'You heard about the British chickening out?' snarled the Secretary of Defense.

'No. What happened?'

Sterling explained about the signal from the *Enterprise*. When he'd finished, Hicks and Muldoon exchanged glances.

'It looks like somebody over there's a lot smarter than we are,' Hicks said.

'You need to explain that.'

'We've got the latest analysis from N-PIC. It now looks like the No-dong missiles on the east coast launch pads are fakes.'

'Jesus.'

'We made those bases the highest priority for N-PIC, and we've had as near continuous surveillance as is possible within the constraints of the Keyhole system. We've analysed the images, and we're sure the missiles on the pads are real No-dongs, but everything else suggests they're not armed or fuelled. We've seen fuelling apparently taking place, but there's been no change in the temperature of the missiles, which means although the hoses were connected, no fuel was actually transferred.

'And we've got suspicions about the warheads as well. They looked right in the satellite photographs, but the maintainers handling them weren't all wearing protective clothing and at Mayang, in particular, mounting the warhead took far longer than we would have expected.'

'Maybe they had a problem with it,' the President said.

'Maybe they did, sir, but the alternative explanation is that they *wanted* us to see and recognize the warhead, to convince us that the missile was being prepared for launch against Japan. It's significant that the North Koreans usually keep their aircraft and missiles under cover until they're ready to actually launch them, but at these four bases the No-dongs have been sitting visible on the pads for the last couple of days. We think these four missile sites were chosen deliberately, because they're near the coast and relatively easy to attack, and that therefore Pyongyang's intention was to entice us to hit them, because that would provide the excuse they needed to cross the DMZ into South Korea. They could then claim they were acting in self-defence, following an unprovoked attack by us or the South Koreans.'

'Devious bastards. So what happened with the British Harriers? Did somebody get a message to them?'

'We've no idea, sir. It's possible someone on the British carrier put two and two together, or maybe one of the pilots worked it out. That doesn't matter. What's chiefly important is that the raid didn't happen.'

'So what now?'

'We're not out of the wood yet, obviously. The North Koreans may not have obtained the excuse they'd like to start an invasion, but that doesn't mean they won't go ahead anyway. In fact, we're reasonably certain that's exactly what they're intending.'

'You've got evidence to back up that assertion?' the Secretary of Defense asked.

'Yes, sir. We've seen troops, tanks and armour at North Korean bases moving towards the DMZ and then holding position, presumably waiting for the word to advance. We've detected other foot-soldiers entering what we believe are tunnels running into South Korea, and there's a lot of activity in the coastal areas on both sides of the peninsula. We think they could be groups of special forces preparing to infiltrate south of the DMZ. But what concerns us most, Mr President, is this.'

Walter Hicks opened his briefcase and took out half a dozen black-and-white photographs. 'These pictures are less than one hour old. This is the North Korean base at Chiha-ri, just north of the DMZ, and we believe this object here' – he pointed – 'is a modified HY-2 Seersucker cruise missile. It's mounted on a trailer and they're just moving it into the hardened shelter.

'The weapon's a Chinese development of the old Russian P-15 Styx anti-ship missile, and it's been exported to a number of countries including Iraq and North Korea. Pyongyang's been playing about with these since the early nineties. Back in ninety-four they test-flew one that covered a hundred miles, and three years later they'd increased the range to over one hundred twenty miles. That's when our military christened the weapon the AG-1.

'Until now we'd no idea what else they've been doing with the Seersucker, but these pictures suggest they've succeeded in developing a land-based variant, and that's real bad news. It's an old design, but it's still a serious weapon. It's big and bulky, but for the North Koreans that's actually an advantage, because they can put whatever they like in it – different guidance system, bigger fuel tanks or whatever – without having to modify the basic shape.'

'What are we talking about here in terms of payload and performance? And will the PAC-3 Patriot batteries south of the DMZ be able to engage it?'

Hicks shook his head. 'To answer your second

question first, Mr President, probably not, because of its flight profile. The Patriot's very good at intercepting medium- and high-level targets, but it was never designed to engage fast low-flying targets like cruise missiles. It's not generally known, but in March and April two thousand three, during the Second Gulf War, the Iraqis fired five obsolete Chinese-built cruise missiles into Kuwait. There were no casualties, and the damage they caused was minimal, but the Patriot radars never even saw them.

'As for the Seersucker's performance, the original HY-2 had a liquid-fuelled motor that gave it just subsonic performance – about Mach zero decimal nine – and a range of about sixty miles carrying a thousand-pound warhead. Its avionics were quite sophisticated, with a radio altimeter, TV guidance system, infrared seeker head and active radar guidance as it closed with the target.

'Those data are based on the Chinese version from the early nineties – I'd be prepared to bet serious money that the North Koreans have made significant improvements in almost all areas. We already know they've doubled its effective range.'

'What do you think they intend doing with them?'

'If I was running this operation,' General Sterling answered the question, 'I'd prepare three or four, strap a low-yield nuclear weapon on each of them and set them to air-burst over South Korea on a line running east–west through Seoul. That would pretty much wipe out the CFC's computers and communication systems and everything else that runs on printed-circuit boards. Then I'd use artillery to soften up the enemy troops, and send in the army. And there wouldn't be a damn thing we could do to stop it.'

Cobra and Viper formation, Sea of Japan

'November Alpha, Cobra Leader. We're heading back to Mother and leaving the tactical frequency for our discrete. We'll listen out on Guard.'

'Cobra Leader, roger.'

'Cobras and Vipers, stud six, go.'

In a few seconds, all four pilots had checked in on their private frequency.

'Cobra Two from Leader. You *are* sure about this? We're going to look like a bunch of real wimps if you're wrong.'

'I'm sure,' Richter said, with a confidence that was only slightly forced. 'Nothing else makes sense, as far as I can see. We'll check out the satellite imagery when we get back, but I'm betting there'll be no sign of fuel going into those No-dongs. They were just bait.'

'I hope you're right.'

USS *Enterprise*, North Pacific Ocean

'Where are they now?' Rodgers asked, as he walked back into the CIC.

'Here, sir. Just passing to the east of the DMZ. They're now at high level, around thirty-five thousand feet and doing about three hundred and fifty miles an hour. It looks like they're just going home.'

'Right. Where are the Prowlers and Hornets?'

The operator pointed out two sets of contacts, established in holding patterns well outside North Korean radar coverage. 'Do you want them recalled, sir?'

'No, keep them out there. This isn't over yet.'

Chiha-ri missile base, North Korea

With no small degree of satisfaction, the commanding officer looked around the missile preparation area inside the tunnelled-out shelter. The three HY-2 cruise missiles, mounted on trailers that also held the firing control panels, were almost ready. Technicians swarmed over them making last-minute checks, but all the flight and avionics systems – and, most important of all, the payload – had checked out and he was certain there'd be no delays when the order to launch them was given.

And behind the three HY-2s were six Scud type B missiles, each topped by a warhead containing fifty frangible bomblets full of sarin gas. The cluster was designed to be released some two thousand feet above the ground, ensuring that the nerve gas – lethal in doses as low as one milligram for an average adult – would be dispersed over a reasonably wide area. Predicting the likely death toll had been no better than a guess because of the huge number of variables in the equation, but Pyongyang was hoping for between five hundred thousand and one million casualties.

So it would fall to the dedicated team at Chiha-ri to strike not only the first blow against the capitalist lackeys in Seoul and their treacherous American friends, but also the second. For the commanding officer, it was more than just an honour: it was the culmination of his life's ambition.

Pyongyang, North Korea

Kim Yong-Su had one task left to perform, for his own protection. He started the tape recorder running, then lifted the receiver of the red telephone and waited for the soft voice he knew so well.

'Yes, Kim?'

'Everything is ready. The commanding officer at Chiha-ri has assured me that the cruise missiles are prepared. Pak Je-San's Foxbat interceptors are fully fuelled and armed, and are waiting for take-off instructions. This is the last point at which we can stop "Golden Dawn". Do you still wish to proceed?'

The 'Dear Leader' hesitated for no more than a few seconds. 'Yes,' he said. 'You may issue the final orders.'

'Very well.'

But before he used his other telephone to make the calls that would order the assault to begin, Kim Yong-Su removed the cassette tape from the recorder, labelled it and then stored it away in his personal safe. Only then did he consult the paper in front of him and dial the first of the numbers on the list.

T'ae'tan Air Base, North Korea

Pak Je-San put down the telephone with a certain sense of relief. Save for the failure of either the Americans or

South Koreans to attack the dummy missiles prepared at the east coast bases, his plan had worked exactly as anticipated. So now it was time for the final act.

He made three short telephone calls to the airfields at Kuupri, Nuchonri and Wonsan in turn, then picked up the microphone and broadcast the order he'd been longing to give for the last six months.

Then he walked across to his office window and stared out. He couldn't see into the tunnelled-out shelters, but already he could hear the rumble as their armoured doors began to slide open, and a couple of minutes later the first of the Foxbats emerged, towed by a tractor. Ten minutes later, the last of the aircraft was pulled onto the hardstanding, and five minutes after that the first MiG-25 roared down the runway and into the air.

And now all Pak Je-San could do was wait.

Chapter Twenty-One

Monday
Cobra and Viper formation, over South Korea

'Cobra Lead, November Alpha on Guard. Request you chop back to tactical.'

'Roger. Cobras, Vipers, stud four, go.'

As soon as all four aircraft had checked in, the AEW Sea King radar operator passed a hostile contact report that was remarkably similar to his previous broadcast issued when the four Harriers had been approaching their targets on the east coast of the peninsula. He had detected multiple contacts taking off from North Korean airfields. The difference this time was that only four air bases were involved, and all the aircraft were climbing to high level.

In all, the bagman reported that he was holding twenty-one contacts on his radar screen. What he didn't yet know was what those aircraft were intending to do.

MiG-25 Foxbat, callsign Zero Six, over North Korea

Lieutenant Gennadi Malakov levelled his Foxbat at just under thirty-two thousand feet and glanced to his right and slightly behind. His wingman was holding position about two hundred metres away, exactly where he expected him to be.

Malakov was a recruit from the Russian Air Force, lured to North Korea by the promise of financial independence, though the chance to shoot down one – or, better still, several – American aircraft had encouraged his decision to become a mercenary.

He couldn't see the rest of the formation under his command but he knew they'd be behind and above him. The pilots had been briefed to fly as three groups of seven aircraft, separated by about one thousand feet of altitude, but until the attack order came all twenty-one MiG-25s would operate as a single entity.

When in service with the Russian National Air Defence Force, the MiG-25 functioned as a 'manned missile'. The interceptor was fitted with Vozdookh and Lazur radio equipment, and these were integrated with the MiG-25's Polyot inertial navigation system. The combined package allowed ground controllers to vector the aircraft to a target or patrol area automatically. Only when about to carry out the interception did the pilot switch on the massive RP-25M Saphir radar – second only to the MiG-31's Zaslon in terms of output power, and known in the West as Fox Fire.

In North Korean service, the same philosophy was followed but, lacking the appropriate ground-based equipment, positive control had to be exercised by the radar stations using radio commands.

'Zero Six formation, Chunghwa. Make your heading zero one zero, speed six hundred kilometres an hour.' The voice of the controller was clipped and precise.

'Zero Six.'

The entire formation turned onto a northerly heading and reduced speed to conserve fuel. The course they were following would take them almost as far north as the border with China before they made the turn towards the DMZ, but this was quite deliberate. Pyongyang had specially instructed that the Foxbats were to remain over North Korea, and well north of the DMZ, until after the first attack had been launched. This was simply to ensure that the MiG-25s would be well clear of the blast radius when the three nuclear devices exploded.

USS *Enterprise*, North Pacific Ocean

'Captain, sir, JTIDS is showing multiple launches from four North Korean airfields. Twenty . . . no, twenty-one contacts presently all heading north. This could be a first wave of bombers forming up to head across the DMZ.'

But in seconds the speed and rate of climb now being detected made it clear that the aircraft had to be fighters.

'Heading north makes no sense, so once they get high enough they'll turn south. Where are the British aircraft?'

'Here, sir, over South Korea, due east of Ch'orwon. But won't the Brits spot them on their radar?'

'No, mister, they won't, because some fuck-wit decided the new Harrier would work better without a radar. That means they're blind up there. OK, contact the Hawkeye,' Rodgers ordered. 'Tell him to pull the Hornets out of their holding pattern and aim them towards – wait one – aim them at Kangnung. Keep them clear of territorial waters until we know for sure the gooks are intending to cross the DMZ. Get the Prowlers moving in that direction as well. And tell the Hawkeye to call the Harriers on Guard. Somebody needs to let them know what's going on.'

Chiha-ri missile base, North Korea

Although he'd been expecting it, the sudden clatter of the teleprinter still took the commanding officer by surprise, and he hurried across his office to read the printed characters. *At last.* The telephone on his desk rang and he picked up the receiver. The caller didn't identify himself, but there was no need.

'You have received the order?'

'Yes, sir.'

'Good. Implement it immediately.'

The CO left the office, almost running down the stairs, and crossed into the missile preparation area. There, as he shouted orders, engines were started on three small but powerful tractors, and the HY-2 cruise missile trailers were towed out of the shelter to their pre-prepared positions. Once in place, the trailers were jacked up, using the tractors' hydraulic systems, to form rigid platforms for the impending launch. Then the towing vehicles were unhitched and driven off.

The technicians were already waiting, and they plugged the power lines into shielded sockets next to the firing positions. The target coordinates had already been entered, so all that remained was to undertake a comprehensive systems check before the launch itself. This took under five minutes per missile and, less than ten minutes after they'd been towed out of the shelter, all three HY-2s were ready to fire.

The technical crews cleared the pad and retreated to launch control – a concrete bunker some one hundred metres distant – to carry out final communication checks with the cruise missiles. And then everything was ready.

The commanding officer glanced round the bunker, nodded his approval, and then uttered the single word: 'Launch.'

On the concrete pads, the liquid-fuelled engines ignited almost simultaneously and, with a roar that seemed to shake the bunker, the three missiles leapt into the air, their paths diverging immediately.

MiG-25 Foxbat, callsign Zero Six, over North Korea

'Zero Six, Chunghwa. All missiles have been fired. Detonation in approximately six minutes. Stand by to turn onto south.'

'Zero Six.'

The North Korean plan was simple enough. The three HY-2s each carried a nuclear warhead, but the weapons weren't aimed at any strategic targets to the south of the DMZ. Instead, each cruise missile had been programmed to fly across the Demilitarized Zone at low level, thus avoiding engagement, and perhaps even detection, by the Patriot batteries. Once well inside South Korea, the missiles would climb to high level where the warheads would detonate, hopefully simultaneously.

Their separation would ensure that the electromagnetic pulse the explosions generated would blanket the entire width of the Korean Peninsula along a line running east–west directly through Seoul. That, they hoped, would destroy every computer, radio, radar, communication system, and anything else that contained a memory chip or printed circuit, throughout the northern half of South Korea. Due to the fall-out, the explosions would probably also kill a large number of people, as might the blast itself, depending upon the altitude and yield of the devices, though nobody in Pyongyang cared about that.

But the North Koreans had a problem. In fact, they had two problems. The first was that cruise missiles are designed to fly horizontally at low level and fairly fast, which was ideal for avoiding the Patriot batteries, but the optimum detonation point for an EMP weapon is as high as possible. It's been estimated that a high-yield device detonated over central North America at an altitude of about two hundred and fifty miles could affect every electrical circuit in the continental United States. Yet the maximum height Pyongyang had calculated the HY-2 could reach with its heavy warhead was only about twenty thousand feet.

The second difficulty was the yield. The power of the EMP is proportional to the prompt gamma-ray output, and in a fission explosion this equates to under four per cent of the total power of the device. This is substantially reduced by the high explosive used to initiate the detonation sequence, which can absorb as much as eighty-five per cent of the prompt gamma-rays. So for a ten-kiloton device – about the maximum power the scientists at Yongbyon had calculated their weapons would produce – the overall power of the EMP would be well below one per cent of the total yield. But that, they hoped, would still be enough.

The Foxbats were the insurance policy. They would hold north of the DMZ ready to take out any aircraft that the Americans or the South Koreans managed to launch. Then, with the American Patriot batteries blinded, their radars burnt out, and the CFC emasculated, the third stage of Pak Je-San's plan would begin.

Cobra and Viper formation, over South Korea

'Missile launch! Right two o'clock range about twenty miles. Two . . . no, three weapons.' Roger Whittard's voice was loud and excited.

'My RAW's not picking anything up,' the Senior Pilot said, 'but I see them too.'

'They're not SAMs,' Richter said. 'They're cruise missiles. This looks like the opening salvo of North Korea's invasion plan. The Patriots won't be able to stop them, but maybe we can. Vipers, you take the one tracking south-west, which looks like it's heading towards Seoul – and we'll handle the other pair. I'll hit the easterly one, OK, Splot?'

'Roger that.'

Richter hauled his Harrier round in a tight descending port turn and pointed the nose almost straight down. Although the HY-2, like most cruise missiles, is subsonic, he knew he had a very limited window of opportunity to engage it. The missile was probably faster than his aircraft, so he had to plan the intercept carefully, and bring his Harrier in right behind it so that the Sidewinder could lock on. Once he'd released the missile, the 'winder would certainly catch it: the weapon has a maximum speed of Mach 2.5.

The altimeter was unwinding at an alarming rate, the ground rushing towards him, but Richter wasn't looking at his instruments, or even the HUD. His whole attention was focused on the scene out of the right-hand side of his cockpit, where a tiny grey dart, trailing a plume of smoke, was heading south-east at close to the speed of sound and very low. It looked to Richter as if it was less than five hundred feet above the ground, which wasn't going to help him any.

Intercepting it would be difficult, he knew. That was one worry. The other was the Patriot batteries that studded the southern side of the DMZ. His Harrier was wearing a squawk issued by air traffic control at Seoul, but he couldn't remember if the PAC-3 radar incorporated SSR identification. If it didn't, his aircraft might be interpreted as an incoming ballistic missile, and it would really piss him off if he himself got shot down by the American or South Korean forces.

'British aircraft over South Korea, this is Hawkeye callsign Alpha Three on Guard, do you read?'

'Alpha Three, Cobra Two, you're loud and clear, but we're a little busy right now.'

'You're likely to get a lot busier, buddy. There are twenty-one interceptors heading straight for you out of bandit country. We estimate they'll be all over you in around ten minutes.'

'Thanks . . . I think,' Richter said. 'Keep us posted, please, Alpha Three. We're chasing three cruise missiles right now.'

He risked a quick glance at the HUD. His Harrier was passing ten thousand feet in a near-vertical dive. The Seersucker was in his two o'clock position at about three miles. It was time he stopped descent and turned to intercept. He was going to have to turn left, allowing the missile to fly underneath him, if he was to stand any chance of getting into a firing position. And the problem was that, as soon as he turned, he'd lose sight of the missile. It really was a one-shot option.

Richter checked the position and speed of the HY-2, then his altitude, trying to do the calculations in his head. Seven thousand feet. Six. Five and a half. He took one more glance at his target, another at the rocky terrain directly below him, then pushed the control column over to the left and eased it back slightly. The g-force pinned him into the seat as the Harrier turned hard to port, its rate of descent slowing rapidly.

He pulled the GR9 level at two thousand feet, heading south-east, and looked all around him. There was no sign of the cruise missile, but it had to be somewhere close by. He daren't turn, because that would bleed off so much speed he'd never then catch it, and he couldn't slow down for exactly the same reason. He just had to hope that his turn had been accurate enough.

Then he saw it. Around a thousand feet below, passing on his left-hand side about a mile away – and travelling much faster than Richter expected. He turned his Harrier gently to port, aiming for an intercept course, made sure the throttle was fully open, and pushed the control column slightly forward.

He selected the Sidewinder on his port wing and immediately checked that the broken circle appeared in his HUD. The HY-2 was on his left, in the eleven o'clock position, on a more or less constant bearing, so he knew his heading was good.

Without radar, he had to estimate the target's range by eye alone, but he reckoned that he was about half a mile behind it. And already he could hear the growl of the 'winder as its infrared seeker began picking up the cruise missile's exhaust plume.

Then the HY-2 pitched up and began climbing. Richter had expected the cruise missile to stay low until it hit its target. The climb suggested something different, and after a moment he guessed what the North Koreans might have planned.

'Flash. All callsigns, Cobra Two. My missile's climbing. It's possible these could be air-burst nukes.'

'Viper Two, this one's doing the same.'

Richter pulled the control column back, starting the Harrier in a steep climb to follow the Seersucker.

In the nose-cone of the HY-2, the radar altimeter recorded an altitude of two thousand metres, and sent a signal to the simple computer – little more than a glorified timing device – that controlled the warhead. It immediately activated the pre-detonation circuit check. The device was designed to explode when it reached a height of six thousand metres, an altitude it would attain in just over eleven seconds.

Chiha-ri missile base, North Korea

The moment the three Seersuckers had vanished, heading for their targets in South Korea, the technicians swarmed out of the hardened shelters and towed away the cruise missile trailers. And, because Pyongyang had made it clear that time was of the essence, in less than a minute the first of the mobile Scud TELs, or Transporter-Erector-Launchers, drove out of one of the shelters and across to the launch pad.

Chiha-ri had been the obvious choice for this phase of the operation. Not only did it host a resident Scud brigade, but it was also the principal technical support headquarters for all of North Korea's Scud missile units. And, crucially, it was a mere fifty miles north of the Demilitarized Zone, close enough to ensure that their targets south of the DMZ would get the least possible warning of the attack. If the weapons carried by the Seer-suckers did their job adequately, there might be no warning at all.

Within five minutes the six Scud launchers were in position and their technicians were making last-minute checks, all of them wearing full NBCD suits and breathing equipment because of the contents of the warheads. Once the weapons were ready, they would be launched without further reference to anyone. The orders from Pyongyang had been most specific.

Cobra Two, over South Korea

The cruise missile's unexpected manoeuvre had cost Richter ground, and he estimated he was now nearly a mile behind it. And, if his guess had been right, the warhead could detonate at any moment.

The growl in his earphones intensified and then the

broken circle in the HUD solidified as the Sidewinder locked on to the target. Richter didn't wait any longer: he fired the weapon. The solid-propellant rocket motor ignited and it streaked towards the HY-2. Just in case, he selected the starboard Sidewinder and made sure it also locked on.

The HY-2's radar altimeter sent a further signal to the computer at five thousand metres, and the three-second detonation sequence began. The North Korean technicians had based their calculations on a missile velocity of three hundred and twenty metres a second, actually a little faster than the Seersucker was travelling.

The detonation sequence had less than one second to go when the 'winder impacted with the rear of the cruise missile. The annular blast fragmentation warhead, containing over twenty pounds of high explosive, then detonated. The blast shattered the rear section of the HY-2, instantly destroying its rocket motor, and less than a tenth of a second later the remaining liquid fuel in its tanks exploded in a massive ball of fire.

The detonation wasn't powerful enough to destroy the warhead, but that didn't matter. It ripped the computer to pieces, wrecked the battery and fused the connections. The final signal never reached the nuclear device. Instead, it was torn from its mountings and began tumbling to the ground nearly twenty thousand feet below.

Richter deselected his second Sidewinder, pulled his Harrier into a steep diving turn to keep out of the blast radius and pressed his transmit button.

'Cobra Two, one Sidewinder expended. Splash one

cruise missile. Break, break. Alpha Three, what's the status of those bogies now?'

'Still inbound, Cobra Two. No, wait. Now they're turning back onto north. It looks like they're in a holding pattern. I'll keep you advised.'

'Roger. Break. Cobra Lead – what's your status?'

'Standby. Right. Two Sidewinders used and the missile is down. I'm turning away. Break. Viper One, sitrep.'

'We just—'

But whatever Charlie Forbes was going to say was lost for ever as a colossal explosion tore through the sky.

Office of the Associate Deputy Director of the Central Intelligence Agency, Langley, Virginia

Richard Muldoon actually ran through the outer office, and barely even paused at the closed door. Walter Hicks looked up in surprise as it slammed open. The two men had got back to Langley only a few minutes earlier.

'Richard?'

Muldoon slowed to a trot and tossed a couple of photographs onto Hicks's desk, then leant forward, resting his hands on the edge of the tooled leather.

'NORAD's just reported another nuke, Walter, less than two minutes ago. This one was over South Korea.'

'Oh, fuck.'

'It was pretty low-yield, definitely under twenty kilotons, and seems to have been an air-burst. The delivery vehicle was one of the Seersuckers out of Chiha-ri. They fired three, but two didn't detonate, and we don't know why. Maybe some kind of defect, or perhaps the Patriots got them, but I've seen nothing from the CFC so far. But this,' he finished, 'is what's scaring the shit out of me. These are straight from N-PIC, and that's the launch pad at Chiha-ri. As soon as the Seersuckers had been fired, they drove out these TELs.

'According to the analysts, they're Scud missiles, probably type B, and there are six of them. The TELs aren't the same as the old Russian MAZ 543 launch vehicles, but they're very similar. They're being prepped ready for launch, so if the nuke that's just gone off was the first strike, these are probably the second. The technicians on the pads are all wearing NBCD suits, which means these Scuds are carrying biological or chemical weapons. My guess is that the nuke was designed to deliver an EMP, and these are the follow-up weapons now that the Patriots batteries have probably lost their radar systems.'

'Aimed where? Seoul?'

'Almost certainly, and we've got nothing in the area that can take them out. They could launch all six of these before we could target a cruise missile or prep an air raid.'

'Fuck,' Hicks said again. 'Wait a minute – what about those British Harriers? The ones that were supposed to hit the east coast missile sites. Are they still airborne?'

'No idea,' Muldoon said, turning to leave. 'I'll go find out. The Hawkeye off the *Enterprise* was talking to them, I think.'

'Richard,' Hicks called to his colleague's retreating figure, 'if those aircraft are still in the area, don't wait for official sanction. Just tell them to get in there and toast the base with whatever weapons they've got. We'll sort out the legalities later.'

Cobra formation, over South Korea

Richter was looking north when the warhead of the third Seersucker cruise missile exploded, but snapped his head around to the left the moment he saw the flash. Even from a distance – and he guessed he was at least thirty miles from the detonation – he knew at once that it wasn't just the fuel in the HY-2's tanks exploding.

A confused babble of voices burst onto the radio as the AEW Sea King bagman and the American Hawkeye controller transmitted simultaneously, but Richter ignored them.

He was far enough away that he hoped the EMP wouldn't have much, if any, effect on his avionics, but he still turned his Harrier away from the blast and opened the throttle to put a few more precious miles between his aircraft and the nuclear explosion. He remembered from his basic NBCD lectures that the intensity of a nuclear blast diminishes more or less with the square of the distance from ground zero, but he had no way of knowing the yield of the weapon, nor how powerful the blast wave was now likely to be.

Then it hit him what seemed like only seconds later.

'Jesus H,' Richter muttered, and then his sole concern was to try to stop his aircraft being blown out of the sky. The Harrier slammed sideways and downwards as the blast wave hit it, the wings losing lift immediately as the aircraft stalled, then spun out of control.

Despite the harness, the violent manoeuvre bounced Richter around in the cockpit, his flying helmet crashing into the back of the ejection seat. Buffeted and dazed, he reacted instinctively, removing his feet from the rudder pedals and pushing the control column forward. The spin stopped in less than two turns and, the moment he was sure he'd unstalled the wings, he pulled back to start regaining height.

As he climbed away he looked at his altimeter, realizing he'd lost over eight thousand feet. Then he swiftly checked everything else, but as far as he could tell the Harrier was undamaged.

'Cobra Leader from Two. You still with me?'

'Affirmative, just about. Break, break. Viper One, Cobra One.' Nothing. 'Viper Two, Cobra One. Radio check.' Nothing.

'I don't think they're still around,' Richter said. 'They were both chasing that cruise missile, and I guess their 'winders hadn't reached it when the warhead detonated. At best, their electrics are probably fried.' He didn't need to explain the worst-case scenario – that the two Harriers might have been caught within the fireball itself when the weapon detonated.

'Cobra One, November Alpha. Request sitrep.'

'Cobra One and Two are still flying but we've lost contact with both Vipers. We shot down two of the cruise missiles but the third detonated. It was a small nuclear air burst and it's possible Vipers were caught in the blast.'

'Roger. I'll relay that to Mother. Intentions?'

'Unless you've any better ideas, we'll RTB.'

USS *Enterprise*, North Pacific Ocean

'Flash signal, sir.'

Rodgers thanked the yeoman and scanned the text. Then he stood up and walked across the CIC to the officer who was controlling the E2-C AEW aircraft.

'Where's the Hawkeye?'

'Here, sir.'

'Right, tell him to call those British aircraft – on Guard if necessary – and pass this message.' Rodgers took a ball-point pen from his pocket and rapidly wrote a few lines on a sheet of paper. 'Then tell him to send the Prowlers and Hornets directly to this position' – he wrote down the geographical coordinates of the Chiha-ri base – 'the Prowlers going in first to clear the path. They're to render whatever assistance the British aircraft need. On my orders, they can engage any target, and respond to any attack against themselves or the Harriers with whatever force they feel is necessary. As from this moment, North Korea is a free-fire zone.'

Rodgers turned away and walked out of the CIC for a quick visit to the officers' heads. The next few minutes were going to be very interesting, and he didn't want to miss a moment of it.

Cobra formation, over South Korea

'Cobra One, Alpha Three on Guard. Do you read?'

'Loud and clear. Go ahead.'

'I've a message for you from Langley, relayed by Starbase. Understand?'

'Alpha Three, this is Cobra Two. Understood. Go ahead.'

'Message reads: "Chiha-ri base at coordinates thirty-eight degrees thirty-eight decimal two five north; one two six degrees forty decimal forty-eight east preparing to launch six times Scud missile with chemical or biological warheads. Can you attack?" Message ends.'

'That's about fifty miles north of the DMZ, boss,' Richter said, 'and it's what we came out to do in the first place.'

'Agreed. And we owe these bastards for Charlie and Roger. Break. Alpha Three from Cobra One, that's affirmative. Turning starboard now.'

Chapter Twenty-Two

Monday
Chiha-ri missile base, North Korea

The Scud B missile dates from 1962, and is an improved and enhanced version of the type A, itself essentially a scaled-down copy of the German V2. Designed from the first to be fully mobile, the Scud is normally fired from a purpose-designed Transporter-Erector-Launcher, a four-axle, eight-wheel road vehicle that tips the scales at thirty-seven tons when fully loaded. The tactic envisaged for the weapon was that it would be fired, and the TEL itself would then be driven some distance away, reloaded from a trailer carrying additional missiles, and launch a second Scud.

The North Koreans had modified several aspects of the missile's operation because of their unique 'underground' military strategy. The launch process for a standard Scud B takes about one hour, and there wasn't a great deal they could do to reduce this. But what they had done was to rejig the sequence of actions so that almost all of the preparations for launch took place before the missile was raised in its cradle into the vertical firing position. This meant they could prepare the weapon in the safety of their hardened shelters and only expose it to danger in the open air immediately before launch.

All the preparations had paid off. The Scud missiles had passed their pre-flight checks with no major problems. Twelve minutes after the last missile had been driven out of the shelter and lifted into the vertical position by the two hydraulic rams on the TEL – this phase of the operation itself taking almost five minutes – the technicians began leaving the area.

In the control bunker, the commanding officer watched the last man walk off the launch pad and waited impatiently for the call from the chief technician. When the phone rang, he snatched it up before the first ring had completed.

'Yes?'

'All missiles are fully checked and prepared, sir.'

'Good. We will commence firing preparations immediately.'

He replaced the receiver and nodded to his assistant. 'Begin the countdown,' he ordered. 'Launch at thirty-second intervals, targets as designated.'

Cobra formation, over North Korea

Richter's aircraft hadn't even reached the southern side of the Demilitarized Zone before his Radar Warning Receiver began screaming. It was picking up multiple transmissions from almost all around him. The 'frying pan' on the HUD was showing over a dozen lines.

'I'm detecting Spoon Rest and Fan Song radars,' Dick Long reported on their discrete radio frequency, 'and that means SA-2s. No problem at this altitude.'

The two Harriers were in battle pair formation, keeping low and fast, no more than five hundred above the ground. The SA-2 surface-to-air missile, NATO reporting name Guideline but known as the S-75 Dvina inside Russia, is optimized to attack high-level aircraft. It was originally designed by the Soviets to counter American B-52 bombers, and is essentially powerless to intercept targets below about three thousand feet, because of constraints in the radar and guidance systems.

Knowing that was one thing, but believing it another. The HUD in Richter's GR9 kept identifying even more fire-control radars as the two aircraft swept across the four-kilometre-wide DMZ.

The boundary between the two countries is marked not by customs posts or duty-free shops, but by a narrow strip of temperate wilderness, seeded with an uncountable number of landmines, that's been virtually untouched for over half a century. Running precisely down the middle of the Demilitarized Zone is the Military Demarcation Line, which marks the frontline that existed when the ceasefire was agreed between the warring states in 1953.

The moment they crossed it, North Korean anti-aircraft gun batteries opened up, and the air in front of the Harriers was suddenly filled with puffs of black debris as the shells began exploding. Both men knew that the chances of being hit by a round from these unsophisticated weapons was very slight. Their worry was SAMs – not the cumbersome SA-2s, but the possibility that some North Korean soldier on the ground below them might be carrying a Stinger or the locally manufactured and equally deadly equivalent, the *wha-sung*. The best defence against short-range weapons like those was speed, so they pushed the Harriers as fast as they dared.

The terrain they were overflying meant they couldn't relax for a moment. The ground was deeply fissured, steep-sided valleys running in all directions, many from east to west. That meant they were continually climbing up over the tops of hills and dropping down into valleys on the other side as they headed north. That required absolute concentration, but it gave surface-to-air missiles and anti-aircraft guns very little time to lock on to them.

That didn't stop missiles being fired, however. Several times both Richter and Long saw the unmistakable smoke trails of SAMs arcing up towards them, but on each occasion either the Zeus worked its magic or they outran the missiles.

The Harrier GR9's Zeus ECM system's Radar Warning Receiver can identify over a thousand different radar emitters and automatically configure the self-defence jammer to meet the identified threat. Zeus also includes a MAW, or Missile Approach Warning, component that's designed to detect a missile launch and activate the Bofors BOL chaff dispensers without the pilot's intervention. It impressed the hell out of Richter.

As they headed deeper into North Korea, the Hawkeye used the Harriers' discrete frequency to relay information the CIA and N-PIC had gleaned from the Keyhole images, data that was being flashed to the *Enterprise* in a steady stream via a communications satellite.

'There's a small residential development at Chiha-ri, but the launch pads are separated and up to the north. The grid reference I passed you is for the launch complex, and it's set in the hills north of the workers' houses, and just south of a small mountain lake. The obvious approach is along the valley from the south-east, but that would take you right over the residential area and alert the air defence batteries, so command is suggesting you come in from due south. There's a range of hills, with tops at around fourteen hundred feet, that runs north–south, and the valley to the west of that is uninhabited. Copied so far?'

'All copied, Cobra One.'

'Roger. That approach will bring you into the Chihari valley at its widest point, but north of most of the houses. Your waypoint there is thirty-eight degrees thirty-seven decimal two four north, one two six degrees forty-one decimal zero five east, ground elevation nine hundred fifty feet. When you pass that you'll see the valley in front of you dropping down to around eight hundred feet. Then you'll have a short transit of one decimal four three miles on a heading of three five six true to the southern launch pads. The hills surrounding the pads top out at sixteen hundred fifty feet. Your suggested escape vector is to maintain a northerly heading, then turn hard left once you're over the lake and continue the turn onto south. That will keep those hills between you and Chiha-ri, and hopefully below the acquisition threshold of their air defence radars.'

'Any details of SAM types, Alpha Three?'

'Stand by, we're checking. OK, the data's inconclusive, but it looks like sierra alpha type three, with the launchers located on the periphery of the complex. They've probably got radar-controlled anti-aircraft guns on the hills above the valley, but we can't confirm that.'

MiG-25 Foxbat, callsign Zero Six, over North Korea

'Zero Six, Chunghwa. Message from command. No reports of CFC aircraft getting airborne, but two low-level high-speed contacts are reported tracking north towards Chiha-ri. They may be attempting to attack the missile complex. You are ordered to detach one combat group to intercept them. Initial heading will be one nine zero. Report when separated and in descent to three thousand five hundred metres.'

Gennadi Malakov decided his group of seven aircraft would handle the incursion, since nothing much else seemed to be happening.

'Zero Six, acknowledged. Combat Group One, descend now to three thousand five hundred metres and turn left onto one nine zero.'

Malakov glanced left and right as he pushed his control column forwards, checking that the other pilots had begun simultaneous descents. The remaining fourteen MiG-25s would hold at altitude until required for another interception, or for recovery to refuel.

'Chunghwa, Zero Six. What aircraft type are the Americans?'

'Unconfirmed, but probably not American aircraft. We believe they're British Harrier fighters.'

'Understood. Zero Six group is in descent and accelerating.'

The fact that, according to the North Korean radar controllers, the aircraft Malakov would encounter in a few minutes weren't American but British didn't bother him. A target was a target, and his training throughout almost his entire military career had been geared towards air combat, a skill that he'd never, until now, been able to demonstrate for real. Unfortunately, pitting seven MiG-25s against two British Harriers was hardly fair – Malakov knew his aircraft could easily destroy a Harrier in one-to-one combat. For a brief moment he thought about disobeying Chunghwa and telling five of the pilots to return to the formation, just to make the contest slightly more even. Then he rejected this idea. He'd just make sure he personally shot down one of the attacking aircraft.

Cobra formation, over North Korea

'Ten miles to target. Prep the weapons.'

Richter clicked an acknowledgement and started preparing his two Mavericks. He was keenly aware that, between them, the two Harriers had only four Mavericks and there were six targets to hit. He was hoping that they could ignite the fuel in one of the Scuds, and that might be enough to take out a second missile. But if they were well separated – and that would be a normal precaution when handling highly volatile fuel and munitions – destroying more than one with each weapon might prove impossible. If it was, they'd have to rely on the CRV7 rocket pods.

Chiha-ri missile base, North Korea

They were only two minutes from the end of the count-down for the first Scud launch when the telephone link to Chunghwa shrilled. The sound it made was different to every other phone in the command bunker, apart from the direct line to Pyongyang, and the commanding officer ran across to his desk to answer it.

'This is Chiha-ri.'

'What is your launch status?'

The colonel looked across at the digital display before answering. 'Ninety-seven seconds from first launch. As ordered, the remaining weapons will be fired at thirty-second intervals.'

'Can you speed up the process?'

'Negative, Chunghwa. We can pause or stop the countdown, but the launch sequence has to be followed. Why?'

'Because our radar reports that there are two enemy aircraft heading directly towards you from the south, now about one minute away. Those missiles must be fired, Colonel.'

The commanding officer didn't reply, simply dropped the telephone receiver on the desk, selected area broadcast and reached for the microphone.

'Air raid warning! Air raid warning! Two enemy aircraft approaching from the south. All anti-aircraft crews stand by. Fire at will.'

His voice echoed around the firing complex from some thirty speakers. The air-defence systems were already fully manned, and had been since well before first light that morning. The chief anti-aircraft weapon at Chiha-ri was a slightly modified Russian SA-3 SAM system. To provide optimum defence against air attack, the North Koreans had installed eight permanent twin-missile turrets around the perimeter of the launch complex, making a total of sixteen Mach 3 missiles.

The SA-3 is controlled by three separate radars, all normally carried on vehicles, but at Chiha-ri they had been mounted in fixed locations on the tallest hill within the firing complex. Initial target acquisition was handled by a P-15 'Flat Face' long-range C-band radar. The target's height was determined by a PRV-11 E-band height finder known to the West as 'Side Net', and a 'Low Blow' I/D-band fire control radar provided initial guidance to the missiles.

Although an old design, the SA-3 is still very capable. In March 1999 a Yugoslav-modified version of the weapon system – having been fitted with thermal-imaging equipment and a laser range-finder – was responsible for shooting down an American F-117 stealth fighter over Kosovo. To date, that is the only recorded loss of this aircraft type as a result of ground fire.

The reason the North Koreans had located the radars at the top of the highest ground in the vicinity was obvious – the terrain was so hilly that an aircraft even half a mile away might remain invisible in some valley. To have any chance of engaging a low-flying target, the radar heads simply had to be mounted as high as possible.

The commanding officer's broadcast was actually redundant. The SA-3 crews were fully alert, scanning their radars constantly, but no contacts were yet being displayed. This was in part because radar coverage of the valley directly to the south of the firing complex was slightly obscured by a hill whose peak was at about sixteen hundred feet, but mainly because the Harriers were still some three miles – or thirty seconds – away and below the radar horizon.

Eighteen seconds later that all changed.

Cobra formation, over North Korea

'Cobras, Alpha Three. Flash message. Seven of the hostiles that have been holding north of the DMZ have detached from the formation and are now heading south. They've increased speed to Mach two and we estimate they're about four minutes away.'

'Roger.' There wasn't much else Richter could say. But four minutes was a long time in a Harrier, and, with any luck, they'd have completed their attack on the missile base and be on their way back towards the DMZ before the approaching aircraft caught up with them. The fact that the enemy fighters were travelling at Mach 2 meant they were probably Foxbats, and he knew they weren't easy to fly at low level. If the GR9s stayed low and fast, they might be able to outmanoeuvre them, even if they could never outrun them.

The two Harriers were now flying in line astern, Richter about a quarter of a mile behind Long's aircraft. The sides of the valley seemed perilously close, and the floor closer still, but both men knew they had to stay as low as possible to avoid being detected by the fire-control radars they knew would be waiting for them at the target.

At that point, they were a mere three hundred feet above the valley's rocky floor, which was now sloping upwards. Dick Long eased his Harrier left, following the curve of the valley, and started to climb. Richter could see a rocky ridge directly in front of them, the course of the valley veering sharply to the left, and followed Long as he jinked around it, turning west, then almost immediately north.

Behind it was another ridge, the highest point – about sixteen hundred feet – lying to the east, the top of it sloping gently westwards. They couldn't go round it, so they'd have to fly over it, which would probably bring them within the coverage envelope of the Chiha-ri radars, but there wasn't any alternative.

Dick Long aimed for the lowest point, pulled his aircraft up and over the ridge with a bare hundred feet clearance, then dropped down into the valley beyond. Richter was right behind him, and according to his INGPS at the crest of the ridge they were one and a third miles from the waypoint the Hawkeye crew had given them, and a little under three miles from their target.

'I'm picking up C-band radar, probably Flat Face. That means SA-3 Goa SAMs.' Even over the radio, the tension in Long's voice was palpable. 'Watch out for the I/D-band Low Blow fire-control radar, but Zeus should handle it.'

'I admire your confidence,' Richter said, increasing speed to close up on the other Harrier as the valley widened below them.

Chiha-ri missile base, North Korea

In the concrete bunker that served as the control position for the SA-3 anti-aircraft missile system, one of the radar operators suddenly called out.

'Two contacts bearing one eight seven degrees range four point six kilometres. Low level, high speed, heading north. Contact now lost.'

'Report all further contacts. Weapons free.'

The two SA-3 turrets on the south side of the Chiha-ri base hummed to life, the launcher swinging the needle-nosed missiles to point south. Once the current location and height of the intruders had been established, and the Low Blow fire-control radar had computed their track, the missiles could be fired.

Cobra formation, over Chiha-ri, North Korea

The Harriers were less than two hundred feet apart as they roared over the waypoint and swept into the next valley. Richter glanced down at the neat rows of buildings laid out in a grid pattern, almost like the suburbs of a small American town, then he focused ahead again.

'Zeus is jamming I/D-band frequencies,' Dick Long reported. 'I see the missile site. I'll go left; you go right.'

'Roger.' Richter eased the control column slightly to the right to increase the separation between the aircraft, and glanced ahead at the launch pads. From just over two miles away he could clearly see at least three Scud missiles standing erect on their TELs. The other thing he could see was that the pads were too far apart for an explosion on one missile to have any effect on another.

'We'll have to use the CRVs as well,' he said.

'Affirmative, but fire the Mavericks first. They're more certain kills.'

Richter clicked an acknowledgement and checked the Multi-Purpose Crystal Display. He aimed the screen boresight – a large cross – at the centre of the closest Scud missile and selected his starboard-wing Maverick. Immediately the missile boresight – a smaller cross –

appeared on the MPCD and within seconds the two crosses aligned, showing that the electro-optical guidance system was detecting sufficient contrast at the point of aim for weapon release. The Harrier twitched slightly as the Maverick accelerated away, its solid-fuel motor propelling it in seconds to a speed of over seven hundred miles an hour.

The Maverick is a 'fire-and-forget' missile, so immediately Richter aligned the screen boresight with the second Scud.

Chiha-ri missile base, North Korea

The Zeus was doing its job well. Every radar screen in the SA-3 control bunker was flooded with spikes, effectively blinding the operators. Without radar guidance, the SAM system was powerless to intercept the attacking aircraft.

But the North Korean troops manning two anti-aircraft gun emplacements on the south side of the missile base didn't need radar for their weapons to function. They could see their targets and immediately began pumping high-explosive shells across the valley towards the incoming Harriers.

Cobra Two, over Chiha-ri, North Korea

As Richter aligned the boresights, the first anti-aircraft shells detonated about a hundred yards in front of, and slightly above, his Harrier. The sudden puffs of black seemed alarmingly close, and he inadvertently twitched at the very instant he released the second Maverick.

'Keep low,' Long radioed. 'They probably can't depress the barrels below the horizontal.'

Richter was already uncomfortably close to the valley floor, but obediently pushed the control column further forward. As he did so, his first Maverick exploded on contact with the Scud he'd targeted, and at almost the same moment Long's missile impacted with a Scud on the left-hand side of the site.

Two down, four to go.

MiG-25 Foxbat, callsign Zero Six, over North Korea

Fifteen miles north of Chiha-ri, Gennadi Malakov slowed his Foxbat down to subsonic speed. If he stayed at Mach 2, the aircraft would overshoot the base and he'd probably never even see the British fighters, far less be able to engage them.

'Radiate, and arm weapons,' Malakov ordered, switched on his Saphir radar and prepared his four R-40T infrared-guided missiles.

Cobra Two, over Chiha-ri, North Korea

Ten seconds after the first two explosions, Richter's second Maverick flew harmlessly past its target and impacted a rocky outcrop just beyond the pad, the detonation impressive but totally ineffective.

'Bugger.' The Maverick has about an eighty-five-per-cent kill probability, but because of the anti-aircraft fire he wasn't certain that he'd got a proper lock-on with the weapon.

Long's second missile scored a direct hit, but that still left three Scuds waiting on the launch pads.

Richter pulled his Harrier round hard to the left, selected the port-wing CRV7 rocket pod and immediately reversed direction. His S-shaped turn brought his aircraft around so that he was pointing almost directly at the second Scud on its TEL. The CRV7 Operational Pod contains nineteen unguided rockets, and has a range of only just over two miles, so he needed to be absolutely sure of his target.

He ignored the anti-aircraft fire, getting steadily closer as the North Korean gunners tracked him, and he stabilized the aircraft. He waited until he was perhaps a mile from the Scud, checked his aim carefully and fired the entire pod. Then he pulled the Harrier into a right turn and pointed it down towards the valley floor, heading north to start a second attack run from that direction.

The CRV7s spread out as they approached the target, something like a blast from a shotgun. Most missed, but six smashed into the TEL. More importantly, three hit the Scud itself, spearing through the thin aluminium skin of the missile and spraying liquid fuel across the concrete, fuel that almost immediately ignited. In seconds, the launch pad was an inferno.

Four of the Scuds were destroyed, but that still left two missiles intact.

Chiha-ri missile base, North Korea

Inside the Chiha-ri command bunker it was noisy chaos. Orders were being shouted and ignored, men were standing staring at their telemetry screens, telephones were ringing but nobody was answering them, and through the armoured-glass windows leaping flames were clearly visible as the remains of the four destroyed Scuds were consumed by their own fuel.

But there were still two missiles left. The commanding officer, unable to make himself heard over the cacophony, drew his pistol and fired two rounds into the wooden floor. Immediately the noise stopped.

'Do your jobs,' he screamed. 'Launch the missiles.'

And with frequent fearful glances through the windows, the technicians bent to their tasks.

MiG-25 Foxbat, callsign Zero Six, over Chiha-ri, North Korea

Malakov could see the Chiha-ri site from five miles away – the four raging fires were obvious, plumes of thick black smoke rising into the air above them. But what he couldn't see was any sign of the attacking aircraft. Perhaps, he wondered, they'd already made their escape, but if they had they wouldn't get far. He'd make sure their pilots never left North Korea alive.

Cobra Two, over Chiha-ri, North Korea

'We've got company,' Dick Long said. 'I'm detecting Fox Fire radar from the north, which means the 'bats are about to join the party, and we've got exactly one Sidewinder between us. This is probably going to get quite exciting.'

'Roger that. Break. Alpha Three, what's the range of those bandits?'

'Inside six miles, now subsonic and in descent.'

Richter was just north of the firing complex, in a left turn to line up on one of the two remaining Scuds. He glanced to his right and could clearly see some half a dozen aircraft heading directly towards him.

'Visual the bandits,' he called, then turned his attention back to the matter in hand. His Harrier had only a single Sidewinder remaining, so engaging the MiG-25s in air-to-air combat would be a very uneven match. But destroying the Scuds had a much higher priority than his personal survival, and he still had one CRV7 pod.

MiG-25 Foxbat, callsign Zero Six, over Chiha-ri, North Korea

'Zero Six, Chunghwa. Eight high-speed contacts approaching from bearing zero eight zero. Range twenty miles, low level. Possibly American. Combat Group Two is heading to intercept, present range fifty-three miles.'

'Acknowledged. Zero Six will deal with the aircraft attacking Chiha-ri. Remainder of the Combat Group, break off immediately and engage the Americans.'

Malakov glanced to his left and saw the other MiG-25s turning and accelerating away from him. That made the contest more even: he could handle the two Harriers himself, once he found them.

And then he saw two fast-moving contacts on his

radar, about five miles ahead. Obviously the attacking aircraft were so low that they'd been lost in the ground clutter, or behind some of the surrounding hills.

But now he had them.

Chiha-ri missile base, North Korea

In the command bunker, the countdown for the first of the remaining two Scuds was down to the last couple of seconds, and the missile was still standing unscathed on the TEL. The commanding officer alternated his gaze between the digital clock that showed the countdown progress and the view of the missile through the window.

As the clock reached zero, he saw what he'd been fearing: one of the attacking aircraft was sweeping in from the north, heading directly towards the launch pad.

Then two things happened simultaneously. The missile's engine ignited with a roar, and the Scud lifted smoothly off the launcher and accelerated into the sky. And a ripple of flame appeared below the right-hand wing of the grey-painted swept-wing aircraft. An instant later several rockets smashed into the now-redundant TEL and the concrete launch pad, but none touched the Scud.

Cobra Two, over Chiha-ri, North Korea

In his GR9, Richter knew the moment he fired the CRV7s that he was too late. Even as the rockets streaked towards the launch pad, he could see the Scud climbing away. They'd failed to stop the launch – or more accurately, *he* had failed to stop the launch when he missed the second Scud with his Maverick. If that missile had hit, he'd have fired his CRV7s at least one minute earlier, when the Scud was still sitting in its TEL.

His remaining Sidewinder was of no use against the missile, because it almost certainly wouldn't be fast enough to catch it: he guessed the Scud was already about three thousand feet off the ground, probably travelling at close to Mach 2 and still accelerating. The 'winder had a maximum speed of Mach 2.5, and a fairly short range. The mathematics of an intercept were compelling and unarguable.

There was, he assessed, just one thing he could do that might work. It was a hell of a risk, but it was the only possible way he could think of that might bring down the Scud. He glanced to the north, but could only see one incoming Foxbat. Presumably the others had spread out or climbed to high level. But one should be enough.

He opened the throttle fully and pulled the Harrier into a high-speed climb.

MiG-25 Foxbat, callsign Zero Six, over Chiha-ri, North Korea

Gennadi Malakov checked his instruments and ensured that the first of his four R-40T infrared-homing missiles had locked on to the British aircraft that was now climbing steeply above the Chiha-ri launch site.

'Excellent,' he murmured, and released the weapon.

Then he turned his attention back to the Saphir radar, looking for the second target. This really was just too easy.

Cobra Two, over Chiha-ri, North Korea

'Paul! Get to low level. You've an Acrid heading straight for you.'

'Copied,' Richter responded, concentrating on following the Scud in its climb. 'It's behind me so I can't see it. Can you call ranges.'

'For fuck's sake, you can't outrun it. It's a Mach four missile.'

'I'm not going to try. Just call when it's about a mile behind me.'

Cobra One, over Chiha-ri, North Korea

Dick Long suddenly guessed what Richter might be intending. He turned his aircraft so that he could see his wingman more clearly and, more crucially, track the massive Acrid missile that was closing on the Harrier at over four times the speed of sound.

Long just hoped Richter knew what he was doing.

Chiha-ri missile base, North Korea

In the Chiha-ri command bunker, the digital countdown for the last Scud passed five seconds to go, and the missile was still untouched on the pad. Two out of six launches wouldn't please Pyongyang, the commanding officer knew, but in the circumstances it was a far better result than he had realistically expected. He looked out of the armoured window towards the TEL and nodded in satisfaction as, with a roar and sudden burst of flame, the last Scud leapt away from the launcher.

Cobra One, over Chiha-ri, North Korea

'Estimate two miles, Paul. Standby. Oh, shit. The last Scud's just been launched.'

'Copied.'

'Stand by for one mile point. Five, four, three, two, one. One mile now, now, now. Get the fuck out of there.'

Chapter Twenty-Three

Monday
MiG-25 Foxbat, callsign Zero Six, over Chiha-ri, North Korea

Gennadi Malakov's attention was directed almost entirely towards locating and obtaining a missile lock on the second Harrier. He was confident that his R-40T would destroy the first aircraft within seconds, as the idiot Englishman was actually making it easier for the infrared-guided missile to kill him, because he was climbing almost straight up. If he'd dived down to low level there would have been a chance, albeit a small one, that he could have got away.

Then he spotted his second target. The Harrier was in a gentle climb on the far side of the missile base. Malakov pointed his MiG-25 directly towards it, selected his second R-40T and waited for the seeker head to lock on.

Chiha-ri missile base, North Korea

Only after the last Scud had lifted off its TEL did the commanding officer finally answer the direct line from Chunghwa.

'We've launched two missiles,' he reported, 'but the attacking aircraft destroyed the other four.'

The brief silence from the Air Command headquarters spoke volumes. 'We will discuss your failure to obey the simplest of orders later, Colonel. Now, order your anti-aircraft guns and missile batteries to cease firing. We are sending in fighters to locate and destroy the British intruders.'

Cobra Two, over Chiha-ri, North Korea

Richter had done a very rough calculation in his head. If the Acrid was travelling at Mach 4, that meant it was covering over half a mile every second. So from the one-mile distance, and with the Harrier flying at around four hundred miles an hour, the missile would hit him between two and three seconds later. It was, he knew, going to be very tight.

He waited for a quick count of two after Dick Long's call, then acted. He slammed the nozzles into the fully-downward landing position, then chopped the throttle back. It felt as if he'd been kicked in the arse by an angry elephant, and the grey haze of g-loc swam in front of his eyes for a second or two before the 'speed jeans' began squeezing the blood back up towards his brain.

The effect on the Harrier was immediate. The aircraft had been climbing almost vertically: the change in nozzle angle stopped the climb and kicked the aircraft onto its back. When Richter cut the power, the GR9 completed the loop and began falling nose-first back towards the ground.

And that was exactly what he had intended. The violent manoeuvre punched his aircraft away from the flight-path of the Acrid. Cutting the power and instantly changing the Harrier's direction of flight as he'd done – a manoeuvre no other aircraft was capable of performing – virtually eliminated its infrared signature. But he'd had to leave it until the last possible moment, so that the Acrid wouldn't be able to lock on to him again. As the Harrier started descending, Richter looked ahead, down towards the ground, and saw the missile powering past him.

The moment the target's infrared return vanished, the missile's seeker head began trying to reacquire the heat source. It didn't detect the Harrier, but right in front of it was the massive exhaust bloom from the Scud missile, half a mile ahead. The Acrid's computer is a fairly basic device, and its target discrimination isn't particularly sensitive, so it immediately began tracking the new contact.

The Scud was still accelerating, but the Acrid was travelling at close to its maximum speed of Mach 4.5, and overhauled it rapidly. Less than three seconds after Richter kicked his Harrier into a dive, the seventy-kilogram high-explosive fragmentation warhead of the Acrid hit the rear of the Scud and detonated.

The result was spectacular. The remaining fuel in the Scud's tanks exploded in a massive fireball, blowing debris in all directions.

MiG-25 Foxbat, callsign Zero Six, over Chiha-ri, North Korea

Malakov didn't see the Acrid destroy the Scud. Though aware of the explosion, he assumed it was just his missile bringing down the British aircraft. He was now waiting for his second R-40T to lock on to the other Harrier but, unlike the first one, this pilot wasn't making it easy. He'd stopped his climb almost as soon as Malakov identified him, presumably because his ECM fit had warned him he was being irradiated, and went back to low level where the Saphir radar was finding it hard to detect him.

The Russian pilot overflew Chiha-ri, then banked left to retrace his route. The Harrier had to be somewhere down below him. It was now just a matter of finding it.

Cobra One, over Chiha-ri, North Korea

Dick Long was looking for a way out, and a way past the Foxbat. The last Scud was already about five thousand feet above the ground and accelerating. There was no way his Harrier could catch it and, even if he could, he had no weapons left that could bring it down. And if he did climb up after it, the Foxbat would launch an Acrid and the Scud would be too high for Richter's trick to work a second time.

That, he reflected sourly, was going to be the one that got away. Destroying five out of the six – even if the fifth one had needed a little help from a Russian missile – was still a remarkably good result. But he doubted if the residents of Seoul would agree with him when the sarin, or mustard gas, or botulinus toxin, or whatever the North Koreans had loaded inside the missile's warhead exploded on the streets of the capital.

The Foxbat was the more immediate problem. The pilot was clearly looking for him, but by flying fairly slowly at very low level, now less than two hundred feet above the ground, Long believed the MiG's radar wouldn't be able to detect him. But then getting away from Chiha-ri clearly wasn't going to be easy.

'Cobra Two. You still here, Paul?'

'Affirmative. I see the Scud, but where's the Foxbat?'

'Overhead Chiha-ri. I'm down in the weeds, south of the base, and he's just overflown me, turning onto north. The anti-aircraft guns have stopped firing, which probably means more fighters are on their way. It's time we got the hell out of here.'

Cobra Two, over Chiha-ri, North Korea

Then something totally unexpected happened. Richter was looking up through his canopy towards the accelerating Scud when a streak of bright light shot across the sky from somewhere to the east of his position and smashed into the missile, which instantly exploded.

'What the hell was that?' he demanded.

'That, my friend, was an alpha india mike one two zero, better known as AMRAAM.' The new voice on the Harriers' discrete frequency was unmistakably American.

'This is Cobra Leader. Identify yourself,' Dick Long snapped.

'This is Blade One, lead cab of eight Super Hornets from the Mobile Chernobyl. My colleagues are having an exchange of views with some MiGs a few miles east, but I thought y'all could use some help over here, that's if you don't mind me joining the party.'

'Did you bring a bottle?' Richter asked, levelling his Harrier three hundred feet above the ground and turning onto north.

MiG-25 Foxbat, callsign Zero Six, over Chiha-ri, North Korea

The explosion of the second Scud immediately attracted Malakov's attention, and he looked up sharply through his canopy. It could, he supposed, have been some kind of a malfunction, though he knew the Scud was a generally reliable, if fairly inaccurate, missile. But the Russian didn't believe in convenient malfunctions. He thought the weapon was far more likely to have been brought down by an air-to-air missile, presumably fired by the remaining Harrier. Or perhaps one of the Americans had done it.

'Chunghwa, this is Zero Six. I've shot down one of the British fighters, but I've just seen a Scud missile explode shortly after lift-off. Where are the American aircraft now?'

'About fifteen miles to the east of Chiha-ri, Zero Six. Wait. No, we now hold three contacts in your vicinity, two intermittent, probably at low level, and one solid.'

'Three?'

'Confirmed. The intermittent contacts are believed to be the British aircraft, so the other may be one of the American intruders.'

That couldn't be right. He *knew* he'd shot down one of the Harriers – he'd seen the explosion. Chunghwa must be wrong, and there must be two American fighters in the area. He returned his attention to the radar display, and simultaneously began a right turn, back towards Chiha-ri. He still had three missiles, so he could handle two Yankees and the remaining Harrier, no problem.

But as he straightened up on north, his Sirena S-3M radar homing and warning system suddenly alerted him. He checked the readout: an APG-79 I-band radar on a bearing of zero eight two. That, Malakov knew, meant an American F/A-18, a much more dangerous opponent than a Harrier. But he also knew that on the first day of the 1991 Gulf War a MiG-25 had shot down an American Hornet – Iraq's only air combat kill during the conflict.

He checked his weapons, engaged the ECM system, then pulled the Foxbat round in a right-hand climbing turn onto east, looking for a target.

Blade One, over Chiha-ri, North Korea

The Super Hornet's APG-79 radar was suddenly flooded by spikes as the MiG-25's ECM equipment blotted out the picture, and simultaneously the ALR-67 Radar Warning Receiver conveyed the unmistakable message that the aircraft was being irradiated by a Fox Fire radar.

The pilot immediately engaged full counter-measures, but that didn't seem to have any effect. He'd heard about the sheer power of the Foxbat's radar and its ability to 'burn through' any ECM system, but this was the first time he'd seen it in action. And it frightened him, because he'd no clue where the Russian-built aircraft currently was. Without his radar, he was both blind and effectively unarmed.

'Cobras, Blade One.' The American's voice was noticeably louder and sounded more stressed than his previous transmissions. 'I'm being irradiated and jammed by this guy, and I can't get a lock on him. Turning away and streaming a decoy.'

He hauled his Super Hornet round in a tight left turn onto east and extended the aircraft's ALE-50 Towed Decoy System, a combat-proven protection against both air-to-air and surface-to-air weapons.

MiG-25 Foxbat, callsign Zero Six, over Chiha-ri, North Korea

Gennadi Malakov's Saphir radar was showing a solid contact twenty kilometres to the east, but the target was already turning away.

The type 'TD' and 'RD' variants of the R-40 missile – the initial 'D' standing for *dorabotanaya*, the Russian word meaning 'more elaborate' – have a range of fifty kilometres, but the earlier 'R' and 'T' types are effective at only just over half that distance. Malakov's MiG-25 was carrying three R-40T weapons, so he knew he had to get closer to be sure of a kill. He pushed the throttles forward to increase his speed, and aimed his Foxbat directly at the fleeing aircraft.

Cobra Two, over Chiha-ri, North Korea

Richter looked left, and there, about three miles to the west, he saw the unmistakable shape of a MiG-25 turning right onto an easterly heading. He glanced east, but the Super Hornet was too far away for him to see it.

Despite that, Richter had no doubt that the Russian aircraft was now in pursuit of the American.

He also knew he himself was in an almost perfect position to intercept it. His Harrier was low level, probably invisible to the enemy aircraft's radar in the ground clutter, and he still had a single Sidewinder. And because the GR9 has no radar, and the 'winder uses infrared homing, the Foxbat pilot would have no way of detecting him, unless his Harrier painted on the MiG's radar. Richter would just have to keep low and hope for the best.

He glanced again at the Foxbat, estimating its speed and heading, then turned right to match its track. He selected the Sidewinder, checked that the broken circle symbol appeared on the HUD, and increased speed so that when he had to climb, he'd be able to gain height as quickly as possible.

'Two from One. Position and intentions?'

'Just east of the missile site, low-level, tracking zero nine zero. I'm just going to try and slip my last Sidewinder up that Foxbat's tailpipe.'

'You what? You *have* to be out of your fucking tree. The Harrier's no match for the MiG, and we've barely enough fuel now to get back across the DMZ. Let the Hornets handle him.'

'Reality check, Dick. Even if we stay low-level, the moment we start heading south that guy's going to see us on radar and then we're in real trouble. If we're going to get out of here, we have to take him down first.'

'And how do we do that?' Long asked.

So Richter told him.

'I hope you know what we're doing,' Long muttered, turned his Harrier east and started climbing.

FOXBAT

MiG-25 Foxbat, callsign Zero Six, over Chiha-ri, North Korea

Malakov was waiting for his R-40T to lock on to the fleeing American aircraft, but he was still very much aware that there were another two enemy fighters somewhere in the area.

His Saphir radar detected a contact in his right two o'clock position, less than four miles away and climbing out from Chiha-ri. It had to be the second Harrier. Malakov instantly changed his priorities. He would pursue the American once he'd dealt with the British aircraft.

He turned towards the new contact. The R-40T infrared seeker head-locked on almost at once and Malakov fired the weapon.

Cobra Two, over Chiha-ri, North Korea

Richter waited until the Foxbat was just ahead of him, then pulled up into a steep climb. Almost immediately he heard the growl as the Sidewinder detected the MiG-25's jet exhaust.

He saw the flare from the aircraft's port wing as the pilot fired an Acrid at Dick Long's climbing GR9. At the moment of release, the Harrier was only about three miles from the Foxbat. The R-40T would cover that distance in roughly six seconds.

'Missile fired!' Richter called. 'Stand by. Evasive action now, now, now.'

Cobra One, over Chiha-ri, North Korea

One of the problems with a heavy, very fast missile like the Acrid is that it's not particularly agile, but in most cases this doesn't matter because no aircraft currently flying can outrun its Mach 4.5 maximum speed, and few can manoeuvre fast enough to get out of its path. But the Harrier could.

Long waited until he heard Richter's call. Then he rotated the nozzles fully forwards, almost stopping the aircraft dead in mid-air, and chopped the throttle back, a virtual repeat of Richter's manoeuvre just minutes before. The Harrier dropped like a stone and the Acrid punched a hole through the air where the GR9 had been three-tenths of a second earlier.

Cobra Two, over Chiha-ri, North Korea

Richter's Harrier was a thousand feet below the Foxbat when the broken circle in the HUD solidified, showing that the 'winder had locked on. He didn't hesitate, and immediately fired the missile. The solid-fuel rocket motor ignited and boosted the Sidewinder to two and a half times the speed of sound in a matter of seconds.

Richter watched critically as it curved away from his Harrier and angled towards the Foxbat, already travelling close to Mach 2. Then he turned his aircraft away, heading back towards Chiha-ri, where Dick Long should also be heading. If the missile killed the 'bat, they might just get away unscathed. If it missed, they were in deep trouble.

FOXBAT

MiG-25 Foxbat, callsign Zero Six, over Chiha-ri, North Korea

Gennadi Malakov wasn't entirely sure he believed his eyes. The grey Harrier had apparently stopped dead in mid-air, then dropped straight down into a valley as his R-40T had been about to impact it. Now he'd either have to reacquire it and use another missile, or simply forget about it and catch up with the American Hornet.

But before he had a chance to make a decision, Richter's Sidewinder smashed into his starboard engine exhaust at a relative speed of about three hundred miles per hour and the twenty-pound warhead exploded.

When they designed the MiG-25, the Mikoyan-Gurevich team had included a firewall between the two engines, but this was intended to protect against an engine failure, not the impact of a missile, and offered little resistance to the high-explosive detonation.

For the briefest of moments, Malakov thought his aircraft might have suffered some kind of mechanical problem, then he realized what must have happened. The Foxbat lurched sideways and the cockpit came alive as fire-warning klaxons sounded and engine instruments began showing the extent of the damage. If it had just been the starboard engine that the missile destroyed, he might have been able to save the aircraft, but the warhead's detonation had also blown lumps of steel through the firewall and into the combustion chamber of the port engine, which almost immediately caught fire.

With both engines destroyed, the MiG-25 was going nowhere but down, and Malakov had no intention of staying with it, so he did what any prudent pilot would have done – he ejected.

Fifteen seconds later, the burning Foxbat crashed into a hill eight miles east of Chiha-ri. And, ninety seconds after that, Gennadi Malakov landed hard, but unhurt, two miles away. An army patrol found him four hours later and automatically shot him as a deserter.

Cobra One and Two

'Now can we go home?' Long asked, as he pulled his Harrier up to join Richter.

'Yes,' Richter said, with a final glance back towards the burning wreckage of the MiG-25. 'Now we can go home.'

Chapter Twenty-Four

Monday
Cobra One and Two

Ten minutes later the two aircraft crossed the DMZ into South Korean airspace and turned west. They knew they wouldn't make it back to the ship with what they had in their tanks, so instead landed at Seoul to refuel.

The airport was in a state of chaos, to put it mildly. The nuclear weapon in the Seersucker had detonated twenty miles away at around nineteen thousand feet, and the EMP had done considerable damage. Radars and radios weren't working properly and, before they approached, the two Harriers had been forced to use Guard frequency, which someone in the Control Tower was monitoring on a standby radio. Fortunately, the pumps on the fuel bowsers were simple electrical devices, and so had been unaffected by the blast.

Just over four hours after they'd taken off from the *Illustrious*, the two aircraft landed back on board.

T'ae'tan Air Base, North Korea

When Kim Yong-Su had explained the reality of the situation to the 'Dear Leader', he'd received the most explicit instructions.

Clearly they couldn't proceed with the invasion. They'd utilized almost all the plutonium in their vaults and, as two of the three EMP weapons had been destroyed, the ability of the South Korean forces to repel them was only slightly affected. To proceed would have virtually guaranteed that the Americans would land troops in South Korea, because obviously the Taep'o-dong bluff hadn't worked. Within minutes of the attack starting, US Navy aircraft had entered North Korean airspace and destroyed fourteen of their MiG-25s and badly damaged three others, for the loss of just two of the Super Hornets.

With his plans in ruins, the 'Dear Leader' was looking for someone to blame, and he didn't have to look very far. The plan had been suggested and conceived by Pak Je-San, and so its failure was clearly his fault. Which explained why Kim Yong-Su had just landed at T'ae'tan with a squad of soldiers in two Mil Mi-8 transport helicopters.

Twenty minutes after it touched down, one of the helicopters was airborne again, heading north with one extra passenger on board, the man lying bound, gagged and blindfolded on the floor. Fifteen minutes after that, the second aircraft took off and followed the first, a woman and two young children lashed together and secured to one of the fuselage side strakes.

HMS *Illustrious*, Yellow Sea

'We paid a very high price, gentlemen,' Captain Alexander Davidson said, 'but, thanks to the two of you, I think the end result was better than we had any reason to expect in the circumstances.' He was standing in the Main Briefing Room, with Roger Black beside him. Dick Long and Richter were slumped in the front row of seats, both looking exhausted.

'We've had confirmation from Seoul,' Black said. 'Their patrols found the wreckage of both Harriers on the ground below the site of the air-burst. The bodies of Charlie Forbes and Roger Whittard were still strapped in. The initial medical evidence suggests they were killed instantly by the blast when the weapon detonated.

'According to the latest signals from CINCFLEET, based on American technical intelligence, North Korea's now abandoned the invasion attempt. They've started withdrawing their additional troops from the area close to the DMZ, and their forces appear to be reverting to normal readiness. Despite the detonation of the North Korean nuclear weapon, it looks as if both sides are going to maintain the status quo. It's possible that the cruise missiles they fired contained their entire supply of plutonium and, without the destructive effects of the EMP to cripple the South Korean forces, they weren't going to risk proceeding.'

Black glanced at his watch. 'The bar's opened already, because of what happened to Charlie and Roger. You should both go down there. The rest of the squadron will want to talk to you about the mission, but be careful how much you tell them. Officially, neither of you ever crossed the DMZ, and all the action took place over South Korea. Sign the bar chits with "Viper", as it'll make accounting easier.'

An old Royal Naval tradition is that on the day an

officer dies, the entire wardroom drinks on his mess bill, which is then written off.

'Why not?' Richter murmured, and stood up.

Office of the Associate Deputy Director of the Central Intelligence Agency, Langley, Virginia

'It looks like they've given up,' Muldoon said. 'The latest pictures show the extra troops dispersing, and there's noticeably less activity at most of the North Korean bases.'

'I've just got back from the White House, and the President's decided we're not going to embark on a military response,' Hicks replied. 'Pyongyang has sent an apology for the nuke that detonated over Seoul. They're claiming that the release was an unauthorized act by a disaffected officer, and officially we're buying that. They've already offered financial reparations for the damage caused, and that includes the two British Harriers that were lost trying to take out the Seersucker.'

'They're buying their way out? But North Korea's virtually bankrupt.'

'I know, so I guess they'll just increase their production of hard drugs for a few years to cover the cost. The problem we have is that if we did decide to eliminate that psychopathic dwarf in Pyongyang, we'd either have to use nukes ourselves or get dug in for another Vietnam, and neither option's politically acceptable in the present climate.'

'So we wait for the next brilliant plan the little shit comes up with?'

'I guess so,' Hicks said, 'but maybe next time we'll be better placed to take him down.'

Camp 22, Haengyong, North Hamgyong Province, North Korea

North Korea isn't a particularly big country, and the flight took only just over an hour. Both helicopters landed a few minutes apart on the square that lies between the armoury and the office of the Camp Director.

Once the rotors had stopped, the prisoners were hustled into the torture and detention centre on the west side of the square. Preparations had been made for their reception, and the order of their arrival had been specified. Pak Je-San was already gagged and strapped to a chair bolted to the floor in front of the clear glass wall of the gas chamber when his wife and two children were led towards the killing room.

The moment he saw them he began pulling at his bonds, but the soldiers who had secured him knew their trade, and his struggles were completely ineffective.

Kim Yong-Su smiled pleasantly at the woman, who was clearly terrified, her hands clutching at her children's shoulders, and opened the airtight door to usher her inside the chamber. He looked, bizarrely, like a doorman at a good hotel welcoming a favoured guest, and within moments the three of them – Pak Je-San's wife and his two sons, aged ten and eight – had stepped inside. There was, after all, no other option for them.

The door was sealed and the internal pressure checked. Pak moaned in anguish as his wife stared helplessly at him through the armoured glass, and his eyes filled with tears.

Kim Yong-Su ordered the cameras to start recording – although it was an execution, useful data could still be obtained – then walked across and took the chair beside him. He settled himself comfortably, then nodded to the chief scientist, who started a stopwatch and opened the valve that allowed the gas to flow down the injection tube and into the chamber.

'We're using soman,' Kim remarked in a conversational tone to Pak, who'd closed his eyes and bowed his head as he heard the rush of the injected gas. 'It shouldn't take long.'

The gas chamber wasn't soundproofed, but the thick glass wall served to muffle any sounds from the inside.

When his wife screamed, Pak looked up and stared at her for what he knew would be the last time. His sons had already collapsed, their slight frames twitching involuntarily as the agent wreaked havoc on their nervous systems. Urine and faeces stained their clothes and the grubby metal plates that formed the floor. Then his wife fell backwards and Pak closed his eyes again. That he couldn't bear to watch.

Four minutes later the gas flow was switched off and the pumps began purging the chamber. Pak looked up again, at the three pathetic bundles that had once been his family, as strong hands began releasing the straps that held him in the chair. Anger burned inside him, but he knew resistance was completely futile.

Three prisoners wearing grey overalls and gas masks opened the door of the chamber and dragged out the bodies. A sharp command brought Pak to his feet, and he shuffled round to the chamber entrance, Kim walking beside him.

'For you, we're going to use tabun,' he explained. 'It's not quite as fast-acting as soman, so you'll have a little more time to suffer.'

Pak Je-San stepped into the chamber and waited for the door to be closed. He'd resolved to simply sit down close to the injection pipe and inhale as deeply as he could, to finish his life quickly.

Behind him he heard a sudden commotion, and looked round in surprise. The door had slammed shut, but Kim Yong-Su was *inside* the chamber. The government official was yelling and banging on the door, but the smiles on the faces of the men outside told their own story.

And despite himself, Pak began to laugh.

HMS *Illustrious*, Yellow Sea

The mood in the Wardroom was subdued. Most officers who weren't on duty were there, standing or sitting in small groups as they discussed the events of the last few hours. Richter was sitting in one corner, half a cup of coffee on the table in front of him, and still wearing flying overalls, a technical breach of etiquette that no one appeared too concerned about. He was wondering if he could be bothered to change before lunch. Or even to eat lunch. All he really wanted to do was sleep.

When the communications rating appeared in the doorway, Richter knew almost instinctively that he was the addressee on the signal the man was holding. He got up, walked over towards him, signed the Classified Documents Register, and ripped open the envelope. The message was short and to the point, and Richter knew immediately that he wasn't going to be getting much sleep in the near future. Or, at least, not on this ship.

RICHTER, ILLUSTRIOUS. RETURN LONDON IMMEDIATE. OVERRIDE PRIORITY <u>FRANTIC</u>. SIMPSON, FOE.

Thirty minutes later Richter was escorted onto the flight deck by the duty SE rating. They stopped just abeam the Merlin's cargo door and waited for the pilot, Craig Howe, to give permission for him to board the aircraft. The moment the marshaller waved him forward, he walked across, ducking as he moved under the rotor disk.

As he strapped himself into the seat, about to lift off for Seoul, Richter wondered just what the hell Simpson had got them involved in now. He'd only heard the 'FRANTIC' priority code-word used once since he'd been at FOE, and had hoped he'd never hear it again. But, he reflected, leaning back and finally closing his eyes, he supposed he'd find out soon enough.

Author's note

EMP and the MiG-25 Foxbat

The existence of the electromagnetic pulse caused by the detonation of a nuclear weapon was not suspected by the American scientific community until 9 July 1962, as a direct result of a classified experiment called Starfish Prime, itself part of a series of tests code-named Operation Dominic. Utilizing a Thor launch vehicle carrying a W49 warhead, this was a high-yield – 1.4 megatons – nuclear test conducted at an altitude of around 250 miles over the Pacific Ocean, which had significant, and previously unsuspected, secondary effects.

Some one thousand miles distant in Hawaii, power lines fused; televisions, radios and other electrical equipment burnt out; and hundreds of street lamps failed. On other Pacific islands, microwave links were destroyed, cutting telephone connections. Only when this damage was analysed did American scientists realize the potential damage that a high-altitude nuclear blast could cause to an advanced and technology-dependent society.

The Russians, in contrast, had known about this effect for at least seven years, following their detonation on 22 November 1955 of a 1.6-megaton thermonuclear device code-named RDS-37, and possibly as early as 1953 when they exploded the comparatively low-yield (400 kilotons) Joe 4 weapon.

What is almost certain is that knowledge of the destructive effects of the EMP guided the design of the MiG-25 Foxbat interceptor's avionics. The Mikoyan-Gurevich bureau's use of valve technology in this cutting-edge fighter, rather than readily available solid-state electronics, only makes sense in this context.

It is also a fact that there were no existing or planned Western aircraft that could fly at anything like the speed the Foxbat could achieve: one was clocked on radar in the early 1970s by the Israelis at Mach 3.2. Despite this, the MiG-25's Machmeter was red-lined at Mach 2.5 and, according to Viktor Belenko, if the aircraft's speed exceeded Mach 2.8 there was a danger the engines would accelerate out of control. This was at least in part because the Tumansky R-15B-300 afterburning turbojets had originally been designed for use in a single-engined and single-use Mach 2+ reconnaissance drone, the Tupolev Tu-123 Yastreb or Hawk.

The Russians have never publicly admitted that the MiG-25 was actually intended to intercept ICBMs, but several unofficial sources have claimed that this was the case.

Camp 22

This is one of about a dozen concentration and slave-labour camps in North Korea, which together hold around 200,000 prisoners. Located near Haengyong in North Hamgyong Province and close to the borders with China and Russia, Camp 22 is the largest, and its description in this novel is accurate.

The 'crimes' most of these prisoners have committed would not be considered offences in any other nation. Many are there because they, or one of their relatives, are believed to be critical of the ruling regime or, equally dangerous to Pyongyang, are Christians or support Christianity. And Kim Jong-Il is absolutely determined to stamp out the 'bad blood' that causes citizens of his country to entertain such heretical notions: as a matter of course, three entire generations of the criminal's family will be seized and sent to the North Korean gulag for any such infraction.

Documentary evidence exists that condemned prisoners are transported to Camp 22 by the Pyongyang regime specifically to be used in human experimentation into the effects of poisonous gases and liquids.

These 'experiments' range from detailed observations of the effects of newly developed substances in the gas chamber to rough-and-ready executions carried out in the most casual manner. In one reported case, some fifty women were selected at random and fed cabbage leaves laced with an unidentified poison that resulted in them vomiting blood and suffering agonizing deaths within about twenty minutes. In other instances, entire families were gassed simultaneously, the parents desperately trying to protect their children as the lethal concoction began its work.

The gas chamber itself is roughly three metres square and two metres high and primarily made of glass. This allows the 'doctors' and 'scientists' outside, who film the proceedings and take notes, to have a clear view of the experiments. In this novel I have made one small change in my description: I have described the observation as being made from the side of the gas chamber, whereas the process is normally watched from above, through the glass roof.

Camp 22 holds upwards of 50,000 prisoners. Those who aren't put in the gas chamber, or tortured to death for the pleasure of the guards, are forced to work on the land or in the nearby Chungbong coal mine. Many there die from their regular beatings or simply through exhaustion because of the appalling conditions.

Women as well as men are sent to this concentration camp and, inevitably, some give birth whilst they are incarcerated. Caring for infants is not a part of the remit of Camp 22, and it has been reliably reported that the guards are instructed to kill all new-born children by stamping on their heads and necks.

Life is hard in the 'Hermit Kingdom', but death is harder still.

Glossary

203 Slang term for the American Colt M16A2 5.56mm assault rifle fitted with a 203 grenade launcher clipped under the barrel. This is the preferred weapon of the SAS, whose troopers refuse to use the clumsy and unreliable SA-80, the standard British Army rifle

AA-6 See 'Acrid'

ACRB Aircrew Refreshment Bar. Informal snack bar where aircrew can eat and drink before or after a mission

Acrid NATO reporting name for the Russian R-40 air-to-air missile, also known as the AA-6. First constructed in the 1960s, the missile had two variants: the R-40T (infrared homing) and R-40R (semi-active radar homing), and in the late 1970s two longer-range versions, the R-40TD and R-40RD were introduced. Production was discontinued in 1991

ADD Associate Deputy Director of the CIA

Aegis Generic term for the American SPY-1F radar and associated missile launch system installed on ships from several navies. The system is optimized for engaging high-flying, high-speed targets

AEW Airborne Early Warning

AIM-9 Sidewinder. Short-range air-to-air missile

Alpha Russian hunter-killer submarine

ALR-67 Super Hornet Radar Warning Receiver

AMRAAM AIM-120 Advanced Medium-Range Air-to-Air Missile

An-28 Antonov twin turbo-prop light transport aircraft, NATO reporting name 'Cash'

An-72 Antonov STOL twin turbofan transport aircraft, NATO reporting name 'Coaler'

Bagman Slang term for an AEW Sea King observer, after the shape of the inflatable fabric dome covering the modified Searchwater radar that dangles from the side of the aircraft like a large grey pustule

Bergen Standard-issue British Army rucksack

Boomer Slang term for a ballistic-missile-carrying nuclear submarine or SSBN

Brimstone Solid-fuel anti-armour missile

Bureau 39 The North Korean government department responsible for the cultivation, transport, export and sale of illegal drugs

Bus Device in the nose of an ICBM that supports the warhead

Buster Full chat, maximum speed

CAG Commander, Air Group. The officer in charge of the air wing on an American carrier

CAP Combat Air Patrol. Defensive air patrol usually mounted by pairs of fighters to protect the aircraft carrier and other vessels from air attack

CBG Carrier Battle Group. American surface group headed by an aircraft carrier

CDS Chief of the Defence Staff

CFC Combined Forces Command. The joint American/South Korean military organization

CIC Combat Information Center. The tactical nerve

centre of a US Navy aircraft carrier where data is
collected and collated for the command

CINCFLEET Commander-In-Chief Fleet

Claymore A directional fragmentation mine that can be
triggered by trip-wires, infrared sensors, or by
command detonation

COMINT Communications Intelligence

ComSat Communications Satellite

COMSEC Communications Security

Cover All American Strategic Air Command's airborne
command post. One Cover All aircraft is airborne at
all times, and additional units are launched in times
of crisis. See also 'E-6B'

CRV7 Ground-attack rocket, fired from an under-wing
pod

DEFCON Defense Condition. A measure of the
alert state of the American military machine.
The DEFCON state runs from Five – the normal
peacetime state – to One, which implies that
America is either at war or about to go to war

DFC Dedicated Flying Course. Course steered by a
carrier when recovering aircraft

DMZ Demilitarized Zone. Buffer separating the two
Korean nations

DNI Director of National Intelligence. The highest
position in the American intelligence organization

DPRK Democratic People's Republic of Korea. Like
most Communist states, it's neither democratic nor a
republic, and certainly isn't run by or for the people

E-2C All-weather tactical airborne warning and control
system aircraft flown from US carriers. Commonly
known as a Hawkeye

E-4B The Nightwatch Boeing 747-200 aircraft designed as a command post for the US President and military chiefs. Known as the National Airborne Operations Center or the National Emergency Airborne Command Post – NEACP or 'Kneecap'

E-6B A modified Boeing 707 that acts as an airborne command post. Known as Cover All, its primary task is relaying instructions from the National Command Authority

EA-6B Electronic warfare aircraft designed to suppress enemy radars and communication systems. Commonly known as a Prowler

ECM Electronic Counter-Measures. Equipment used to counter any form of electronic surveillance or tracking devices, such as radar

EMCON Emission Control. EMCON policy is a statement of intent governing the use of radios and radar

EMP Electromagnetic Pulse. Surge following the detonation of a nuclear weapon, capable of destroying unshielded solid-state electronic devices

F-5 Shenyang F-5. Chinese-built version of the Russian MiG-17 fighter

F/A-18 Twin-engine, multi-role fighter/attack aircraft that has replaced several earlier types. Commonly known as a Super Hornet

Fan Song Tracking and guidance radar for the SA-2 SAM system

Fat Albert Slang term for a C-130 Hercules transport aircraft. Also known as a 'Herky-bird'

Five See 'MI5'

Flat Face Long-range C-band radar that forms part of the SA-2 SAM system

Flight Level Height of an aircraft in thousands of feet based upon the standard pressure setting of 1013.25 hPa (hectopascals) or 29.92 inches (for some American aircraft)

Flyco Flying Control Position. Located on the port side of the bridge of a CVS-class aircraft carrier, Flyco controls all launches from, and recoveries to, the ship

Fox Fire NATO reporting name for the very powerful RP-25M Saphir radar carried by the Russian MiG-25 Foxbat interceptor

Foxbat See 'MiG-25'

G-loc G-induced loss of consciousness. Caused by excessive g-force that drains blood away from the brain

GBU-28 American bunker-busting bomb

GCHQ Government Communications Headquarters. Britain's principal electronic intelligence-gathering service, based at Cheltenham

GIA *Groupe Islamique Armé*. Radical Islamic terrorist group operating in Algeria

GPS Global Positioning System. Satellite navigation equipment

GR9 Designation of the current Royal Navy Harrier fighter

GRU *Glavnoye Razvedyvatelnoye Upravleniye*. The Chief Intelligence Directorate of the Soviet General Staff, the Russian military intelligence organization

Guard Military UHF emergency frequency of 243.0 megahertz. The equivalent civil VHF frequency is 121.5 megahertz

GWO Group Warfare Officer

Hawkeye See 'E-2C'

Head-shed SAS slang term for the Regiment's headquarters at Hereford. Also known as 'The Kremlin'

Herky-bird Slang term for a C-130 Hercules transport aircraft. Also known as a 'Fat Albert'

HIFR Helicopter In-Flight Refuelling. A method of refuelling a helicopter whilst in the hover beside a ship that's too small to allow the aircraft to land-on

Homer A radar console manned by a specialist Air Traffic Control officer on a CVS-class aircraft carrier

HUD Head-Up Display

IAEA International Atomic Energy Agency

IAP *Istrebitel'nyi Aviatsion'nyi Polk* (Fighter Aviation Regiment). Russian air-defence interceptor squadron

ICBM Intercontinental Ballistic Missile

INGPS Inertial Navigation/Global Positioning System fitted to the GR9 Harrier

JARIC Joint Air Reconnaissance Intelligence Centre. The Royal Air Force's photographic interpretation unit, located at RAF Brampton, near Huntingdon

JIC Joint Intelligence Center. Intelligence collection and collation facility on a US aircraft carrier

JTIDS Joint Tactical Information Distribution System. Secure electronic data dissemination system that links airborne assets with surface units

Keyhole American KH-11 or KH-12 reconnaissance satellite

KH-12 Type of surveillance satellite normally known as 'Keyhole'

Kiloton Yield equivalent to the explosion of one

thousand tons of TNT and normally applied to the power of a tactical nuclear weapon. The yield of strategic nuclear weapons is measured in megatons, or millions of tons of TNT

Kyocera Make of satellite telephone

Legoland See 'Vauxhall Cross'

Little F Royal Navy Lieutenant Commander (Flying)

Mach Measure of an aircraft's speed relative to the speed of sound. Mach 2 is twice the speed of sound, Mach 3 three times the speed, and so on

Maverick AGM-65 air-to-surface tactical missile

MI5 Military Intelligence 5 – the Security Service – responsible for counter-espionage in the United Kingdom. Also known as 'Five' or 'The Box' (from its old postal address of 'PO Box 500, London')

MI6 See 'SIS'

MiG-25 Mikoyan-Gurevich supersonic interceptor, NATO reporting name 'Foxbat'. The fastest fighter aircraft ever manufactured, capable of speeds in excess of Mach 3, though red-lined at Mach 2.5

MIRV Multiple Independently-targeted Re-entry Vehicle. System of multiple warheads contained within a single missile's nose-cone, and often including decoys

Mode Charlie Automated height readout that forms part of an aircraft's SSR fit. See also 'Squawk'

MPCD Multi-Purpose Crystal Display. Part of the GR9 Harrier's HUD

MRE Meal, Ready-to-Eat. US Army field ration

MVD *Ministerstvo Vnutrennikh Del.* Actually the Ministry of Internal Affairs, but normally used to mean the Russian police force

NBCD Nuclear, Biological and Chemical Defence

NIS National Intelligence Service. South Korea's intelligence agency

NMCC National Military Command Center, located in the Joint Staff area of the Pentagon

NOFORN No Foreign Nationals. CIA acronym restricting sight of a document to American citizens

NORAD North American Aerospace Defense Command. In many ways the centre of America's defensive armament, NORAD is located in the heart of Cheyenne Mountain in Colorado, and has links to sensor networks and other hardened facilities all over the United States

N-PIC National Photographic Interpretation Center. Part of the Science and Technology Directorate of the CIA and based at Building 213 in the Washington Navy Yard

NSA National Security Agency. America's extremely secretive electronic intelligence agency, analogous to Britain's GCHQ. Sometimes known as 'No Such Agency'

NVG Night Vision Goggles

ODNI Office of the Director of National Intelligence

OHP Overhead projector

OP Observation Point

Oplan 5027 The 'master plan' conceived by South Korea and America to repel a North Korean invasion

Orbitron A satellite-tracking program available for free download from the Polish website www.stoff.pl

PAC-2/PAC-3 See 'Patriot'

Patriot Patriot Advanced Capability versions 2 and 3.

A high-performance air-defence guided missile system

Pave Paws AN/FPS-115 long-range phased-array radar system operated by the 21st Space Wing of the USAF Space Command for missile warning and space surveillance. Radars are located at Beale, Cape Cod and Clear, Alaska

Pigeons Magnetic heading to steer and nautical miles to run to reach a ship. Passed to a pilot on recovery to the ship in the format 'Pigeons two seven five at forty-two'

Pinky or Pink Panther SAS Land Rover

Predator A long-endurance, medium-altitude UAV. The RQ-1 version is used only for reconnaissance, but the multi-role MQ-1 can be armed with Hellfire missiles

PriFly Primary Flight Control. The location on an American aircraft carrier from which flight operations are supervised

Prowler See 'EA-6B'

RAW Radar Warning Receiver

Reporting names The NATO reporting name system is a convenient shorthand that avoids awkward pronunciations and also immediately identifies the type of asset being talked about, simply by the first letter of the name. Fighters are designated by names beginning with 'F' – Foxbat, Fulcrum; bombers by 'B' – Bison, Badger; helicopters by 'H' – Hind, Hormone, and so on

RFA Royal Fleet Auxiliary. Merchant ships that operate under special rules and act as supply vessels to Royal Navy ships

RTB Return to base

SA-2 The most widely deployed SAM system ever manufactured, known in Russia as the S-75 Dvina, and by NATO as 'Guideline'

SA-3 Isayev SAM system known in Russia as the S-125 Neva or Pechora. NATO reporting name 'Goa'

SAM Surface-to-air missile system

SAR Search and rescue

SAS Special Air Service. Also known as 'The Regiment'

Security Service See 'MI5'

Shadow 2000 UAV Short-range tactical UAV manufactured by the AAI Corporation

Sidewinder See 'AIM-9'

Sig 226 Schweizerische Industrie Gesellschaft (SIG)-Sauer P226. A full-size combat pistol chambered for the 9mm Luger cartridge

SIGINT Signals intelligence

Sirena S-3M Radar homing and warning system fitted to the MiG-25 Foxbat

SIS Secret Intelligence Service. Frequently but inaccurately known as MI6, and responsible for espionage outside the United Kingdom. Also referred to as 'Six'

Six See 'SIS'

SLBM Submarine-Launched Ballistic Missile

Speed jeans Anti-g trousers worn by fighter pilots to help prevent g-loc

Splot Senior pilot of a Royal Navy squadron

Spoon Rest Target acquisition and warning radar that forms part of the SA-2 SAM system

Squawk Secondary surveillance radar (SSR) return. Selecting ('squawking') a particular SSR code will display a four-digit number or the aircraft's callsign on a radar screen and allow an aircraft to be identified immediately. Selecting one of the emergency squawks – 7700 (emergency), 7600 (radio failure) or 7500 (hijack) – will generate a flashing symbol

SR-71A Blackbird American high-speed, high-altitude surveillance aircraft, which still holds numerous absolute speed records. It first flew in 1964, nine years after the first flight of the U-2, and had a long and highly successful career before being officially retired in the early 1990s

SSBN Sub-Surface Ballistic Nuclear. American designation of a ballistic missile-carrying nuclear-powered submarine

SSR See 'Squawk'

Starbase/Starship Slang terms for the USS *Enterprise*

STOL Short Take-Off and Landing aircraft

Storm Shadow Anglo-French air-launched cruise missile

Stovie Royal Navy slang term for a Harrier or other fighter pilot

Super Hornet See 'F/A-18'

Superdollars Near-perfect copies of American banknotes produced in North Korea that even experts find difficult to detect. They're known in the USA as PN-14342 notes, the numbering derived from Secret Service nomenclature

SVR *Sluzhba Vneshney Razvyedki Rossi.* The successor to the First Chief Directorate of the KGB, responsible for espionage and intelligence operations outside Russia

TACAMO Literally, 'Take Charge and Move Out'.

A system of survivable communication links and
platforms, including aircraft, designed to ensure that
in the event of a nuclear exchange, proper control of
US forces could still be exercised

TEL Transporter-Erector-Launcher. The vehicle used
to transport and fire a missile such as the Scud

Telebrief Communication system used on Royal Navy
aircraft carriers to allow a pilot to receive last-minute
tactical updates from the Operations staff

TFT Thin-Film Transistor. Technology used in flat-
panel computer screens

Trappers Examining officers who assess a pilot's flying
ability and competence

Trident Submarine-launched ballistic missile-carrying
nuclear warheads

U-2 High-altitude surveillance aircraft developed by
Lockheed in the 1950s

UAV Unmanned Aerial Vehicle

USStratCom United States Strategic Command

Vauxhall Cross The headquarters of the Secret
Intelligence Service fronting the Thames in London.
The building's bizarre design has spawned a number
of uncomplimentary nicknames. To those who work
inside the building, it's known as 'Legoland'

Wadi Dried-up watercourse in a desert

Wings Commander (Air). The head of the Air
Department on a Royal Navy aircraft carrier or
air station

FOXBAT

North Korean military ranks (in ascending order)

Chung-wi	Lieutenant
Tab-wi	Captain
So-ryong	Major
Chung-yong	Lieutenant-colonel
Tab-ryong	Colonel
So-jang	Major-general

extracts reading groups

competitions books new

discounts extracts

competitions

books new

events books

extracts

new reading groups

interviews

discounts events

new books events

events new

discounts extracts discounts

www.panmacmillan.com

extracts events reading groups

competitions books extracts new